Beerbohm Tree

Sir Herbert Beerbohm Tree was an actor-manager of flamboyant versatility, who was most instrumental in restoring magnificence to a theatrical scene that had largely, by the 1880s, become tawdry and trivial. His parentage – his father was a naturalized British subject but of mixed German, Dutch and Lithuanian extraction – gave him an exotic and cosmopolitan personality, and the stage always seemed to be his destiny, although he arrived there after a period as a clerk in his father's grain business and on the amateur stage.

He was soon to make his mark, being particularly noticed for those parts that demanded a gift for character in its most eccentric aspects. Throughout his career, he was to combine this facility for convincing disguise with the passion he brought to the romantic and fantastic heroes of melodrama. One of the earliest performances that built his following was as Svengali in *Trilby*.

Soon, in his thirties, Tree embarked on his career as theatrical manager when he took over the Haymarket Theatre. Ten years later he built Her Majesty's Theatre as headquarters for his operations, which became ever more grandiose and spectacular. He developed and elaborated the sumptuously illustrative Lyceum tradition of Shakespearian production, lavishing fortunes with spendthrift abandon on magnificent theatrical effects, much to the enjoyment of late-Victorian audiences. But Tree was not limited in taste. Shakespeare shared his stage with Tolstoy and he was to encourage, with some success at the time, a revival of modern poetic drama led by the dramatist Stephen Phillips. His most notable essay into what was bold and original for its period was his production of Shaw's *Pygmalion*.

His true gift lay in comedy and character, and his aspirations as a tragic actor, despite the overwhelming settings he provided for such plays as *Antony and Cleopatra* and *Julius Caesar*, could not always be fulfilled. But he left a permanent legacy to the British theatre, put his daughters on the stage, and well deserved his knighthood in 1909. He was also responsible for the founding of that Academy of Dramatic Art from which generations of fine actors have graduated.

The Lively Arts
General Editor: Robert Ottaway

A Mingled Chime · Sir Thomas Beecham
Memoirs · Alexandre Benois
Dance to the Piper · Agnes de Mille
The Movies, Mr Griffith and Me · Lillian Gish
Chaliapin · Maxim Gorky
A Life in the Theatre · Tyrone Guthrie
My Grandfather, His Wives and Loves · Diana Holman-Hunt
Groucho and Me · Groucho Marx
Beerbohm Tree · Hesketh Pearson
Renoir, My Father · Jean Renoir
Liszt · Sir Sacheverell Sitwell
Fun in a Chinese Laundry · Josef von Sternberg

Forthcoming titles include

Ego · James Agate
On Human Finery · Quentin Bell
Unfinished Business · John Houseman
The Baton and the Jackboot · Berta Geissmar
Theatre Street · Tamara Karsavina
Mr Jelly Roll · Alan Lomax

BEERBOHM TREE

His Life and Laughter

*

HESKETH PEARSON

FOREWORD BY
SIR JOHN GIELGUD

COLUMBUS BOOKS
LONDON

This trade paperback edition
published in Great Britain in 1988 by
Columbus Books Limited
19-23 Ludgate Hill
London, EC4M 7PD

First published by Methuen and Company in 1956

Copyright © Michael Holroyd

Foreword copyright © Sir John Gielgud CH 1988

British Library Cataloguing in Publication Data

Pearson, Hesketh
Beerbohm Tree: his life and laughter.—
(The Lively arts).
1. Tree, Sir Herbert Beerbohm   2. Theatre
—England—Biography
I. Title   II. Series
792'.092'4   PN2598.T7

ISBN 0–86287–902–7

*This book is sold subject to the condition that
it shall not, by way of trade or otherwise,
be lent, resold, hired out or otherwise circulated
without the publisher's prior written consent
in any form of binding or cover other than that
in which it is published and without a similar
condition including this condition being imposed
on the subsequent purchaser.*

All rights reserved.

Printed and bound by The Guernsey Press
Guernsey, CI

To
my friend
Douglas Jefferies
who walked-on with me at
His Majesty's Theatre in
1911-12

ACKNOWLEDGMENTS

I must first express my thanks to Mr Denys Parsons and Mr David Tree Parsons for urging me to write the Life of their grandfather, a work I had long wished to undertake. Tree's daughter Felicity (Lady Cory-Wright) not only placed at my disposal some twenty-four trunks of her mother's private papers but helped me in every possible way. Without her assistance my book could not have been authentic, nor would it have included the letters, diary and notebooks of her father, extracts from which are quoted here by permission of the trustees of his estate. This bare acknowledgment is inadequate. Tree's youngest daughter Iris (Countess Ledebur) told me much of value; while the late Max Beerbohm, Tree's half-brother, was good enough to answer all my questions and to add several things that enrich my biography.

My gratitude is also due to those who have given me their memories of Tree, to Mr Douglas Jefferies, the late Frederick L. Whelen, the late William Mollison and Mr Richard Hatteras. For much interesting information I am indebted to Mr Baliol Holloway, Mr W. Somerset Maugham, Mr Reginald Pound, Mr Arthur Brough, and to the Borough and Reference Librarians of Folkestone Public Library, Mr Reginald Howarth and Mr Peter Davies. Professor L. Eyrignoux kindly let me have the biographical data he had collected about Stephen Phillips, and letters were lent me by Mr F. B. Cockburn, Mr Elmer Gertz and Mr Kerrison Preston; while further help was received from Miss Christopher St John, the late Allan Wade, Mr Colin Hurry, Mr Richard Ainley, Mr Frank Allen, Mrs Edward Fordham, and Baroness von Hutten.

Sir Max Beerbohm, the artist, and Mr Robert H. Taylor, the owner, generously allowed me to reproduce the cartoon, *Genus Beerbohmiense*.

I acknowledge with thanks permission to quote the following: Extracts from letters of Sir W. S. Gilbert (the owner of the copyright); a letter and an unpublished passage from a play by Oscar Wilde (Mr Vyvyan Holland); two letters and several passages of dramatic criticism by Bernard Shaw (The Authors' Society); passages from my own book, *Modern Men and Mummers* (Messrs Allen & Unwin

Ltd); passages from *Herbert Beerbohm Tree*, edited by Max Beerbohm (Messrs Hutchinson & Co.).

I should add that without the assistance of my wife I could not have sifted the mass of documents and other material that had to be examined.

CONTENTS

1. Introducing Herbert Beerbohm Tree   1
2. City and Stage   5
3. A Diary   14
4. Love Letters   27
5. Gilbert, Irving, Stevenson and Others   43
6. Haddon Chambers and Henry Arthur Jones   51
7. Shakespeare, Oscar Wilde and Ibsen   59
8. Domestic and Foreign   74
9. Hogwash   84
10. America Again   94
11. Her Majesty's   101
12. Man and Manager   105
13. Shakespeare Spells Success   116
14. Phillips, Fitch, Caine and Kipling   134
15. Home and Dome   142
16. Tolstoy, Dickens, Thackeray, Sheridan and Brieux   152
17. The Ways of Glory   162
18. Bernard Shaw   172
19. Strange But True   183
20. Actor and Producer   189
21. Personal   201
22. Uniting the States   221
23. Quick Exit   233
Appendix   235
Authorities   240
Indexes   243

Herbert Beerbohm Tree, aged about 60

FOREWORD

I never saw Herbert Tree, either on or off the stage, but I find him most vividly brought to life in this fascinating biography. He was something of a legend to me in my stage-struck boyhood, and I remember my surprise when my mother refused to take me to see him in his stage version of *David Copperfield*. As I knew her to be a willingly emotional playgoer, I was amazed when she said she could not willingly suffer again the pathos of the scene between Little Emily and Daniel Peggotty, played by Tree, who also doubled as Micawber.

The splendid stories and witticisms in circulation, both of Tree himself and his clever and long-suffering wife Maud, were ever much appreciated by both my parents, and I was eager to lap them up. How I longed to have been able to see the lavish spectacles, Shakespearean and otherwise, with which Tree had dazzled his audiences before I was old enough to go to the theatre. My parents greatly admired Tree as a character actor, describing his mastery of make-up and his ability to alter his physical appearance – especially in a double bill when he played the bulky detective in *The Red Lamp* and the slim romantic poet Gringoire in the same evening.

What an extraordinarily versatile creature he must have been, a doting husband and father (despite his many irregularities in sexual exploits) and a deeply kind, eccentric and creative artist of remarkable originality and enterprise. I once played the part of Charley Bates at a charity matinée in which some of the scenes from the Tree version of *Oliver Twist* were hastily put together, with Constance Collier and Lyn Harding appearing in their original parts of Nancy and Bill Sikes, and culminating in their sensational murder scene. The part of Fagin, once played, of course, by Tree, was taken by Gilbert Childs, a popular comedian then appearing in a musical revue called *The CoOptimists*; but I fear he failed in achieving much success despite several showy opportunities. The shadow of his distinguished predecessor, to say nothing of the fact that we were acting in such nostalgic surroundings – the stage of His Majesty's, so proudly referred to by Tree as 'my beautiful theatre' – must have been something of a daunting challenge for him upon this occasion.

The death of Queen Victoria, ushering in the rakish years of the new king's reign, seems to have led to a surprisingly permissive fashion for discreet adultery, especially among the actor-managers in the West End. Tree was evidently the leader in this field (though he was certainly matched by Gordon Craig in fathering a numerous brood of illegitimate offspring). But, just as Queen Alexandra remained the respected (and respectable) matriarch in the Royal Family, so the submissive wives of the Edwardian actor-managers remained undisputed and acknowledged mistresses of their home dining-tables and obligingly turned the other cheek, though the needless extravagance of their husbands in expensive cab-fares to meet the requirements of professional punctuality must have put a considerable strain on purses and pocketbooks alike. 'Ah, Herbert,' Lady Tree is said to have remarked on one occasion. 'Late again. Another confinement in Putney?'

Tree's talented family were destined to outlive Sir Herbert for many years. When I was acting in the twenties and thirties, I knew Lady Tree slightly, as well as his two tall and eccentric daughters, Viola and Iris. Lady Tree was by this time a striking, somewhat bizarre personality with a beaming smile. Her crooked mouth and jaw (disfigured years before in the motor accident described by Pearson) gave her a strange distinction, and she had many stage successes as countesses and French Revolutionary hags. She also played Mistress Quickly in a production of *Henry the Fourth* in which George Robey was a controversial Falstaff. She draped brightly coloured scarves over her red hair ('So kind of you,' she said, 'to call it *my* hair') and wore flowing robes.

We would sometimes meet at charity matinées, where she would study her lines through a huge magnifying glass, and was reputed to be heard, while waiting in the wings for her entrance, muttering strange gasps and groans and mouthing the shapes of the syllables she needed to solve difficult clues in the *Times* crossword puzzle. Vivien Leigh, who acted with her in *The Mask of Virtue* (in which she herself was to score her first London success) told me a delightful story of the dress rehearsal. Lady Tree broke off suddenly in the middle of one of her speeches and, shielding her eyes with her hand, looked searchingly into the empty auditorium. 'Is the director in the house?' she called out, and, as the person in question emerged from the back of the stalls: 'Yes, Lady Tree?' – 'Mr X,' she remarked politely, 'do you think you could kindly oblige us with a little more light? I think perhaps you don't realize that my comedic effects are purely grimacial!'

No wonder she was such a fitting partner for so witty a husband. What a good idea to republish this amusing and rewarding record.

John Gielgud

Herbert Beerbohm Tree

by His Contemporaries

'A damned good sort!'—William Terriss

'Tree—the charming fellow—I could murder him with great pleasure.'—Gordon Craig

'He was a man and a gentleman who will never be replaced in this profession.'—Henry Dana (Tree's manager for twenty-one years)

'He was a wonderful man, and I like to fancy he was perhaps sometimes rather fond of me—I was most certainly of him and shall always be.'—Sir Gerald Du Maurier

'Was ever a more hospitable fellow, or a better host?'—C. Haddon Chambers

'To his last day he was a boy in spirit. He would not have been old if he had lived to be ninety. He had the secret of perpetual youth of the Spirit.'—Sir Gilbert Parker

'Tree was the despair of authors.'—G. Bernard Shaw

'I was very fond of Herbert.'—Ellen Terry

'That splendid, radiant, conquering personality.'—Reginald Turner

'The world will never be the same place again.'—W. J. Locke (on Tree's death)

'London was not itself when he was away—he was an essential factor in the great machinery—a vitalizing influence and focus ... His memory will never fade. He was greatly beloved—and he deserved it all and more.'—Sir Alfred Fripp

'Herbert aimed at and attained the highest.'—Sir Edward Elgar

'I like him so much that nothing could induce me to write a play for him.'—Sir Arthur Pinero

'Tree had a remarkably attractive and fascinating personality; he was one of the most impulsively generous of men, and, in a curiously charming way, one of the oddest and most erratic.'—Alfred Sutro

'A charming fellow, and so clever: he models himself on me.'—Oscar Wilde

'I feel as though I had lost my own father, and I know I shall never again have so good and kind a master.'—Alfred G. Trebell (Tree's dresser at His Majesty's Theatre)

'To me he was always a genius. He and Edward Carson were the two ablest men that I ever knew well.'—Charles F. Gill

'The essential humanity of his character always appealed to me, and he seemed to mellow into greater breadth and sympathy with the years.'—Roy Horniman

'Throughout my friendship with him I have never known him to fail in sympathy and goodness.'—Constance Collier

'It is impossible not to like Tree because he is a great big baby, and impossible not to be irritated with him for the same reason.'—Sir George Alexander (1910)

'There was nothing but love and a perfect understanding between us.'—Sir George Alexander (1917)

'He was the most generous man I ever knew, and on the scene of life as well as on the stage he did nothing common, nothing mean.'—Maurice Baring

'The friendliest, most enthusiastic, most hospitable, and most infuriating of creatures.'—Mrs Patrick Campbell

'A loyal, affectionate and most delightful friend . . . a brilliant and charming personality.'—Sir Hall Caine

'England is the poorer for having lost his bright gay spirit and his genius.'—Lady Cunard

'The most lovable man I have ever met; the most aggravating man, too.'—Louis N. Parker

'Of all the actors I've known I would rather have spent a fortnight in Tree's company than with any of the others.'—Henry Arthur Jones

'What a great chap he was! . . . he really was a giant among minnows in the theatrical world.'—Frederic Norton

'I had always, as had my dear father and mother, an affection as well as a fervent admiration for Sir Herbert.'—George Grossmith Junior

'If I ever talked to a man who made me feel like his grand-uncle and seemed certain to live for ever, he was that man.'—G. Bernard Shaw

'A more brilliant and graceful companion has not been left us in these days of storm and stress.'—Frederic Harrison (1917)

'His was—nay *is*—one of those buoyant characters of which the strength and beauty and variety are only brought into high relief when they are withdrawn from sight.'—Sir George Arthur

'He was more than "the Chief" to me. He was a generous friend.'—Oscar Asche

'The magic of his personality brightened me every time I came near it, and the unworldliness of him was always attractive. He really was bigger than other people.'—Sir James Barrie

'So great an artist and so good a man.'—J. E. C. Welldon (Dean of Manchester)

'A dear friend and a great man.'—Sir Landon Ronald

'He was a great man, and I had a great affection for him.'—Sir Nigel Playfair

'. . . that wealth of vitality and that unfailing reservoir of true kindness and affection.'—Lord Oxford and Asquith

'He was so full of life and courage and will always remain a great memory.'—Irene Vanbrugh

'One of the best friends I have had the honour of knowing since my youth.'—Willy Clarkson (Tree's wigmaker)

'Herbert was (then and always) a hero to me.'—Sir Max Beerbohm

'The greatest man who ever lived . . . except perhaps Our Lord.'—Harriet (Tree's devoted sister-in-law)

'He leaves a gap impossible to fill.'—Sir John Hare (1917)

CHAPTER 2

City and Stage

Many remarkable men are mongrels, the crossing of breeds frequently tending to queer results. The richest personality, the wittiest character, the most intelligent and versatile actor-manager in the record of the British stage, Herbert Beerbohm Tree, had German, Slavonic and English forebears. It was generally believed by his contemporaries that he was Jewish, but there is no trace of such descent in his paternal pedigree. Moreover, his great-aunt Mathilde spent many years at the court of the Emperor William I and married General von Unruh, military governor to the Crown Prince Frederick, while another Beerbohm married General von Pape, who was standard-bearer at the Emperor William's funeral. These alliances would have been impossible in the nineteenth century if the Beerbohms had been even partially hebraic, since anti-semitism was rife in the Prussian military caste. But as the peculiar charm, courtliness, sensitivity and intelligence of a cultured Jew were united in Herbert Tree, it is possible that he inherited these racial characteristics from the distaff side of his father's or mother's ancestry.

The Beerbohms may have been of Dutch extraction, but the sole evidence of this is that the name was spelt 'Beerboom' on some old marriage ribbons. The family first appears in history at the beginning of the eighteenth century, when a Frederick Beerbohm was a merchant in Pomerania. His son, Ernest Joachim, after a mercantile training, settled at Memel, a Baltic seaport near the Russian frontier, where he married the sister of a timber merchant named Roerdanz and became a partner in the business. The firm supported Frederick the Great against Russia, in recognition of which Ernest Joachim was given a property called Bernstein-bruch. His eldest son, Ernest Henry, was born in 1763, and at the age of 22 married Henriette Amalie Radke, aged 18, who was of Slavonic descent. These two lived through a period of much turmoil, the officers of various nations being quartered at different times on Bernsteinbruch, where the members of incoming and outgoing royal families were also entertained. Ernest Henry Beerbohm kept a diary in which the thrills and horrors of those days were noted. 'Mere starving human skeletons, wrapped in rags,' he described the fragments of the French army as they passed through Memel on their retreat from Moscow: 'Several to protect themselves from frost had wound straw round their bodies and limbs, as one sees pumps protected in winter—now cursing their great Emperor, calling him a tyrant.' In spite of the miseries they witnessed and the general sense of insecurity caused by the overthrow of monarchies, the collapse of dynasties, the vindictive triumph of advancing armies, and the mutinous despair of retreating troops, Ernest Henry and Henriette Amalie lived very happily together and produced eleven children, the youngest of whom, Julius Ewald, born in 1810, was to be the father of our actor.

Julius was educated at Schnepfeuthal in Thuringia, received a business training in France, arrived in London at the age of 20, and became a corn merchant in the city. At the age of 39 he married Constantia Draper, whose parents were of Yorkshire and Lincolnshire stock. Her father, John Draper, a Yorkshireman, the son of a solicitor, was for many years a clerk at Lloyd's. A deeply religious man, an ardent bibliophile and a lovable character, he had no worldly ambitions of any kind. Constantia gave birth to three sons and a daughter, and died before the age of 30. The second son of Julius and Constantia was named Herbert Draper, and was born on December 17, 1852, at 2 Pembridge Villas, Kensington. In after-life he seldom spoke of his youth, though in 1913 he was heard to remark: 'I was born old and get younger every day. At present I am sixty years young.' This was a variation of his saying: 'Those whom the gods love never grow old.' Two stories of his childhood have been preserved. The first suggests that he was already an actor in his nursery, where he was put into the corner and reproved by his nurse: 'Ah, Master Herbert! what we want is deeds, not actions.' The second seems to justify his statement that he was born old, or at least knowing. A middle-aged friend of his father paid a call, and the five-years-old child was brought down from the nursery for inspection. 'Well, my little tiddlywink,' was the visitor's greeting. '*You*'re a tiddlywink—and a rascal too,' retorted Herbert.

His seventh and eighth years were spent with his elder brother at Mrs Adams's dame-school at Frant, near Tunbridge Wells; and early in the twentieth century, when laying the foundation-stone of the Tunbridge Wells theatre, he mentioned that 'there was a wood, I think it was called Mad Cap Wood, where in my boyish days I dwelt with the fairies which many years after I may unconsciously have conjured up in my production of *A Midsummer Night's Dream*, for the works of our maturity are often but the games of our childhood.' From the recollections of contemporaries we learn that he was for a time at Dr Stone's school in King's Square, Bristol, where he surprised his companions with clever recitations; and later at the Westbourne Collegiate School in Westbourne Grove, London. While at the last he attended Bible classes given by a philanthropist in Pembridge Square, Bayswater.

No doubt he appeared to be learning very little at these establishments, and his father determined to send the three boys to a German school, where the discipline was less lax, the teaching more severe. They were despatched to their father's old school at Schnepfeuthal, and here they quickly discovered that life could be grim. There was punishment instead of pleasure, woe instead of joy. Having been taught that the Sabbath was holy, Herbert was shocked that the other boys played games on Sunday, and he refused to take part in them, thinking, 'Poor fellows, they're all going to hell. Only I may be saved.' But he was soon made aware that the wickedness of youth was harmless compared with the villainy of man, the masters seeming to wallow in cruelty. He was wretched incessantly from waking to sleeping, and even his dreams were troubled. Sometimes he rebelled, and once, during a hated music lesson, he smashed the piano in his rage; but the penalties for resistance were so frightful that such outbreaks were rare. His German schooling left him with a shuddering detestation of education in all its forms. In the years ahead he would often interrupt the lessons of his own children, saying, 'Education is useless—I don't believe in it,' to the consternation of the governesses

and the delight of their pupils. And he crystallized his conviction in a phrase: 'As humour is above wit, so is intelligence
above intellect and instinct above knowledge.' His years in
Thuringia also cured him of the common youthful ambition to
be a soldier.

Julius Beerbohm, now thoroughly established in the City and
a member of the Baltic Exchange in Threadneedle Street, had
founded a journal, *The Evening Corn Trade List*, which daily
recorded the movements of ships and cargoes in that trade and
was published at his office in Bishopsgate Street. He wished his
three sons to benefit from his business, and they were duly employed as clerks, one of Herbert's jobs being to help edit the
journal. But none of them took to the work. The eldest, Ernest,
pined for open spaces, and ultimately became a sheep-farmer in
Cape Colony, where he joined hands with a dark woman who
was always described as 'a brunette' by the family at home. The
youngest, Julius, developed a taste for unexplored regions, chose
Patagonia for the purpose, inspected it thoroughly, and described
the experience in a book. In time he became a somewhat shaky
financier and a writer of poems which were considered excellent
by those who heard him recite them but too daring for publication. Their father, the corn merchant, was a shrewd, courteous,
cultured, dignified man, humorous, tolerant, and, except in
business, absent-minded. He raised no objection to the pioneering
proclivities of his eldest and youngest sons, and gave them the
necessary financial assistance; but he drew the line at a stage career
for his second son Herbert, whose sole ambition from the age of
17 was to become an actor, in those days regarded as a disreputable
being, though successful ones were welcome in the better class
of Bohemian society.

So for eight years Herbert stuck to his desk in the City, express-
ing his real inclination in amateur theatricals. Though fond of his
father and anxious to please, he could not take the smallest interest
in bills of lading, the price of corn, the shipment of cargoes, or
the value of money. Given letters to post, he would sometimes
put them into the letter-box of a neighbouring office. Told to pay
cheques into the bank, he would forget all about them as he
walked the streets reciting a part or a poem, and find them in his

pocket when he went to bed. To the end of his days he could not master elementary arithmetic, stating his opinion that 'the vagaries of finance have ever been a puzzle to me, and I know it is only hypocrisy on the part of mankind to accept the theory of an obscure mathematician who said that two and two make four'.

He appears to have been baffled by religion as well as arithmetic, for he tried to convince himself of the truths of positive theology by preaching in the Sunday-school of a Bayswater church, though whether he did so to practise elocution or to save his soul is uncertain. Probably the former, because at about this period he wrote an agnostic's prayer: 'O God! give me the faith to believe in those things which the common sense Thou hast given me tells me are not true.' His preaching came to an end when the children in the Sunday-school, feeling no doubt that his preaching lacked conviction, called him 'Ha'porth o' carrots', a satirical comment on his personal appearance. At that time his hair was bright red and usually untidy; he was rather over six feet tall, slim in build, limp in carriage, shy in manner. His eyes were intensely blue, which in moments of abstraction changed to what looked a greyish green. With pale eyelashes, a nervous intellectual face, a prominent nose, and a mouth that twitched spasmodically as if to check laughter, he was clearly a noticeable youngster, if also a subject for Sunday-school mirth.

Soon performing for several amateur dramatic clubs, the Erratics, the Irrationals, the Bettertons, the Philothespians, he early won notoriety for his imitations of famous actors and often gave them at social clubs and smoking concerts. Indeed, he first became known for the cleverness with which he parodied the characteristics of leading players, just as in later life his fame was consolidated by his ability to copy the oddities of recognizable human types. Many years afterwards his own mannerisms of speech and movement were frequently ridiculed in music-halls, and having witnessed one of these burlesques he remarked: 'A man never knows what a damned fool he is until he sees himself imitated by one.'

Among the Philothespians of the late seventies were two other young men who wished to escape from their desks in the City. One was George Alexander, a clerk in a draper's warehouse; the

other was Lewis Waller, a clerk in his uncle's firm; and both were
to achieve fame on the stage. It seemed as if the leading actors of
the future were to be recruited from the world of commerce; and
this drift synchronized with the arrival of Tom Robertson's 'cup-
and-saucer' comedies, which, produced by the Bancrofts at the
Prince of Wales's Theatre in the sixties, revolutionized the stage
by superseding the old stilted prose or blank-verse melodramas
and by demanding an entirely fresh and naturalistic technique
from the actors. In fact, Robertson's plays, more than anybody or
anything else, made the stage a respectable calling, for his ladies
and gentlemen had to be acted by people who could pass as
socially presentable. The days of the disreputable, drunken, rant-
ing, 'stock company' actor were clearly numbered with the
production of *Caste* in 1867; and the rising generation of performers wished to be recognized as gentlemen no less than as
artists, a desire that sometimes took peculiar forms, as when
young Herbert Beerbohm recited a ballad by G. R. Sims called
'Told to the Missionary' and substituted the word 'dog' for that
of 'bitch' in the original.

The histrionically ambitious youths who were working in
the City during the seventies spent all their spare shillings at the
Prince of Wales's Theatre in Charlotte Street, where the Scala
Theatre now stands. The Robertson comedies were constantly
revived by the Bancrofts, who were the first to produce modern
plays in a realistic style. Before their time the scenery was as far
from the illusion of reality as the acting. An old-style drawing-
room was made up of wings, flats, canvas doors, carpetless floors
and roof-borders, its furniture chiefly consisting of white chairs
with red damask seats and a strip of gold tinsel down the legs to
make them look luxurious. Into a setting of this sort there entered
a stage lover, usually past middle-age, dressed like a waiter in
a cheap restaurant off duty, whose strange actions and uncouth
diction seemed appropriate in such a place. The Bancrofts transformed all that as completely as Robertson's comedies changed
the course of the drama. Bright, jolly, well-dressed young lovers
could now be seen in real rooms with good furniture, behaving
naturally in plays that seemed lifelike. The effect was fascinating
and wholly novel, while the comic acting of Marie Wilton

(Mrs Bancroft) was as delightful and unique as the scenery and plays.

It was also the Bancroft management that gave Ellen Terry her first chance to reveal her singular genius. In their production of *The Merchant of Venice* in April, 1875, she played the part of Portia, and Herbert Beerbohm, aged 22, went to see the third performance, writing in his diary:

> I never saw so empty a pit at the Prince of Wales—not more than a dozen people, and it only started Saturday last. All the papers made unfavourable criticisms, and they were certainly justified by the performance. Coglan as Shylock was simply inoffensive, tame and respectable . . . Ellen Terry as Portia made up with her art for what the others lacked. I cannot understand how she can smile so naturally. Her by-play was marvellous. She looked like one of Leighton's women, queenlike. In the trial scene she astonished me by putting on the manners of a youth, and leant against one of the . . . [the diarist could not think of the right descriptive name, so left a space] like a young barrister of the present day. Her genius was immediately recognized and rewarded accordingly. Archer was fine as Antonio—rather too gentlemanly—he could not have spat at Shylock.

The production was the work of E. W. Godwin, the father of Ellen Terry's two children, Edith and Gordon Craig, and when young Beerbohm had made himself known as Tree he declared that *The Merchant of Venice* at the Prince of Wales's Theatre was the first production of a Shakespearean or classical play 'in which the modern spirit of stage-management asserted itself'. The experiment thrilled him, and he quickly made the acquaintance of Godwin, with whom he was on very friendly terms for some years.

Travelling about to rehearse plays and then perform in them, to say nothing of spending his free evenings in the theatre watching professional actors, frequently exhausted Herbert's salary before it was received, and he lived on loans. We catch a glimpse of him in those days through the eyes of a friend, T. Murray Ford, who described him as

> a lanky youth acting with amateurs at Dalston and Haggerston. He was reserved, almost sullen, but keen and deep in love with his art . . . His father had told young Beerbohm that he must stick to

business and leave acting alone, and the lad was on his beam-ends at times, and not too proud to borrow an occasional half-crown from the waitresses of Crosby Hall.

The one-time palace of Richard III, Crosby Hall, was then situated close to Bishopsgate Street, and until its removal to Chelsea Embankment in the first decade of the present century it was used for some thirty years as a public restaurant.

The need to supplement his salary became urgent, and as he had won a reputation for playing totally dissimilar parts he was sometimes asked to appear in professional companies for a day here or two days there. He received a fee for such performances, though on one occasion the fee was paid by himself. Engaged to act in a drama at the Town Hall, Hythe, he wired to the manager that he was leaving Charing Cross by a train just after four o'clock. By the time the telegram arrived the figure '4' had changed to '8', and the frantic manager sent the town crier through the streets to inform the expectant public that owing to the illness of a principal actor the first performance of the play would not be given until the following evening. The Town Hall was closed when Beerbohm reached Hythe, and he indignantly went in search of the manager, who promptly fined him £5 for the cost of postponement.

It became so necessary to obtain professional engagements while still an amateur that he paid for the printing of a diminutive paper-covered booklet containing the opinions of critics on some of his performances. Copies were no doubt distributed in promising quarters, and theatrical managers read without noticeable excitement that the *Era* had 'never seen a better bit of amateur acting' than Mr Beerbohm as Achille Talma Dufard in *The First Night*, that the *Surrey Comet* thought him 'inimitable', that the *Islington Gazette* considered him 'unique', and that *Figaro* judged his performance 'full of artistic touches'. Already the critics were remarking his versatility as an actor, his skill in make-up, and the *Sporting and Dramatic News* made the remarkable prophecy that 'his acting showed an originality and fertile humour which, with hard work and careful schooling, may really lead to great things in the line of grotesque eccentricity which is particularly his'. This booklet was dated 1877, and the name on the cover was 'Mr

H. Beerbohm Tree', which shows that he had determined more than a year before the event to become a professional actor under that cognomen.

His father did his utmost to persuade the young man against such a course. Acting was all very well if one reached the top of the tree, said the father, but the room up there was restricted, and it was a miserable business at any point short of that. Hence my name, said the son, who meant to climb to the tip-top. It is probable that Julius Beerbohm would have put his foot down more firmly if he had not added considerably to his family by marrying again. His second wife, Eliza Draper, was the sister of his first, and their wedding took place in Switzerland. She bore him four daughters and one son. His absorption in the growing domestic circle weakened his opposition to the will of Herbert, and he reluctantly gave way.

The youngest child of his second marriage, born in 1872 and christened Henry Maximilian, was also to be drawn towards the stage, becoming a dramatic critic long after Herbert was famous. But Max Beerbohm never criticized the acting or productions of his half-brother Beerbohm Tree.

CHAPTER 3

A Diary

After appearing for a charity as Grimaldi in *The Life of an Actress* at the Globe Theatre in February, 1878, Tree was asked to join the Bijou Comedy Company for a short tour opening at Folkestone, and he hesitated no longer. He was never a stage-struck actor, but it would be true to call him theatre-struck. Even at this early period he wished to have a playhouse and a company of his own, and though, naturally, he wanted to be seen in leading characters, his imagination soared above the average actor's ambition to be the main attraction. He was too intelligent to think of plays solely in terms of parts. That he had already made his name as an amateur is proved by the advertisement in the *Folkestone Chronicle* on Saturday, May 18th, 1878, which heralded the appearance of the Bijou Comedy Company the following week in seven plays, and announced that the management had secured 'the services of Mr H. Beerbohm Tree', who would appear in the various pieces, giving on Wednesday and Friday '(by special desire) his inimitable Dramatic and

---

Town Hall, Folkestone.

On MONDAY, MAY 20th, 1878,

THE

Bijou Comedy Company

Will appear in a varied programme

For Six Nights Only!

Besides the well known members of this Company, the management have much pleasure in announcing that they have secured the services of

MR. H. BEERBOHM TREE,

Who will appear during the week in the various pieces, and on Wednesday and Friday will give (by special desire) his inimitable Dramatic and Mimictic Recitals.

Stalls (price 3s.) may be secured at Goulden's Library, Rendezvous Street, Folkestone.

Mimictic Recitals', in which he imitated Irving, Toole, Salvini, and other leading actors.

According to the local paper, Tree received 'repeated and special applause' for his performance as Milky White in a play of that name on the opening night, May 20th, and later that week gave a very powerful rendering of the blind and aged Colonel Challice in *Alone*, when the critic noted 'the excitable movement of his fingers, the staring of the eyes, as if straining to regain the sight once enjoyed, the quick movement of the head, as if hearing the fall of a leaf, by ears quickened by the loss of his greatest faculty'. Although these details appeared to suit the part, they were largely due to the fact that the actor did not know his words and kept snapping his fingers in his efforts to remember them, turning his head to the prompt-box for assistance, and straining his ears for the whispered communications of the prompter.

The attendances at the Town Hall were poor and the newspaper apologized to the company.

> The performers are highly educated ladies and gentlemen [wrote the critic]. Alas! how many members of companies that pretentiously go the round of the provinces lack even the rudiments of early instruction. We have heard actors tripped up at a difficult word, and the letter 'h' scattered in all directions. The Bijou's are graceful, easy and natural actors. No rant; or efforts to create an impression by stagey effects, instead of real talent, are resorted to. They are evidently brought up in the usages of society, and display themselves to great advantage, especially in drawing-room scenes and in those *tête-à-têtes* which so often display the charms of real acting, but which many professionals, although clever perhaps in other things, know not how to manage.

The critic was glad to see that Church of England clergymen and several Nonconformist ministers were present at the entertainments, and expressed a hope that religious bodies would henceforth discard their prejudice against the stage, which was now devoted to moral instruction. When next the Bijou Company visited Folkestone, he hoped their performances would be advertised under the patronage of the vicar, the clergy, the churchwardens, and the ministers of Dissenting denominations.

This newspaper notice throws light on a phase of stage-history. The provinces had been accustomed to the appalling acting of 'stock companies', of which we read such depressing accounts in Macready's diary. The average 'stock' actor, having to 'swallow' a part in a couple of hours, and to play a different one nearly every night, found it necessary to adopt a single line of business. He would specialize either in old men or in villains or in low comedians or in heroes, and whatever the part, whatever the play, he never varied the performance. All the senile parts had the same crotchets and quavers; they doddered and they piped. All the heroic parts were hearty, bombastic, and prone to attitudes. All the villains frowned, tugged their moustaches, snarled, moved stealthily, and gave vent to a sinister chuckle at appropriate moments. All the low comedians produced the same gags that had done service in every play and went on repeating them until the audience ceased to think them funny, after which they made noises. Already, in the Folkestone critique, we see the influence of Robertson and the Bancrofts, and the arrival of a different class of actor, drawn from business not born in the buskin.

Following this short tour, Tree got his first London job under the management of Henry Neville, who in due course would get many jobs under the management of Beerbohm Tree. What was described as a 'Grand Revival of *The Two Orphans*' took place on September 23rd, 1878, at the Royal Olympic Theatre, when the part of Lafleur was played by 'Mr H. B. Tree'. It was preceded by a farce called *The Rendezvous*, in which 'Mr H. B. Tree' appeared in the character of Smart. In those days the English stage was flooded with French dramas and farces. The Victorians felt that there was something either wicked or daring about anything French, and to see a Parisian play was almost equivalent to a trip to Paris. What must have helped Tree considerably in his early years as an actor was that he could talk both French and German fluently, and his speech and mannerisms were slightly exotic, as a consequence of which he was often cast for alien parts, and whether he played them well or ill he gave an impression of verisimilitude. Unlike the famous actors of the past, he trusted to intuition instead of education. Henry Irving had performed more than six hundred parts in a dozen years before he made a success in London, and had experienced the humiliation of being hissed by audiences and mocked by critics. Although Tree used to assert that he had played over a hundred parts before he became an established London actor, the number included those he had acted as an amateur. He always relied on his own cleverness in reproducing the oddities of human beings, and on the impulse or inspiration of the moment in depicting pathos. With an uncanny power of observation, he was a subtle and instinctive mimic, trusting entirely to spontaneous sensibility when playing 'straight' parts. 'Genius', he used to say, 'is an infinite capacity for not having to take pains', and he believed that acting was more a matter of temperament than training:

> The adroit actor should be able at will to adapt his individuality to the character he is portraying. By the aid of his imagination he becomes the man, and behaves unconsciously as the man would or should behave; this he does instinctively rather than from any conscious study, for what does not come spontaneously may as well not come at all.

This dependence on natural ability and innate capacity was sufficient for him, but no other actor of genius would have shared his confidence. It was the philosophy of the amateur, not the professional; and though in his case the outcome was unique, we shall find that the resultant vices were as spectacular as the virtues were transcendent.

At the conclusion of the season at the Olympic he went on tour again in various companies, playing French marquises, Italian counts and German barons successfully enough to receive 'burnt offerings of fried fish' from his admirers on Saturday nights at the Garrick Theatre in Leman Street, Poplar. He enjoyed the life, meeting all sorts of people, accepting and giving hospitality. Always short of money, he constantly anticipated his salary and once replied to the remonstrances of the business-manager, 'Thrift is a virtue it is easy to urge upon others.' He read a lot about the stage, studying the criticisms of Hazlitt, Leigh Hunt and Charles Lamb, of whom he confided in a notebook: 'Dear Charles Lamb occasionally drivels, *vide* his remarks on keeping up a kind of good-humoured understanding with the audience.' He wrote down all the passages he could find that described famous bits of acting. He read plays, and decided that he liked Goldsmith's *The Good-natured Man* quite as much as *She Stoops to Conquer*. He enjoyed the novels of Scott, Dickens and Thackeray, and he even got through the works of Charles Darwin and John Stuart Mill. Late in life he pretended that he had never read anything. 'I never read: I'm afraid of cramping my style,' he said. But his early note-books prove that he had laid a satisfactory foundation for a style which, apart from occasional witticisms, might have been anyone else's.

Then, and always, he enjoyed the pleasures of the table; but though he considered that 'It is better to drink a little too much than much too little', he never abused the blessing of good wine. He knew that 'a good man is the better, a bad man the worse, for drink', but that even a good man is no better for being drunk. He had however a true toleration for drunkards, because they amused him. While in Dublin on one of his early tours, he was invited to a convivial gathering where his health was proposed by a fellow in words which he treasured in his memory:

Sir, you have a great future behind ye. I feel that you will achieve a great career if ye can avoid one rock that I see looming ahead. That rock, sir, is a whirlpool that has upset the apple-cart that has undermined better men than you are, sir, or are ever likely to be, sir, and that rock is—Drink.

At which point the speaker collapsed and was carried from the room. Tree managed to avoid the rock and escape the whirlpool, but he always sympathized with those who were wrecked by the first and absorbed by the second.

During his early years on the stage he kept a diary, and when in the mood, or when anything seemed worth recording, he made an entry. Late in life, while preserving many of the small note-books in which he had jotted his own and other people's sayings, he destroyed the volumes containing his diary, declaring that he soon broke the habit of keeping one because it would have made his life too self-conscious. He extracted a single passage from the record of 1875 and kept it among his papers. It dealt with Ellen Terry's Portia and has already been quoted. But somehow the diary for the year 1880 escaped destruction, and those passages which reveal aspects of the writer must appear here. It happens that the year 1880 saw the end of his first wanderings in the provinces and the beginning of his London career, so these entries have an especial interest.

We find him at the end of January staying at Scanin's Hotel in York and playing the old Marquis de Pontsablé in *Madame Favart*. The company went on to Scarborough, where he put up at the Imperial Hotel, his salary being raised to £14. 14s. a week, in those days extremely good pay for a relatively unknown provincial actor:

> Synge and Burt wanted me to sign for 6 months. This I declined— upon being pressed told them that in case I should die before the expiration of that term, I should feel I had not fulfilled my earthly duties and my conscience would therefore not permit me to undertake such responsibilities.

On Saturday, January 31st, 'I played wretchedly, having dined late and very heavily with Synge. Moral: Don't dine late!' It was Hamilton Synge's company, and Burt was acting-manager. The next day, Sunday, after being photographed 'in various positions', he drove with three friends in a landau to Bridlington, where they dined and 'returned through the night to Scarborough'.

Monday, February 2nd:

> Started for Bradford at 8.15. Miss Newton, who had been very kind, left us at York. Rehearsed at Bradford—our new Madame Favart, Cornelie d'Auka, very imperfect—as also was the Hector (Strathmore)—melancholy performance at night—I had to prompt both newcomers—slept at Victoria Hotel (bill for one day £2.15.) —then took lodgings at 4 Salem Street which shared with Burt— lodgings very nice and clean.

Sunday, February 8th.

> Dinner: Burt, Cornelie d'Auka, Alexander, and Strathmore— most pleasant evening—agreeably surprised at d'Auka—a woman with plenty of good in her. Walter Fisher arrived from London to join company again—wonder whether he will keep straight this time.

The Alexander here mentioned was to become Sir George Alexander and Tree's only serious rival as an actor-manager. He ran the St James's Theatre for twenty-seven years, producing Oscar Wilde's first and last comedies, *Lady Windermere's Fan* and *The Importance of Being Earnest*, and Arthur Pinero's most popular plays, *The Second Mrs Tanqueray* and *His House in Order*. He was touring in Robertson's *Caste* when Tree ran across him in 1880.

A cryptic entry in pencil on February 9th suggests a love-affair: 'Found letter—Crash!—Here goes another illusion for ever!—Be firm this time.' It also suggests that he had not been firm last time. Hostility towards the stage must have been shared by some of his family's friends; hence the next entry:

Wednesday, February 11th.

> Went to see Constance Ambler—found her most charming. Laura Percival staying with her. Talked over old times. Didn't like to call before, for fear she should have inhaled provincial prejudices against actors which I should have been compelled to resent, but received the kindest treatment.

On Friday the 13th he reports that 'During this week and the foregoing about £150 must have been lost at Bradford—owing to a variety of circumstances—chiefly probably owing to the bad quality of the performances at the beginning. Audiences very cold.' On Sunday the 15th came the news that the Theatre Royal at Huddersfield, where they were to perform on Monday, had been burnt to the ground. Much agitation in the company was allayed after a decision that they would play in a hall.

Sunday night:

> Dined with Strathmore; a man named Connolly whom I had seen and admired in a little music-hall at Dublin came in and amused us intensely by his comicalities—gave description (wordless) of a pawnbroker receiving a man's coat, showing the value of detail in 'business'. At Dublin he kept the audience in a roar for about ten minutes in this way without saying a word and I thought him the cleverest low-comedian I had ever seen. On asking him whether there was any money in Huddersfield, said 'Yes, if you take it there.' Connolly told a good story about Paul Hering the clown, illustrating that the ruling passion is strong in death—for he replied on his death-bed, when the doctor was leaving him promising to call the next day, 'All right, I shan't be out'—this when he could barely move in his bed.

Monday, February 16th. 'Arrived [Huddersfield] after unpleasant journey, consequent on last night's dissipation. At the White Hart Hotel—wretched place. Stage rigged up in the Armoury Hall—small but enthusiastic audience.' His residence at the White Hart made him 'Wish we hadn't come here. Mem: Always go to the best hotels. Life too short for bad ones.'

The company were at Nottingham on the 23rd, performing at the Theatre Royal. Tree had nice lodgings at 5 Lower Talbot Street, where he read Jules Verne's *Master Zacharius* and decided to dramatize it. While in the town he saw the pictures at Nottingham Castle. They proceeded to the Theatre Royal, Newcastle-on-Tyne, where he had very good lodgings at 2 North Street, Saville Row; and on Monday, the 8th March, they started a fortnight's engagement at the Prince of Wales's Theatre, Liverpool: 'Arrived at Mrs Crosby's, 13 West Derby Street (excellent lodgings)—received big reception on reappearing on this stage after 4 months.'

In spite of many evenings passed in a 'merry' or 'jolly' manner, he did not forget his father's birthday on March 9th: 'He was greatly surprised and pleased that I had remembered the occasion. Had renewed offer to go to Prince of Wales's Theatre (London) at once. Greatly puzzled as to my best course—decided to go to London on Saturday night.' He went; put up at the Euston Hotel; saw his family; and interviewed Genevieve Ward, who was about to revive her huge success *Forget-me-not* at the Prince of Wales's, then owned and managed by Edgar Bruce. Tree found her 'most agreeable', promised to see Bruce on Monday morning, and dined that Sunday at Kettner's with his brother Julius and his friend A. K. Moore. He returned to Liverpool without seeing Bruce, who sent him a telegram, to which he replied 'giving terms'. On Thursday the 18th Julius and Moore arrived at Liverpool, and that night Synge gave a supper-party:

Grand evening. Julius recited several poems of his own—were he able to publish them, I feel sure they would create a sensation. I recited several poems well and having been worked up was going to recite 'The Raven'. The lights were turned down—but I *could* not recite—owing to Neville's heavy and very audible breathing. After making several starts I informed the company that I could not recite the poem. Everybody asked the reason of this sudden determination and great amusement was caused when I explained the reason. This shows how a most trifling circumstance may upset one even at a moment when one feels one might be equal to a great effort.

It also shows his main weakness and his peculiar fascination as an actor: he never became fully professionalized.

On Friday, March 19th, he heard that

> Bruce accepts my terms. I informed Hamilton Synge that I was desirous of leaving the *Favart* company. He greatly annoyed, but not wishing to stand in my light. He had told me and Julius that, if I remained, he would commission Julius to write a play for me, probably on the subject of *Don Quixote* or Jules Verne's *Master Zacharius* (both subjects chosen by me) and that he would take a London theatre for its production. Am terribly worried what decision to make. Don't wish to annoy Bruce—there is still an uncertainty about the production of the piece. On the other hand my friendship with Synge might be at stake. Consulted and meditated a great deal as to which would be the best course. My fear of becoming a one-part actor after playing one part for so long a time weighs heavily in the balance . . . Went to Liverpool races.

That his internal struggle did not affect his sense of humour is proved by the next day's entry. At supper with a friend he remarked that posterity would supersede matrimony by a higher form of morality. The friend was not so sure about that, or indeed about anything, and gravely enquired: 'You think, then, that our posteriors will be platonic?'

The company were at the Grand Theatre, Leeds, on Monday, March 22nd, for twelve nights, and from his 'good lodgings' at Mrs Swann's, 8 Brunswick Terrace, Tree 'dispatched letter to Edgar Bruce accepting engagement Prince of Wales's Theatre at £10 per week for season'. On Tuesday he 'informed Hamilton Synge that I had decided to leave the company and think I have acted for the best'. After a further twelve nights at the Prince's Theatre, Manchester, he was able to write on Saturday, April 17th: 'Last performance of Pontsablé in *Madame Favart*—thank God! Took an affectionate farewell of the company, who were extremely kind and who left me wishing me great success.' The next day, Sunday, he rehearsed his part of Prince Maleotti in *Forget-me-not* with Genevieve Ward at her house, and on Monday the 19th he 'played Prince Maleotti for the first time; was successful; had a good make-up, which was generally praised'. Then came a new part:

Friday, May 7th:

Dress rehearsal of *L'Aventurière*—a really great success—was terribly nervous—and each time that I had finished a scene felt I had failed to do what I had wanted in the way of effect. I was therefore really surprised to find what an impression had been made. This has been of the utmost value to me professionally.

Monday, May 10th. 'Today took place the performance of *L'Aventurière* before the Prince of Wales—a big success—see notices—have received nothing but congratulations on every side.'

At the end of the month

Genevieve Ward presented me with a 'Souvenir de *L'Aventurière*' in the shape of a handsome silver cigarette-case and match-box, accompanied by the following note: 'May the accompanying little souvenir remind you of the stride you made in your profession as Monte Prade and of my thanks for your zeal in the enterprise.'

He had been reciting at private houses; but after doing so for a gentleman named Samuelson at 2 Charles Street, Lowndes Square, he determined 'I will never recite again for money, if I can help it. There seems to be something undignified in this kind of work and it is only the remuneration that has tempted me in this case.' He got £5 5s. for it, which was half his salary at the theatre, but he was beginning to place self-respect above earning-capacity. Edgar Bruce was delighted with his work and offered him a three-years' engagement, but he thought it best to temporise. He was asked to meet all sorts of interesting people: Clement Scott, the dramatic critic; Dion Boucicault, the dramatist, who sang 'The Wearing of the Green'; Coquelin, the actor, who recited several things at a party given by Mrs Tennant at Richmond Terrace; Madame Modjeska, the Polish actress, who recited so expressively that Alma-Tadema remarked, 'I never knew that I understood Polish till now.' Tree did not think much of Sarah Bernhardt in *Adrienne Lecouvreur*, and thought nothing at all of Mounet-Sully, whose shouting and grunting made Irving's eccentricities of voice and gesture mild by comparison.

Early in July he appeared at the Imperial Theatre as Sir Andrew Aguecheek in *Twelfth Night*:

'Odell played Malvolio splendidly and the performance was

altogether pronounced creditable. Enjoyed playing Sir Andrew. Introduced following business at exit after drunken scene.—Try to get to door, but find myself in another place at each attempt—happy thought: seize candlestick—see two candlesticks, and try to get hold of imaginary one—burn fingers at the other—then, happy thought: there's only one candle—close one eye—seize candlestick and walk straight out of door without swerving. Powles, who supported Odell financially, lost £120 through this performance, of which the total expenses were £150. Made £18 this week—still hard up—why?'

In those days the London theatres closed from July to September, and Tree had an offer to play the Miser in *Les Cloches de Corneville* and the First Lord in *Pinafore* at Brussels and Antwerp during the vacation; but apparently he did not take it. At the request of Genevieve Ward, he acted on several occasions in a playlet called *La Pluie et le Beau Temps*, which she gave at private houses, for example at Hamilton Aïdé's:

The Prince of Wales was present and appeared highly pleased. Madame Modjeska and Forbes Robertson played a 'Proverb' by H. Aïdé called 'All or Nothing'—rather wishy-washy. The Prince sat at supper between Mrs. Langtry and Madame Modjeska—the latter rather astonished me by smoking a cigarette.

The season at the Prince of Wales's finished on Saturday, July 24th, and the diary is blank until Wednesday, October 20th, when we find this:

In consequence of repeated differences with Miss Ward, gave up part of Dirksen in *Anne Mie*. I have during the past fortnight been subjected to repeated insults at rehearsal. Every obstacle was thrown in my way and at times I could hardly proceed with rehearsals, so much was I affected. Thank Heaven, I did not forget myself and have been repeatedly complimented by the company on my patience and reticence under a most trying and provoking ordeal. Wrote a letter (copy kept) to Clement Scott on the subject. Edgar Bruce behaved extremely well and is most anxious to retain my services—he also promised me the part of De Taldé in the production of *Damscheff*.

It is perhaps worth mentioning here that Genevieve Ward was the last of the Siddonian actresses: she had the grand manner of the old school, and no one who saw them could ever forget her Volumnia in *Coriolanus*, her Margaret in *Richard III*, performed with tremendous effect when she was well past seventy. She was 42 years old when she made the success of her lifetime in *Forget-me-not*, which she played over two thousand times in different parts of the world. Having compelled Count de Guerbal to marry her at Warsaw in 1855, she left him for ever immediately after the ceremony, and for the rest of her life remained extremely susceptible to slights, usually fancied, from the male sex. When she was nearly eighty years old she took serious offence at a thoughtless but quite unintentional action by the present writer, who, at a curtain-call, held the hand of the leading girl instead of hers. It is therefore likely, as she had shown herself pleased with his success as an actor, that Tree had been paying too much attention to a younger woman in the company.

There is nothing more in the 1880 diary except a list of parts played by the diarist up to date, and a brief memorandum of 'Things to bear in mind', of which there were two: 'Be careful of a peculiar habit of dropping and waving the hands in an uncertain manner—have been told this is a mannerism of mine', and 'In shrieking, don't shout, but draw the breath in.'

Although he again toured the provinces in various plays during the next three years, he acted in London as well, making an impression as Scott Ramsey in *Where's the Cat?* at the Criterion Theatre and as Lambert Streyke in *The Colonel* at the Prince of Wales's. Both these characters were lampoons of Oscar Wilde, then being caricatured in *Punch*, the editor of which, F. C. Burnand, wrote the latter play. Tree was clearly marked out for exotic parts, and he had no objection to burlesque. Indeed, he wrote a parody of Wilde's affectations which was published in *Punch* under the heading 'Oscar Interviewed' on January 14th, 1882. As an æsthete Oscar parodied himself, and would have read with amused toleration the remarks attributed to him by an interviewer on his arrival in New York:

Quite; I have been too ill, too utterly ill. Exactly—seasick in fact, if I must descend to so trivial an expression . . .

I took the Newdigate. Oh! no doubt every year some man gets the Newdigate; but not every year does Newdigate get an Oscar . . .

I am not quite sure what I mean. The true Poet never is. In fact, true Poetry is nothing if it is intelligible . . .

A few years later Tree met Wilde, and from that moment was one of the few contemporaries who fully appreciated his genius.

The oddity of Tree's personality did not appeal to everyone, and in spite of his occasional successes in London no one would have prophesied for him a brilliant future. The managers preferred the type of actor whose appearance and personality attracted women, such as H. B. Conway, who became a *jeune premier* under Irving at the Lyceum and an idol of female playgoers. David James, lessee of the Vaudeville Theatre, had made up his mind about the good-looking Conway and the queer-looking Tree, writing to his acting-manager:

> And now, my dear Smaile, please understand me, I will give Tree £15 a week—not a penny more. H. B. Conway can have £25, as I think he will draw it, but £15 is every shilling as much as Tree is, or ever will be, worth, and I shan't go beyond that, so please do not write me again on the subject.

But David James was mistaken.

CHAPTER 4

Love Letters

Early in 1881 Herbert Tree attended a Fancy Dress Ball; and as he had been acting old men on the stage, he went in his ordinary dress clothes disguised as himself. In the course of the night he was introduced to a girl of eighteen named Maud Holt. Destined for a scholarly career, she was studying and teaching Latin, Greek, mathematics and science at Queen's College, Harley Street, with the object of going on to Girton College, Cambridge. But already she was stage-struck, having played Shakespeare's Ophelia and Beatrice in amateur performances. After her introduction to Herbert she also became actor-struck, and used to go out of her way in order to pass the Garrick Club, hoping that, as it was full of actors, she might meet him either entering or emerging therefrom. He had seen her play Beatrice, and in May, 1881, she wrote to ask if he would come to see her in another part. He replied on the 26th from the Prince of Wales's Theatre, Birmingham, where he was appearing in *The Colonel*, that he had asked Edgar Bruce to send someone to report on her performance. Her success made her wish to adopt the stage as a profession; but he advised: 'Don't go on the stage unless you feel you *must*.' She persisted; and in September he wrote to say that a Society had been formed to start a new theatre, of which E. W. Godwin would be Art Director, and that he had continually brought her name before the meetings of members. That winter he called at her rooms over a shop at 10 Orchard Street. Sitting by the fire he recited poetry and told stories. He called again and she sang to him. Soon they were sending poetry to each other, and he must have been too demonstrative, for on February 3rd, 1882, he finished a letter: 'I have nothing brilliant to say and I don't think you like me to say affectionate things.' But she undeceived him on this point, and on the 7th he wrote:

My dear Maud

For so I may now call you, I hope. I write simply to tell you how happy I am and to say how I appreciate your kindness. I really cannot say anything sensible. I feel rather light-headed (I suppose it's excitement) and I have been laughing on the stage most disgracefully—I had a few oysters before the theatre. I do so want to see you again . . . may I hope to see you tomorrow? I know I don't deserve it—but then it will be all the kinder of you! I hope you will take care of your cold. How strange it seems—all this—does it not?

Believe me ever
Yours sincerely
Herbert.

Five days later he asked her to be his wife. Though suffering tremors at the thought of what her relations and what the people at the College would say if she stated her intention to marry an actor, she did not take long to make up her mind, and on the 14th February they walked from her rooms to Clanricarde Gardens, where his father and stepmother lived, to announce their engagement. She liked his family as much as they liked her, and thereafter Herbert and Maud lunched every Sunday at the house of his people. He was then sharing rooms with his friend A. K. Moore at 29 Maddox Street, where parties were given in Maud's honour and she sang Herbert's favourites in her repertoire: 'Echo', 'The Creole Love-Song' and 'Es war ein Traum'. A few passages from his letters to her in the early days of their engagement indicate his feelings. The style, broken up with dots and dashes, is hurried, for he seized any free moment during rehearsal or performance to let her hear from him:

I am so happy tonight—everything seems radiant—everything is tinged with you.

How nice it would be if all were like today—all bright—all sunshine—all sowing—no reaping—all laughing—no weeping—that's poetry—at least rhyme—perhaps reason.

My dearest, Thank you for your kind sweet letter—it was such a pleasure to me. 'Mein Alles Du'—how pretty that is, and how pretty of you to say it!—I have been rather unhappy all day—that is to say I have had a blank feeling—I suppose it's not seeing you . . . I met a poor fellow going home last night—he endeavoured to sell me some wonderful little birds he had put on some strings and which have the appearance of flying up and down—I gave him a shilling—but being

no longer 'pleased with a rattle, tickled with a straw' I declined the
toy. It would have done you good to have heard his blessing—he
said too he hoped I might never be in want of what I had given him
(poor fellow!). Indeed I hope I never shall!—it is a dreadful thing to
think of—is it not? So you see I did *one* good act yesterday—and
what a cheap luxury—only a shilling—the price of a cigar! And then
I walked and talked a long time with him, and got quite a shilling's-
worth of character in return. Then I came home and read the end
of 'Enoch Arden'—I confess to one little tear—and that was shed over
the last three lines which seem to me beautifully suggestive:

> 'So past the strong heroic soul away.
> And when they buried him the little port
> *Had seldom seen a costlier funeral.*'

That is *simple* . . .

I felt rather 'out of it' this evening—but then we are neither of us
demonstrative in the presence of others. I will make up for the want
of ardour another time . . . I scarcely even now can take in all the
importance of our situation, dear. I pray, at times, that all may be
happy for you—as happy as I know you deserve—I am striving towards that with all my might—How good you are to me!—Don't
think this gush—It is written because I can't help it. I know how
much your happiness will depend on me—on my seriousness . . .
My last thoughts tonight and my first thoughts tomorrow will be
of you. Good-night, God bless you—Ever affectionately yours
Herbert.

I couldn't go home tonight to study—I knew I should be unhappy
and I am sufficiently cowardly to avoid those unpleasant musings
which I know my inner man was preparing for me.—My dear, I
am so sorry to think that you should not be entirely happy about me
—even though your thoughts may be unreasonable . . . My dearest,
do not think badly of me—I don't mean this for my own sake so
much as for yours.

In May, 1882, they acted together in a one-act play at the home
of his parents, and in the course of the evening he seems to have
behaved more like a producer than a lover, which explains this:

I should not like you to know me as I was tonight—you see the
excitement and whirl of acting makes one break through one's own
ideas of what is correct—I don't want you to know this—and I can't
help it.—I am so sorry you should have witnessed that exhibition of
brutal temper.

One of the reasons he did not wish her to become an actress was that she would see a side of him not apparent in the ordinary intercourse of life:

> In regard to your going on the stage, my mind is still filled with doubts.—However, probably I have not sufficient in me to give you true happiness—that happiness which I should have liked above all things to have been capable of giving you—and so you shall do as you please.

He could not help paying attention to women, especially attractive ones, and his flatteries may have been mistaken for affection by a suspicious nature. The leading lady in *The Colonel* was Myra Home, who afterwards married Arthur Pinero; and when he bought a scarf at Liberty's for her birthday, Maud was glacial enough to make him change his opening mode of address, though he warmed as the letter lengthened:

> My dear Maud
> I must send you a few lines to tell you how sorry I am that I should again be the cause of making you unhappy—Oh, pray don't think seriously what you spoke hastily, dearest.—Only it is so difficult to act strictly according to the cruel letter of what is considered the right thing to do. I assure you most solemnly that I have not broken through the spirit of what is right in doing what I have done—Indeed my only reproach is that I should make you unhappy—you who are so good, so very good to me.—To lose you, dearest, would be to lose everything—it seems as if it would all go 'black-out'. I promise you I will do as I said.—Pray forgive what has gone before —and *above all*, dearest, don't worry yourself. I will walk past Orchard Street tonight after the theatre—if you would see me for only a minute, dear, I should be much happier—I shall be passing at about 15 minutes past 11. I want you to have a long restful night, dearest, and tomorrow we shall, I hope, be quite happy together, with no misgivings.—Pray destroy this letter as I should not like you to be reminded of this blot of the past in what I hope, my darling, may be a bright future. I shall think of you a great deal tonight. God bless you, my sweet—Ever your affectionate Herbert.

There was another cause of disagreement, which, though insignificant, shows that neither was prepared to sacrifice individuality for a quiet life. She admired the poetry of Browning, while he made it clear that he could not share her admiration:

> My dearest,
> I am going to make a confession—will you break with me for it?

—or will you still hope to convert me from the error of my ways? —I am dissatisfied with myself for not feeling what you feel—I want to and I can't—it is like writing on oily paper—you can't do it—it is a feeling of mental impotency. Yet I have a sense of the beautiful —an appreciation of the fine—have I not shown it?—But Browning is to me mystically meaningless—a scientific word-painter—Why not be simple?—Shakespeare was!—How grandly commonplace! I have turned over poem after poem—hoping to educate myself by one for the understanding of another—but it will not come—my mind seems Browning-barren—I would far sooner talk to you—I mean it does me more good.—Is all this very dreadful? What will you think of me? But I must tell you—will you read some poem to me?—perhaps I may see it differently by the light of you.—I want to like the poetry because I know you do—but to me it is mathematical at present.—There I have said it.—Shall you jilt me for it? —It is late, darling—I will say goodnight—I had hoped to be able to feel better by reading this—but it leaves me sober. Sweet dreams! Herbert.

She tried him with Tennyson, and this time he was able to agree: 'I enjoyed "Maud" immensely—of course *there* is genius.—I have taken the liberty of marking some favourite passages amongst which is that ending "the delight of low replies".'

The month of June brought misunderstandings between them. He had taken rooms in a cottage, which he shared with George Alexander, in Heath Street, Hampstead, and was receiving lessons from Hermann Vezin, a player who had made a reputation in the previous generation and who was recognized as an authority on elocution. As so often happens when an actor begins to make a name on the London stage, discreditable stories, either invented or embroidered on fact, were told about Herbert, and Maud was inclined to believe them when he was not present to allay her suspicions. In the first days of June he reproved her:

I am sorry if I was stupid today—but it really hurts me just a little when you say such things as you did, even though they might be said in jest.

I don't love you less, dear, for having these moments of womanly pique which in a man one would call unreasonable. I will only say that I think you were mistaken in thinking me careless of you—I was only *not demonstrative*—that is all—I wanted to be nice to you—but you wouldn't let me—and after a time I had a feeling of disappointment. So I hope the latest Railway Mystery is cleared up! It was not I who murdered your love—it was your love that committed suicide.—I was very sorry, darling, to leave you this evening—on Sunday I hope we shall have a long day together. I will endeavour to turn the bright side towards you—it is alas not always day!—but it is not that the sun does not shine—rather it is the earth that revolves and makes the night.

He was acting at Brighton late that month and staying at the Old Ship Hotel:

I wish, my own, that you were here, and we would take long nocturnal walks by the 'sad sea waves'. I shall go on the beach every night and think of you.—I hope nothing very dreadful was said about me. Never mind, darling, what has passed.

If any lies have been told about me, I hope you won't believe them. Tell me what you have heard—I have no fear.

I must see you in order to know what it is that has evidently upset you.—I really don't know anything that I have done to make you worried.—I am only sorry, my darling, that you should have so much trouble with me.—But it will be far better to know everything that has been said.—I hope you will not be too readily influenced by narrow-minded advisers.—Surely you could tell me.—It must be something very serious if you cannot write.—You can rest assured of one thing, my sweet—and that is that I shall not alter towards you and I hope that I may live to make you very happy and to make you forget all the cloudy past in the bright future. I wish I hadn't left town, and all might have been well.—Whatever may be the cause of your worry, I think it extremely unkind and puritanical of those people to make you unhappy and I shall say so to them, if I have the opportunity.—I shall think of you tonight.—Herbert.

My darling Maud. Your telegram reached me this afternoon and I at once telegraphed you to Bexley to tell you how happy I was to know that you had forgiven me— . . . I was so entirely upset yesterday that I was unable to coherently speak of the matter which has caused you, my own, so much trouble and grief. You shall not regret your forgiveness—the forgivers are more blessed than the deceivers—although I can hardly be said to have deceived.—I do think you were carried away by those feelings for which I love you the more—but which perhaps spring from your inexperience of the world.—I have done nothing since our engagement for which you could really blame me.

In July Maud's sister was ill at Aix-les-Bains and needed someone to look after her. Maud was asked to go, and Herbert, deeply disappointed, wrote: 'Your dear sister may perhaps have a greater claim upon you than I have—so pray go and don't think too much of me in the matter.' His lack of enthusiasm for her sisterly duty may have vexed Maud, for he closed another letter with the words: 'I hope by this time that you are in a sound beautiful sleep dreaming that you are married to a fairy-like being without human failings,—unlike your disappointing Herbert.'

While nursing her sister at Aix she received daily letters from Herbert, telling her all the news: that he had been to see Edwin Booth in *Richelieu* and thought him splendid in the curse of Rome scene but commonplace in many parts of the play; that he had talked with Ellen Terry; that he had been to the theatre with E. W. Godwin; that he was rehearsing a one-act tragedy called *Merely Players* by Edward Rose and getting the critics to see it; that he longed for his 'dearest, dearest Maud'; that he wished to see her at Aix and would come the moment the season finished unless she opposed his wish; that he would not bother her in the least if he came; that he begged her to be happy and not to worry too much about things; and that her letters were the only bright incidents in his life. The one-act tragedy was duly produced—'I had a tremendous call before the curtain'—but the critic of the *Morning Post* did not like it, and Herbert tried to console himself with the reflection that 'one cannot always expect everything rose-coloured'. More stories about his past life were filtering through to Maud, and on July 28th he wrote a dignified letter:

My dear Maud,
My last letters will have shown you that I was beginning to be anxious at not hearing from you.—This morning I was greatly upset at receiving no tidings of you—but I have since learned from my mother and your sister, Mrs Floyd, that your previous misgivings have reasserted themselves, and that they have made you very unhappy.—That my folly should be the cause of upsetting you, no one could more seriously lament than I do.—But the time has come for me to speak and act with decision.—That I love you very dearly my letters of the last few days will have told you again, and I assure you most solemnly that my loyalty to you has been and will be unchanging, if you choose to ask for it. But I am grieved and pained to think that your confidence in me should be less firm.—Do the few miles and the few hours that separate us make so great a difference in your feelings?—and is this the love which you had taught

me to treasure?—I confess I cannot reconcile all this wavering with the courage of my Maud.—What have I done to deserve this bitter disappointment?—I was foolish—perhaps weak—but not vicious or dishonourable.—I gave you to understand, when I first asked you to care for me, that my past life had not been entirely unworldly. I repented what I had done, and you forgave me.—I have endeavoured to make every reparation for the error committed before I knew you, and I have been true and loyal to you.—There was never at any time the slightest claim upon me, and I have recently taken steps to remove even the possibility of a shadow in the future. Can I do more? Have I hitherto been impatient of your reproaches, and the attacks of your friends?—To whom do you owe your allegiance— to them, or to me?—It is for you now to say—I do not care to enter into competition with them—nor will I allow you to despise me, as you would grow to despise me, did I not demand your entire trust, and a love which is not regulated by acquaintances.—As this may be demanding too much, I am anxious to release you from such a bondage—for I assure you that if I honour and value your love, I also honour and value my own dignity.—Your affectionate Herbert.

Before this letter was posted he received a wire from Maud: 'Come if like directly.' He sat down at once and enclosed the letter in another note which ran:

My dearest: Since writing this, I have received your telegram.—I shall come to you at once.—Nevertheless I think it right to send this letter—I hope you won't think it harsh—and certainly I think it best not to keep it back.—I shall be with you, then, very soon—my dearest. I shall telegraph you tomorrow when I leave London.— Meantime God bless you. Your loving Herbert.

On arrival at Aix he put up at the Grand Hotel and dropped her a line: 'My dearest . . . can I see you soon? . . . What a lovely place this is! I have already bathed myself in sulphur.' She did not immediately reply, and again he altered his epistolary tone, the uncertain grammar revealing his agitation:

My dear Maud
Perhaps you do not want me after my last letter.—Anyhow, it may be that it would preferred [sic] that I should not see you. If this is so, I will not trouble you—I will not inflict myself on you, and if you will only give me a hint I will leave by the very first train. I have already given you a great deal more trouble that [sic] I am worth—so let me go.—It may be better for you, and I assure you that I shall not blame you—I shall only feel how sad it is.—Think it

all well over before you decide, and if you come to the conclusion that we must part, you had better not even see me, but send me one line.—Anyhow I only intended making a very short stay.—I did not wish to be unkind in saying what I did in my last letter to you —but it will be much better for us all not be [sic] undecided any longer. Believe me I think of your happiness in saying this, for you don't deserve to suffer. Herbert.

I don't know what to do or say—I wish the two hours of suspense were over! Don't hesitate to do whatever you think for the best. H.

She thought it best to see him, and he spent a very happy fortnight at Aix. They walked in the woods, making love and reciting poetry. Having nothing to forgive, she forgave him for everything, which pleased him so much that in an indulgent mood he encouraged her to believe he would do anything she asked. They arranged to get married as soon as she could leave her sister, and he promised to find rooms in which they could start life together.

On returning to England he went to stay at an old house which his father had taken for the summer, Thurnham Court, some four miles from Maidstone. Built in the time of Elizabeth at the foot of the Kentish Downs, it is a sort of literary landmark, for at one time Byron leased it in order to be near Lady Oxford. From there he wrote on August 20th:

My darling Child

I have just returned from a walk which I took in order to be alone with you—that is to think of you and what you said to me in your letters. I have re-read your dear letter and wished, oh how much I wished, that you were walking by my side. I went down by a field of waving corn, the sun just setting, to a little wood near here— there was an old withered fir-tree by which I sat and thought of you, my dearest. It does indeed seem hard that we should be separated now that we might be *so* happy together—we may not have the time to wander about in the fields for a long, long time to come, and it would be so pretty now in the spring-time of our love . . . When happiness is within one's reach, one cannot help sometimes wishing that one might snatch it . . . How I wish I were driving to the station tomorrow to fetch you—we should have such a nice long drive (4 miles) by ourselves and we would drive very slowly up the hills, so as not to tire the horse, wouldn't we? . . . This is a most charming place—a very old-fashioned house with lots of rooms— and a beautiful lawn-tennis ground on which we are going to play tomorrow—would that you were too! . . . We have had such a quiet happy day today—I did not go to church—but I *thought* church this evening.—I have been idly sketching, and reading *The Newcomes* . . . Ever your own Herbert.

Five days later he heard that her sister was worse and that she could not leave her. He was in despair:

I feel so unhappy and dreary—so 'numb'—and the day is dreary too —a drizzling rain with no prospect of sunshine . . . Yes dear, those were happy times that you speak of—but it hurts me that you should think the earlier days the happiest. I thought some days at Aix were happier even than those—did you care for me more *then*? I do indeed hope that our future days may be happier than any that have gone before—I will try and make them so—but today all is hopeless —all this weary waiting—all these upsets—and then I am not well again today . . . How I wish you were in my arms now to drive away this horrid feeling of emptiness longing to be filled . . . I continue to have the most horrible dreams—always fancying that either you have gone from me, or I from you . . . I am still reading *The Newcomes*—it is very pretty—but nothing can cheer me up today.—All is ???!?!!?—Sir George Hampson, the owner of this place, called the other day and I left a game of lawn-tennis to say a few words to him.—After I had gone he said to my mother, 'Your son is a most puzzling lad—his opinions are those of a man of 25— and he looks a boy of 17!' Very odd, but quite true—I thought this would amuse you. Good-bye, my very dear one—Your utterly demoralised but still loving Herbert. Come as soon as you can—that is all.

Her next letter was more cheerful and he discussed with his family the advisability of asking the local clergyman to publish the banns the following Sunday, telling her that

Three Sundays would have to elapse in order that it might be the 'third time of asking', although I have asked you a good many more times. But I do wish us to be married here—the church is close by, and all is so peaceful, and you would as it were issue to the church from the bosom of my family. So let it be—let us be married within two or perhaps three weeks—*and let this be decisive*—Tell your sister so . . . Good-bye, my tantalizing love. . . .

On Sunday, August 27th, he wrote again:

My Sweetheart . . .
    Come as soon as you can, dearest—DO!—Oh, I longed for you to be by my side last night. I was riding home alone over the hills at sun-

set—I was as happy as it is possible for a human being to be *without* his dear love beside him—feeling the glow of health, having that sense of freedom and buoyancy and elation of body and mind and seeing all around the most glorious landscape the eye could behold. The sun was setting in the west and lighting up myriads of little clouds with bright gold and crimson—in the east a rainbow peeping through some dark clouds with an occasional glimpse of blue sky —On my right the wooded hills, dark blue clouds rising above, and on the left the corn in the fields looking really *golden*—the ploughed fields *purple*—part of the landscape overshadowed by clouds—and part lighted up by the straggling sun-rays.—It was really glorious and I murmured a little blessing for my darling far away.—*Do come* —so that we can ride together in the sunset . . .

Maud's answer gave him a shock. Her character contained a strong element of puritanism and no little determination. An impartial observer, reading her letter and his rejoinders, would have foreseen certain consequences of a marriage between two people who were alike in resolution and opposed in temperament. The project of a new theatre having been dropped, he had become a member of a Costume Society, the leading spirit of which was the architect E. W. Godwin, whose amorous affairs were as notorious as his public appearances in a wide black hat and a long black cloak were striking. Herbert hoped to make a good deal of money out of the Society, but Maud was more concerned over the morals of its founder, against whom she had already warned him, extracting some sort of undertaking that he would keep out of Godwin's way as much as possible; his nature being such that he would seem to promise anything for the sake of peace and the harmony of the hour. He had referred to the meetings of the Costume Society in his last letter, and this is what Maud sent in return for his description of the setting sun over the Kentish weald:

I have *no* sympathy about the Costume Society—and I am *quite* opposed to the idea of your engaging in anything that occupies you the greater part of the day. These are minor considerations however compared with the *intense* objection I have to your being engaged in any scheme *whatsoever* in which you work hand and glove with Mr Godwin—I have your promise about him—yet how can you be working with Messrs Wiles and Godwin at the head of your concern without being thrown into almost hourly companionship with both?

Today for the first time Emmie asked me who this Mr Godwin was—and when I told her 'the architect' she was *quite* horrified—utterly disgusted at the idea of my ever having known such a man. She knows something about him, I suppose—at all events says he is such a man as she would no more shake hands with than with a snake, and is as sorry as you know I am for *you*, whom she so likes, to know such a man. Do not now therefore think that all I said to you on our new life that day unreasonable and foolish. I was right. I was right. I was *right*. I do *not* ask things of you unreasonably—and I *do* ask you not to be this man's friend—not to have yourself put down with him. I warn you, you will have to choose between him and me. This is a subject on which you know how strongly I feel. But if you are seriously taking up this new scheme—for after all I cannot ask you to forgo it because of Mr Godwin, any more than I can forbid you London which holds Mr Godwin—I shall very certainly keep on a great deal of my teaching. This I think only the sensible thing to do. I *must* be alone at night. I need not be alone in the daytime and shall be really glad, as you know, not to lose my work entirely—I shall not of course keep on very much—my High Schools and a *very* little College—taking up only four afternoons a week, and perhaps *one* morning. I think perhaps this after all will be happy for us. We shall be then very much more together than most married people—and of course I will not dream of rushing about and tiring myself over my work as I used—I promise you this. So, after my little outburst, dear, I come round to your way of thinking, and shall by this post arrange my plans for keeping my work. . . . I think of you, my heart's darling, every hour of the day—and love you more every day!! Yours devotedly, Maud.

Herbert's answer was written at once, in pencil, from the Criterion Theatre, where he was about to open in a new play:

My dearest Maud

I have just received your note here at the theatre. I must say that I am surprised at its tone, and I absolutely *forbid* you to take up your college work.—I wish you on no account to take it up again, and certainly I think your *threat* a somewhat ungenerous proceeding, considering that I only took up that other work to be able to make you happier. I don't like you when you act like this—it is not like your own self.—Understand me, I am perfectly serious and determined on this point.—If you ask me to give up the Costume Society I will do so—but I will not have you speak to me in this manner—it is not right, or becoming, and you will, I hope, feel this.—I hope that I am not writing in an unbecoming spirit—forgive me if I speak my mind somewhat strongly.—What has your sister heard about

Godwin?—Let me know.—Of course you are my first consideration and I would never expose you to anything to which you should not be exposed—you know I love you too well. It so happens that I have avoided Godwin since I have been back except to meet him in business matters. I did not mean that I should devote all my afternoons to business as *you* threaten to do. Maud, I hope you will be sorry for this. It is a jarring note that you have struck.—You know how I would give up anything and anybody for you.—I send you back your letter, for I don't like to keep it and I don't like to tear it up—but *you* will do so, will you not? You have grieved me.—I shall telegraph you tomorrow to retract what you have said in regard to College work. You would not have done this, had you guessed how much it has upset me.

He slept on the matter, at Charing Cross Hotel, whence he penned the following (September 1st):

My dearest Maud

I wrote the enclosed during last night's rehearsal, and—although I was very excited at the time—I shall let the letter go as it is. The reflections of the morning leave my mind unchanged, and I am going to telegraph you this morning that the College scheme is out of the question—You understand me, I mean this.—It is for me to use my judgment in regard to my own business affairs.—I merely took up the Society, as by that means I had hoped to add several, perhaps many, hundred pounds a year to my income.—It would not have taken up very much of my time.—Should you in any matter temperately advise me, you know what weight your opinion or your inclination would have with me—but I cannot think that in taking the tone you have in regard to this matter, you are acting quite in the way best calculated to make us both happy in the future—and it is this that grieves me.—Possibly you may have written in temper —and, in order to influence me, said more than you actually meant. —Pray, *pray* don't let anything of this kind allow our love to moult one feather.—I fancy I know the source whence your sister has heard such damaging reports in regard to G.—You know how I feel instinctively with you in all things—and you know how I talked about this very matter on the last day at Aix.—But G. has been in many ways a very good friend to me—and I should not like to actually hurt his feelings by 'cutting' him in a heartless manner—you understand me.—Maud, I expect you to allow me to have a certain authority over your actions—or endless misunderstandings may arise —I am to be the bread-winner, not you—I should not like you to further worry yourself with my work—and if you once set this precedent, there is no knowing where your *whims* may lead you to!

—It must be understood that you cannot act in these matters on your own responsibility—and I am sure that your sisters will agree with me—if you have any doubt, ask them.—I say again I am sorry this has occurred.—Now let the matter drop—I am sorry to have worried you with all this lecture. . . . It is very good of you, dearest, to think so much about me.

Apparently she did let the matter drop, and no more lectures were necessary. He was living in a whirl of rehearsals, morning and night, and in the afternoons rushing about in a hansom cab looking for rooms and telling Maud of his experiences:

I was much amused at one of my interviews today.—I had received a letter informing me that 'a lady of good family' wished to let a place which would exactly suit the taste of the 'party' who advertised. I arrived at Kensington Palace Mansions and was ushered into a desert of a reception room, where I was received by an imposing maiden of eight and forty summers, who asked me how I liked the 'apartment'. I told her that it was rather too large for my taste (I felt sure there would be violent gusts of east winds springing up in the various corners of the room)—she then ushered me into two other apartments of still larger dimensions, informing me that she herself was of as good family as anyone could desire. I felt very much inclined to tell her that I did not wish to take a family but a flat. —I then said, no, I should like some rooms *en suite*—a flat, in fact. 'Ah', she said, 'you cannot expect bedrooms on the same floor in *this* class of house'—and added that flats were going out of fashion. —She thereupon went into her room again—I believe to fetch her pedigree to show me, by way of reference, when I made a dash for the front door and told the cabman to drive in an easterly direction as fast as he could.

Eventually Herbert took rooms on the first floor of No. 2 Old Burlington Street for three guineas a week.

On September 2nd he heard the 'glorious news' that Maud was returning home with her sister. 'Oh, how happy we shall be when we are once more together', he wrote. He had been living in a state of suspense, and during rehearsals had kept asking the hall-porter if there were any letters for him. Henceforth, he declared, all their days must be passed together: 'I have a large balance in the bank, so never mind about your stupid little debts—once marry me and I am responsible.' The raptures of their reunion over, and the wedding hurriedly arranged, he wrote a last premarital letter from the rooms in which they were to start life together:

My dear Childie,

I am writing you a few lines after the theatre to beg you to take great, *great* care of yourself for the next few days—be very careful at crossings, so as not to be run over—for you know what expenses I have incurred in the way of procuring a licence, which is *not* transferable, by the way.—Do consider this! My love, how I wish you were here now—but, oh joy! it is only 4 more days before you will be my own, entirely—when no chaperone can say 'Nay'!—My darling love, I feel quite serious tonight and shall think of you and pray for you so nicely tonight. To think that this is probably the last letter I shall ever address to you in your own name—how strange it seems.—We shall, I pray to God, be very happy together—only be to me as you are now—and I *know* we shall be happy.—How sacred a step it is— sometimes one forgets to see it all in the light I now see it. I *will* try to be a good husband, my darling, and take care of you, as you want to be cared for; and you on your part will overlook as many short-comings as you can.—I want to see you very early tomorrow.—I have no stamps here, so I will leave this letter at Orchard Street. —I am glad to tell you that I played tonight, perhaps better than I have played in my life—and there were shouts of 'Bravo, Tree!' at the fall of the curtain, and of which I felt very proud. I only hope the Other Gods will shout 'Bravo, Tree' when the curtain shall fall on our little domestic drama.

Good-night, my darling love, forgive me all that you have to forgive, and think of me as

Your own loving
Herbert

Their marriage took place in the church just beyond the garden wall of Thurnham Court on Sunday, September 16th, 1882. Maud stayed with his family the previous night, but he was acting on Saturday and could not get down till the morning of the wedding. As Herbert's brother Julius was in Spain, the duty of 'best man' was delegated to his ten-years-old half-brother Max, who was so much impressed by the importance of his office that he inspected the triumphal arches under which the bride and bridegroom would pass from the house to the church. These had been made of leaves and flowers by the gardener, and Max, who thought them worthy of so great an occasion, was a little indig-nant when the gardener's brother said: 'They're not what you

might call awful grand, but they're what you might call rustic.'
With a full sense of the significance of his office, Max posted himself under one of these arches an hour before Herbert's expected
arrival; and when the carriage drove up and Herbert stepped out,
the 'best man' noted with pleasure that his top hat was glossy
enough, but with alarm that he looked pale and excited. 'Have
you lost the ring?' gasped Max, who felt that such a godlike person might easily have mislaid it. But the ring was present with the
bridegroom, and the ceremony was conducted with a smoothness
that won the approval of the 'best man', who was particularly
pleased with the sillabubs at the wedding-breakfast, and amused,
though shocked, by Herbert's remark that the name of the dish
sounded biblical—'And Sillabub, the son of Sillabub, reigned in
his stead.' But this no doubt was said to quicken Max's literary
talent, which had impressed his big brother less than a month
before when, on his tenth birthday, he had drunk his own health
a little too liberally in champagne-cup. 'Max', said Herbert por-
tentously, 'it is bad to be tipsy at ten.' To which Max returned:
'How can one be tipsy when we are conscious they are not?'

No honeymoon being possible while Herbert was busy acting,
the pair went straight to No. 2 Old Burlington Gardens, the first
of their many homes. Like so many marriages, theirs was to
consist of quarrels, reconciliations, infidelity, fidelity, tenderness,
coldness, sympathy, hostility, the change of moods, the differing
of outlooks, the inevitable clash of opposing wills. But through all
their ups and downs she continued to love him and he never
ceased to love her, if not exactly on the lines of the Church
marriage-service.

CHAPTER 5

Gilbert, Irving, Stevenson and Others

Very soon they were looking for a house, and shortly before Maud got her first job on the stage (January '83) they took one in a fashionable quarter: No. 4 Wilton Street, Grosvenor Place. Here they entertained many of the leading figures in the theatre of the time: Hamilton Aïdé, Cecil Clay, W. S. Gilbert, Charles Brookfield, E. W. Godwin, Comyns Carr, Hugh Conway, and others. Occasionally Maud went to see her sister, and a letter from Herbert during one of her absences has been preserved:

> My darling,
> In order that the word of the prophet may be fulfilled, I take up this pen.—The night is cold, the pillar-box looms coldly distant like the morning sun, but my resolve is firm, and I will hie me thither.—The guests, Vezin, Godwin and Claud Ponsonby, have just departed.—We have had a pleasant chatty evening—plenty of scandal, you may imagine.—The corpses of soda-water bottles and those of departed spirits are strewn around me, and I am alone.— Alone, I am not lonely,—for you at all events are with me in spirit. —No sound but the indistinct but approaching tread of the policeman in search of dynamite. *Frankly*, I have no postage stamp!—But you will get this letter in the morning, and be reminded *doubly* of me by the extra postage charged. Come back early, dearest,—I have many things to do tomorrow . . . Good-night, my darling, I hope you have spent a very happy evening, but not too happy to make you grieve to return to
>
> Your loving Herbert

For a short while he was out of work and they had to let the house, taking lodgings off Haverstock Hill, but they were soon back again, and in March '84 he made the first big hit of his career in a farce called *The Private Secretary*, an adaptation from the German of Von Moser by Charles Hawtrey. For a generation

The Private Secretary and *Charley's Aunt* were the two most popular farces on the English stage, and it is generally believed that Tree was the first actor to play the Rev. Robert Spalding in the former. The fact is that, though he 'created' the figure of the ludicrous parson, the original impersonator was Arthur Helmore, who acted the part in the provinces for a trial run of two or three weeks, and later became known as a society entertainer. Tree's appearance as Spalding was quite accidental. Edgar Bruce let his theatre to Hawtrey on condition that the members of his company should be engaged for the various parts in the farce. Tree, under contract with Bruce, was furious at being compelled to play such a ridiculous part in such a silly play, and in revenge deliberately and outrageously burlesqued the curate, devising preposterous 'business', conceiving absurd catchwords, gagging to his heart's content, and practically inventing the part during rehearsals. One touch was added at the last moment. Maud was standing with him in the wings before his first entrance. Suddenly an idea struck him: 'Quick, quick! I must have a bit of blue ribbon in my button-hole.' (In those days a blue ribbon was the badge worn by teetotal fanatics.) Nothing of the kind being at hand, Maud tore a strip from her white sleeve, dashed to the painting-room, dipped it in a pot of the right colour, and got back just in time for his entry. At first the farce was not successful, but gradually it picked up, and when Tree, tired of making a fool of himself, threw up the part, *The Private Secretary* was playing to full houses. The new Spalding, W. S. Penley, adopted all Tree's gags and antics, and played the part, off and on, until he pretended to be the Aunt of Charley in *Charley's Aunt*, making another huge success of that.

Tree abandoned Spalding for a totally dissimilar character, Paolo Macari in *Called Back*, the dramatic version of a 'thriller' by Hugh Conway. By playing the handsome, audacious Italian spy after the timid and comical cleric, he caused a sensation and definitely established himself as a front-rank actor. His performance was the talk of the town, and set a new fashion in melodramatic acting: thenceforward all stage villains were acted in the flamboyant manner of Tree; they became subtle and cynical and coloured instead of being obvious and heavy and unrelieved. The play ran for months; Herbert and Maud took a house in Cheyne Walk, Chelsea; their first child Viola was born (July '84); and there was plenty of money to spare. Maud spent some weeks of the summer at Ramsgate with her baby and the nurse, writing regularly to 'darling Herbie', retailing all the gossip of the hotel, advising him not to go on playing Macari in *Called Back*, which looked like running for ever, and begging him not to keep late hours, not to neglect his food, not to do anything she would not like. She lived for the week-ends when he could join her: 'Oh! darling one, I do wish you were here. I do miss you so, and long for Sunday. Never again will I be persuaded to go away without you.'

After his two sensational successes, Tree appeared without much distinction as Mr Poskett in Arthur Pinero's *The Magistrate* and in a revival of *Engaged* by W. S. Gilbert, whose operas with Sullivan provided the most popular entertainment of the eighties. When the curtain fell on the opening performance of *Engaged*, the author went to see Tree, noted that he was perspiring freely, and remarked: 'Your skin has been acting at all events.' Tree was chiefly concerned over the moustache he was wearing and said that he ought to have grown one for the part. 'You will be able to grow an enormous moustache before you can play this part,' said Gilbert, dryly. It is to Tree's credit that he retailed these quips in conversation and recorded them in his private papers, wherein he also reported a duologue between himself and the dramatist during a week-end that he and his wife spent with the Gilberts in the early days of their acquaintanceship:

'Have you had any offers during the week?' asked Gilbert.

'Yes, three.'

'Which have you accepted?'

'None.'

'Surely that is very immoral with a wife and child to support?'

'Possibly, but my ambition is in a different direction.'

Tree then expatiated on the necessity of doing the best of which one was capable. At the conclusion of their argument, Gilbert said:

'Look at me; I have been writing down to the public all these years.'

'No, you have been doing the best that is in you, and very fine it is,' returned Tree.

'I will show them what I can do!' exclaimed Gilbert: 'I am writing a comedy.'

The comedy was *Brantinghame Hall*, which failed because he was clearly unaware of what he could do at his best.

Tree decided that Gilbert had far more wit than humour, found him very personal and rather touchy as a man, but admired his operas as the most characteristic entertainment of their time. The Trees were on very friendly visiting terms with the Gilberts, who made much of their small daughter, Viola. Possibly too much, because at the age of two she declined to kiss W. S. Gilbert, being reproved by papa, who urged, 'Oh, kiss Gillie, darling— Daddy loves Gillie.' 'Then Daddy kiss Gillie,' was her logical reply.

It was no doubt his desire to strive for the best within him that made Tree accept an invitation by F. R. Benson to play Iago and Sir Peter Teazle during an August week at Bournemouth in 1886. In the years ahead F. R. Benson's Shakespearean repertory was to be as famous throughout the provinces of England and Scotland as were Tree's Shakespearean productions in London, which gives interest to this association at the outset of their careers. Benson, always generous, offered Tree half-profits and a guarantee of £10 for the week, Maud Tree to play Portia and Lady Teazle. Tree took the precaution to be coached by Hermann Vezin in the traditional 'business' of Iago, and his performance was interesting enough for Benson to ask him to repeat it at Oxford and Cambridge. But he was dreadfully nervous, his tremors being obvious to Mrs Benson while waiting to make her entrance as Desdemona. 'Why do we choose a calling that causes us such unutterable agony?' he asked her. The two wives spent some hours on the beach watching Viola play. The baby handed a pebble to her mother, who said fervently, 'Clever, *clever* girl!' and then to her friend, 'You always tell children and men they are clever; I don't know why but I know it's expected.' Mrs Benson complained that her husband, whom she had just married, was not content with the breakfasts she provided. 'What do you give him?' asked Maud. The dishes were enumerated. 'Oh, you feed him too well! I give Herbert a rasher of bacon, and he thanks God he has got a wife.'

That autumn Tree appeared at the Haymarket Theatre in a play called *Jim the Penman*. He had expected to be cast for the protagonist and was deeply disappointed when offered the small part of a German baron, Harzfeld. But he acted it with such distinction that it became the chief feature of the play. During the run he fulfilled his promise to Benson and travelled down to Oxford and Cambridge for matinées of *Othello*, his nervousness at the former being such that he was discovered in the dressing-room nibbling at a stick of greasepaint while smearing his face with a mutton cutlet. Immediately after the performance he sprang into a hansom-cab dressed as Iago and caught the train, being able to change his clothes in a compartment hurriedly emptied of its occupants, who thought him an escaped lunatic.

He was now a member of the Garrick Club, of which he became extremely fond and where he became increasingly popular. He liked the somewhat gloomy atmosphere and enjoyed the varied conversation of the members, one of whom resigned in consequence of a scene, explaining the cause to Tree in an unfortunate phrase: 'When I joined, all the members were gentlemen.' 'I wonder why they left,' said Tree. He loved the company of Henry Kemble, a descendant of the famous actor John Philip Kemble, brother of Sarah Siddons. Henry, known in the profession as 'beetle', amused everyone with his pessimistic attitude to life and usually managed to make his repartees felt by those who attempted to score off him. Tree was dining with him one evening when George Meredith joined them and began to chaff Kemble with much eloquent *blague*. Kemble got up and left the table with a misquotation from *Pilgrim's Progress*: 'Then came one talkative by the way.' Tree recorded another story of Kemble in his private papers:

A young graduate from Oxford, who had edited a comic paper at the university, thought he could be facetious with Kemble at a Garrick Club supper. Kemble was always a dangerous butt, and putting on his black cap addressed him thus: 'Young man, in the course of a long life I have never heard anyone utter such foolish things as you have tried to pass off as wit tonight.' On leaving Kemble turned to

apologize to the young man for his harshness and said, 'I am sorry I
made a hasty remark to you. I said that I had never heard anyone
make such foolish observations as you did tonight. I was wrong. I
once did. It was nineteen years ago in a public house in Oldham.
Good-night, sir. The next time we meet I shall not be there.' And
he made his exit.

Henry Irving often went to the Garrick Club after his performances at the Lyceum, and a few members would gather round
him to talk and drink until their 'eyelids could no longer wag',
sometimes until, as Tree put it, 'the sun peeped over the horizon
with an inflamed eye'. One night, the wine having flowed freely,
Tree felt that he had better see Irving safely home. In the hansom-
cab Irving became repetitive. 'For-r-ward the oriflamme!' he
exclaimed at regular intervals, Tree's attempts at conversation
being received with a like apostrophe. Arriving at Irving's house,
Tree offered to escort him to the door, as the road was under
repair and several obstacles had to be avoided. Irving rejected his
help, felt his way unsteadily along the railings, reached the door,
turned, and with an ample gesture challenged the sleeping uni-
verse: 'For-r-ward the oriflamme!' He then disappeared within.
But he was not unaware of his companion's thoughtfulness, because a day or two later he confided in a friend: 'Nice fellow,
Tree; clever actor . . . Hm . . . Pity he drinks.'

Even before he became a manager Tree was constantly looking
for good plays, and unlike the other actors of his time he preferred
something intelligent or original or poetic to the popular pot-
boiler, though he never forgot that the pot had to be boiled, that
good work had to be financed by popular work. In the eighties
Robert Louis Stevenson and W. E. Henley were writing plays
together, and Tree hoped they would turn out something that
he could recommend for production. In the spring of '85 he heard
that Stevenson had written a play entitled *The Hanging Judge*.
Liking the sound of it, he travelled down to Bournemouth to see
the author, and left an account of his visit, together with descriptions of Stevenson and Henley, among his private papers:

> We started from Waterloo station on a bleak cold morning about
> 6 o'clock on Sunday. I was very tired, having had little sleep and two
> performances the previous day. I arrived at Bournemouth and asked
> for a carriage. The people seemed to regard this as a kind of . . .

[word omitted] to which they were unaccustomed. At last I got a discharged porter to carry my bag. Stevenson lived in a place called Bonelly Castle. I pictured it as a stately structure with a moat and drawbridge. It turned out to be a semi-detached stucco villa. When I arrived there I was wet through from the rain. I saw no knocker or bell. Then I discovered a gelatinous string swollen by the rain. I pulled at it and a bell tinkled in a distant court-yard, waking a belated chanticleer. Then Mrs Stevenson opened the door to me, telling me Louis was not well and was resting, and that he would read the play to me later on. I was very worn out and listened to the play which turned out to be a rather turgid affair, and I remember that in order to keep myself awake I went to Mrs Stevenson's dressing-table and took her hat-pin, with which I continually prodded my leg to prevent myself from falling asleep.

He thought Stevenson very polite, nervous, graceful, charming, mellifluous of speech, that he spoke 'like one of his own books —his sentences were quite literary, but he seemed to enjoy their embroidery. . . . By the by, he told me he hated writing love-scenes—it was like putting on skates—he turned Mrs Stevenson on to them.'

Later Tree met Henley and Stevenson together, finding them a great contrast, Henley's talk being crude, his manners brusque, their only resemblance being a love of good wine and food.

I suggested to them to make Robert Macaire a philosopher in crime. I stayed with them in Bournemouth. I made a number of suggestions for the play, and they wrote it, offering that I should be a part author. They were good enough to say my suggestions were invaluable. This I declined—as I had done nothing, I was not entitled to the recognition. I had occasion to regret my modesty, for when we came to produce the play I wanted to make some alterations, as I considered the construction somewhat faulty. My suggestions were pooh-poohed. The play was produced and the notices given to my performance were more flattering than were the references to the play, and I think this was unjust. Henley wrote to me somewhat violently, saying I had evidently done the butter-slide trick with the play; to which I replied that if he would not cease his correspondence I would do the play no more. Henley was really a fine fellow, but somehow the world seemed to revolve around him. Still, I have always liked him in spite of his bludgeonesque manners. One day I met him in the street in Edinburgh. He asked me, 'Why did you not come to see me?' To which I replied, 'My dear Henley, I forgot for the moment that we were on speaking terms.'

Tree did another Henley–Stevenson play besides *Macaire*. This was *Beau Austin*, produced shortly after he became a theatre-manager, and received with respectful attention by a picked audience which, according to Sidney Colvin, was 'miles above the average intelligence of the British public'. The notices in the press were complimentary; but as most of the tickets were of a similar kind, the play was soon withdrawn. No other manager took such a risk, so it is agreeable to learn from a letter written by Stevenson's wife that they liked the daring actor: 'We have just had a visit from Beerbohm Tree, whose name, I am sorry to say, is treated with shocking levity by Louis. He seems a very nice, modest, pleasant fellow, and we were much pleased with him.'

CHAPTER 6

Haddon Chambers and Henry Arthur Jones

'Everything comes to him who doesn't wait,' said Tree, who lived up to his maxim by seizing the first opportunity to become manager of a small theatre, the first opportunity to become lessee and manager of a larger theatre, and the first opportunity to build and own a theatre spacious enough to fulfil his ambition. All else in life being subsidiary to his main desire, which was to produce plays that took his fancy, he carefully cultivated the friendships of men who could help him to that end. A barrister who wished to write plays, Stuart Ogilvie, and another barrister who advised on plays, J. Comyns Carr, helped Tree, the first with cash, the second with counsel, to start his career as a manager at the Comedy Theatre in Panton Street on April 20th, 1887, with a melodrama, *The Red Lamp*, in which he played Demetrius, head of the Secret Police. Not a soul in the house recognized the rather clumsily proportioned, white-haired, drowsy-eyed, sinister figure, who walked with the aid of a stick but moved with feline softness and celerity. It was a wonderful disguise, and from it playgoers might have guessed that the new actor-manager, a master of make-up, would try to escape as often as possible from his own personality.

The adventure was successful, and he took the Haymarket Theatre, a risky tenancy just then. In 1880 the Bancrofts had relinquished the Prince of Wales's, which was let to Edgar Bruce, and had gone to the Haymarket Theatre, remaining there until they retired from the stage in 1885. Then, for two years under a different and somewhat indifferent management, failure had followed failure at that house, the only success being *Jim the Penman*. Tree therefore stepped into a shaky concern, but caution was not in his nature. He lit the auditorium with electricity, halved the

price of seats in what was called the pit circle, abolished a number
of boxes, improved and extended the gallery and dress circle, and
in short catered for the poorer playgoing public.

He opened at the Haymarket in the autumn of '87 with *The
Red Lamp*, preceded by a one-act romance, *The Ballad Monger*,
adapted from Theodore de Banville's *Gringoire*, in which he
played a philosophical poet and reformer, a complete contrast to
the practical and cynical policeman in the other play. As Gringoire
the imaginative 'straight' actor was revealed, and some critics,
notably Bernard Shaw, always preferred him in such parts to the
clever 'character' actor applauded by audiences which often mistook imitation for impersonation.

We need not follow Tree's managerial exploits in detail. He
produced a number of plays that cannot interest us now, and a few
that, for one reason or another, retain their interest. An estimate of
his acting and methods as a producer will be attempted in due
course; and for those who wish to have the complete record, a list
of all the plays he presented will be found in the appendix. But
here we are concerned with his personality, and only such authors
and plays as materially affected his career or brought out the
significant features of his character. His second production at the
Haymarket, for example, is worth mentioning solely because he
was sufficiently amused by an incident to jot it in a notebook at
the end of his life:

> On the first night of *Partners* Kemble was a little garrulous. He was
> made up as my faithful clerk and walked about the stage mumbling
> complaints.   At that moment a huge property made of wood and
> looking like an iron safe was brought in by the property man and
> deposited on the stage. Kemble said, 'Why have a wooden safe when
> an iron one would do?'

We shall meet Henry Kemble again.

What put the new management firmly on its feet was the
production of *Captain Swift* by C. Haddon Chambers in 1888.
Chambers was a young Australian, who was living in rooms over
a Bayswater milk-shop and trying to earn a livelihood by writing
magazine stories. He had met Tree, who stopped him one day in
Panton Street and asked, 'Have you ever thought of writing a
play for me?' 'No, but I will,' he replied, and went home at once

to start one. After a struggle of four months, he took *Coincidence*, as it was then called, to the Haymarket. Tree promised a reading, and the author's optimism changed to pessimism as the months went by and he heard nothing. Then he learnt from Outram Tristram, author of *The Red Lamp*, that the closing scene in a play by Hamilton Aïdé, which had just been given a trial matinée, was similar to that in his own. Tristram also said that the scene had not been in Aïdé's original manuscript but had been incorporated at rehearsal. Suspecting sharp practice in Hastings, the stage-manager, Chambers jumped into a hansom, drove to the Haymarket, and got a promise from Tree that he would hear the play read the following day. The reading went as far as the end of Act 2, at the conclusion of which Tree was half-asleep. Pulling himself together, he expressed an urgent need for a Turkish bath, and promptly departed for Leicester Square. But Chambers had not rounded up refractory cattle in the Australian prairies merely to be defeated by the whims of a London actor. He followed Tree, and finished the reading in the 'hot room'. The manager consented to do the play.

But there was danger ahead. The stage-manager, Hastings, called the piece 'Damned rot!' no doubt having his private reasons. Comyns Carr, the literary adviser, foretold disaster; and as he had influenced Stuart Ogilvie to back the Haymarket enterprise, his advice carried weight. Carr set forth his reasons with such eloquence that Tree glanced sympathetically at Chambers, who returned the glance with a wink, which made Tree laugh. 'What are you laughing at?' from Carr irritably. 'I am laughing because I have an idea. If Chambers doesn't object, we'll give his play at a trial matinée.' Tree liked the author as much as the play. Chambers was a light-hearted devil-may-care fellow, with a breezy attitude towards life which gave a tang to his work. Bernard Shaw called him 'a rough and ready playwright with the imagination of a bushranger; but it is imagination, all the same, and it suffices'.

Everyone seemed to have a say in the rehearsals. An old actor, Macklin, was allowed to introduce an appalling line that pleased him; Carr thought of a phrase which gave the author cold shudders; and another old actor, Pateman, wanted something changed in his part: 'Excuse me, Mr Tree, but *must* I say that line?' 'What line is that?' 'The line "After all, he was only a common bastard!" Isn't it a bit thick?' 'What would you rather say?' 'I think "a common love-child" would sound better.' But Tree managed to convince him that a vindictive servant would be more likely to use the briefer word. So many suggestions were forthcoming that the manager at last yelled: 'Is this my stage or is it not?' and he cannot have been soothed by his wife's reminder, 'It certainly is yours in this play, Herbert,' because Captain Swift swamped every other part.

The matinée was a success, though Tree nearly wrecked the show in the last act by turning his part into a comic crook. He altered this when the play was put into the evening bill; and he became for the first time in his life a sort of matinée idol, to see whom little mobs of women waited at the stage-door. Elizabeth Robins, later to make a name in Ibsen plays and to write successful novels, was fascinated by Tree's performance, and when about to meet the actor in private life expected to see a dynamic hero with dark-fringed eyes. Instead she saw a person with hardly any eyelashes at all: 'What he has are a pale reddy-yellow . . . he is colourless . . . he has a cold.' Fortunately he appeared to better advantage on the stage, and the bushranger who is converted from evil to good, from irresponsibility to duty, from heartlessness to love, by staying in a nice English home, became extremely popular with audiences that liked to believe in the ennobling nature of British domesticity.

Incidentally the play was perfectly staged and marked the first step of Tree's fame as a producer. The realistic interior scenery initiated by the Bancrofts at the Prince of Wales's had been perfected by John Hare during his management of the Court and St James's Theatres, and was now elaborated to the smallest detail by Tree at the Haymarket. Hare made audiences recognize the difference between the furniture of a house in Bloomsbury and a house in Bayswater. With Tree one could almost tell the difference between a room in the home of a stockbroker and a room in the home of a bank manager. But the play's success was due to sentiment, not upholstery. On all the programmes and advertisements appeared Shakespeare's words: 'There is some soul of goodness in things evil', and Tree's ability to give a convincing performance was due to his belief in this soul of goodness, a feeling he shared with the playgoing public. Some three years after the production of *Captain Swift*, he was asked to read 'A Modern Idyll', a short story by the editor of *The Fortnightly Review*, Frank Harris, and his letter to the author displays his belief as well as his critical acumen:

> Hill House
> Northrepps
> Norfolk
> 14 July/91

My dear Harris

I am sorry to say I did not find time to read your story before I left town. I have now read it, and think it a most powerful piece of writing—terribly modern in its unblinkingness of the great fact.—You have indeed committed a most successful rape of poetic justice—but personally I find it saddening—how could it be otherwise?—Why don't you write a companion story reversing the order of things?—ugliness culminating in beauty—a flower blooming on a dunghill—and so make your peace with idealists—I mean with women and with

> Yours sincerely,
> Herbt Beerbohm Tree

P.S. There were some passages which struck me as quite beautiful, notably the description of the sermon—and the undercurrent of self-consciousness while doing a 'fine thing' seemed to me a very truthful touch.

When Tree wrote this he was enjoying a holiday after his second big managerial success at the Haymarket: *The Dancing Girl* by Henry Arthur Jones. The three most successful dramatists on the London stage in the nineties were Henry Arthur Jones, Arthur Pinero and Oscar Wilde. The first specialized in sermons, the second in stagecraft, the third in wit. Jones, the son of a Buckinghamshire farmer, had a severe puritanical upbringing, started to earn a living at the age of 13, and became an efficient commercial traveller. Though he had written stories as a boy, he first entered a theatre at the age of 18, at once caught the infection, and nine years later abandoned salesmanship for the drama. His first play to make money happened to make a fortune. Written with Henry Herman, *The Silver King* became one of the three most popular melodramas of the age, the others being *East Lynne* and *The Sign of the Cross*. Tree did one of his plays, *Wealth*, in '89, but both management and author were the poorer for it, and two years later came *The Dancing Girl*, wherein the soul of goodness in things evil was again manifested with a favourable effect on the box-office receipts, over three hundred performances being the record run of a serious modern drama in the West End. 'I can never say how much I owed to Tree in *The Dancing Girl*,' said Jones many years afterwards; but one would never have suspected this at rehearsals.

Jones was a courteous, friendly and genial fellow by nature, but he held definite views on how his plays should be performed, displayed a dogged persistence in obtaining his end, and exhibited a choleric temper when thwarted. If he felt a thing strongly he expressed it vehemently, and he refused to budge an inch when convinced he was right. His obstinacy made Tree bristle with irritation, and noisy scenes alternated with dead silences when the author dashed into the street to cool himself and the actor rushed to his dressing-room for restoratives. Now and then the tension was relieved by an interchange that made the company laugh, which abated the fury of the disputants:

H. A. J.   No! No!! No!!!

H. B. T.   Don't repeat yourself.

H. A. J.   I must if you won't listen.

H. B. T.   Repetition breeds listlessness. By the time you said your last 'no' I had forgotten what the first was about.

H. A. J.   Very well. I'll be content with one. NO!

H. B. T.   No what?

Unable to contain himself beyond the walls of the theatre, Jones broke out in the press, writing in opprobrious terms of the actor to whom he afterwards felt more indebted than he could express.

Two years later the scenes were renewed with increased acrimony during rehearsals of *The Tempter*, a pseudo-poetic costume drama by Jones in which Tree played the part of the Devil, 'a weak-kneed devil' said the author, who thought highly of his play. Edward German wrote music for it and nothing was spared to make a sensation, least of all the tempers of author and actor.

The number of times the former stamped in rage from the theatre was only equalled by the number of times the latter threw up his part and stopped rehearsals. At one of his exits Jones ran up the centre gangway, turned at the top, shook his fist at Tree, and screamed that he would never return. 'In that case we shall be able to get on with the rehearsals,' the manager shouted back. A solicitor's letter arrived on behalf of the author. A solicitor's letter was despatched on behalf of the manager. The author's solicitor called; the manager's solicitor met him. The antagonists were brought together, shook hands, and everything was forgiven and forgotten. At the next rehearsal they were elaborately polite to each other, but the strain told on them, and the ensuing explosion was louder than ever on account of the suppression that had preceded it. Somehow the play got produced; but the first-night audience began to disperse long before the final curtain descended after midnight; the critics, in the fashionable wit of the period, called the show 'The Attempter'; and its withdrawal from the stage was the only quiet episode in its history. W. S. Gilbert, a fellow-dramatist, summed it up in a letter to Maud Tree in a style that would have gravely affected the author's blood-pressure:

I thought *The Tempter*, as a play, gross and damnable—its literature, the literature of the servants' hall. 'Thou dost not love me as thou used to do'! ! 'Thou used'! Oh merciful father that stayest thy hand though thy rebellious children deserve the blow, save and protect us from this plague of Jones (which we have nevertheless rightly incurred for our many backslidings) through the merits of thy beloved Son, Jesus Christ. Amen. This is a form of prayer to be used in all churches and chapels throughout the United Kingdom and in the town of Berwick upon Tweed. 'Thou dost not love me as thou used to do'! It is as true in fact as it is false in grammar. '*Thou used*'! ! ! Farewell. I can no more!

Six years later, at his new theatre, Tree produced a fourth play by Henry Arthur Jones, *Carnac Sahib*. Their tempers failed them at rehearsals as completely as the play failed when it was produced. The scenes were so stormy that the stage was emptied for long periods while the manager was being nursed back to normal by his staff and the author was trying to restore his tranquillity in the street outside. At one point Tree, who had been trying to say

certain lines in a manner required by Jones, called out in a voice
of extreme irritation, 'Then how do you want it done?' Jones,
twitching with rage, replied with calculated clarity, 'Ask Wyndham to show you how to do it,' and made a rapid exit. Charles
Wyndham, the best 'straight' comedy actor of his generation, was
a rival manager, and nothing more infuriating could have been
said. Next morning the author was refused admission to the rehearsal, and the solicitors of both parties were employed for some
time in writing letters to each other.

Authors were not the only people to make the new actor-
manager suffer. For many years he was regarded by his fellow-
managers as a sort of lucky interloper, one who had come to the
front too quickly and easily. They distrusted his humorous light-
heartedness as a man, his facility as an actor; they did not consider
him as a serious artist. The great figure in the theatre of that time,
Henry Irving, was very jealous of rivalry, making no attempt to
disguise his poor opinion of Tree as an actor; and as Irving had
become practically canonized by the time Tree was beginning to
make his presence felt, the critics, most of whom had been
lavishly entertained at the Lyceum and whose favourable opinions
had been bought by options on dramas they may or may not
have translated for the great actor, were chary of praising the newcomer lest they should displease Irving. A slight incident will
illustrate Irving's malice and the sort of stonewall attitude against
which Tree had to fight. A French play had been adapted by
Sydney Grundy, entitled *A Village Priest*, and produced at the
Haymarket in 1890. It caused some controversy because its plot
partly hinged on the violation of the Confessional, but Tree's
touching performance of the priest carried it to success. One of
the actors, Charles Allan, made a single appearance as a gendarme
and had nothing to say but two words: '*Allons! Marche!*' Irving
saw the play and afterwards went on the stage for a chat with the
actors he knew. Tree was naturally bursting for a word of praise
from the great man, who was not bursting to give it. Having
talked lightly of this and that for several minutes, Irving shook
hands with Tree, said 'Good-night—hm—Allan excellent—hm—
God bless you!' and left the other to his private thoughts.

CHAPTER 7

Shakespeare, Oscar Wilde and Ibsen

Being the man he was, Irving's attitude to Tree just then may be explained, if not excused, by three achievements on the part of the Haymarket manager in the same line of business which the Lyceum manager had made his own. Tree had in fact committed *lèse-majesté*, a sort of high treason against the sovereign of the stage, by playing a French priest as sympathetically as Irving had played an English parson in *Olivia*, by doubling two parts in *A Man's Shadow* as successfully as Irving had doubled two parts in *The Lyons Mail*, and by producing a Shakespearean comedy, *The Merry Wives of Windsor*, which had aroused as much enthusiasm as Irving's production of *Much Ado About Nothing*. A man who could start his managerial career by challenging comparison with the monarch of the profession was clearly a man to be feared. Here was no Bancroft, Wyndham, Hare or Kendal, who would stick to one class of play and one style of acting. The Haymarket management would be more catholic in choice of work, more versatile in performance, than the Lyceum; it would do modern plays as well as the poetic and melodramatic shows associated with Irving; it would vie with the Lyceum in grandeur of production and surpass the Lyceum in the acting ability of its companies; all of which must have been dimly apprehended by Irving as he listened to the plaudits of the Haymarket audience and watched the long lean figure of his rival taking numerous 'calls' before the curtain.

Tree's achievement in *A Man's Shadow* had immediately preceded his village priest. In it he played a hero who is accused of a crime committed by his double, the villain. He made the dramatic effect, but naturalistic error, of differentiating the two parts so strongly that neither man could have been mistaken for the other in real life, just as Irving had done in *The Lyons Mail*. The general public of course admired his clever 'character' villain.

More alert playgoers recognized the quality of his 'straight' hero, which, in Bernard Shaw's words, gave him 'an opportunity for a remarkable display of his peculiar talent as an imaginative actor', and which, as we shall hear, helped Shaw to display his peculiar genius for fitting an actor with a part worthy of him.

The leading figures in the social and political worlds were now patronizing the Haymarket, and Mr and Mrs Gladstone appeared in a box on the last night of *A Man's Shadow*, at the conclusion of which the famous Liberal statesman went on the stage to congratulate Tree. In the course of their conversation Gladstone asked: 'What are the political convictions of your profession?' Tree replied cautiously that there were many intelligent men on the stage but that he thought the profession was almost solidly conservative. 'That is deplorable,' said Gladstone. Tree hastily reassured him: 'But the scene-shifters are radical to a man.'

A fact not generally appreciated is that Tree was the father of the repertory movement in England. Long before the days of Granville Barker the manager of the Haymarket did a series of Monday evening and Wednesday afternoon performances of plays that were generally regarded as above the average playgoer's intelligence. One of these was the Henley–Stevenson *Beau Austin*. Another was his first Shakespearean production, *The Merry Wives of Windsor*. His enthusiasm for the project of putting on plays that were distinguished but uncommercial was due to an element in his nature already remarked: he remained an amateur in his attitude to the theatre, loving it as a means of experiment, hating the tedium of acting the same part night after night, and living up to his saying: 'It's no good giving the public what they want. Give them what you want them to want, and in time they'll want it.' Everyone prophesied failure for *The Merry Wives*. It was then an article of belief in the theatre that 'Shakespeare spells ruin'. Irving had proved that it was not so; but Irving adapted Shakespeare's plays to fit his own personality, using the poet as a means of providing magnificent parts and settings for himself. His success therefore proved nothing more than the immense popularity of two 'stars', Ellen Terry sharing the honours with him. Tree lacked Irving's mesmeric power and had no Ellen to fall back on. Instead he gathered about him, now and always, a first-class company, many of whom made their reputations while under him, allowed everyone a commensurate share of the entertainment, and by doing as much of the text as possible even permitted Shakespeare to shine as a dramatist. He also gave the musicians a chance, engaging an excellent orchestra under a composer-conductor, Raymond Roze, and letting the music of Nicolai and Sullivan lend charm to the proceedings.

A first performance was given at the Crystal Palace, where Tree acted Falstaff under difficulties. A leak started in the tube whereby air had been pumped to increase his paunch, and he had to fight against a diminishing corporation as well as frayed nerves. But the disaster did not lessen his sense of humour, and years afterwards he entered a note in his pocket-book:

> When I first played Falstaff at the Crystal Palace and made such a failure, I remember Richard Butler came up to us, as Brookfield and I were standing together—Brookfield played Slender—and said to me: 'What a splendid Slender *you* would have made!' It was a double insult.

The play was put on for a series of matinées at the Haymarket during the run of *Captain Swift* in 1888, going into the evening bill the following year, and being revived so frequently that Tree's Falstaff became his most popular Shakespearean part. Some of the critics complained that he moved too lightly for so bulky a man, but he replied that he had once seen the Tichborne claimant going upstairs and carrying his twenty-four stones so nimbly that the actor was right in making Falstaff gambol. As time went on he managed to get the fruity voice and gurgle of the fat knight, and altogether it became a most enjoyable show, rich, riotous, rollicking.

But the Falstaff of *The Merry Wives* is only a button of mirth on the belly of humour contained in the Falstaff of the historical plays; and when Tree presented the first part of *Henry IV* at the Haymarket towards the end of his tenancy in 1896, the genius of comedy escaped him and he reproduced the object of ridicule. Shaw's criticism, though harsh, was not unjust:

> Mr Tree only wants one thing to make him an excellent Falstaff, and that is to get born over again as unlike himself as possible . . .

the hopeless efforts of the romantic imaginative actor, touching only in unhappy parts, to play the comedian by dint of mechanical horse-play: all that is hopeless, irremediable ... if he were wise he would hand over his part and his breadbasket to Mr Lionel Brough, whose Bardolph has the true comic force which Mr Tree never attains for a moment.

Lionel Brough was the best low-comedy Shakespearean actor on the stage, and he remained with Tree until his death. Tree never feared comparisons, and at this time two of the finest romantic actors of the period were graduating under him, each to become an actor-manager: Lewis Waller and Fred Terry. In *Henry IV* Waller as Hotspur won the chief acting honours. Shaw's view that Tree was best when most himself on the stage was opposed to the opinion of his critical successor on *The Saturday Review*, Max Beerbohm, who writes to the present biographer:

> Shaw's remark about Herbert's *métier* being 'straight parts' seems to me great nonsense. I remember he once said to me that Herbert wasn't really a comedian, but a romantic actor—a theory which I flatly rejected. Herbert had of course a strong element of romance, but the main thing about him was that he was an immensely versatile and *richly creative* comedian. His Svengali and his Malvolio abide in my mind as two of his especial triumphs.

The truth is that Tree was equally successful in character comedy and quiet pathos. Where he failed completely was in purely romantic work, of which he gave the worst example in 1892 when he produced *Hamlet*.

Actors cannot be prevented from seeing themselves as Hamlet, and so they always romanticize the part. Johnston Forbes-Robertson was the only actor within living memory to conceive the part and speak the lines in an entirely natural, unromantic and beautiful manner. Irving's performance made a sensation but that was largely because, like Fechter, he spoke the lines pensively instead of declaiming them in the traditional style of Kemble and Macready. Shaw said that Irving's Hamlet had 'moments of violent ineptitude separated by lengths of dulness; and though I yawned, I felt none the worse next morning'. But Irving's acting amounted to hypnotism, and Shaw was in a minority, a patient who would not react to the treatment. There had been no notable Hamlet since the Lyceum version, and Tree's was therefore another challenge to Irving's supremacy. The play is a perennial favourite with the public, and the Haymarket Theatre was filled for over a hundred performances to see this new bearded teutonic Hamlet, but only a few critics thought that Tree had done more than give a performance of Beerbohm in a flaxen wig. One of the few, Frederic Harrison, founder of English Positivism, wrote of a revival of the play which Tree presented against a most effective background of tapestries: 'His Hamlet without scenery was the finest interpretation I have ever seen', and he had seen the part played by Mounet–Sully, Macready, Phelps, Barry Sullivan, Salvini, Fechter, Ristori, Irving, Edwin Booth, Sarah Bernhardt, and a dozen others. Tree emphasized the sentimental lover-like aspect of Hamlet by returning quietly to kiss a tress of Ophelia's hair after the scene in which he rages at her, by reappearing alone with an armful of flowers for her grave after the quarrel with Laertes at her burial, and by dying to soft music as the chorus of angels sang him to his rest and brought the curtain down. A pleasant departure from the usual gloomy setting was the church-yard scene, which was made attractive with blossoming trees, singing birds, and a flower-decked hill in the background. Tree's wriggle across the stage during the play-scene in a series of belly-flops introduced a welcome but unconscious note of comedy.

The chief novelty of the production was the music written by George Henschel. Shaw's experience of past Hamlets had led him to believe that the music for the play consisted of the March from *Judas Maccabaeus* when the Court enters, the Dead March in *Saul* when Hamlet dies, and a few popular overtures between the acts. As a critic of music in '92 he was invited to the Haymarket, and because of this revolutionary innovation his opinion of the producer

> rose to such a pitch as to all but defeat the object of my visit to the last rehearsal; for instead of listening to Mr Henschel's interludes, I spent the intervals in explaining to Mr Tree exactly how his part ought to be played, he listening with the patience and attention which might be expected from so accomplished an actor.

However, Shaw heard enough to declare that Henschel's preludes went deeper, and his incidental music was simpler and more effective, than Grieg's for *Peer Gynt*.

If Tree had not felt satisfied with his interpretation of Hamlet, he would scarcely have enjoyed the remarks he heard about it. 'I don't believe there are ten or eleven actors in London who could play it better,' said a member of the first-night audience. His fellow-manager, John Hare, went round to his dressing-room after a performance. Tree was sitting at his mirror removing his make-up. 'Well, what did you think of my Hamlet?' he asked. 'Quite frankly,' replied Hare, 'I didn't much care for it.' Tree absorbed this and then tried again: 'No . . . but it's a good part, isn't it?'

A phrase that has become a common quotation was inspired by his conception. The well-known Quaker singer, David Bispham, reports in his book of 'Recollections' that he heard W. S. Gilbert say to Tree on the stage of the Haymarket Theatre after the first performance of *Hamlet*: 'My dear fellow, I never saw anything so funny in my life, and yet it was not in the least vulgar.' This remark quickly went the round of the clubs, eventually being quoted in its accepted form: 'Funny without being vulgar.' Tree made the best of it by repeating the gibe to friends and laughing heartily over it. He even went so far as to claim it as his own, writing to Gilbert on March 25th, 1893:

. . . . By the bye, my wife told me that you were under the impression that I might have been offended at some witticism of yours about my Hamlet. Let me assure you it was not so. On the contrary, it was I believe *I* who circulated the story. There could be no harm, as I knew you had not seen me act the part, and moreover, while I am a great admirer of your wit, I have also too high an opinion of my work to be hurt by it.

> Believe me
> Yours sincerely
> Herbt Beerbohm Tree

It is not likely that an actor would invent such a cutting quip at his own expense, especially when it mocked his art in a vulnerable place. Gilbert was prolific of such smart sayings at the expense of players, and he probably invented this one; but when it began to appear in the papers, Tree doubtless perceived that it would redound to his credit both as actor and man if he assumed the responsibility.

Another wit of his acquaintance, while too kind-hearted to hurt him, could not help joking about him; but Tree had already joked at the wit's expense in *Punch*. The moment that *Lady Windermere's Fan* became the chief topic of conversation in social circles, Tree asked Oscar Wilde to write a play for the Haymarket. While toying lazily with his next drawing-room drama, Wilde met Tree and said: 'As Herod in my *Salomé* you would be admirable. As a peer of the realm in my latest dramatic device, pray forgive me if I do not see you.' Tree was persistent and remarked that his Duke of Guisebury in *The Dancing Girl* had been highly praised. 'Ah! that's just it,' returned Wilde. 'Before you can successfully impersonate the character I have in mind, you must forget that you ever played Hamlet; you must forget that you ever played Falstaff; above all you must forget that you ever played a Duke in a melodrama by Henry Arthur Jones.'

Tree: I'll do my best.

Wilde: I think you had better forget that you have ever acted at all.

Tree: Why?

Wilde: Because this witty aristocrat whom you wish to assume in my play is quite unlike anyone who has been seen on the stage before. He is like no one who has existed before.

Tree: My God! he must be supernatural.

Wilde: He is certainly not natural. He is a figure of art. Indeed, if you can bear the truth, he is MYSELF.

The first two acts of *A Woman of no Importance* were written in London and Babbacombe, the last two in a still extant farmhouse near Cromer, where Wilde took his family for a few weeks in the late summer of '92. While there he read of the death of Julius Beerbohm at the end of August, and immediately wrote to Tree:

> Grove Farm
> Felbrigg
> Cromer
> (*c.* Sep. 1, 1892.)

My dear Tree,

My wife and I were much shocked to read of your father's death. I remember having had the pleasure of meeting him at supper at the Haymarket, and how proud he was of your success in art. Pray accept our sincere sympathies.

As regards the play: I have written two acts, and had them set up by the typewriter: the third is nearly done, and I hope to have it all ready in ten days or a fortnight at most. I am very pleased with it so far.

The American rights I have already sold the refusal of—I fancy they want to produce at the Chicago Exhibition two new plays, one by Sardou and one by me. But the English rights are quite free. If you will send me your dates I would read it to you somewhere about the end of this month.

I find Cromer excellent for writing, and golf still better.

Yours
Oscar Wilde

It would have been amusing to watch Wilde playing golf. The game probably finished on the first green, by which time it had become a conversation; or if continued for another hole or two, the strokes doubtless took the place of commas in the talk. Tree was occasionally persuaded to start a game, but when he made a decent drive off the first tee he said, 'That's good enough for today,' and went no further; when he topped the ball, 'That's more than enough for today,' and went home.

All his friends knew how fond Tree was of his father, and messages of sympathy followed him on his provincial tour that autumn. Henry Irving had paid a tribute to Julius Beerbohm at one of Tree's supper-parties, and now he sent a wire from Winchelsea, where Ellen Terry lived: 'Sincere sympathy, dear Tree. Have just heard sad news.' Tree kept a copy of his reply:

4 Sep. 1892

My dear Irving

It was very kind of you to send me that sympathetic message.— Yes, my poor father's loss has been a great blow to me—the more so as I have never allowed myself to look the inevitable in the face. —He had a great admiration for you and the beautiful little speech you made, with so much tact of heart, touched him very deeply— nor shall I forget it, for to me it was one of those few moments which burn themselves into a life's memory.

My father's was a very sweet and at the same time deep and re-served nature. To him death had no terror, for he possessed the most precious of all gifts—a simple and staunch religious faith. Of all gifts this is the one which I think is most to be envied, and to me, who am without it, the tragedy of his death is the more awful.

We buried him yesterday—my wife sent a wreath with the words 'Wearing the white flower of a blameless life'—and I believe it applied to him.

Yours sincerely
Herbt Beerbohm Tree

The Haymarket company having reached Glasgow in October, Wilde arrived to read his play, and for three days there was much laughing, eating and drinking at the Central Station Hotel, where a contract was drawn up and signed. Tree was enchanted by the piece, which he later described as 'a great modern play', and complimented the author on the development of the plot. But Wilde thought nothing of that. 'Plots are tedious,' he said. 'Anyone can invent them. Life is full of them. Indeed one has to elbow one's way through them as they crowd across one's path. I took the plot of this play from *The Family Herald*, which took it—wisely, I feel—from my novel *The Picture of Dorian Gray*. People love a wicked aristocrat who seduces a virtuous maiden, and they love a virtuous maiden for being seduced by a wicked aristocrat. I have given them what they like, so that they may learn to appreciate what I like to give them.' He had clearly been re-reading *Dorian Gray* because he lifted many of the witty sentences therefrom and put them into the mouths of various characters in the play. As he did not like Dickens, it is strange that he should have remembered *Little Dorrit* well enough to let his Archdeacon echo the manner of Mr Casby in that novel, just as, later, he gave Lady Bracknell in *The Importance of being Earnest* a phrase of Rosa Dartle's in *David Copperfield*.

Wilde and Tree were very much alike in some respects. Both possessed happy natures, enjoyed life, and revelled in nonsense. With most people every birthday makes them feel older. With Wilde and Tree every day was a rebirthday, making them feel younger. They loved wit and humour, laughing at their own jokes as much as at other people's, and no less heartily when the joke was against themselves. They also loved good wine, good food and good company. Tree had an enormous admiration for Wilde as a wit, talker and personality, and wrote down a few of his sayings, for example: 'Extravagance is the luxury of the poor, penury the luxury of the rich.' Some of Wilde's American stories also found their way into Tree's notebooks:

> 'Oscar Wilde told me that when he went to America he had two secretaries—one for autographs, the other for locks of hair. Within six months the one had died of writer's cramp, the other was completely bald.'

> 'Wonderful man, Columbus!' said a New Yorker.
> 'Why?' asked Wilde.
> 'He discovered America.'
> 'Oh, no! it had often been discovered before, but it was always hushed up.'

Wilde's play was originally called *Mrs Arbuthnot*, and Lord Illingworth, the part played by Tree, was at first called Lord Brancaster. Territorial nomenclature had an irresistible attraction for the dramatist, who usually gave his characters the names of places he knew or where he was staying when the plays were written. In the typescript of *Mrs Arbuthnot* both Hunstanton and Brancaster appear, neither place very far from Cromer where he finished the play, and the name of Illingworth resembles that of a village on the road to the Norfolk coast.

Rehearsals started at the end of March '93, and Tree thought Wilde fussy over minor points. In the script used by the author at rehearsals there are several jottings in his handwriting: 'Tree's question far too theatrical' (when Illingworth asks Mrs Allonby how long she gives him to convert the puritan)—'Don't like your false exit' (Illingworth's at the end of Act 2)—'Tree not emphasize this' (Illingworth on youth at the beginning of Act 3). Wilde wanted his actors to be natural, and he was a bit worried over Tree's tendency to attitudinize. His frequent interferences were multiplied in the memory of Tree, who must have confused him with Henry Arthur Jones when telling Vyvyan Holland, fifteen years afterwards, that a week before the play's production he gave orders that the author must not be admitted to the theatre during rehearsals on any pretext whatever. Considering the urbanity and charm of Wilde, his eminence as a playwright, the fact that he was constantly cutting lines and re-writing scenes at the request of the manager, whose unqualified admiration for him was so frequently expressed, we may safely assume that nothing of the sort happened in his case. Tree's recollections of all his rehearsal rows with so many authors were a trifle muddled. He always thought that authors should attend rehearsals solely for the pleasure of seeing how perfectly he produced their plays. His present biographer once asked him about *A Woman of no Importance*:

'I suppose you produced it?'

'Of course.'

'With the assistance of Wilde?'

'With the interference of Wilde.'

Sir Max Beerbohm agrees that his brother would never have treated Wilde in the cavalier fashion mentioned above, writing: 'I was at several of those rehearsals, and Oscar was always there. Herbert had known him for many years and, as you say, always delighted greatly in his company.' But Tree's momentary vexation was amusingly manifested in an episode he related to Mr Holland. Playwright and actor met one day outside the theatre. Tree was in a frock-coat, wearing a carnation and carrying, brim upwards, a brand-new top-hat with a bright red lining. 'My dear Herbert, what a charming lining you have in your hat,' said Wilde, eyeing it appreciatively. 'My dear Oscar, do you really like it?' 'Yes, I think it is perfection.' 'Then it is yours,' said Tree, ripping out the lining, handing it to Wilde, and vanishing into the theatre.

That Wilde would accept an actor's advice is proved by the omission of Illingworth's speech to his natural son Gerald Arbuthnot at the commencement of Act 3. The dramatist had allowed his own feelings to run away with his character, and had made the cynical self-possessed peer almost passionate in a diatribe on Puritanism:

My dear boy, the real enemy of modern life, of everything that makes life lovely and joyous and coloured for us, is Puritanism, and the Puritan spirit. *There* is the danger that lies ahead of the age, and most of all in England. Every now and then this England of ours finds that one of its sores shows through its rags and shrieks for the nonconformists. Caliban for nine months of the year, it is Tartuffe for the other three. Do you despise a creed that starves the body, and does not feed the soul? Why, I tell you, Gerald, that the profligate, the wildest profligate who spills his life in folly, has a better, saner, finer philosophy of life than the Puritan has. He, at any rate, knows that the aim of life is the pleasure of living, and does in some way realize himself, be himself. Puritanism is the hideous survival of the self-mutilation of the savage, man in his madness making *himself* the victim of his monstrous sacrifice. Profligate, Gerald, you will never be; you will choose your pleasures too carefully, too exquisitely for that. But Puritanism you will always reject. It is not a creed for a gentleman. And, as a beginning, you will make it your ideal to be a dandy always.

Tree did not think that a crusade against Puritanism in favour of profligacy should be launched in the middle of a scene in which the speaker is delivering worldly-wise epigrams, and Wilde cut the last part of the speech (beginning 'Why, I tell you, Gerald'), substituting for it 'Puritanism is not a theory of life. It is an explanation of the English middle classes, that is all.' But Tree was not satisfied and wanted the rest to go. All of it went, and did not reappear in the published play.

Perhaps the fact that Wilde had partly portrayed himself as Lord Illingworth made him feel that Tree was not an ideal actor for the character. During the rehearsals he met Squire Bancroft outside the Garrick Club, and some twenty years later Bancroft recalled their conversation for the entertainment of his guests at dinner:

'I hear you have written a play for the Haymarket Theatre.'

'Say rather,' corrected Wilde, 'that the Theatre Royal, Haymarket, has asked me for a play.'

'Well, at any rate, Tree is doing it.'

'Alas! yes.'

'But won't he be good in his part?'

'Good? No.'

'Surely not bad?'

'Bad? No.'

'Indifferent, then?'

'No, not indifferent.'

'Then what on earth will he be?'

'In the strictest confidence . . . but you won't repeat this?'

'Not a word.'

'Then I will whisper it in your deaf ear. Tree will be . . . we must face it manfully . . . he will be Tree.'

The first performance, on April 19th, 1893, was received with enthusiasm and loud calls for the author, who was in a box, from which he announced: 'Ladies and Gentlemen, I regret to inform you that Mr Oscar Wilde is not in the house.' Tree's dressing-room was crowded with admirers and resounding with super-latives when the author entered. An interchange of congratulations was followed by:

'I shall always regard you as the best critic of my plays,' from Wilde.

'But I have never criticized your plays,' from Tree.

'That's why,' from Wilde.

Tree was very good in his part, liking it so much that he used to throw off his own witticisms in the style of Lord Illingworth, and Wilde remarked: 'Ah, every day dear Herbert becomes *de plus en plus Oscarisé*; it is a wonderful case of Nature imitating Art.'

The comedy has some speeches and sentences of an old-fashioned sentimental kind that would make a modern audience laugh, such as 'Child of my shame, be still the child of my shame!' Nevertheless, if acted at all, it should be acted as written. Within the last few years Wilde's three other comedies have been done successfully in their original acting versions, but a recent revival of *A Woman of no Importance* was a well-merited failure because someone who thought himself cleverer than the author 'adapted' it. There should be a law for the protection of period pieces.

Tree, the last of the great actor-managers, was the first of the really intelligent ones. Outside their special faculties as actors and managers, the rest were not distinguished for mental alertness or imagination. Even David Garrick, whose inclusion in the Johnson circle proves his companionable qualities of high spirits and comical patter, lampooned the age by 'improving' Shakespeare's plays—that is, violating them—showing thereby that, even within his own province as producer, he lacked sensibility and common sense. Kemble and Kean were solely interested in themselves, Macready was primarily interested in earning enough money to live like a gentleman, and Irving built up his extraordinary person-ality with parts cut out of Shakespeare's plays, with third-rate continental melodramas, and with inferior native products, dis-playing not the smallest interest in the revolutionary work of contemporary playwrights, nor indeed in anything outside the Lyceum Theatre. The other actor-managers of Tree's time, Hare, Wyndham and the Kendals, made no notable contribution to stage-history; though some distinction was won by George Alexander, who spotted reputable money-makers in Wilde and Pinero, by Johnston Forbes-Robertson, who did two of Shaw's plays and several of Shakespeare's, by Martin Harvey, who did the same; and much distinction by F. R. Benson, who inoculated the provinces with Shakespeare, producing all but two of the plays, and turned Stratford-on-Avon into a national Mecca.

Apart from his unique record of spectacular Shakespearean productions, Tree perceived the genius of Ibsen at a time when the other actors and nearly all the critics were describing his works as a sort of intellectual cloaca, and appreciated the poetic quality of Maeterlinck's early plays when most English people were laughing at them, though one or two French critics were acclaiming him as 'the Belgian Shakespeare', which makes us wonder how often contemporary judgment ought to be called temporary aberration. Tree recognized the valuable work being done for the stage by Brieux, and justly estimated the brilliance and originality of Shaw's comedies long before the Vedrenne–Barker management had popularized them. He produced one work by each of these four dramatists, starting with *L'Intruse* by Maeterlinck in 1890, and following the run of *A Woman of no Importance* with a matinée of Ibsen's *An Enemy of the People*. The latter was the first production of an Ibsen play in England by a leading West End actor, and it was successful enough to be revived at intervals for occasional performances. Tree played Dr Stockman in a humorous manner that would have surprised Ibsen, but he improved on his first conception of the part and it became a favourite of his.

Shaw's critical campaign against the actor-manager system was mitigated by this enterprise, and he admitted that Tree's 'notion of feeding the popular drama with ideas, and gradually educating the public by classical matinées, financed by the spoils of the popular plays in the evening bill, seems to have been the right one'.

At a revival of *An Enemy of the People* early in 1906, a General Election was in progress, the Liberals were sweeping the country, and when Stockman spoke of the 'damned compact Liberal majority', 'this devil's own compact majority', the beliefs of which were 'like rancid, mouldy ham, producing all the moral scurvy that devastates society', the audiences thought that the player was 'gagging' in the interests of the Conservative Party, the action being held up by hoots and cheers. But this was nothing new. Tree had risked a performance at Chicago in the spring of 1895, and free fights had taken place in the theatre to the loud accompaniment of 'boos' and 'bravos', the performance being suspended at several points.

Undaunted by the critics and the opinion of all respectable playgoers, Tree contributed three guineas towards the purchase of a drinking-cup as a present to Ibsen on his seventieth birthday. It was a solitary gesture on behalf of the English theatre, and Shaw wrote that Tree 'must feel rather like a man in morning dress at a smart dinner-party, for no other manager compromised himself by meddling in the business'.

CHAPTER 8

Domestic and Foreign

At various times in her life Maud Tree found what she thought an ideal home for Herbert, and the list of her different addresses reads like a house-agent's list of desirable residences. They were stationary for about three years (1888–1891) at 16 New Cavendish Street; then they spent a year at The Grange, near Jack Straw's Castle, on Hampstead Heath; after which their longest period was spent at 77 Sloane Street, where they remained for ten years and where their second and third daughters, Felicity and Iris, were born. Between their more durable domiciles they occupied flats or rented houses or stayed in hotels.

In the early years of their marriage Maud formed a close friendship with W. S. Gilbert and his wife, with whom she went on a holiday to Egypt, and she exchanged many letters with the famous librettist, who always started his with: 'My dear N.K.L.' (Nice Kind Lady). She even begged him to continue his collaboration with Sullivan and encouraged him to do so by passing on a remark the composer had made to her, which brought this:

> Grim's Dyke
> Harrow Weald
> 16 June '93

My dear N.K.L.

Thank you, really, for your letter which was written, I know, out of sheer good nature and good will—and intended to put me into better heart with my work. Well, it has done so, and so your kindly object has been attained. Probably you don't know how highly I value any indication of interest on your part in me and in my work.

Sullivan never says much to me, and what he *does* say I usually knock a lot off of, for discount. But what he said to you he, no doubt, meant and it is very gratifying to know that he thinks so well of what I have done. I have made two attempts to pick up the dropped threads, but so far in vain. Before I make a third attempt I shall read your kind letter again, and that will give me heart. I don't think I am a vain man or I shouldn't have so poor an opinion of what I do.

We enjoyed your visit immensely—it was kind of your husband to come. I sincerely hope you don't find us so humdrum as to prevent your coming to make a stay with us.

Yours affectionately
W. S. Gilbert

Opinions greatly differed about Maud's acting. She was good in comedy of a gentle and delicate kind, but stagey in emotional parts and entirely unsuited to 'leading lady' types in modern or classical plays, though her Ophelia was highly praised, probably because she sang the snatches in the mad scene effectively. As she was extremely ambitious, trouble was bound to ensue in her husband's theatre, for she wanted to be cast for parts which he knew were not within her compass, and he never made the mistake of thinking that the wife of a leading actor was necessarily a leading actress. In her memoir of her husband she honestly records several instances of her tears and tempers when she did not get what she wanted. '*Why* Marion Terry? *Why* not me?' she once asked. 'You see, the part needs extraordinary sympathy,' he told her. She admits to 'a sudden ungovernable rage. I am ashamed to say what absurd form my fury took: suffice it that Herbert got up from the table where we had been supping so happily, and left the house without a word.' He pacified her by letting her play the Pompadour in his next production.

Again there was no part for her in *Hypatia*, a drama based on Charles Kingsley's novel and lavishly produced with scenery by Alma Tadema and music by Hubert Parry. She did not allow Herbert to forget her disappointment, frequently letting him see her, 'with careful traces of recent weeping', as he passed from the stage to his dressing-room. It is interesting to recall that an actor who would one day become famous in films, George Arliss, applied for a small part in *Hypatia*. He heard that there were three monks in the play, obtained an interview with Tree, and asked if he might be cast for the first monk. 'Oh!' said Tree, 'Mr Allan is playing that.' 'Well, then, the second monk.' 'Let me see. Mr Allan is playing him too.' 'Then let me play the third monk.' 'Alas! Mr Allan plays him too. You see, we've rolled the three monks into one.'

According to Irene Vanbrugh, there were many emotional up-heavals while *The Tempter* was being prepared, in addition to those caused by the author and manager. Maud was much upset that Julia Neilson in the leading part was being rehearsed with greater care than herself, and the proceedings often terminated with floods of tears. Herbert was usually sympathetic, showing his solicitude in letters of this period by telling her that she must abandon a part if she feels uncomfortable in it, as he does not want her 'to do anything that is against the grain'. Occasionally he felt that he had spoken too harshly to her on the stage, and following one such occurrence he despatched a letter after her by hand:

My dearest Maud, I don't want you to worry about what I said today—but I wanted to make an impression on you, for I have a very strong feeling about the matter—and I want you always to be your own sweet self and not another person. I have been working all the afternoon and am tired—I will come home early, dear. Love— your Herbert.

Though she was often seen to advantage at the Haymarket, she felt at moments that she would be more comfortable elsewhere, and wrote to obtain Gilbert's advice about getting a job with D'Oyly Carte. He replied:

36 Princess Gardens
S.W.
1 Feb. '94

My dear N.K.L.
A merry February and a happy New Month.
I should certainly write to Carte if I were you. You see he gets so many applications of the kind from *me* that the edge of his enthusiasm may be a little dulled by this time—but the joy of receiving a per-sonal application from someone in the same rank of life as himself —I mean a London manager's wife and not a contemptible author —will stir him up to special exertions. At the same time I will do all that a contemptible author (who does lovest thou as he didn't ought to wont) can do to enlist his sympathies.

Your amusing friend
N.K.G.

But within two months of her letter to Gilbert she was given her best part at the Haymarket in *Once Upon a Time*, a play founded on Hans Andersen's story 'The Emperor's New Clothes' and adapted by Tree and Louis N. Parker. Having attended a per-

formance Gilbert wrote to say that he had never seen her so well
cast and advised her to keep to comedy and pretty little bits of
pathos: 'A perfect ray of sunlight whenever you came on the
stage. If I were a younger and more enterprising man I would tell
you exactly how you looked—and hope for the happiest results.'
He did not care for the play, giving one of his objections: 'Why
does Magdalena love the King? He hasn't a redeeming quality.
He is a base tyrant of the meanest type. Is it because he shows himself to her in his pyjamas? If I showed myself to ladies in *my*
pyjamas could I hope for such a result? If I thought I could—but
no—that way madness lies.' Tree had miscast himself as the King,
and the play would have been defined by him as a repertory piece.
'When is a repertory not a repertory?' he once asked, supplying
the answer: 'When it's a success.' The failure was rather serious
for the manager just then because it followed three similar ventures, and Gilbert was repentant:

3 Ap. '94

My dear N.K.L.

I am heartily sorry to hear that you are in so low a state about the
new piece. How my nonsense must have jarred upon you! I'm really
sorry that I played the buffoon at so serious a juncture. I hope you
will forgive me—and that you will come down here to do it. Why
don't you both—all three—come on Sunday until Monday evening?

Now do let your husband be advised by me, for once, and produce Tom Taylor's version of *Le Roi s'amuse*—it is called *The
Fool's Revenge*—it is badly written but theatrically effective—it is
grossly indecent—and in short has every chance of success. There's an
admirable part for him in it—a splendid part for Jowlier [Julia
Neilson]—I believe a very pretty part for yourself—and a Fred Terry
part. You could do it in three weeks easy and I believe it would pull
in crowded houses till the end of July. Moreover it hasn't been done
for a quarter of a century in London.

We have lovely weather down here—I wish you would come.
My wife sends her best love and all sympathy.

Yours always affectionately
W. S. Gilbert

He wrote again on the same day to express his willingness to
polish up the play without any other reward than the satisfaction
of feeling that he had contributed, however remotely, to what he
felt sure would be a successful production. But Tree had already

arranged to do Sydney Grundy's new drama *A Bunch of Violets*, in which Maud had another good part. This was no repertory piece. It packed the theatre for over three months, a run which in those days meant a large profit. Gilbert was delighted, and suggested that the Trees should take a cottage within a mile of Grim's Dyke at five guineas a week for the summer months. 'Pray come whenever you can. The gooseberry bushes are thickly hung with stomach aches—and while the cuckoo delights by day, the nightingale and the screech owl do their best to make night lovely.'

But Maud took Viola to the seaside that summer, and Herbert spent a few weeks at Marienbad for his rheumatism, going for long walks and learning *Hamlet* in German. He was concerned over Maud's health, writing to her: 'Do take great care of yourself and be very happy all the time', and he found time to send a parental admonition to his 'Dearest Villi Vi', a pet name for his ten-years-old daughter:

> I hope you are taking great care of Mother—she is not very strong just now and you must treat her very kindly.—I hope you always *try* to be unselfish—I know it is not quite easy for you, but must learn it as any other accomplishment—like playing the piano, for instance.—Now, dear Viola, do remember this. Don't always think only of catching butterflies and enjoying yourself. Think of Mother who has worked so hard this year, and who is not as strong as you are.

A short summer visit to Marienbad became an almost annual event with him. It improved his digestion and allayed his rheumatism, teaching him the simple truth that 'The greatest pleasure is the cessation of pain'.

Every dramatist who thought he had written a good part for Tree was now sending his play to the Haymarket, and among them was an eminent politician, Joseph Chamberlain, who however insisted that the authorship should not be disclosed. Tree did not think that the play would succeed on its own merits, nor that it was good enough to do for its own sake, and it is possible that the manuscript still lies in the Chamberlain archives. Royalty was also beginning to take an interest in the Haymarket Theatre, and Tree was commanded to give performances of *The Red Lamp* and *The Ballad Monger* at Balmoral Castle on Monday, September

24th, 1894. He was doing his usual autumn tour of the provinces at the time, and after the visit to Balmoral the company had to travel to Dublin, opening there with *A Bunch of Violets* on Tuesday the 25th. Having received the personal congratulations of Queen Victoria and eaten a hasty supper, they left Balmoral at 1.30 a.m., drove ten miles in darkness to Ballater, and arrived at Holyhead at 4.5 on Tuesday afternoon. A special steamer had been chartered for the crossing, which was rough enough to make Tree lie down. A stewardess was particularly attentive, asking at intervals how he felt. When he said that he was a little easier, the reason for her solicitude became apparent: 'Then will you kindly write me an order for three for the Theatre Royal tonight?—I will hold the basin while you do it.' The boat reached the Dublin quayside at 7.40 p.m., the players having dressed and made-up for their parts before disembarking. In the belief that the whole world was taking a keen interest in their journey, that cheering crowds would greet them on arrival, and that the sporting population of the Irish capital were betting heavily for and against the curtain going up that night—all of which misinformation duly appeared in the English press—the company were a little dashed to see three men and a boy standing on the quay. As Tree and Haddon Chambers climbed into a jaunting-car, the boy raised a cheer, upon which the actor smiled and said to the driver, 'They seem to be very excited about this affair over here.' Having flicked his sleepy horse with the whip and shouted 'Get up, you bloody swine!' the driver turned to Tree and asked, 'Is it the smallpox you mean?' All the same, they had the satisfaction of starting the play at the advertised hour, eight o'clock.

Following the autumn tour, Tree paid his first visit to America in January, 1895, the company preceding him. Maud had him all to herself during the voyage, and was later to confess: 'How I adored and looked back upon the long-drawn days of that week! Days that never came again . . .' When their boat arrived at New York 'I was discovered in our state-room weeping among our boxes, because my happy, cherished hours were over. Herbert dried my tears and promised me that everything should come again; but it never did.' Max Beerbohm accompanied them as a salaried private secretary to Herbert. Max was frequently ill, and

Lionel Brough had the opposite cabin. Brough was a little too hearty for one in Max's condition, constantly entering his cabin to cheer him up with club-room stories, and imparting to the atmosphere a powerful bouquet from the bar which left his victim with the impression that they had shared a cabin all the way.

They stayed at the Waldorf on Fifth Avenue and 33rd Street, then the most luxurious hotel in the city. Herbert and Maud entertained, and were entertained, for some days before they opened at the theatre. He took to the place eagerly, liking everything about it and nearly everyone he met. The hot rooms, the cold streets, the low voices of the men, the high voices of the women, all appealed to him. Max, too, enjoyed himself, and amused Herbert endlessly, his opinions being as quaint as his compositions were careful. One day he suggested an effective line to bring the curtain down on a play. 'Where are you going?' asks the heroine. 'I am going to the Thirty Years' War,' answers the hero. Herbert made a note of it. But the letters Max wrote in reply to those received by his brother were so laboriously considered and exactly worded that the pile of unacknowledged ones became unmanageable and the duty was transferred to someone with less nicety of style, Max retaining his full salary.

Herbert even enjoyed being examined by press reporters, though he once remarked, 'I have been interviewed in America and after that I fear no foe,' and coined an epigram: 'An American's home is an interviewer's castle.' He and Maud hardly had a moment to themselves. One party followed another, and Maud was impressed by the high spirits and fine clothes of everybody, writing home to Viola that the parties in New York were much smarter than those in London:

> In my best brocade I feel quite shabby, though I put on all Lady Granby's jewels! *All* the grand ladies here are as joyous and full of fun as Margot Tennant—they dance about (most beautifully) and mimic people and shout and sing like children—so do the *very* smart, *very* stiff-collared, *very* correct young men—I suppose their climate makes them so lighthearted.

Herbert also wrote to Viola about their doings:

> We went to a dog-show today and all the dogs howled at us to buy them—but we had to pass them by—big golumphing St Bernards

and little wippety Spitzes.—Darling, mind you are very good and
obedient and sweet. Always count ten when you are going to be
angry—I have to count fifteen.

His advice was prompted by a memory. Viola, in a pique, had
once broken a window. 'This, my child, is wickedness,' said
Herbert. 'No, father, this is heredity,' she replied.

Their season at Abbey's Theatre began on January 28th with
The Red Lamp and *The Ballad Monger*. They remained in New
York for a month, presenting *Hamlet*, *The Merry Wives*, *An
Enemy of the People* and *A Bunch of Violets*. Then came a fortnight
at the Opera House, Chicago, a fortnight at Broad Street Theatre,
Philadelphia, and a week at Tremont Theatre, Boston. In the
course of a lecture to the Harvard students Tree first gave, what
he was often to repeat, Hamlet's speech 'To be or not to be' in
the voice of Falstaff, whose speech on 'Honour' was delivered
in the voice of Hamlet, the actor believing that the philosophy in
both was identical. During their three days at Washington they
were received by President Cleveland, the approach to whom was
far more formidable and intimidating than the preliminaries to
an audience with Queen Victoria, for they seemed to pass through
cordons of armed police, soldiers, servants, secretaries, to traverse
innumerable rooms and corridors, and to mount imposing stair-
cases, until they arrived at an enormous writing-table piled with
papers, from behind which rose a large man with simple speech
and engaging manners. While at Washington they gave a supper-
party to three writers: Thomas Nelson Page, Colonel John Hay
and Rudyard Kipling, the last of whom entertained them with
stories of his Vermont farm. Three nights at Baltimore and a
short final season in New York brought their visit to a close.

The quantity of speeches, banquets, parties and what-not that
engrossed Tree were too exhausting even for one of his vitality,
and he spent the first two or three days of the return-journey in
bed. When he got up he was as lively as ever and organized a concert for the last evening of the voyage with his usual enthusiasm.
An actor, who had volunteered to recite Mark Antony's funeral
oration, wished Tree to hear him rehearse it. Having taken up his
position at the far end of the saloon, he folded his arms, stood with
great solemnity for a while glaring at Herbert and Max, and then

began. 'Fr-riends,' he rumbled like distant thunder. 'R-romans,' he roared like an erupting volcano. 'Countrymen,' he howled like a typhoon in full blast.

'One instant, Mr ——,' interrupted Herbert.

'Well, Mr Tree?'

'An idea has just struck me. Didn't Antony address the crowd from *above*?'

'From the rostrum, Mr Tree.'

'Rostrum—yes—rostrum. My idea is this: How would it be if you spoke your speech from that little place up there?' Herbert pointed to the organist's gallery.

The actor weighed this carefully, nodded gloomily, and began to ascend the staircase.

'One instant, Mr ——,' cried Herbert. 'Another idea. What did Antony *wear*?'

'A toga, Mr Tree.'

'Toga—yes—toga.'

Snatching a tablecloth, Herbert proceeded to drape the actor, who gravely continued the speech without noticing that his two listeners were in danger of apoplexy.

On the night of the concert the speech was duly vociferated from the gallery, but the actor, feeling perhaps that his gestures were incommoded by the tablecloth, left the toga to the imagination of the audience. At a certain point in the oration he descended from the organ-loft, and there was, says Max, 'a rather awkward moment when he reappeared at the foot of the winding staircase. Major-General Sir Somebody Something, who was acting as chairman and sitting in the middle of the front row, sprang up and went to shake him warmly by the hand. The Major-General was warded off with a fierce gesture. The end was not yet. Antony had but, as in the play, come down among us to read Caesar's will. "If you have tee-arrs, prepare to shed them now," and so forth.'

An incident that was to have a great effect on Tree's future career occurred while he was in America. While acting in Philadelphia he asked Max to see a play being performed at another theatre and report on it. This was Paul M. Potter's stage version of George du Maurier's *Trilby*, a novel which had made a sensational success in England and America, where it was published by Harper & Brothers. Max's report at supper that night was concise: the play, said he, was utter nonsense and could only be a dismal failure in London. Impressed by his brother's opinion, Tree dismissed *Trilby* from his mind. But it so happened that at the conclusion of his season at Abbey's Theatre he had one spare evening before embarking, and instead of going that day to see Niagara Falls he went that night to see *Trilby*, which had just arrived for its first New York production at the Garden Theatre, where it was performed for one week, from the 15th to the 20th April. When the curtain descended on the second act, Tree left his box, saw the adapter, and at once purchased the English rights.

Max's view of *Trilby* may have been slightly coloured by his view of New York, which he described as 'a terrible, horrible place' with its numbered and unnamed streets, its overhead railways, its tall houses, its shriekings and whistlings, and the constant clatter of horses' hoofs over the cobblestones. But the harbour was 'rather fine' and the rough paven streets in the neighbourhood of the docks reminded him of Nuremburg. He thought the people 'very nice', and became friendly with the dramatist Clyde Fitch: 'He loves my writing, which is a bond. I have never seen or read anything of his, which is awkward.'

Though an uncertain business-adviser to his brother, Max managed to sell four of his own articles to *Vanity* for 25 dollars apiece (a total of £20 in those days) and he disposed of several drawings. Each article was about 1,000 words long and he considered the pay 'not bad'. The first to be published was on the famous dandy Count D'Orsay, an appropriate theme in view of Max's report to his mother: 'I look very well dressed.'

CHAPTER 9

Hogwash

The American tour had not been a financial success, the critics had not been flattering, and Tree decided that his reappearance at the Haymarket must be sensational. In those days the most famous popular playwright in the world was Victorien Sardou, who wrote comedies, dramas, histories and melodramas with a facility only equalled by the skill with which he contrived startling situations. Several of his melodramas were written for the sole purpose of enabling Sarah Bernhardt to display her vocal accomplishments; but his plays were liked in England on account of their thrilling qualities, and it became a matter of faith with British dramatists that Sardou was the grandmaster of stagecraft, most of them copying his methods and trying to repeat his success. Until Bernard Shaw described his artificial plots and unnatural characters as 'Sardoodledom' and wrote of *Fedora* that it 'made up an entertainment too Bedlamite for any man with settled wits to preconceive', the Frenchman was the major saint of English play-providers whose sole object was to get rich quickly by titillating the public palate.

Admirers of Ibsen and the new drama were in violent reaction against the Sardou influence, and Shaw's criticism of Tree's production of *Fedora*, which took place at the Haymarket in May '95, was the first nail in the coffin of what then passed for brilliant stagecraft.

The Bancrofts had made a success of the play back in the eighties, and Tree's sensation consisted of Mrs Patrick Campbell in the leading part and Mrs Bancroft's return to the stage after her retirement in a lesser part. Stella Patrick Campbell was then at the height of her fame as an emotional actress. She had driven critics and playgoers to hyperboles with her performance as Paula in Arthur Pinero's *The Second Mrs Tanqueray* at the St James's Theatre in '93. George Alexander had discovered her as an actress

just as he had given Wilde his first chance as a playwright, and
Tree was quick enough to benefit from both revelations, getting
Wilde's second comedy for the Haymarket and offering Stella
Campbell £60 a week the moment he saw her as Paula. Alexander
had paid her £15 a week to play Mrs Tanqueray, but he raised her
salary to £30 shortly after she made a resounding success of the
part. He had an option on her services for his next production,
The Masqueraders by Henry Arthur Jones, but her engagement
with Tree followed, and she appeared in a Haymarket failure:
John-a-Dreams by Haddon Chambers. Tree then lent her to John
Hare for Pinero's *The Notorious Mrs Ebbsmith* while the Haymarket company were in America. She made another hit as Mrs
Ebbsmith, but when Tree returned she had to leave the Pinero
play, which, as she said, 'unfortunately did not survive the change
of cast', and take the part of Fedora.

Sardoodledom was again triumphant, and Shaw advised Mrs
Campbell to use soap and water instead of whitewash for her
arms, because her embraces wrecked Tree's clothes:

> She knelt at his feet and made a perfect zebra of his left leg with
> bars across it. Then she flung her arms convulsively right round
> him; and the next time he turned his back to the footlights there was
> little to choose between his coatback and his shirtfront. Before the
> act was over a gallon of benzine would hardly have set him right
> again. Mr Tree had his revenge at the end of the play, when, in
> falling on Fedora's body, he managed to transfer a large black patch
> to her cheek, which was strikingly in evidence when she bowed her
> acknowledgment of the frantic applause with which the evening
> ended.

Sardou's melodramas made great demands on the vocal organs,
and Mrs Campbell had not yet learnt how to shout, scream and
coo with the Bernhardtian technique. After a few weeks of fever-
ish success, she lost her voice; Maud Tree took her part at twenty-
four hours' notice; and the play, as Stella would have put it,
'unfortunately did not survive the change of cast'.

Opposite the Haymarket Theatre there stood a decaying opera
house known as Her Majesty's, built on the spot where Sir John
Vanbrugh had once designed and managed a theatre. This opera
house was about to be demolished, and Tree determined to obtain
the site with the purpose of erecting a theatre in which he could

realize his dreams. He took the risk without the money, and thereafter much of his time was occupied in raising the sums required. His decision was made, it must be remembered, before his next production at the Haymarket had so firmly established him as a successful actor-manager that he could personally contribute towards the great design; and not a little of his holiday at Marienbad in the summer of '95 was spent in writing letters to financiers, solicitors, and such-like folk, in the furtherance of his plans. At the same time his letters to Maud were full of optimism and encouragement. Several passages reveal his mood and his nature:

24 July '95.

I hope you are taking great care to enjoy yourself—you have had a wearing season and ought to have a really good holiday and you have certainly earned it. —You will only feel by and bye what an enormous impression you made in *Fedora* . . . I have been writing out limitless notes for Du Maurier to work upon—but I do hope he may be induced to come here . . . Marienbad is quite beautiful and the air is fresh and cool . . . Now, dear Maud, once more do enjoy yourself—make up your mind to and you will—and don't make troubles for yourself!—How about money?—have you sufficient?— if not I will send you a cheque at once—let me know.—I enclose cheque £10 meanwhile. Fond love—Your affectionate Husband.

26 July '95.

Did I tell you the Laboucheres are here? I am seeing a good deal of him—he is very charming and entertaining . . . I have been working a good deal at *Trilby* and yesterday I read the play to a German manager . . . I am feeling very well indeed—I am probably going to take mud-baths to get rid of this year's rheumatism.

No date.

I am delighted that you are keeping well—mind you take great care of yourself.—What I meant was that sometimes you *allow* yourself to mope.—Pray don't fancy that you need give up hope— there was never a time when there was so much hope for your future in regard to the stage, for you have made enormous strides during the past year, and especially this season.—Leave everything until we see how *Trilby* turns out, and we will arrange something special for you at the Haymarket, even if you do not get a really fine part elsewhere in the meantime . . . I feel this Marienbad cure will set me up for the entire year, and I know it is important that

I should have all my powers for the coming campaign—especially as Robertson is now in the field. [This was Johnston Forbes-Robertson, who was about to join with Mrs Patrick Campbell in a series of seasons at the Lyceum Theatre, during which they did *Romeo and Juliet, Hamlet* and *Macbeth*.] I have been reading *Othello*—I think we ought to do that—but I can't make up my mind as to whether I should do Othello or Iago—the former appeals to my imagination more—but perhaps Iago would be more suited to me—I wish you would read the play through again.—I did not know Irving thought of *Coriolanus*, but really I don't think that would do for me, nor for him either for that matter.—*Julius Caesar* is what I should like to do and I intend reading it again.—I find I have plenty to do here in the way of work and writing—I have to prepare a lecture for *Hamlet*; I am working at *Macaire* as well as at *Trilby*.—About the latter I have sent my suggestions to Du Maurier and he approves of them. —Do tell Viola to be very careful about bathing, and not to swim or float too boastfully ... Good-bye, dearest Maud—I did not mean my lecture to be unkind—I can't imagine how you could have taken it so. Yes, I will be gentle—indeed often I try to be and sometimes I fancy you won't let me be ... Your loving Herbert.

No date.

The theatre is let, so we are better off—and the tour is sure to be remunerative—mind you don't stint yourself ... I find I have a fearful lot of writing to do in connection with the theatre ... Take great care of yourself, Maud dear, won't you?—and buy yourself all you want—I really think the future is going to be brighter for us.

No date.

Arthur Cecil accompanies me on my walks—yesterday I walked five hours and I do an average of three or four hours a day ... I shall probably get home about the 14th [August] and have a couple of days with Du Maurier—I am extremely anxious to buy the German rights of him ... I am sorry to say the bicycling does not progress. [Nor did it. Tree was not built for a bicycle.]

He was always begging Maud not to worry about trifles, but to 'eat, drink, sleep and be happy!' She was inclined to despondency, he to elation. On his return he spent two days at Folkestone with George Du Maurier, and they went through *Trilby* together, the author agreeing to the actor's interpolations and amendments. It is a pity that Tree did not write a play round his own personality instead of making the characters conceived by other authors fit himself. He possessed the ability to do so, for two episodes he added to *Trilby* were theatrically effective, and the combination of his wit and dramatic instinct should have resulted in a superb actor's play. The two short scenes he wrote for *Trilby* are in his own handwriting along with the original prompt copy. The first introduces Svengali early in Act I:

Svengali: You called me? (*A little scream from Trilby*) Bon jour, ma belle.

Taffy: Hullo, Svengali.

Trilby: How you startled me!

Laird: We were talking of you, Svengali.

Svengali: You flatter me.

Billee: Come, Svengali, play us some music.

Svengali: No!

Taffy: What's the matter today, Svengali?

Svengali: I have been insulted.

Laird: What has happened?

Svengali: They have dared to ask me for my rent—*canaille*—I will not bear it! A dirty 200 francs! A bagatelle! What is 200 francs? Have you 200 francs?

Taffy: No, but you have 200 francs of mine. If you can repay them it will be devilish convenient.

Svengali: Do not insult me, or I shall be angry—I am a proud man, though I am poor.

Taffy: Would you be insulted by five francs?

Svengali: (*indignantly*) Five francs! I—I—five francs—to me—Ah! —well (*takes money*), not as a gift—I will repay it—that will make 205 francs—I will give three per cent—I would not be under an obligation to anybody—I will see what I can do for you one day.

Laird: Come, come, Svengali—give us some music.

Svengali: (*half aside*) The pig—dogs—to insult me with five francs! Ah bah! (*pockets money*).

Trilby: Yes, Svengali, do play to us——

Taffy: Trilby has a touch of neuralgia.

Svengali: Ah ha! la grande Trilby!—I will forget the world—I will make music for you and take away your pain and keep it myself. . . .

The second scene that Tree wrote occurs near the end of Act 2 when Svengali tells Gecko that they are going to take Trilby away, separating her from Little Billee, Gecko being in love with Trilby but knowing that she loves Little Billee:

Gecko: Is this right?

Svengali: Right—what is right? Pah! (*snaps fingers*).

Gecko: Svengali, I have served you as a dog, but rather than injure her I——

Svengali: Fool that you are (*takes him by the ear*)—You owe everything to me—and now when the ball is at my feet you kick it away—you little whippersnapper—whom I picked out of the gutter when you were starving.—This Littrebilli whom I hate shall not take her.—You talk to me of religion—of your God—That for your religion—I laugh at it—I laugh at all the world—I am myself, Svengali—I know my power, nothing can frighten me—I am my own God—(*laughs*)—and you dare (*raises his arm—suddenly puts his hand to his heart—staggers—gasps*) I—I—what is this—help—help—Gecko —I faint—I cannot see—brandy—quick—I—I (*Gecko runs out—Svengali feels his heart—it seems not to beat*) I will not die—(*Goes to window—throws it open—gasps—comes down agonized like a rat in a trap*) God! Do not let me die—Death, death, no, no (*gasps*), let me live another year, another month—I will repent—Oh God of Israel— 'Stemang Yisrael adonai Eloheno Adonai Echod.' (*Continues gibbering. Re-enter Gecko with brandy—Svengali drinks.*) Ah—ah! (*looks before him, feels himself recovering, puts hand to heart, begins a low laugh.*) I am not dying, Gecko—I feel my heart—unloose my neckcloth—I am not dying——

Gecko: No, no, Svengali, you are better, eh? (*sympathetically*).

Svengali: Yes, I am better—it was nothing but excitement—a little faint—my father died like that when he was seventy— I shall recover—more brandy—(*rises, smothered laugh*)— Ah! I am not dying—ha, ha, ha—we will, my Gecko, you and I——

Gecko: What were you doing on your knees when I came in?

Svengali: I was offering up a prayer for Little Billee—ha, ha—poor Little Billee—we will live—you and I—we will wander Eastward—you and Trilby and I—we will cage the song-bird till it sings velvet and gold and beautiful flowers and pearls and diamonds and rubies—and we will be rich—I will ride in my carriage and smoke the big Havana cigar—and I will wear a big fur coat—all the winter—and all the summer too——

When the play came to the Haymarket this particular episode was picked out for Shaw's especial opprobrium, which shows his

acuteness, no other critic noticing that it was out of key with Du
Maurier's work:

> I derived much cynical amusement from this most absurd scene;
> but if I were Mr Du Maurier, I should ask whether the theatre is
> really in such an abject condition that all daintiness and seriousness
> of thought and feeling must be struck out of a book, and replaced
> by vulgar nonsense before it can be accepted on the stage. I grant
> that the public deserves nothing better from Mr Tree. It has done
> its silly best to teach him that it wants none of his repeated and
> honourable attempts to cater for people with some brains.

The public showed on this occasion that it wanted nothing
better from Tree. *Trilby* was produced in Manchester during his
autumn tour, and started a run of many months at the Haymarket
on October 30th, 1895. It was the biggest financial success of his
career, being repeatedly revived. Everyone liked it, even W. S.
Gilbert having nothing to say against it. 'I enjoyed last night very
much indeed,' he told Maud. 'Svengali's make-up is marvellous—
we could *smell* him.' It was astonishing how Tree with the utmost
economy of means could alter the entire appearance of his face.
'It takes father far less time to make himself ugly than it takes
mother to make herself beautiful,' said Viola. No one could
account for the celerity with which it was done or the amazing
effectiveness of the result. While Irving used to spend an hour or
more to make himself look like another edition of Irving, Tree
transformed himself completely in ten minutes. Yet, though the
Svengali disguise was remarkable, the performance was an epit-
ome of Treeisms: the quick slinking walk, the flashing eyes, the
hand on hip, the fluttering fingers, the foreign gestures, the slightly
guttural accents; in this part even his faults were turned into virtues, and the total mesmeric effect, as if Trilby's singing entirely
resulted from Svengali's power, was a triumph of suggestion. An
instance of his absent-mindedness proved how completely his
acting had gripped the audience. The piano on which Svengali
performed was a dummy, the real instrument being played off-
stage by Raymond Roze. One evening Tree jumped up from his
seat three or four bars before the completion of the tune, the music
continuing with no visible player. Not a soul in the house appeared
to notice what had happened. But Tree was made aware of it by

the look of horror on the stage-manager's face in the prompt corner. He met the emergency by pointing to the piano and saying, 'See what Svengali can do!' which broke the spell with a shout of laughter. This incident was recorded by Tree's business-manager, Fitzroy Gardner, and remained in the memory of a future actor-manager, Gerald Du Maurier, son of the author, who played the small part of Zou-zou at a salary of £4 a week.

As we shall hear, Tree quickly got tired of his parts and played them perfunctorily when the excitement was over, but he took longer to tire of Svengali than the rest because he could amplify his creation without evoking the wrath of an author, himself being one of them in this instance. But he soon got bored with waiting at the theatre merely to show his face in a frame for the further hypnotizing of Trilby by a picture of Svengali after the latter's death. At his last revival of the play Douglas Jefferies was asked to make up another actor to resemble Tree as Svengali for this picture. The likeness was satisfactory, Jefferies being a skilful artist. But one evening the actor did not turn up and Jefferies was asked to make himself up for the purpose.

I did my best to give my features the right appearance of dominating Hebraic villainy [he writes], but on going down the stairs met Tree on his way out of the theatre. He stopped me, gave me a long gaze of anxious wonderment, and then said 'Oh my God! *The Saviour!*' Not a perfect impersonation, I gathered.

As the novel had been so popular, and the author had provided illustrations, the picture of Trilby herself was clear in the public mind, and for a while both Tree and Du Maurier were stumped for their heroine, who had to be tall, beautiful, young, perfectly formed, and an actress. At last they heard of a girl named Dorothea Baird, aged 18, who had been with Ben Greet's Shakespearean company for a year and had played Viola and Beatrice. When they called to interview her, they found her lying on a sofa, surrounded by books and studying the part of Desdemona. She was exactly right; they engaged her on the spot; and her reputation was made almost as soon as she stepped on the stage as Trilby. 'Miss Baird very swell and charming,' wrote Gilbert; 'all the more so, to my mind, for the absence of actress-like *savoir faire*.' She eventually married H. B. Irving and played the leading female parts in his revivals of his father's old plays.

After *Trilby* had been running for six months, Tree put on the first part of *Henry IV* for a series of matinées, and the outstanding merit of his production was, said Shaw, 'that the play has been accepted from Shakespeare mainly as he wrote it . . . there is no alteration or hotch-potch, and consequently no suspicion of any attempt to demonstrate the superiority of the manager's taste and judgment to Shakespeare's,' whose plays had recently been emasculated by Henry Irving to make his own parts stand out and by Augustine Daly to make Ada Rehan's parts shine forth.

But the acting of Falstaff and Svengali did not exhaust Tree's energies, which were mainly expended on the details of building his new theatre, planning the policy for its opening, obtaining the necessary capital, and arranging for a second visit to America. His last appearance at the Haymarket took place in July '96, and while his wife went to Spa for a holiday he spent the summer weeks rushing to and from the City, writing letters, seeing all sorts of people, and helping Gilbert Parker in the preparation of a play to be produced in America and afterwards in London. Temporary offices for the half-erected Her Majesty's Theatre were opened at 22 Panton Street, and as the drains were up in that neighbourhood he tried to neutralize the smell by smoking all the time he was working. He reported everything that was happening to Maud, telling her that one man would put in £2,000, another £1,500, a third £3,000, and so on:

> I have two more big men in tow and by Saturday I hope to see day-light through the whole scheme . . . Take great care of yourself, darling, won't you?—Gardner has been most good through this business and is quite devoted. How about your visit to Cassel?— Love to dear Viola. Write me every day and tell me how you are feeling. Your loving Herbie.

Fitzroy Gardner was his business-manager at this time. Ernest Cassel was a famous Anglo-German financier, a large subscriber to the undertaking.

The success of *Trilby* enabled Tree to provide much of the

capital required for the new building. But he had no illusions about the play. When someone praised it as a wonderful contribution to the theatre, he described it succinctly as 'hogwash'. Which had, roughly, been the opinion of brother Max.

CHAPTER 10

America Again

As with all successful men, there was a great deal of self-will in Tree, amounting in some instances to sheer perversity. His mind once made up, no advice could shake it, his obstinate course ultimately being deflected by external forces. He had come to the conclusion that Gilbert Parker's dramatization of his novel *The Seats of the Mighty* was an ideal piece with which to open, first his American tour, and next Her Majesty's Theatre. He may have liked the book, or its title, or his part, or the author, or all of them. The book was certainly a good specimen of its class, the title was appropriate for his new theatre, the part suited his eighteenth-century style, and the author was an agreeable fellow. But scarcely anyone except the producer and the author believed that the play would succeed; and the desire to prove himself right, the rest of the world wrong, is very strong in a man who enjoys self-confidence and trusts his own instinct or judgment. His first big success at the Haymarket, *Captain Swift*, had justified his own faith in it against that of his advisers; and he determined that *The Seats of the Mighty* should do the same at Her Majesty's. In this case the warning he received in the United States merely hardened his inflexibility.

Maud was expecting her third child, so she could not accompany him to America. Had he believed in omens, an experience on the boat which took him across the Atlantic might have shaken his optimism. He made a note of the circumstance:

When I was travelling to New York on my second American tour there was a terrible storm and we were driven out of our course for three days and the company were battened down. I had a deck cabin and was seasick all the time. A deputation knocked at my door on the third day and Lionel Brough said: 'Get up, all danger is past—you must pull yourself together—I say it respectfully—but be a man.' I made an effort and crawled out of my bunk, when a sudden lurch of the ship felled me to the ground insensible. When I looked around I saw an object lying there—it was labelled 'Life Saving Apparatus'. The lurch of the ship had detached it from the wall, and it had nearly killed me who had escaped the perils of the storm. I said: 'How like a Life Saving Apparatus!'

Soon after his departure someone had written to tell his wife that he had been seen in affectionate proximity with another woman; and during the final run-through of Gilbert Parker's play, which was produced at Lafayette Square Opera House, Washington, he scribbled her a note referring to this painful topic:

27 Nov. 1896

My own sweet darling Maud,

Last night all your letters reached me—I never knew, dearest, how deep and beautiful your love for me was—I will try and be a little worthy of it.—

I am writing you now on the eve of the production—it is now 5 o'clock and we have still Act V before us—but I must tell you how happy and how sad your letters have made me—I will answer them all one by one tomorrow. Do not worry, sweet one, about that horrid letter—it is evidently some enemy of yours—for what but a cruel and depraved wretch could send such a letter, knowing your condition. Please don't give it another thought—you can rely on my love and my loyalty to you.—

Gilbert Parker tells me of your sweet thought about the violets. The play is to be done tonight—all is well prepared, and I am calm —it is a great night—with great issues. I will wire my dear wife after the performance. God bless you and our dear ones. I shall say a little prayer tonight for you all before I go on the stage,—and I shall be encouraged by the knowledge of your great love.—

Dear Maud—
Your loving
and lonely
Herbert

The Washington critics were kind enough about the play, but the New York critics fell upon it ruthlessly, pulled it to pieces, and did not encourage the author and producer to put it together again. Tree's American agent, Elisabeth Marbury, strongly advised him to shelve it for good, to forget all about it, and save the situation with other items of his repertory. 'I am bearing it all with a fortitude which I cannot help admiring', Herbert informed

Maud. He decided to put on *The Dancing Girl* and to follow that with *Trilby*, but he refused to abandon *The Seats of the Mighty*:

> I have been working very, very hard and Gilbert Parker has been an angel of helpfulness. Of course we shall continue to work at the play, and I am sure we shall get it right for England . . . I am not flirting with anyone and you may rely on my being good.—I have been worrying myself about that horrible letter—if you get any more, do not worry yourself by reading them, promise me, but send them to Webb or to George Lewis. I have an idea whence that one came. I told G. Parker all about it—and he said that these things are quite common. If I had known, I would have made you come with me.

William Webb was his solicitor, George Lewis the most famous lawyer in London.

The failure of Parker's piece made Tree anxious about his finances, yet he longed for Maud to join him: 'Darling, what a beautiful surprise to see you walk in one morning!' The Waldorf Hotel in New York let him stay on at reduced rates, otherwise he would have gone to a less expensive place. He tried to explain the hostile reception of the play by telling Maud that 'there is a strong anti-English feeling in the press here', but when he put on *The Dancing Girl* the critics were friendly, so we must assume that they had become pro-English within a week:

> 8 Dec. '96
>
> My darling Maud
>
> I wrote you four days ago, but it was too late for the boat. Today I received your last sweet letter. Take great care of yourself, darling, now, and mind you are not unhappy.—I took your picture to bed last night and Viola's and Felicity's and prayed for my darlings.—
>
> We produced *The Dancing Girl* last night with really *great success*. I think it will draw money. *The Seats of the Mighty* is too subtle for them.—Poor Parker is naturally upset—but I have the fighting to do, and in the battle I forget the defeat of the other day.—We are to do *Trilby* next week—and they say it will draw enormously.—
>
> Mind you keep up Sir Algernon West and Wernher—it is most important now to get strong people at my back—even if they put into the general concern, apart from the mere building . . .
>
> It has been a terribly worrying and busy time—but the outlook is all right now. Good-night, darling, your loving Herbert.

A week later came *Trilby*, and his Svengali brought the audience to their feet with shouts of 'Bravo'. He got three calls after

Act 1, four after Act 2, seven after Act 3, and he had to make a speech. The courage with which he had faced failure, and the energy with which he had won success, aroused the admiration of Gilbert Parker and Elisabeth Marbury, both of whom sent letters to Maud about it. 'Herbert bore the march of the Javelins with a Spartan fortitude', wrote the former. 'He seems so strong and brave that I do not think he needs much outside support', wrote the latter. Herbert himself reported: 'The work is hard but I am keeping up wonderfully well amid it all. For one thing, the climate is so wonderfully invigorating that one does not feel fatigue—everybody here is beginning to come forward to show us good feeling.' With all his anxieties he found time to do a young actor a good turn: 'I dare say you have heard that Gerald Du Maurier and Miss Sylva are engaged to be married—I hear Miss Sylva's mother objects—so I shall write to her all about it and appease her mind.'

He refused to climb down in face of hostile criticism and arranged to repeat *The Seats of the Mighty* at some of the places he visited. Parker touched up several scenes, and other cities were given a chance to reverse the New York verdict; but the feeling remained sternly anti-English when that play was performed and steadfastly pro-English when *Trilby* and *The Dancing Girl* were given. He was more concerned over the fact that Maud was about to deliver a child than that the critics were about to deliver judgment, writing from the Stenton Hotel, Philadelphia, on January 5th, '96:

My darling Wife

It was a great relief to me to get your telegram yesterday—I have been terribly worried because I have not heard from you for over a week.—I think of my darling always—and wonder whether she is suffering as I am.—It was madness to let you stay behind—and I am very sad without you.—All is going *brilliantly* here—we are to have a great week.—Oh, my dear sweet Maud, by the time you get this letter all will probably be over—I hope you will not suffer— you know that I shall always be thinking of you and wishing that I could be by to hold your dear hand.—Sometimes I think I cannot stay—but that I must take the first steamer to London, regardless of everything.—Maud darling, I hope you have not been making your- self unhappy about me—you must know that you are sure of my love—I cannot bear to feel this distance between us and to think that I cannot bring you happiness and take your pain to myself.

Everybody speaks lovingly of you here, and they all miss you.—New York was a terrible time for us—and I am glad to have shaken its dust from my feet.—Gilbert Parker is here, working on his play.—

I hope we shall have a little tour before opening the new theatre and that you will come too.—Kate Rorke played Ophelia very well—but of course she was not near you. God bless you darling Maud and Viola and Felicity! Your loving Herbert.

Meanwhile Her Majesty's Theatre was gradually being completed and Maud was on the committee which dealt with the building, decoration, upholstery, and so forth. The architects and other artists concerned could not always see eye-to-eye with one another, and Herbert wrote: 'I am afraid you must have had an awful time to contend with their respective *amours-propres.*' He was trying to raise money for the theatre in America, and she was doing the same in England. In addition, he asked her to see Henry Arthur Jones, Haddon Chambers, Sydney Grundy and other dramatists, as he would be needing plenty of plays, though he insisted that *The Seats of the Mighty* would be a success. So anxious was she to forward his ambition that she even approached the leading dramatist of the day, Arthur Pinero, suggesting that he should provide a piece on the Indian Mutiny. He replied tactfully that he had been thinking of doing something for the new theatre, but that everything depended on his getting a likely idea. If he were to write on the Indian Mutiny, he would have to read a lot first and then visit India, as he could not deal with second-hand facts. However, he had several plans buzzing in his head, and one of them might prove suitable for Her Majesty's Theatre. But his reply was dictated by courtesy. He would not allow anyone to interfere with his production of his own plays, and he knew there was not room for two autocrats in the same theatre. Following a terrific battle, one would remain in possession, the other would leave on a stretcher, and he did not fancy the latter mode of conveyance.

Herbert also wanted Maud to find a first-class manager, and his request was implemented by Elisabeth Marbury, who confided in her that a firm and intelligent direction in the business department was essential: 'What Mr Tree needs is a *Manager*—a man who is able, experienced, *honest, sober* and *tactful*; a man full of energy and of invention. He *must* be protected. Do your best to find someone ere he returns.' They found him in Henry Dana.

An accident that happened to Henry Irving on the first night of his *Richard III* production necessitated the withdrawal of the play. 'Poor Irving!' wrote Herbert from the Stafford Hotel, Baltimore, on January 12th, '97:

> I wired him a sympathetic cable, and received a kind reply from him —I sincerely hope that the reports about his accident are exaggerated —I wish I were in London to take the theatre off his hands.—I am still thinking of *Julius Caesar*. What do you say about engaging Forbes-Robertson for Brutus?

The idea grew upon him, and he wrote again:

> Cannot we arrange to do *Julius Caesar* at the Lyceum with Forbes-Robertson and Waller and myself, keeping the scenery from *Coriolanus*?—or shall I buy it from Irving, as he is not likely to do it. What do you say about this?—That is if the *Coriolanus* scenery would do.

But Irving was to need his scenery, and in due time Tree engaged the same painter to design his production of *Julius Caesar*.

It was of the utmost importance, thought Maud, that the English press should announce the success of Herbert's American tour, and she intimated as much to Elisabeth Marbury, who pointed out that so many newspaper critics and members of rival English companies knew differently that it would be 'very hard to make the public take the impression we want to give'. But the tour was neither a success nor a failure. It paid expenses and left a little in hand, thanks principally to *Trilby*. Herbert was more worried by Maud's confinement than anything else.

Clarendon Hotel
Brooklyn, N.Y.
18 Jan. '97

My darling
　　Here we are at Brooklyn—a dreary but respectable spot. We shall do very well on the week—next week Boston—and then for England, home and you! How good it sounds—but oh dear Maud, what a terrible time of suspense it has been, and but for your telegrams I do not know what would have become of me—for I have been on the rack having the most awful visions.—But I hope I may

soon get another telegram telling me that your suffering is over—
and that you are happy.—I shall soon be with you again, darling.

I had a breakdown a few days ago, but I have rested all I can—
and am now quite well again—I feared it might be serious . . .

Good-bye, darling.   God give my sweet a good time.

Your loving Herbie

On January 29th he scrawled a last note from Parker House,
Boston:

My darling Wife

I was overjoyed to get your telegram today—'splendid progress'.
—I do pray all will go on well—I long to see the little one—I hope
you are very, very happy, dearest.—I was terribly anxious all this
time—but I am soon to be with you.—

Tonight we do *The Seats of the Mighty* and I am quite worn out
with rehearsal and fret—but I think the piece will be a success with
the Boston people.—I wish you were here.—I can't write more, dear
—I have just been trying to rest—and must go to the theatre. Get
well and strong, darling

Your loving Herbie

I'll write a long letter after tonight.

But the long letter never arrived, possibly because he did not
wish to vex her with an account of Boston's cool reception of the
play. He reached home a week after the birth of their third child,
Iris. They had longed for a son, 'but the frost of our disappointment', wrote Maud, 'was soon melted away by the calm and
inextinguishable sunshine of the newcomer'.

While in America, Herbert had made good an omission of his
previous visit. He went to see Niagara Falls with Gilbert Parker,
who anticipated an exclamation of awe and astonishment. But
Herbert must have been thinking of the impressive stage effects of
natural phenomena which he hoped to produce at Her Majesty's
Theatre, because he remained silent for a long time. 'Well?'
prompted Parker at last. Herbert emerged from his meditations.
'Well, *is that all*?' said he.

CHAPTER 11

Her Majesty's

'The more one cares, the less one dares,' said Tree to a lady who asked why he had never made love to her. But he cared more and dared more for his 'beautiful theatre', as he always called it, than for anything else in the world. No other actor in history, having gained Tree's position on the stage, would have taken such a risk; and for that matter no other actor has ever built himself so fine a theatre. The enterprise was financed by a company known as The Playhouse Ltd. The capital was composed of debentures. Tree subscribed £10,000, his debentures ranking after the rest for the payment of interest. Ernest Cassel, a large subscriber, obtained others, such as Lord Rothschild, Carl Meyer, Mrs Bischoffsheim, and half a dozen more, all of whom had reason to be satisfied with their investment. Tree was the proprietor of the theatre, having to pay just under £6,000 a year for ground-rent and interest on mortgages and debentures. The original estimate for the structure was £55,000, and this was exceeded by less than £300.

The building, of Portland stone relieved by red granite, was designed by C. J. Phipps and the interior decorations were by Romaine Walker, the period effect being a mixture of Louis XIV and XV. It was quite the handsomest playhouse in London, and the atmosphere within was that of a Temple of Art, not a lavishly be-mirrored commercial saloon. 'You feel that you are in a place where high scenes are to be enacted and dignified things to be done,' wrote Bernard Shaw. 'And this is the first quality a theatre should have.' The patrons were treated like guests. No charge was made for cloakrooms; the programmes were free and not disfigured by advertisements; and the occupants of the pit were shown as much courtesy as those in the stalls. The orchestra, discreetly hidden beneath palm leaves, was of a far higher quality than any that had been heard in a London theatre before, and the music played during the intervals was good enough to subdue the chatter of the audience, and even to prevent people from crowding the bars, as they did elsewhere.

With the completion of the building Tree was as excited as a child over a new toy. He would seize a friend or acquaintance or even a stranger and walk up towards Coventry Street to display the theatre from the north, and down towards Pall Mall to exhibit it from the south, and along Charles Street to show the side view, and back again to the pavement opposite the entrance to admire it from the front. One day, after lunching at the Garrick Club, he eagerly invited Squire Bancroft to come and gaze at his wonderful creation. Presently they were standing in the colonnade of the Haymarket Theatre, and Bancroft was surveying Her Majesty's through his monocle. 'Well?' asked Tree at last. Still looking upwards, Bancroft said in his hollow, impressive voice: 'A great many windows to clean.' It was not the only criticism the proprietor encountered. Taking advantage of the fact that he had warrant to call the theatre Her Majesty's, the stewards were dressed in liveries resembling those of the Royal Household. The Prince of Wales, a stickler for forms and ceremonies, was furious when he noticed this, and the stewards were thenceforth clothed in uniforms which did not remind His Royal Highness too much of Buckingham Palace.

The theatre was not ready for use when Tree returned from the States, and he went on a short provincial tour, in the course of which he suffered a frenzy for economy, writing on March 17th to Maud: 'I am terribly sorry, darling, but this has been an awful time and one must seize on every penny to stave off the attacks of creditors. Soon I hope all will smile again.' As his note was despatched from the Metropole Hotel, Brighton, his creditors cannot have been very much upon his mind. Meanwhile he had engaged as business manager Henry Dana, who fulfilled all the requirements mentioned by Elisabeth Marbury, and who remained with him to the end. During those twenty years Dana and Tree never exchanged even a casual letter of contract, each knowing that he could rely on a verbal understanding. Dana's severely practical outlook was the necessary curb to Tree's exuberant idealism.

The great day came when, as Ellen Terry declared, the position of the Lyceum as a unique institution under Irving was changed by the opening of Her Majesty's under Tree; and while other people debated, after Irving's death, whether this actor or that was his true successor, Tree could proudly claim: 'I covet no man's mantle, for the public has given me one of my own.' But the beginning of his intrepid adventure was discouraging. The American reception of Gilbert Parker's play had failed to shake his belief in it, and he chose it for the inauguration. On April 28th, 1897, *The Seats of the Mighty* was performed before an audience that included the Prince of Wales, a good sprinkling of the aristocracy, and a representative of republicanism in the person of Henry Labouchere. The operations were commenced by Maud Tree, who nervously delivered an ode composed for the occasion by the Poet Laureate, Alfred Austin. It was pompous, patriotic, un-poetical, and in rhyme. Then came the National Anthem, with an additional verse, sung by Clara Butt alternately with the Queen's Hall choir. There followed an announcement, loudly cheered by those who had not paid for their seats, that the Prince of Wales's Ratepayers' Relief Fund would receive the entire takings for that performance. After which the play was given. At the conclusion of the entertainment Tree addressed the audience. 'This is a great moment in my little life,' he began. But one of the critics present provided a comment on his speech which gave him a wry laugh.

> Mr Tree told us that he would never disgrace the name the theatre bore [wrote G. B. S.]; and his air as he spoke was that of a man who, on the brink of forgery, arson and bigamy, was saved by the feeling that the owner of Her Majesty's Theatre must not do such things.

It was characteristic of Tree's bohemian *bonhomie* that after all his preparatory exertions, all the ceremonial in connection with the first night, all the receptions, congratulations and feasting that followed it, he accompanied two friends to the cabman's shelter in Piccadilly, then known as the Junior Turf Club, at three o'clock in the morning, and stayed there drinking coffee and playing dominoes with the men until 6 a.m., when one of the cabbies was called away on a job and the party dispersed.

The Seats of the Mighty did not fill the seats of Her Majesty's, and this time it was final. Even Tree could not run a play to dwindling audiences, though he often stated in writings and speeches that he acknowledged no outside influence in the choice of plays or their manner of presentation. Replying to the press attacks on one of his elaborate Shakespearean productions, he wrote:

> So far from pandering to the public taste, I claim that an artist works primarily for himself—his first aim is to satisfy his own artistic conscience. His output is the result of the impetus in him to work out his own ideals. Even were the public satisfied with a less competent treatment of the poet's work, I should still have presented it in the way I did.

The secret of how he could reconcile with his artistic conscience the choice of Garrick's silly and vulgar version of *The Taming of the Shrew* has gone to the grave with him. Allowing for the fact that his taste in ordinary plays may sometimes have been questionable, the presentation of *Katherine and Petruchio* was the only serious artistic blemish on his thirty years of management. He kept the theatre going with revivals for a time, and then, probably in a panic, he gave his worst performance in his most lamentable production that November. Fortunately no one wished to see what Garrick thought of Shakespeare.

But in the summer of '97, during a yachting holiday off the Isle of Wight, he had been re-reading *Julius Caesar* carefully, writing to Maud: 'I like Brutus best—he is so much deeper—but I still feel that Antony has the colour—the glamour of the play, don't you?' It was lucky for him that his mind could be so occupied while trying to memorize the part of Petruchio, for at the end of the year he was financially on his beam-ends.

CHAPTER 12

Man and Manager

Speaking of J. L. Toole, a famous comedian of the time, Tree said: 'His manner was never the barometer of another's prosperity.' The same can be said of Tree, who treated everyone alike, from dukes to dustmen, from Somebodies to Nobodies. An autocrat in the theatre while a play was being produced, he was a Tolstoyan democrat in his personal attitude to all ranks of people, and his sense of human equality, the rarest of senses, made him both generous and helpful. His deeds of kindness were not widely advertised as Henry Irving's were, but several have been recorded by those who served under him. Oscar Asche, for instance, makes the point that when Tree lent any of his actors to other managements, they were allowed to arrange their own terms and keep the balance in their favour. This was unusual. He was the first manager in London to pay the poorer members of his company for rehearsals; and he could not resist an appeal for help, badgering his stage-manager to swell the list of 'walkers-on' with hard-up actors. Once he saw a disreputably dressed ex-actor reciting to a pit queue and taking his hat round for pence. He got so little that Tree drew him to one side, asked if he would care to play a small part in the play then being prepared, and added him to the salary-list.

The manager was especially sympathetic with actors who had succumbed to what was then a great temptation and were in what he called 'an advanced state of alcoholic decomposition'. Many of them, having been paid on Friday, were in a fuddled condition on Saturday night, but arrangements were made to keep an eye on them, to hold them erect if they showed a disposition to fall, and to have their words spoken by someone else if they were inclined to falter. One of them, in Tolstoy's *Resurrection*, was supposed to say that a girl had eyes like a Persian cat, but after liquidating his salary he nearly always came out with 'eyes like a Persian carpet', which amused Tree so much that he looked forward to Saturday nights. When it was hinted that he took too favourable a view of these delinquents, he would explain that 'Wine helps genius, and genius helps itself to wine', or dismiss the subject airily with 'If you drink too much wine you get drunk, but if you drink too much water you get drowned.' Such was his kindliness of nature that when a member of his staff stole some money to pay for gambling debts, and had to be prosecuted because others of the staff were aware of it, he privately arranged for the man's escape abroad and future financial support, deriving much humour from the fact that he was also paying detectives to search for his late employee. He also laughed heartily when a fellow who had forged his name to a cheque, and whom he had refused to prosecute, accused him of compounding a felony. It worried him if a backer lost money on a production, and once, when a revival of *Trilby* did well, he repaid a sum of £2,000, though he need not have done so, since the backer takes the risk of loss along with the chance of considerable profit.

He was frequently pestered for loans by impecunious actors, and found one such incident sufficiently diverting to record in his private papers:

> A minor member of my company who was doing 'super' work once said to me he would like to talk to me on business after the performance. I made an appointment. He then said that he wanted fifty pounds. I said, 'It is a curious coincidence, but that is the sum I myself covet.' He said, 'Don't be flippant! I will not accept the amount except as a matter of business, and insist on paying 3% interest on the loan; and I'll be damned if I will be under any obligation to the management.'

From this it will be seen that Tree, unlike Irving, was accessible and amiable to everyone in his company. He never became self-important and was unchanged by success. Though called 'the Chief' by his staff, he never behaved as such, his irresponsibility, sense of humour, and tendency to play the fool, which he shared with other geniuses, being wholly at variance with the dignity and gravity supposed to be inseparable from greatness. 'The only man who wasn't spoilt by being lionized was Daniel,' he said; but himself was another. 'The process of acquiring a swollen head is a pleasant one,' he declared; 'it is only the subsequent shrinkage that hurts.' As his never swelled it never shrank. 'When people stand on their dignity, they have no other pedestal,' was a further saying. Such a posture was unnatural to one whose pedestal was his personality.

His nature, as his brother Max said, was radiant, his mere presence adding something bright and animated to any group of people. It was not so much what he said or did that produced this effect; it was rather that his vitality infected others; his happiness was catching, his gaiety compelling. Before his arrival at, say, a committee meeting, the members seemed to feel what Dr Johnson called 'the tediousness of time'. He brought with him the excitement of time. One of his phrases ran: 'A committee should consist of three men, two of whom are absent'; but his presence imparted vivacity even to a committee, so that every member appeared to be present. The obverse of his transcendent ability to revive moribund people was shown in an unreasonable dislike of miserable people and sudden irrational antipathies to whatever jarred upon him. He wanted to see human beings happy; and when by some unfortunate twist of temperament they were unable to be so, he did not like to have them near him. Passionate outbreaks, violent tempers, infuriating behaviour of all kinds he could pass over and forget with ease, being too much absorbed in what he was doing to bear malice; but a settled melancholy or a steady refusal to enjoy life antagonized him and alienated his sympathies. When his feelings were hurt by inconsiderate behaviour or the vehement reaction of a contrary temperament, he looked and felt bewildered, sometimes even blushing with the shock to his susceptibility; but the effect was temporary, and in a short while he would be fraternizing and joking with the person whose anger or callousness had but recently outraged him. He was often inconsiderate and sometimes cruel to others, but these faults were due to the histrionic side of his nature, the wish to show-off or an uncontrollable desire to score off someone who irritated him. He bore no fundamental ill-will, and his momentary expressions of harshness were the lapses of a man whose nervous system had been strained and who was scarcely conscious of their hurtfulness.

Like so many artists, he was sensitive to hostile criticism and comment, but affected indifference, saying, 'It is only while man advances that he encounters opposition. The microbes of criticism desert the moribund.' And on the same subject: 'Detraction is the tribute which the little pay to the great.' In this way he comforted himself. 'Have you read the criticisms? I dare say I shall glance at them later on,' he remarked one morning to his manager, who noticed that all the papers were opened at the pages where the criticisms appeared and knew that 'the Chief' had carefully read them all. The leading dramatic critics of those days were not slow to point out his defects. Having overpraised Irving, they underpraised Tree as a reasonable compromise. Clement Scott, an emotional person who in the opinion of a contemporary carried a bludgeon in one hand and his hat in the other, used the first on Tree and doffed the second to Irving. A. B. Walkley, a bookish individual who had cultivated his mind at the expense of his emotions, was acid enough to be described by Tree as 'a whippersnapper of criticism who quotes dead languages to hide his ignorance of life'. But the actor made no attempt to conciliate his critics. 'I shall soon be able to retire on the blackmail I have not paid,' he said. Occasionally the journalists were extremely unfair, passing the limits of fair comment, and once the victim was so much incensed that on December 17th, 1898, his wife sent a confidential letter to T. P. O'Connor, whose paper *M.A.P.* (Mainly About People) had published something unpleasant, telling him that Herbert was very indignant over certain damaging and untruthful statements, that he thought it *infra dig.* merely to contradict them, and that 'he is inclined to take much more serious action in order to set himself right in the eyes of the Public'. But Tree was the last person to take serious action over anything outside his work in the theatre, and in quiet moments he knew that criticism, however useless in itself, was good for business. 'To the worst of critics and the best of friends', he wrote on a photograph which he gave to one of them, who complained of the inscription and was told: 'When you put more butter into your criticisms, I'll say you are the best of critics and the worst of friends.'

Like most people, he enjoyed being flattered. 'I can stand any amount of flattery so long as it's fulsome enough,' he told brother

Max, but he was not taken in by it. 'Flattery makes the great little, the little never great,' he said, and when someone, in Disraeli's phrase, laid it on with a trowel, he indicated briefly what it sounded like: 'He has his tongue in his cheek and his cheek in his tongue.' Again like most people he could face a crisis with equanimity but was easily irritated with trifles. 'It is fleas not elephants that annoy,' he said, though he was well aware that trifles disappeared when no notice was taken of them: 'If your hat blows off, never run after it. Somebody will always run after it for you.'

Perhaps his most engaging quality was the combination in him of the civilized man and the eager child, each being at times uppermost. He described a gentleman as 'one who doesn't care whether he is one or not', also as 'one whose courtesy is not regulated by his interests', and his own nature was covered by these definitions. But his essential childishness was displayed in all sorts of ways. He laughed, in a falsetto peal, with abandonment. He cried easily and unashamedly when moved by beauty or an act of kindness. He talked excitedly, running his fingers through his hair. He only thought of money as something to spend on his comfort or his work. He was never habituated to fame, every symptom of which, from applause in the theatre to recognition in the street, came to him as something fresh and surprising. He could not take an interest in his personal appearance, his necktie being usually on one side, his top-hat lustreless, his hair disordered. He asked questions in order to answer them himself. He could be as fatuous as funny, as witty as silly. He liked the company of young men, himself always the youngest among them, and would rather be with anybody than alone. He disliked the country because it seemed empty of people, and would start looking for a time-table soon after glancing at the fields. 'But you're not going already?' Maud would say. 'I must get back to the theatre,' was his invariable reply. He could fall asleep on all occasions at a moment's notice, and wake up in twenty minutes as fresh as a child. He liked dramatizing situations, and his daughters remembered how he used to come home, lean on the mantelpiece, ruffle his hair, and declaim in tragic tones, 'We'll soon be ruined.' He took a juvenile pleasure in his own sayings, and when reminded of one would cry delightedly: 'Did I say that? Did I say that?' Sometimes he would coin a happy phrase at rehearsal, calling at once to his secretary to make a note of it. In this way his facetiæ were preserved, and he would repeat them at appropriate moments as if they had just occurred to him. Here are a few, either written down after being said or said after being written down, in either case specimens of his conversational brevities:

'One fool makes more noise than a thousand wise men.'

'Let sleeping dogs lie, but why let lying dogs sleep?'

'Cynicism is the humour of hatred.'

'The jaded jester quarrels with his bauble.'

'Earned increment is sweet, but that unearned is sweeter.'

'Is life worth living? It depends on the liver.'

'Every man is a potential genius until he does something.'

'Hell is desire without hope.'

'In pursuing the phantom of pleasure man loses the substance of happiness.'

'He slept the deep sleep of the unjust.'

'People are too apt to treat God as if He were a minor Royalty.'

'The national sport of England is obstacle-racing. People fill their rooms with useless and cumbersome furniture, and spend the rest of their lives in trying to dodge it.'

'Never say a humorous thing to a man who does not possess humour: he will always use it in evidence against you.'

'Silence is the wisdom of fools.'

'Our domestic morality is founded on the axiom that boys will be boys but that girls mustn't be girls.'

Examples of his more nonsensical style:

'Do you say that in the asphalt or the concrete?'

'My nose bleeds for you.'

Of an actress whose reputation as a lover was higher than her reputation as an artist: 'She has kissed her way into society. I don't like her. But don't misunderstand me: my dislike is purely platonic.'

To a man who was staggering in the street under the weight of a grandfather clock: 'My poor fellow, why not carry a watch?'

It is improbable that anyone who knew Tree well really disliked him, for his amiability disarmed antagonism. He was inclined to flatter himself on making enemies, but their enmity was aroused by his success, not his personality. 'I often wake up in the morning determined not to tell the truth,' he remarked, 'but before the sun has set I find myself the richer by another enemy.' This was merely the vanity of a man who likes to feel it within his power to affect the minds of others; and his further saying that 'The man who is afraid of making enemies doesn't deserve to have friends' derived from a similar source. Thus even his vanity was that of a child, and largely consisted of make-believe. It is often said that actors and actresses are more vain than the rest of mankind, but they give that impression because of their *naïveté* and because their constant contact with fellow-players brings it to the surface. One has only to read the memoirs of authors, scientists, politicians, soldiers, and other eminences to recognize that the vanity of actors is a relatively childlike complaint. Some critics used to accuse Tree of being a charlatan. But all men are charlatans more or less, for they pretend to resemble the pictures they have formed of themselves or that other people have imposed upon them. The charlatanry of actors is more obvious solely on account of their profession, which is one of pretence. Tree could not help acting off the stage as well as on it. In his early days as a manager he had cultivated a vague manner, an absent mind and a dreamy form of speech, simply as a protection against importunity. This became his second nature, with surprising results. Yet, though he seemed to have no idea of time, he was seldom late for an appointment; though he never appeared to read papers, he always knew what was going on; though he was hardly ever observed to open a book, he gave the impression of being well-read; and though he scarcely ever noticed the countryside when travelling, he could describe it afterwards. He was, said his daughter Iris, 'like an exile from some country whose name he had forgotten', but his native place was London, his real home the theatre.

It was the element of fantasy in his nature that seemed to differentiate him from his fellow-men, giving him the quality of a dreamer, and the comical aspect of that fantasy humanized it while emphasizing his peculiarity. He told ludicrous stories with much gravity, the gestures of his disproportionately small hands stressing their oddity. Sitting at the dinner-table, in his own house or at the Garrick Club, something in the conversation would remind him of a story; and as he told it he would gradually clear a space on the table in front of him, pushing away one by one the knives, forks, spoons, condiments, dishes, and whatever else interfered with his freedom to gesticulate and illustrate his theme, until at last, another course being due, his part of the table had to be re-laid. Occasionally, when alone, he would remember one of his stories and commit it to his private papers, from which we will extract some typical samples:

A lady very unfairly said: 'You evidently do not remember me.' I said: 'Could I ever forget that day that we met?' She said: 'It was not in the day.' Then I said: 'Could I ever forget that night?' She said: 'Oh,' and still persisted before a number of people that I did not remember her. She said: 'Well, what is my name?' By way of admonishing her I said 'I will not mention your name, but I will make a bet with you that I write down your name on a sheet of paper. I will bet you twenty pounds to ten shillings in the presence of all these people that I will write down your name on this sheet of paper. Will you take the bet?' She said: 'No, but I am glad,' and smilingly turned away. I said: 'By the by, what is your charming name?' She was very angry at the loss of twenty pounds.

A luggage tout at Dublin station, to whom I gave a shilling to get rid of him, said, 'Ah, Mr Tree, Sir Henry Irving gave me two shillings and sure you're twice as good an actor as he is,' adding at I withdrew, 'in your own estimation.'

I was travelling in a train. The carriage was full, save for one seat opposite me. I was smoking a cigar, and had my feet on the opposite seat. Much to my annoyance a little clerk hopped in at a station and sat down in the one vacant seat, and pulling out his last cigarette lighted it. I said: 'Are you aware that this is not a smoking carriage?' On which he threw his cigarette out of the window. Looking up, he saw me smoking my cigar. 'But you are smoking, sir,' he said. 'Yes,' I replied, 'but I thought you might have conscientious scruples.'

Sitting in the window of the Garrick Club, I made a bet that the next hundred persons who passed would all be unhappy, for all the lost souls of London pass through Garrick Street. Ninety-nine melancholy persons passed. Then came the hundredth, skipping. 'You have lost your bet,' said my companion. 'No,' I replied, 'he is a victim of St Vitus's Dance.'

Lord Glenesk was visiting Disraeli, and the peacocks to which Disraeli was devoted were scratching up the primroses. Glenesk turned to Disraeli and said: 'Pardon me for interrupting your conversation, but do you notice that the peacocks are destroying the primroses?' Disraeli answered: 'I prefer the peacocks to the primroses.' When the question came up of immortalizing his memory by a flower, I suggested the appropriateness of the primrose. This is the origin of the Primrose League.

When we were in Chicago, Lionel Brough was walking with me and we were looking at the shops. He would always buy things he thought were bargains. That night he was to play the part of Ives in *The Dancing Girl*. It was the first tragic part he had ever played, and he wanted to do thorough justice to it. We were passing a shopwindow of artificial teeth. I saw one set labelled "Try our five-dollar jaw.' I drew his attention to it. The thought at once seized him that he ought to possess those teeth, and he went in. It seems that the shopman explained to him that the particular virtue of this set of teeth was that it was self-acting like a free wheel—when a certain number of mastications had occurred, the teeth went on biting automatically. Brough said it was a fine invention, and would be a splendid thing for him, because it would make his articulation (which by the way was excellent) perfect. He had the most useful teeth drawn that afternoon and appeared with this brand new set of teeth that evening. All went well up to the scene where he has to denounce the Duke of Guiseberry for having eloped with his daughter. His elocution was simply stentorian, but too violent, for in his denunciation the teeth flew out of his mouth on to the stage. It was a most awkward moment, and he made his exit up the great flight of stairs at the back, leaving me alone on the stage.—But the teeth, so violent had been his elocution, hopped after him up the stairs, bit him on the soft of the back, and I finally made the sign to drop the curtain. It was with some difficulty that we extricated the teeth from Lionel's flesh. The story is almost true. When I told it at some public dinner in proposing Lionel Brough's health, he got up and denounced it as a gross exaggeration.

Tree's chief merit as a talker was that he revelled in the exercise and could always prevent the conversation from lagging. Whether as host or guest or club member, the talk in his neighbourhood was taut, for he had a way of listening as if he felt certain the speaker of the moment were about to say something clever, which may have been embarrassing but undoubtedly kept up the standard. The qualities that endeared him to his friends at the Garrick and kept them lingering at the Club long after they should have been in bed were his good comradeship, buoyancy and fun. It is worth recalling that Henry Arthur Jones, who had known every distinguished actor of his period, and who had quarrelled frequently and fiercely with Tree to the point where sedatives or stimulants had to be applied, confessed at the end of his life that he would rather have spent a fortnight in Tree's company than in that of any other actor; and his feeling was echoed by Wilde, Shaw, and all the other dramatists of the day, though most of them had anything but happy memories of the times when their plays were being produced.

As a companion, then, Tree had no rival on the stage, but this made him a poor man of affairs, because the chief joy of good companionship is that the hours pass unheeded. He could borrow money to put on his shows when his own account at the bank was overdrawn, but that was largely because his backers liked him personally, trusted his judgment as a producer, and enjoyed a gamble when there was a good chance of winning. Though the consequences of failure were often serious, Tree did not bother much about them, telling Philip Carr that, while watching the soap in his bath going round and round until it disappeared, he sometimes wondered, each time he went round himself, whether he would be sucked in or just manage to go round once more. Apart from his ability to raise the wind, he had as little practical capacity as a man can have without being run over by a steamroller in the street or having his watch stolen while winding it up. This did not matter because he had an excellent staff of men and women whose loyalty was won by his personal charm and his childlike appeal to their compassion: they would do everything for him because he could do nothing for himself. Another reason why his boredom with business counted for little was, to quote Bernard Shaw, that

A man may enter on the management of a theatre without business habits or knowledge, and at the end of forty years of it know less about business than when he began. The explanation is that a London West-End theatre is always either making such an enormous profit that the utmost waste caused by unbusinesslike management is not worth considering, or else losing so much that the strictest

economy cannot arrest the process by a halfpenny in the pound . . .
Tree was accustomed to make two hundred per cent every day when
he was in luck. With such a margin to play with, it was no more
worth his while to economize or remember uninteresting things
than it was to walk when there was a taxi at his beck.

It is therefore not surprising to learn from one of his business
managers, Fitzroy Gardner, that when told the overdraft at his
bank could not be increased because it was barely covered by his
securities, he brushed aside the difficulty with: 'Tell them we will
transfer the account to another bank.' The running of one production at the Haymarket Theatre cost £190 a performance, and
the business manager, feeling that this was excessive, begged Tree
to go carefully through the accounts in detail and see what could
be saved. He did so, finally deciding that a penny newspaper
should be supplied to the Green Room instead of the usual one
costing threepence. Gardner once reproved him for his too generous hospitality, and he said he would bear it in mind. A few days
later, seeing Gardner going out to lunch, Tree led him to a
confectioner's shop in Charles Street, said, 'Please give this gentleman a glass of milk and a sausage roll, if they don't cost too
much,' placed sixpence on the counter, and disappeared. Next day
he invited Gardner to a particularly extravagant lunch at the
Carlton Hotel. His sense of economy was only in evidence when
something amused him. A 'property' loaf of bread was proudly
displayed for his inspection at a rehearsal. Hearing that it had cost
10s. 6d. to make, he pointed out that a real loaf only cost a penny,
that its appearance was more realistic, and moreover that it could
be cut and eaten. His objection to talking business and the magnetic attraction the theatre had for him were amusingly illustrated
when he arrived at the stage-door one Sunday, which he was supposed to be spending in the country, saw his business manager
standing in the street outside, and tiptoed past him into the
building.

CHAPTER 13

Shakespeare Spells Success

Since Tree's management of Her Majesty's Theatre was mainly notable for the unexampled splendour of his Shakespearean productions and the institution of an annual Shakespeare Festival, it was fitting that his first successful enterprise there should be the presentation of a play by Shakespeare. He had long wished to put on *Julius Caesar*, and on January 22nd, 1898, his dream was realized. Laurence Alma Tadema, to be knighted the following year, was responsible for the scenery, costumes, and so on, and it was generally agreed that no play of Shakespeare's within living memory had been mounted with such magnificence or acted so well, and that no crowd like that in the Forum scene had been so skilfully and realistically handled. For the first time the majority of the critics and playgoing public recognized that Sir Henry Irving's successor as pageant-master, if not as actor, had arrived. It may not be inapt to compare very briefly their respective contributions to the stage-history of Shakespeare, since such comparisons were rife at the time, and usually beside the mark.

Sixteen of Shakespeare's plays were produced by Tree, twelve by Irving. Neither actor was expert in the delivery of the verse, neither could achieve vocal climaxes in a lengthy rhetorical crescendo, neither had studied the classical technique of speech and action; neither, in short, was a true Shakespearean actor like Forbes–Robertson, who had been coached by Samuel Phelps and had learnt the technique handed down from Burbage to Betterton, and so, via David Garrick and Mrs Siddons, to Macready. Irving and Tree had developed their own peculiar personalities, acquiring specialized methods which concealed their physical and vocal shortcomings and enhanced their merits. But Irving had studied to create his stage personality with a singleness of purpose that was foreign to Tree's temperament; and such was the mesmeric force of Irving's acting, the peculiar beauty of his queer halting delivery of the lines, that he could impose himself upon a part like Shylock or Iachimo and make it richer and more compelling than the original. He could spellbind an audience; and though the effect was not Shakespeare's but his own, no one but a fanatical devotee of the verse wished it otherwise. Tree's personality was quite as arresting as Irving's, but it was totally different. His wide cultural interests made it impossible for him to live solely for the aggrandisement of a stage figure, and so he had not taken his job with the other's deadly seriousness. Lacking the intensive training to which Irving had subjected himself, he depended too much on the impulse of the moment. Having once got his effects right, Irving could repeat them night after night without variation, which is what a thoroughly professionalized actor ought to do; whereas Tree's performances depended on his moods; he was incalculable, and therefore essentially unprofessional.

There can be no doubt that Irving, with all his faults, was a greater actor than Tree, whose stage personality, for the reasons already given, was more amusing and surprising than his predecessor's. Irving enthralled an audience; Tree entertained it. Some of the mystery and glamour attached to Irving's personality may have been due to the gloomy gas-lit scenes on the Lyceum stage, but his histrionic power to electrify the house was unquestioned, and will remain so.

In the presentation of Shakespeare, as opposed to the exploitation of an actor's individuality, Tree must be given the palm. His acting versions were as much like the original texts as the elaborate scenery allowed, whereas Irving's had been 'arranged' to exhibit the leading actor. Furthermore, Tree surrounded himself with the best players of his time and gave them every opportunity to outshine himself, while Irving's company were chosen and drilled, their speeches abbreviated, to make his own part stand out. Irving would never have produced *Julius Caesar* because it contains three or four leading characters, each as good as the other; and it is significant that when he had an accident on the first night of *Richard III*, the play had to be taken off because the Lyceum company could not be depended upon to draw enough money to pay for the heating of the theatre.

The most acute critic of the age dealt with Tree's superior acting versions and the all-round ability of his company.

> Mr Tree must stand acquitted of any belittlement of the parts which compete so strongly with his own [wrote G. B. S.]. Before going to Her Majesty's I was curious enough to block out for myself a division of the play into three acts; and I found that Mr Tree's division corresponded exactly with mine.

He went on to say that Lewis Waller's opportunities as Brutus, Franklin McLeay's as Cassius, and Louis Calvert's as Casca, were only limited by their abilities to take advantage of them. 'That's where Tree is dangerous', Shaw warned Ellen Terry, who had defended Irving's policy: 'he surrounds himself with counter-attractions and lets them play him off the stage to their heart's content as long as he takes the money at the doors. Good policy, Ellen: look to it.' Ellen was sceptical about Tree letting his company play him off the stage. 'I'd like you to see what is written in his heart upon that subject,' she rejoined. But Shaw stuck to his point. Lewis Waller, he affirmed,

> is *ten* times as good as the very best man you have supporting Henry at the Lyceum; and the public think him thirty times as good, small blame to 'em. He has authority, self-respect, dignity, and often brilliancy: you do not see him dodging about the stage with one eye on 'the governor',

as the actors did at the Lyceum. Ellen was doubtless right that Tree did not enjoy being acted off his own stage, but Shaw was not wrong about his policy. Though vain, Tree was not conceited. He did not believe that the public paid merely to see him, and throughout the whole of his managerial career his casts were as good as he could make them. A list of the players who appeared under him, some of whom became managers, would include nearly every 'star' of the time, and it is fair to say that no other famous actor on record would have borne for thirty years in his own theatre the intermittent indignity of receiving less personal applause than such popular favourites as Ellen Terry, Madge Kendal, Stella Patrick Campbell, Irene and Violet Vanbrugh, Winifred Emery, Lena Ashwell, Constance Collier, Phyllis Neilson–Terry, Fred Terry, Lewis Waller, Oscar Asche, Henry

Ainley, Matheson Lang, Lyn Harding, Robert Loraine, Basil Gill, Godfrey Tearle, Arthur Bourchier, Laurence Irving, Weedon Grossmith, Owen Nares, and a score of others.

Tree chose to play Antony in *Julius Caesar* because he was more suited to that part than to Brutus or Cassius, though he was simple enough to confide another reason to his notebook: 'For the scholar Brutus, for the actor Cassius, for the public Antony.' The rhetoric was quite beyond his declamatory powers, but, as Shaw said, 'he contrived to interest the audience in Antony instead of trading on their ready-made interest in Mr Beerbohm Tree. And for that many sins may be forgiven him nowadays, when the playgoer, on first nights at all events, goes to see the cast rather than the play.' The rehearsals had that comically chaotic character that was usual under Tree, who had an infinite capacity for making other people take pains. The stage staff appeared to be rushing about ordering this and disordering that, interfering, contradicting, misunderstanding. More will be said hereafter about Tree as a producer, and all that need be mentioned now is that at one point during a dress-rehearsal the crowd got completely out of hand, the scene-shifters were arguing, the scenery was swaying, the assistant-producers were bellowing, and the stage-manager, Herbert Shelton, was distractedly dashing hither and thither, waving his arms about and yelling at everybody. Overcome by the general hubbub, and moved by the contortions of his stage-manager, Tree knelt on the stage and offered up a prayer: 'Dear Lord, do look at Bertie Shelton *now*!'

Tree's passion for realism took curious forms. He insisted that Charles Fulton, who played Caesar, should lie supine as the murdered man throughout the Forum scene, and refused to have a dummy for the purpose. Fulton protested that he suffered from colds in the winter and that the stage was draughty: 'What will people say if the corpse sneezes?' Tree assuaged his fears: 'They will call you Julius Cnaesar.' Another touch of reality was his invention of hairy tights, which made it unnecessary for the males to put bole on their legs. In this case art did not improve upon nature. But his sense of reality was sometimes dormant. A pedant pointed out that in the Forum scene there was a statue of Caligula, who was born half a century after Caesar's assassination. 'Well,

that only shows what wonderful people these old Romans were,'
said Tree.

It was the biggest thing he had yet attempted, and there were
oversights in the production and under-rehearsal with the scenery
which his sternest but fairest critic noticed.

> Every carpenter seems to make it a point of honor to set the cloths
> swinging in a way that makes Rome reel and the audience positively
> seasick [wrote Shaw]. The Roman soldiers take the field each man
> with his two javelins neatly packed up like a fishing-rod. After a
> battle, in which they are supposed to have made the famous Roman
> charge, hurling these javelins in and following them up sword in
> hand, they come back carrying the javelins still undisturbed in their
> rug-straps, in perfect trim for a walk-out with the nursery-maids of
> Philippi.

But there was to be no more comment of that sort on Tree's
future productions, for in May '98 the most knowledgeable, individual, provocative and entertaining critic in the history of the
drama retired from business to write plays of his own. Nearly all
the leading actors were greatly relieved when G. B. S. vanished
from the stalls. 'I should be delighted to pay his funeral expenses
at any time,' said Sir Henry Irving. 'First-night nervousness was
bad enough, but the night before his criticism appeared was
worse,' said Tree. 'Now the playwright may sleep in peace, and
the actor may take his forty winks without anxiety,' said Charles
Wyndham. 'We pretended he was not serious, but our fingers
trembled as we turned to his articles. A good riddance, but how
we shall miss what he might have said about the others!' sighed
Stella Patrick Campbell. The relative detachment of Wyndham's
valediction may have been due to the fact that Shaw regarded him
as the finest living actor of modern comedy; Wilde thought the
same, and so did Henry Arthur Jones. All three wrote parts for
Wyndham, who acted with success in some of Jones's plays but
never appeared in the comedies of Wilde or Shaw.

Whatever the provocation, there was a strange lack of resentment in Tree, who remained on friendly terms with Shaw after
the most scathing criticism and returned good for evil when W. S.
Gilbert accused him of making blank verse sound blanker than it
need have done. Shortly before *Julius Caesar* began packing

Her Majesty's Theatre, Gilbert told a newspaper reporter that poetic drama was dead in England because none of the actors knew how to speak blank verse; and in referring to the Shakespearean productions of Irving, Tree and George Alexander, he declared that not one of them could make a poetic speech of thirty lines interesting to an audience and all of them mouthed the verse like Eton and Harrow schoolboys on Speech Day. The *Era* defended the actors by criticizing the critic: 'Mr Gilbert's abnormal self-esteem has with advancing years developed into a malady ... His good nature has been obscured by the abnormal protuberance of his bump of self-esteem.' Irving retaliated in a public speech with the sarcastic remark that Gilbert was 'a librettist who soars to write original comedy'. Tree did his utmost to make the *Era* climb down by printing a handsome tribute to Gilbert's work as an original dramatist; and while admitting that 'to sacrifice an epigram on the altar of tact is the last martyrdom of man', he believed in making the sacrifice. But Gilbert's blood was pressing him to conflict and he brought an action for libel against the *Era*, claiming £1,000 damages. Edward Carson represented the *Era*, and his cross-examination of Gilbert was quite as funny as any scene in the Gilbert and Sullivan operas, the writer scoring off the barrister; but the jury could not come to an agreement and each party to the suit sustained the damage of costs. Gilbert's recognition of Tree's good-nature was made known in a letter he wrote to Maud from Sorrento on April 12th, 1898:

My dear N.K.L.

Thank you for your gracious and sympathetic letter—which only reached me two days ago, as I have been at sea since 1st April when we started for Naples, going through the Bay of Biscay (which you may remember), then by Gibraltar and Marseilles. We have had a perfectly ideal voyage, as smooth as a lake all the way from the Thames—a capital set of passengers (I am in love with most of the lady passengers) and everything admirable.

I have not worried myself at all about the trial. I resolved not to look at a newspaper and, in short, I determined to clear my mind of it altogether. After all, I have done what I wanted to do. I was charged with having made an unworthy and malicious attack upon a body of men, many of whom I hold in high regard, and it was (as it seemed to me) incumbent upon me to refute the charge. The only way of doing this was to bring an action. The case would have been

mine but for the judge who was simply a monument of senile in-
capacity. To the very last he hadn't the faintest notion as to what the
trial was about. My case was comparatively trivial, but it is fearful
to think that grave issues, in which a man's fortune or a woman's
honour may be involved, are at the mercy of an utterly incompetent
old doll. Lawson Walton conducted my case with admirable dignity
and restraint. Carson conducted his in the spirit of a low-class police-
court attorney. But I believe he did me no harm. I was particularly
impressed with your husband's kindness in trying to make peace.
As one of the men whom I was represented as having pointed at, it
showed no little magnanimity on his part and one does not forget
such things. We return about 20th April. Love to the kids and to
yourself.

Always affectionately yours
W. S. Gilbert. N.K.G.

P.S. I am not at all surprised to find that the press strongly dis-
approve of actions for libel against newspapers.

Julius Caesar, which had not been seen in the West End for half
a century, was a financial and artistic success. It ran for five
months, and though the expenses were great Tree made a clear
profit of £11,000. That summer he spent some weeks at Marienbad and Bath. He was worried over the behaviour of his brother
Julius, who was constantly on the verge of making a fortune,
which as constantly eluded him, and having failed to bank a
million he would borrow a fiver. Once he got a business to
finance him in a scheme to drag the Nile for the jewels of Pharaoh,
who must have mislaid them. Everything with him was on a big
scale. After dropping a few thousands in the City, he would try
to pick them up at the gaming tables of some continental spa.
Herbert sent a message through Maud to Julius's wife: 'Give
Evelyn my best love—and tell her to try and keep J from the
tables.' But Julius believed in his luck, and nothing could divert
him from a financial flutter when there was anything to flutter
with. He had no little of the Beerbohm charm, which explained
his success in obtaining support for his ventures. His long yellow
moustache, blue eyes, languid manner, nonchalant air, smart
clothes, drawling speech and imperturbable deportment were
his chief assets; but there were times when his brother had to pull
him out of the holes he had dug for himself. One such moment

occurred when Herbert was at Marienbad this August, for we find
him writing to Maud:

> I wired you this morning—then I wired you again owing to the
> bad news about Julius. Another £500 has turned up and I at once
> wired to Webb telling him I would return immediately on receipt
> of a wire from him. Is not all this tragic? I do not know where it
> will end—but an exposé would be too awful. Yet I must consider
> myself as well as him, and I don't know where the money is to
> come from, unless I cripple myself in the future in order to save him.
> —I scarcely dare hope that he will be prepared to cover these sums.
> —I am sorry, darling Maud, that you should be worried about these
> things—but when one can be on the spot, one at all events can know
> the worst, and knowing it is less terrible than fearing it.

Owing to the Julian crisis, Herbert had to leave Marienbad and
finish his holiday-cure at Bath. He stopped in London on the way
to see his solicitor Webb, and found that Julius would settle his
more urgent liabilities within a week. But he also discovered that
Julius was trying to borrow £300 from their sister Constance. 'I
have put my spoke in that wheel,' Herbert told Maud. 'Con
wants him to have the money.—I gave him very clearly to understand that I would not be too yielding.' Julius survived this crisis
to become involved in others. He died in 1906, his final hope of a
fortune having rested on a preparation called Westrumite, which
was supposed to lay motor-dust but which ended in smoke.

While at Marienbad in the summer of '98 Herbert was also
worried over the behaviour of a leading actor in his company,
Lewis Waller, who as Brutus had made the chief acting hit in
Julius Caesar. A competent play-tailor of the time named Sydney
Grundy had fitted Tree with a drama founded on *The Three
Musketeers* by Dumas. At the same time another literary clothier
had cut a play out of that identical book for Lewis Waller. Tree
announced his version, called *The Musketeers,* for early production.
Waller announced his version, called *The Three Musketeers,* for
imminent performance. Tree had already made his arrangements
for casting and scenery. Waller hurried on his arrangements of a
similar kind. Tree felt that Waller was being unfair. Waller felt
that Tree was claiming a monopoly. They had scarcely spoken to
each other on the subject before Tree went to Marienbad, where
he worked on Grundy's version, removing scenes here, adding

scenes there, and becoming, as usual with works of this order, a part-author. He was very anxious for Maud and the children to join him. 'Now that the worries of the theatre have faded into the middle-distance one can breathe the mountain air more freely', he told her, adding

> Dear, your loving words make me very happy and yet sad.—It is true I have not understood you for some time, but I dare say that is my own fault. Before I went away I had a different feeling—for I thought you so gentle to me.—I feel sometimes as if my nature were turned wrong side out.

In his next letter he implied that he would have offered money to prevent the appearance of the rival version of the Dumas play, but that 'Waller had been pretty rude about it all, so that it was difficult to approach him.' He now hoped that some compromise could be reached. Maud wanted to have a cottage in the country. He replied that she could do just as she liked, but 'For myself, I am inclined to think that if we can rig up a set of rooms in the theatre, we might take a place near London that we could drive out to—but let us see which way the theatre cat is jumping.' He went on with a piece of advice:

> I think it is time you should tell Viola all things about life—they were discussing the question here the other day and were agreed that mothers should tell children what others will tell them less nicely. I hope you won't mind my saying this—I sometimes feel anxious about it.

He then adverted to the success of *Julius Caesar*: 'What a wonderful season it has been—looking back upon it we should feel very proud. I hope that we may be equally fortunate next season.' In another letter he begged her to come to Marienbad: 'It would do you so much good and you could take a little mild cure—just for the complexion.' The weather was glorious, the people were nice, and he was working steadily at the play, going to bed every night at 9.30 and getting up every morning at 6.30.

But his brother's business called him to London, and Maud took a cottage (West Lodge, Aldwick, Bognor) which became the family's summer residence for several seasons. From the Grand Pump Room Hotel at Bath Herbert wrote: 'As to £1,000, I think that sum would be a very large one to quash the Waller version

... I would give £500 and no more. I am sure you will agree with me that this is sensible.—I saw Waller for a moment, but did not mention the matter.' The situation was complicated because Waller had fallen in love with Maud, who had played the boy Lucius to his Brutus in *Caesar*; and, by an odd twist in human nature, Herbert, who loosely interpreted the marriage vow where himself was concerned, strongly objected to any romantic attachment for another on his wife's part. It is doubtful whether Maud ever felt more than a sincere friendship for Waller. She never ceased to love her husband. But she would scarcely have been human if she had not felt flattered by the feeling she had aroused in Waller, the stage hero of every female playgoer and budding actress, a man who, in the words of Justice Shallow, could have 'had the best of them all at commandment', and whose devotion to Maud was no doubt partly due to her puritanical invincibility.

The situation became acute early in the autumn of '98, when Waller produced his version in the suburbs and provinces and made a sensation as D'Artagnan. The part suited him perfectly and was totally unsuited to Tree. About two years later Waller acted Shakespeare's Henry V with a splendour of declamation and ease of manner unrivalled by any other actor since his time; and within the limits of stage representation his D'Artagnan was the impetuous, humorous and picturesque figure of Dumas. He brought the play to the old Globe Theatre in London, and his performance would have drawn the theatre-going world if Tree had not acted swiftly. On tour at the time, Tree asked his business-manager to see Waller's version and pronounce upon it. Henry Dana did his utmost to get seats but failed, and at last, much to his discomfort, had to approach Waller himself. The theatre was full, but he saw the play from a chair in the gangway and gave it as his opinion that the forthcoming production at Her Majesty's would suffer from the competition. Tree immediately offered Waller a large salary to play Buckingham in his own production of *The Musketeers* and a highly advantageous contract for two years. Waller accepted the bribe, probably because he did not then feel equal to the cares of management, always preferring security and quiet to risk and excitement, and perhaps because it meant that he would see a lot of Maud. His play was taken off to full houses; Tree's was put on at Her Majesty's; and everything appeared to be satisfactory; especially as the Grundy version ran for over five months.

But everything was not as satisfactory as it appeared to be. Beneath the glittering surface of theatrical success a human drama was in progress. Herbert's lapses from a state of monogamy had produced an effect on Maud that might have been expected in one of her temperament and upbringing, and resulted in angry domestic scenes. Such unhappy conditions are the outcome of diverse natures and part of the inescapable sadness of life. To blame human beings for being human is to blame their Creator for making them so. If Herbert had not been the one kind of man he was, he would not have been the other kind of man he was. The flaws in people are the obverse of their virtues, weakness in one respect occasioning strength in another. Everyone who enjoys life wishes to live it in his own way, and Herbert enjoyed every minute of it. Maud's nature on the other hand was dutiful and sacrificial. Apart from the urgencies of sex their characters were complemental, and so, with all their unfortunate differences, they remained indispensable to each other. But at times their disharmony seemed to deaden their mutual affection and admiration. One such period occurred during the run of *The Musketeers*. The leading actress, who played Miladi, was a famous American beauty named Mrs Brown Potter, while Maud appeared in the relatively small part of the Queen. Mrs Potter left the cast some weeks before the play came off, and Maud felt slighted because she was not asked to play Miladi. Probably Lewis Waller encouraged her to expostulate, for at a later date he told her that her husband had never helped her as an actress, which was not true.

Herbert was greatly distressed, and in a heated exchange between them over the part of Miladi he tried to make her see that, if she had been asked to play it after Mrs Brown Potter had given it up, she might justifiably have regarded the offer as a slight. This did not soothe her, and she refused to attend a party he was giving on February 1st, '99. It was a moment of much unhappiness for both of them, their misery being intensified by the strength of their underlying affection for each other. He begged her to reconsider her refusal; and as her good nature usually prevailed in the end, she no doubt did as he wished and made a lively hostess at his party.

On September 20th, 1899, Tree produced Shakespeare's *King John* at Her Majesty's. He had first put it on during his season of matinées at the Crystal Palace Theatre in 1889-90, recording an incident of Henry Kemble's participation therein:

> At the first performance of *King John* at the Crystal Palace, when I played King John for the first time, for Hastings' benefit, I was somewhat disturbed when I saw Kemble walking down to the refreshment room in company with Comyns Carr and Charles Brookfield. I did not know my words very well and arranged with the prompter that he should be dressed as the Court Fool and sit on the steps of the throne with the prompt book discreetly hidden from the public. After the second act, I was going up to my dressing-room and met Brookfield, who was also playing. I said 'Thank God, all has gone smoothly so far.' He replied, 'Wait till Kemble comes on!' In the next scene Kemble appeared as Cardinal Pandulph—(he has to pronounce the curse of Rome on King John). He began with great concentration and rocklike sturdiness: 'Hail you anointed deputies of Heaven!' When he came to the lines
>
> > And meritorious shall that hand be called,
> > Canonized and worshipp'd as a saint,
> > That takes away by any secret course
> > Thy hateful life,
>
> he used the word—giving tremendous emphasis to each syllable— 'And meriotorious shall that hand be called.' Sitting on my throne I burst out laughing. As I was leaving the stage he came up to me and said, 'Mr Manager, I want a word with you. You nearly queered my scene by laughing. But I knew perfectly well what I was doing. The fact is I dropped a syllable in the previous line and was too good an artist not to pick it up in the next.'

Tree's acting was described as panther-like, the scene in which he instigates Hubert to kill Arthur being especially commended. There was a bed of flowers, the heads of which he flicked off with his sword as he mused, and at the close of the episode he fell on his knees at a prie-dieu before a stained-glass window, an ironic touch that must have amused him. In the hope that W. S. Gilbert might change his views on Herbert's ability to speak blank verse, Maud got him a seat for the first-night, receiving this acknowledgment:

> Grim's Dyke
> Harrow Weald
> 21 Sept. '99

My dear N.K.L.

Many thanks for the stall and for the trouble you took about it. It is a splendid show and is sure to do. The play is not one that I passionately adore, but the pill is so handsomely gilded that everyone will swallow it.

The stage management is superb.

I had to go before the last act, as
   'I had a train to catch, O!'
I heartily wish you every success.

> Always affectionately your
> W.S.N.K.G.

The acting honours were carried off by Lewis Waller as the Bastard, the calls for whom at the final curtain must have made Tree wonder whether he had not paid too high a price for the privilege of playing D'Artagnan without competition.

King John was followed early in 1900 with another success: *A Midsummer Night's Dream.* In the effort to achieve reality, the wood near Athens was well rabbited; but these creatures must have felt more at home in ancient Greece than in modern England because they disregarded the antics of the lovers and were seemingly content to nibble stage grass. The woodland glade was a masterpiece of silvan scenery, and Tree's Bully Bottom was a critical comment on the actor-manager system, the 'star' actor, as it were, pulling his own leg. Henry Arthur Jones, who had suffered from the system, became repetitive in praise: 'Tree as Bottom had a blank wall of vanity—it was impassable—you couldn't get beyond it. He conveyed the absolute stolidity of the character. How well he managed to convey Bottom's enormous vanity.' Maud had been reciting Kipling's 'The Absent-Minded Beggar' every night at the Palace Theatre for charities in connection with the Boer War, which had broken out the previous autumn, but after ten weeks of it she returned to her husband's theatre to play Titania. The preparations appear to have been more perplexing than usual, because the final dress-rehearsal was such a fiasco that the leading players, exhausted and irritated, sat up with Tree till six in the morning while he tried to pull the show together. As so often happens on the stage, the last-rehearsal disaster became the first-night triumph, probably because the actors were on their mettle.

We must here skip some of the intervening productions, to which we will return in succeeding chapters, and go forward with Tree's Shakespearean work in the first decade of the twentieth century. The death of Queen Victoria in January, 1901, necessitated a reversion to romantic comedy, and the first production at the now to be renamed His Majesty's Theatre (by permission of King Edward VII) was *Twelfth Night*, first given on February 5th of that year. Maud was offered the part of Olivia but hungered for that of Viola, and even went so far as to ask Charles Wyndham to tell Herbert that she was ideally suited for it. Wyndham replied tactfully that he could not write to her husband but that if she would arrange for Herbert to be at the Garrick Club one evening he would talk the matter over. But Tree had already cast Lily Brayton for Viola, and Maud, having refused Olivia, said she would like to play Maria. After a few rehearsals she was found to be miscast and had to abandon the attempt. Such embarrassments did not help to create concord in the home.

The scenery was to be a very important feature, and Joseph Harker, the artist, lunched with Tree to discuss it. Emerging from the Pall Mall restaurant together, they started to cross the road; but Tree stopped in the middle of the Haymarket and said: 'Now don't forget. The keynote of this play is to be joy—joy—JOY', adding in an undertone 'with economy.' But there were no signs of economy when the curtain went up.

On the whole Tree's *Twelfth Night* was his most satisfactory Shakespearean production. Olivia's garden with its grass terraces, hedges and statuary (copied from a picture in *Country Life*) was more realistic and beautiful than anything of the kind previously staged, and the acting was as rich as the scenery was sumptuous. The author himself must have approved of Lionel Brough as Sir Toby Belch, Norman Forbes as Sir Andrew Aguecheek, and Courtice Pounds as Feste, but he might at moments have wondered whether the Malvolio was partly his or wholly Tree's. The performance was superbly comical, but it was not in the character of Olivia's steward as conceived by his maker. Tree was followed

about by four little Malvolios, who aped their master in costume
and carriage, and who lined up behind him, stiffly to attention,
whenever he spoke, a simple and effective march accompanying
the arrival and departure of steward and retinue. Tree was constantly inventing comic business, such as a careful inspection
through his glass of the statue of a nude female figure, varying
his reactions to it from strong disapproval to leering delight. One
inspiration he retained. Descending the steps of the terrace, head
in air, with stupendous self-importance, he tripped and almost fell
headlong, but recovered his balance in the nick of time and managed to descend in a dignified sitting posture. To show that it had
been his intention to take a seat at that precise spot, he calmly lifted
his eyeglass and inspected the surroundings at leisure, the effect
being fantastically funny. Indeed, the whole impersonation left
an unforgettable impression of Beerbohm Tree's Malvolio, with
incidental verbal music by William Shakespeare.

Without noticing the regular revivals of Shakespeare at His
Majesty's, one of them must be recorded. It took place in the
summer of 1902, to synchronize with the Coronation of the new
monarch, and was perhaps the most joyous and riotous thing of
its kind ever seen on the stage. With considerable difficulty Tree
got Ellen Terry and Madge Kendal to play Mistress Page and
Mistress Ford in *The Merry Wives of Windsor*. The great Irving–
Terry partnership at the Lyceum was breaking up. Ellen heard
that another actress had been engaged for some of the parts she
was getting too old to play, and so felt free to accept the offer
from Irving's rival. She was then 55, Madge Kendal 53, Tree in
his fiftieth year, but they romped through the play like children
and incidentally taught the younger generation how to act
abandonment without losing control. Tree also displayed his skill
as a grease-paint artist; he never padded his cheeks for the part of
Falstaff, yet they looked plump enough for the body beneath.
Ellen revelled in her part and confessed that the first-night was the
jolliest she had ever experienced. Watching her husband at rehearsal with Ellen Terry on one arm and Madge Kendal on the
other, Maud said: 'Look at Herbert between two ancient lights!'
but they shone more brightly than any other 'stars' in the theatrical firmament. Maud, by the way, had bought a Panhard motor-

car, and one Saturday evening at six o'clock she and Herbert and Ellen started off for a week-end at Aldwick. The theatre was closed on Saturday nights, as the two Merry Wives refused to be merry twice a day. Stopping at Horsham for dinner, all went well until they reached Bury Hill, half-way up which the engine stopped and the car started to run backwards, halting in a ditch. While the driver walked to Arundel to fetch a horse-carriage, they sat on the downy turf by the roadside and told stories, Herbert coining a phrase which has not lost its significance: 'In our endeavour to cover the ground quickly, the ground is apt to cover us.' They reached Aldwick at five on Sunday morning.

In the autumn of the following year Tree gave a majestic production of *Richard II*, his own performance as the King containing some of his most inspired bits of acting. One of the scenes, the Lists at Coventry, was made more than usually difficult because the combatants were provided with real horses whose behaviour was unpredictable. It was rehearsed again and again to give the animals confidence. Tree was in the stalls with his stage-manager at the first dress-rehearsal of this scene. The Marshal directing the operations made an entrance, followed by his attendant, a youth who had obviously taken several hours over a 'character' make-up which completely disguised him. 'Good God, chief! who on earth is that with the Marshal?' exclaimed the stage-manager. 'Ssh!' whispered Tree, 'that's probably Mr Snelgrove.'[1] Shakespeare's historical plays are improved by pageantry, but Tree could not resist the temptation to give an elaborate stage-picture which the poet had merely suggested in a short speech. The entry into London of Bolingbroke and the deposed King is described by the Duke of York. Tree substituted a crowded street scene through which the victor and the vanquished rode on horseback, the mob yelling vituperation and hurling stones at the ex-King.

One still remembers that great white horse, and the look of hunted terror with which Richard turned his head as the crowd hooted him [wrote Shaw many years later]. It passed in a moment; and it flatly contradicted Shakespeare's description of the saint-like patience of Richard; but the effect was intense ... Again, one remembers how Richard walked out of Westminster Hall after his abdication.

[1] For the benefit of readers in Tierra del Fuego, it should be said that Marshall and Snelgrove is a well-known London firm dealing in women's wear.

Next came *The Tempest*, in September, 1904, a presentation so gorgeous that several critics raised the lament that poetry was being sacrificed to pomp. The opening scene showed a complete ship rocking in a realistic sea, the breakers roaring, the waves splashing over the deck, the wind tearing at the sails. The panto-mimic scenes towards the end were Shakespeare's, and the pro-ducer did his best to make them effective. Those who disliked stage illusion need not go to the theatre, said Tree: 'The book-worm has always his book.' But the majority of playgoers seemed to like what he liked and to feel that, as Caliban, he was justified in returning to an empty stage at the end of the play to look yearningly after the ship that carried the rest of the cast away from the island; though the more mordant critics hinted that he did so in order to 'steal' the final curtain.

Little need be said of *Much Ado About Nothing*, which followed immediately. With the exception of *Othello*, it was his least successful Shakespearean production. He could not even make Benedick funny in his own way because he found nothing very amusing in the lines he had to speak, which proves his intelligence as a man, his failure as an actor, who should at least give the impression that he thinks himself clever. Winifred Emery as Beatrice did her best to make the wit sound witty.

Wishing to give Ellen Terry a worthy part in celebration of her fifty years on the stage, Tree put on *The Winter's Tale* in the autumn of 1906. He did not appear in it, entrusting Leontes to Charles Warner, a realistically intense actor who had made a world-wide reputation as Coupeau in *Drink* (founded on Zola's *L'Assommoir*), which he played over a thousand times. *The Win-ter's Tale* was a lovely production, containing a rural scene with cottage, stream, waterfall, willow-tree, etc., the mere sight of which made jaded Londoners plan country week-ends. But the loveliest thing in the production was the Hermione of Ellen Terry, whose words were music and whose movements were poetry. She often forgot the lines of her part, but she substituted her own language, which sounded just as good as Shakespeare's.

This comedy was shortly followed by *Antony and Cleopatra*, a difficult play for Tree's spectacular methods and the text had to be 'arranged' to suit the scenery, which was lavishly Oriental.

The return of Antony to Alexandria, dismissed by Shakespeare in a brief speech, gave Tree an excellent opportunity for annoying the pedants. The occasion was illustrated by a superb tableau which a modern film producer could not equal in colour, sound, movement and dramatic suggestion, wherein excited crowds, priestly processions, dancing flower-decked maidens and marching soldiers preluded the arrival of Cleopatra to voluptuous music and Antony to the sterner notes of Rome. Perhaps it is needless to say that Tree's Antony was not a performance on which the critic can dwell with profit. Constance Collier's Cleopatra looked like Shakespeare's and had some fine moments. But the outstanding performance was that of Enobarbus by Lyn Harding, the most versatile actor of his time. Here again Tree was eclipsed in his own theatre, and there were occasions when the audience shouted for Harding so lustily that the lights in the house went up and the National Anthem was played.

Such drastic treatment was unnecessary when *The Merchant of Venice* was presented in 1908. Tree's Shylock was as picturesque and impressive as his production, though his partiality for realism provided two disconcerting moments. After arranging the loan at the beginning of the play, Antonio and Bassanio departed, and the moment their backs were turned Shylock sent a large gobbet of saliva sailing through the air after them. The effect was more humorous than venomous. Then, too, Tree overdid a very effective touch initiated by Henry Irving, who used to show the Jew returning at night-time after the revels, and knocking on the door of his house, from which his daughter Jessica had fled to marry a Christian. The curtain fell on the silent figure waiting with his lantern for the door to be opened. Tree spoilt the drama of this moment by pushing at the door, finding it open, and entering the house. At first he was heard within calling 'Jessica!' imperatively, but soon his cries became urgent, and at length hysterical. Sobbing and howling, he rushed from the house through the streets in search of his daughter.

But a man's mistakes are as great as himself, and Tree's were as peculiar as his character was singular.

CHAPTER 14

Phillips, Fitch, Caine and Kipling

From the sixteenth century onwards nearly every poet had attempted to write blank verse plays. The lure of the stage, or the desire for an immediate audience, is strong, and even in the nineteenth century, when the theatre was abandoned to the worst kind of drama, Keats, Shelley, Byron, Wordsworth, Coleridge, Swinburne, Browning and Tennyson all wrote plays. But either the plays were too good or the playgoers were too bad, and the poetic drama appeared to be dead until the arrival at the end of the century of a young poet named Stephen Phillips. The chorus of praise with which he was received showed up the dearth of effective blank verse in the past hundred years.

Phillips was the son of a parson. He had been educated for the Civil Service, but a love of poetry inherited from his mother inclined him towards the stage and he joined F. R. Benson's Shakespearean company. Apart from his sonorous rendering of the Ghost in *Hamlet*, he made little impression as an actor, but he was liked in the company, not because he could recite pages of Milton but because he developed a passion for cricket. The vicissitudes of a touring actor's life fretted him, and he left the stage to become an army 'crammer'; but the regularity of a tutorial life bored him and he drifted into the literary profession. In 1897 *The Academy* awarded him a hundred guineas for 'the most important contribution to the literature' of that year, and his *Poems* evoked exclamation marks from the critics, who compared him with Milton, Rossetti and Swinburne. Their praises rose to pæans when George Alexander produced Phillips's *Paolo and Francesca* in 1899, his first blank-verse play being compared with Sophocles, Dante and Racine, and William Archer declared that 'Sardou could not have ordered the action more skilfully, Tennyson could not have clothed the passion in words of purer loveliness'. As on two previous occasions already noted, Alexander paved the way for Tree, who commissioned Phillips to write a poetic tragedy, the result being *Herod*, produced at Her Majesty's in October, 1900, and dedicated 'To Herbert Beerbohm Tree: in life a true friend, and on the stage the Herod of my dreams'. Thus at the age of thirty-three Phillips stood at the apex of his career, the Eliot and Fry of his age, with two plays successfully produced by the two leading actor-managers of London, his achievements greeted by the literary and dramatic critics in language usually reserved for the greatest poets of the past, and a claim to be the only writer of blank-verse plays since Shakespeare to make as much money as the providers of topical comedy and melodrama.

But success went to his head and ultimately ruined him both as man and artist. His character was not sufficiently balanced to recognize the fleeting value of praise, nor robust enough to withstand the corrupting influence of money. The initial cause of his weakness partly resulted from an unhappy nonage. An intense affection for his sister created a longing for love and an inability to return it, this basic frustration making life at times insupportable. He became morbid, morose and melancholic. He lived in a world of childish fantasies and nightmares propagated by a keen perception of horror, which derived from a sense of guilt and a dread of the unknown. He disappeared for long periods, no one knew where; his money vanished, no one knew how. Protracted seasons of inertia followed short phases of activity, the first deadened by drink, the second stimulated by it. Such moments of gaiety as he enjoyed were boisterous and tinged with hysteria. Like Tree, he was addicted to practical joking, but what was an expression of light-heartedness in Tree was a sign of self-insufficiency in Phillips, who had little humour. Obscurely conscious of his thwarted nature, he once declared that the romantic attitude towards life led to suicide or insanity. In his case it led to the public house.

All this is reflected in his plays before he had succumbed to the fate he feared yet could not avoid. His verse is rhetorical, Marlowesque, always straining for strength. Sometimes it springs to life in a line or a scene, but usually the poet is lost in verbal violence, drugged by grandiosity of speech. Nevertheless, much of it was theatrically effective when declaimed in the grand manner, and the development of the action displayed a feeling for drama, the absence of which has kept the works of greater poets from the stage. A good example of Phillips's less bombastic rhetoric may be given from *Nero*, where Seneca speaks of what might happen to the artist-emperor when he realizes his unlimited power, and

> Uses for colour this red blood of ours,
> Composes music out of dreadful cries,
> His orchestra our human agonies,
> His rhythms lamentations of the ruined,
> His poet's fire not circumscribed by words,
> But now translated into burning cities,
> His scenes the lives of men, their deaths a drama,
> His dream the desolation of mankind,
> And all this pulsing world his theatre.

Tree produced four plays by Stephen Phillips, *Herod* (1900), *Ulysses* (1902), *Nero* (1906), *Faust* (1908), each of them running for more than a hundred performances, which in those days, and in that theatre, meant a considerable success. They were staged with a luxuriance that matched the language, and audiences gasped at scenes that made Jerusalem and Rome more marvellous on the stage than they appeared in the National Gallery. It would be interesting to know how much Tree contributed to the plays as well as their settings. He certainly helped Phillips a lot, and no doubt hindered him too. They did much preliminary planning together before the production of each. 'Mr Phillips and I are working hard on *Herod*', he wrote to Viola from Marienbad in August, 1900; 'I think you will like the play—it seems wonderful to me—the best thing, outside Shakespeare, I have ever known.' They talked *Herod* all day long, and Tree admitted 'I have never worked so well and I have never had a wry word'. He described the tragedy as 'a grand play to go bankrupt on'. It seems that he wanted James McNeill Whistler to design the scenery, but an interview with that artist convinced him that the setting would merely provide a pleasing background for an exhibition of Whistler's pictures, and he abandoned the idea. As eventually designed and executed the single scene included a most imposing bronze staircase leading to the royal apartments. At the close of Act 2 Tree as Herod made a slow exit up this staircase, reciting as he went the names of the places recently added to his dominions by Caesar:

> Hippo, Samaria and Gadara,
> And high-walled Joppa, and Anthedon,
> And Gaza unto these, and Straton's towers!

It was a striking finish to the act, and at one performance, as the curtain slowly descended, a friend turned to Sir Henry Irving: 'Well, what do you think of that?' Irving replied: 'Ah . . . Hm . . . a very fine . . . hm . . . flight of steps.'

Tree worked with Phillips on *Ulysses* and *Nero* while he was appearing in other plays, and the author had some difficulty in preventing the actor from introducing lines of his own which, if funny, were not quite in the period, such as an epigram he wished to put in the mouth of Nero: 'All men are equal—except myself.' At the rehearsals of *Faust* he took so many liberties with the text that Comyns Carr, who collaborated with Phillips in this one play, wrote to say that both of them felt rather strongly that no alterations should be made unless they were present and without their agreement. Tree got bored with the part of Mephistopheles and one evening varied the monotony of the Brocken Scene, which was full of weird and wonderful horrors, by handing Henry Ainley, who played Faust, a boiled lobster. Ainley retaliated at another performance by presenting Tree with a bottle of Jeyes' Fluid. But Tree finally scored by having the chalice from which Faust drank screwed to the table, and Ainley had to sup it up like a horse at a trough. Just as the Victorian lady, after witnessing a performance of *Antony and Cleopatra*, remarked, 'How unlike the domestic life of our own dear Queen!' so an actor at His Majesty's who had once served under Irving might have exclaimed: 'How unlike the stage behaviour of our old Chief!'

Long after Stephen Phillips sank in the world's esteem and became destitute he was helped by the Herod of his dreams. 'He lends me money which I always mean to repay, and he is the only man I know who takes the will for the deed,' he confided in a friend. Tree did not 'compound for sins he was inclined to by damning those he had no mind to', but was tolerant of all human frailty and generous to any artist who was down and out. On hearing that Oscar Wilde needed financial assistance at the beginning of 1900, he at once sent money with a letter:

> No one did such distinguished work as you [he wrote]; I do most sincerely hope . . . that your splendid talents may shine forth again. I have a lively remembrance of your many acts of kindness and courtesy, and was one of those who devoutly hoped that misfortune would not submerge you.

Very few people acknowledge past kindness when they are in a position to return it, especially when they have a moral excuse for not remembering it.

Sandwiched between *Herod* and *Ulysses* a very different class of work was seen at His Majesty's Theatre. An American author, Clyde Fitch, had written a play on Count D'Orsay, calling it *The Last of the Dandies*. Two things about it appealed to Tree: an excellent part for himself, and a boating-scene which enabled him to introduce a river with real water. Though the water may have helped, the success of the play was due to the actor, and it was perhaps his only production in which everything depended upon his own performance. He had an exceptional talent for suggesting emotion beneath an artificial exterior, and he could manage to admiration the delicately affected prose of a 'period piece'. Even so, with all the scenic effects, the exquisite clothes, the lovely furniture, and the perfect impersonation of D'Orsay, it was touch and go with the play. A drawn-out first-night left the management in doubt, but by the end of a week Tree had learnt his words, the show was running smoothly, and success was assured. 'I hope you will be pleased with the production and with me', wrote Tree to Fitch: 'the former is quite beautiful, and the latter pretends to be.'

An odd thing occurred in the course of the run. A little shabbily-dressed old lady called at the theatre to see Tree. She would not state her business and was at first refused admission. But her persistence won, she entered his dressing-room, and the following duologue ensued:

'I wish to tell you, Mr Tree, that the final scene in your play is not historically correct. I refer to the death of the famous Count D'Orsay. He is presented as dying in very meagre circumstances.'

'May I ask where you live, madam?'

'In the workhouse, Mr Tree.'

'And—er—may I enquire what you know of Count D'Orsay?'

'I am his daughter, sir.'

The old lady then produced letters and a birth certificate from her reticule, all of which proved her to be what she claimed.

'Would you like to hear the story of his death?' she asked.

'Very much.'

'Well, it was in this way. We were not rich, but my father had his appointment in Paris, and a pension from a famous duchess, so that we were at least comfortable. I was playing to him one night —he was very fond of music. It was a gallop, a bright, rattling tune. I had been playing some time when of a sudden he called out "Faster," and again "Faster," and yet again "Faster." My fingers flew over the notes. The gay tune rattled on. "Faster, faster," he still cried, until suddenly—', the speaker stopped for a moment and bent her head, 'suddenly I heard a fall and a groan. I turned. My father, Count D'Orsay, was dead.'

Tree gave the old lady a pension for the three-months' run of the piece.

An interval of Shakespeare followed *Ulysses*, the title of which the stage-hands pronounced 'Useless', and then came *The Eternal City* by Hall Caine, one of those born writers who should never have been allowed to hold a pen in his hand until he had learnt the use of a blue pencil. His home was in the Isle of Man, where, to judge by his novel *The Manxman*, the natives speak a strange tongue, chiefly made up of pseudo-poetic clichés. The sale of his novels was prodigious, his only competitor in that respect being Marie Corelli. He believed that he had been sent into the world with some kind of mission, in which moral uplift and purifying thoughts had their part. He took himself very seriously, and when he read one of his plays to a theatrical company the members felt like a church congregation listening to the lessons. His manner impressed Tree so much that some years later, when the Votes for Women movement became critical and the suffragettes were kept alive in prison by forcible feeding, he suggested that they should be sent to the Isle of Man, with forcible reading by Hall Caine. During rehearsals he dealt humorously with the solemn playwright. At one moment he had to throw Constance Collier roughly to the ground. 'Stop!' called the author, raising his hand. Everything, including the music, stopped; and Hall Caine, running his hand through his hair, spoke as in a dream:

'I see in my mind an actor, seizing a woman fiercely, and with tense muscles and bated breath hurling her right over his head.'

'I remember,' interposed Tree as in a reverie, 'seeing a famous actor seize a famous actress, lift her up by her feet, and dash her head against the ground, not once, not twice, but three times.'

'In what play was that?' demanded Hall Caine.

'I understand that it was called *Punch and Judy*,' said Tree.

Reality was not an ingredient in the work of this dramatist, and Tree did not bother to introduce it. To show his contempt for a character in the play who was sitting for his bust, Tree as Baron Bonelli struck a match on the wet clay of the half-finished work. Asked by a sculptor how he could do anything so absurd as to light a match on wet clay, he replied: 'You artists are too critical. It will never occur to the audience that one cannot do so.' 'But how did you?' 'Simple enough: I have had a bit of metal let into the clay at the back of the bust—same as you see in railway carriages.'

He was always on the outlook for popular stories that could be dramatized, and before the turn of the century he went down to Hindhead where Conan Doyle read him a five-act drama on Sherlock Holmes. The actor in Tree was more attracted to the part of Professor Moriarty than to that of Holmes and wanted to double them. Doyle pointed out that as a crucial scene in the play took place between the two characters it would be difficult for the same actor to play both. Tree saw the point and then made the surprising suggestion that he should play Sherlock in a beard. Doyle asked, 'What of the well-known illustrations?' Tree answered, 'The public will know that I am disguising myself for a purpose.' 'What purpose?' 'Ah, that is for you to say.' Doyle failed to say it, and nothing came of the suggestion. Eventually the American actor William Gillette wrote and acted in a Holmes play.

Rudyard Kipling's novel *The Light that Failed* was another possibility, and Tree discussed it with Louis N. Parker, who would have liked to adapt it for the stage; but Tree, who knew

Kipling, felt that Parker would not be tactful enough in dealing with the author, and the job was left to a woman, 'George Fleming', whose adaptation was seen in 1903 with Forbes–Robertson as the hero. That same year Tree produced a dramatic version by Kinsey Peile of Rudyard Kipling's short-story 'The Man Who Was' and made a sensational appearance in the part of Limasson, repeating it again and again in the years ahead. He described the following incident to the present writer:

'Kipling came to see me after a performance of *The Man Who Was*. We greeted one another cordially; he sat down; I sat down, expectant. There was a long silence, which I broke by asking whether the playlet had given him satisfaction. He frowned, and at last said, as if to himself, "One." "One what?" I enquired. "Two," he said. This was no reply to my question, but I left him in peace. Then: "Three," he continued. It looked as if he were about to enter the sphere of Higher Mathematics where I could not follow him; so I closed my eyes and waited for his return to everyday life. "There are three distinct ways of acting the character which I conceived and you have delineated," he announced, "but you have chosen none of them." My eyes opened in protest. He went on: "Instead you have done something far more interesting. You have created a character of your own, but the title of the play should be changed to *Who Was The Man?*" A trifle cryptic, but I thought it safer to ask no questions, and I decided to take it as a compliment.'

It is doubtful whether Kipling would have paid him a compliment on some of his later performances of the part. He was the first actor-manager of note to appear on the Music Halls. This happened early in 1912, when he played *The Man Who Was* for a month at the Palace Theatre, then regarded as the only Music Hall which respectable theatre-goers could visit without danger of contamination. He received £1,000 a week, but before a fortnight had elapsed he was tired of the part and pining for his own theatre. However, he managed to amuse himself at the end of the scene. As he lay dead under the Union Jack while the Last Post was being played, he blew up the flag from his face with every breath he expelled, the rest of the company doing their best to appear unconscious of this uncorpselike proceeding.

CHAPTER 15

Home and Dome

By 1900 Tree had fashioned a commodious residence for himself in the dome of Her Majesty's Theatre. It consisted of two rooms, a large one which he fitted up as a banqueting-hall, and a smaller one which he used as a sitting-and-living-room, in the wall of which was a concealed bed. All round the rooms were painted murals depicting scenes from his productions. The furniture in his sitting-room was comfortable without being cumbersome, and there were plenty of books. He declined to surround himself with such presents as most famous people wonder how to get rid of without hurting the feelings of the givers, and when the absence of one was noticed he would explain that a friend had begged for it so earnestly that he had not had the heart to refuse. For all practical purposes the dome became his home, but he would spend occasional days or nights with his family in town or country. He was happier in his theatre than elsewhere, and though a naturally timid man he would pass many nights when himself in the roof and the watchman in the basement were the only occupants of the building. In the large outer room he gave innumerable supper-parties after first-nights and on occasions that could be described as special if they had been less frequent. He loved entertaining, and was an admirable host. He liked to be surrounded with happy faces and to hear the laughter of carefree people. Sometimes the talk would be witty, sometimes sensible, but gaiety was the prevailing note, and so long as his guests enjoyed themselves their conversation could be as non-sensical and commonplace as they wished. After all, if people only opened their mouths when they had something interesting to say, it would be a very quiet world.

Eminent poets, painters, composers, actors and politicians were sooner or later invited to parties at the theatre, and Maud used to call these occasions 'Herbert Tree At Dome'. One of the bonds

142

between these two was that she could usually be depended upon for a smart sally. 'Life is very disappointing,' she once said. 'Nothing comes off except buttons.' When her husband defended a well-known doctor with 'Anyhow, he has attended many of the greatest living Englishmen,' she corrected him, 'Dead, you mean.' A hostess complimented her: 'How charmingly you've done your hair, Maud!' 'Sweet of you to call it *my* hair,' she returned. An American said to her, 'England is an island off France.' She instantly retorted, 'America is a continent off colour.' An old friend of hers was Violet, Duchess of Rutland, and the Tree family often spent Christmas at Belvoir Castle. Her liking for the aristocracy as such was not shared by Herbert, who liked people in whatever class solely for what he found in them to like, but he came across some interesting folk in the circles Maud frequented. At one time or another he was on friendly terms with H. H. Asquith and his wife Margot, with A. J. Balfour, Lloyd George, Winston Churchill, F. E. Smith, Edward Carson, Henry Labouchere, Joseph Chamberlain, and many others of whom he said that they had 'paddled too long in the putrescent puddles of politics'. He left a memory of Joseph Chamberlain among his papers:

I went to stay with the Chamberlains at Highbury on his sixtieth birthday. He was a most charming and natural person. After dinner we were talking about John Bright, and in his library he took down a copy of his speeches and read to me, imitating John Bright's manner. He was a very young man for sixty—for he could not help running like a boy when a cow got loose from a paddock. He showed us over his orchid house—he was an enthusiastic grower and always wore an orchid in his buttonhole. On arriving on a Saturday night, I told him that I had impersonated him on the way to his home through Birmingham. He had sent his carriage for us to drive to Highbury in, and in passing through a congested part of the city where a market was going on, I told him the people recognized his carriage and began cheering him. I was very anxious that they should not think him ungracious, so I bowed right and left to the people, taking off my hat to them, and they cheered lustily.

One day I was lunching at Chamberlain's house, Prince's Gardens. After the ladies had left the table, the men smoked—I remember John Morley was there, and many other distinguished politicians. I was the only layman present. The conversation turned upon the affairs of the world, and after some warm argument Colonel John Haye, who was then American ambassador, said: 'Gentlemen,

gentlemen, do remember that in international politics there is such a thing as morality.' There was a momentary silence, then everybody round the table roared with laughter.

I remember Chamberlain telling me that it was good for one's character always to do what one had made up one's mind to do, even if it was quite unnecessary—for instance, if he made up his mind to take a walk and it began to rain, he would take a walk nevertheless.

I do not think he was a highly imaginative man, but he was a man who saw with great clearness what was near him . . . I heard him deliver a speech at the Guildhall. He had a remarkable voice and was very sparing of gesture.

Tree used to tell a story about one of Chamberlain's fiercest critics, Lloyd George, who, shortly after becoming Chancellor of the Exchequer, paid a visit with his wife to His Majesty's Theatre, and afterwards had supper in the dome. Having expressed an interest in the art of facial expression and make-up, Lloyd George said:

'I particularly noticed that moisture appeared in your eyes during an emotional passage. Can you do that every night?'

'Did you also happen to notice that I hid my face in my arms just before the passage you speak of?' asked Tree.

'No, I didn't; but what has that to do with it?'

'Only this. I was able during those few seconds to transfer some of the contents of a tube of glycerine from my pocket to the corners of my eyes.'

'Good heavens!' exclaimed Lloyd George: 'what a fake!' and he burst out laughing.

'Is it more of a fake than the forced tears of an actor who can work himself up into a condition that tickles his lachrymal gland?'

'Or of an orator, you would like to add?'

'I never voice my suspicions.'

'Well, I don't mind admitting that I can cry to command,' said the Chancellor, 'but it isn't always easy.' Turning to his wife, he added: 'Don't forget, dear; when I'm not in form, a spot of glycerine on a spare pocket handkerchief.'

The talk went on, Lloyd George asking innumerable questions, and Tree finished the story by saying: 'I never met a man who showed such a keen interest in my art. I hope he isn't thinking of going on the stage. Like Bottom, he'd want to play all the parts.'

Tree preferred the company of artists to any other, and we find him at all sorts of places where they congregated. Sarah Bernhardt and Coquelin had a six-weeks' season at His Majesty's in 1902, and were entertained in Sloane Street by Herbert and Maud, the other guests being Madame Réjane and Alma Tadema. Sarah, who liked to make an effective entrance, kept the rest waiting until they were in a fit condition of nervous expectancy, and then swept in with the words '*En retard comme toujours!*' This inconvenienced Maud, whose dishes were endangered, but a different fate was reserved for Herbert when he attended a house-warming given by Maurice Baring in North Street, Westminster. 'I never saw such a mixture of people,' noted Tree; 'cabinet ministers, surgeons, artists, and fashionable folk. The party continued till late in the morning. On my way out I saw H. G. Wells, Hilaire Belloc and Harry Cust poaching eggs in a hat over a spirit-lamp. I thought it intensely humorous—until I discovered it was my hat they were poaching the eggs in. Then I thought it very vulgar.' He expostulated with them, but each provided a sound reason for the investigation. 'I wanted to see whether the eggs would poach before the bottom of the hat fell out,' said Wells. 'It was an experiment to determine which would win in an equal contest, fire or water,' said Belloc. 'Art for art's sake—no shinier hat was obtainable,' said Cust. Tree could only do justice to the situation in French: '*La raison n'est que la fille naturelle de la folie fatiguée.*'

Something more serious for him than the wreck of a top-hat occurred on a visit to Claude Lowther at Hurstmonceux Castle. Lowther lived the luxurious life of a bachelor who made a hobby of the arts. His check suits were sometimes of so pronounced a pattern that Maud once called him 'Colonel Loud Clother'. He had written a play, *The Gordian Knot*, which Tree out of friendship had presented at His Majesty's and which had been heartily booed by the pit and gallery, the calls for 'Author' showing unmistakably what sort of reception he would get. Tree was very courageous in such matters and came before the curtain. 'The author is not in the house,' said he, 'but I am always here, ready to receive your hoots.' As a consequence he was applauded for what he considered the worst performance of his life. Their friendship remained unimpaired, and Tree frequently visited Lowther at

Hurstmonceux. One day when he was there a crowd of trippers arrived to view the castle. On being told that it was not open to the public that afternoon, one of the party approached the owner, who was strolling in the gardens with his guests, and asked if he were Colonel Lowther. 'No, that is the Colonel,' said Lowther, indicating Tree, to whom the visitor then spoke: 'I am sorry, Colonel Lowther, to have brought my party here on the wrong day, but since we are here would you allow us just to look at your beautiful gardens before we return?' 'Certainly,' said Tree, 'and pick as many peaches as you like.' The real Lowther heard this and promptly introduced himself as Herbert Tree of His Majesty's Theatre, saying, 'I shall be delighted to put a box or stalls at your disposal whenever you care to apply for them.' Afterwards Lowther told Tree that some of the party had asked him whether he could not let them have seats for the Coliseum instead. Tree laughed delightedly.

Though not a country-lover, Tree enjoyed riding, swimming and walking, and did not mind covering the ground in a motor-car, though he drew the line at unnecessary speed, telling his chauffeur: 'Better arrive five minutes too late alive than five minutes too soon dead.' They had an amusing cockney driver, who usually had a reason for the risks he took. In July, 1904, Tree left London for Dover in the car, *en route* for Marienbad, and recorded what happened. Descending a hill near Gravesend it became clear that the driver had lost control of the car, the brakes having ceased to work.

> With a steep incline on one side, and rocks on the other, one cart coming up hill in front of us and one down, we seemed to be hurtling to certain death. By great good luck we smashed into one cart and then came to a standstill against the other. Our car was throbbing in its death-throes. My cockney chauffeur got out. I looked at him with a cold grey eye. 'The car is done for—we were nearly killed,' I said. With a reassuring wink, he replied, 'Not a bad ad., governor.'

Tree never wearied of Marienbad. He liked the place, the people and the peace. Walking among the hills and through the woods he felt invigorated. Ideas for plays, never to be written, occurred to him. Phrases for other people's plays, often inserted, struck him, such as this for *Nero*: 'Wines from Bessarabia, cooled with the snows raped from a virgin Alp.' King Edward VII visited Marienbad at regular intervals, and on the 20th August, 1907, Tree wrote to his daughter Iris: 'Tell Mother I lunched with the King today and we got on very well. Sir Squire Bancroft and Mr Hawtrey were there too—the King in excellent temper.' Yvette Guilbert, the famous French *diseuse*, was invited to one of these lunches, and Tree kept on insisting that she should play Lady Macbeth. 'No, no,' said the King; 'she has no rival in her own field; let her remain Yvette Guilbert. No tragedy!'

Like so many born comedians Tree saw himself in tragic parts and would always produce a tragedy in preference to a comedy.

Yet his nature was humorous and he could not resist a joke at moments when other people were being solemn. While laying the foundation-stone of the Croydon Theatre he remarked that speech-making was far more difficult than stone-laying, and to emphasize the point recited:

> Oh, that as easy were the use of verb and vowel
> As is the deft manipulation of a trowel!

Everyone thought this an apt quotation from some famous poet and applauded it. After the ceremony an old gentleman addressed him: 'Of course, Mr Tree, being a literary man I am naturally familiar with that poetic quotation, but I cannot remember who wrote it.' Tree, who had painfully given birth to the couplet, replied: 'What, sir! do you never read your Pope?' Clearly the old gentleman did not. But too many people had read Shakespeare for Tree to risk attributing lines of his own to that poet when unveiling a memorial tablet on the site of the Globe Playhouse in Park Street, Southwark. This occurred on October 8th, 1909, and Tree lunched with the directors of Barclay Perkins, on the wall of whose brewery the tablet had been placed. At the luncheon someone mentioned an oft-repeated saying of Max Beerbohm's, and as it has invariably been misquoted, the actual incident, authorized by Sir Max, may be given here.

'And what work are you engaged on at present?' asked a newspaper interviewer in 1895.

'Oh, I am writing a volume of "Lives of the Brothers of Great Men",' replied Max; 'Mr Ralph Disraeli, Mr Jacob Bright, Mr Willie Wilde, and so on.'

'You yourself are a brother, are you not, of Mr Beerbohm Tree?'

'Oh yes. He is coming into the series.'

In the early years of the century Max was a leading dramatic critic, having taken Shaw's place on *The Saturday Review*, but he never attended His Majesty's Theatre as a critic, liking his brother too much to criticize his productions and far too much to praise them dishonestly. They constantly saw each other, usually at lunch. The Carlton restaurant, next-door to the theatre, was Herbert's favourite feeding-ground, but occasionally he went to the Café Royal, of which he said: 'If you want to see English people at their most English, go to the Café Royal, where they are trying their hardest to be French.' The dinners in the dome were brought in from the Carlton, and a chef was usually hired to cook for Maud's parties. The family left the Sloane Street house in 1904, and after a short interval in North Street, Westminster, moved to Walpole House, Chiswick Mall, where they remained for six years. It was a lovely Charles II house, for which they paid a rent of £110 per annum. After that, they went first to Hillside, Rottingdean, and next to The Wharf, Sutton Courtney, finishing up with six years at 1 All Souls Place, which Herbert thought hideous and only to be endured if hidden by splendid flowers, and a country residence, Glottenham House, Robertsbridge, Sussex. Herbert's sister Constance said that Maud got her own way in everything. This was certainly true where houses and their appurtenances were concerned, and it was probably true about all except the one thing for which she would have bartered every-thing else. She could no more help making scenes over her hus-band's infidelities than he could help avoiding the issue between them. Neither was peculiar in that respect, for most women pine for bondage, most men for vagabondage, and the two desires are irrreconcilable. He was exceptionally susceptible to female allure-ments, and in his case absence made the heart go wander. 'Falling in love is largely an affair of habit,' he said.

Inevitably their alienation resulted in charges of callousness on her part and rebuttals on his. Like so many husbands, he would not recognize his own conduct as a reasonable excuse for his wife's behaviour. Perhaps he did not see that her attitude resulted

Herbert Beerbohm when working in the City

Maud Tree (in the Nineties)

Genus Beerbohmiense, species Herbertica Arborealis, species Maximiliana.
Cartoon by Max Beerbohm of his brother and himself

Julius Beerbohm, father of Herbert Tree and Max Beerbohm

Tree as Svengali, His Majesty's Theatre

Tree as Malvolio in *Twelfth Night*. His Majesty's Theatre

The Forum, Rome

Antony's speech ('You all do know this mantle'). Tree's production of *Julius Caesar*. Her Majesty's Theatre, 1898

Tree as Richard II (Deposition scene)

The Man Who Was
Tree's production at His Majesty's Theatre, 1903

Tree as Fagin in *Oliver Twist*. His Majesty's Theatre, 1905

Caesar's House, Rome
Tree's production of *Antony and Cleopatra*. His Majesty's Theatre, 1906

The Market Place, Alexandria
Tree's production of *Antony and Cleopatra*. His Majesty's Theatre, 1906

Tree as Beethoven. His Majesty's Theatre, 1909

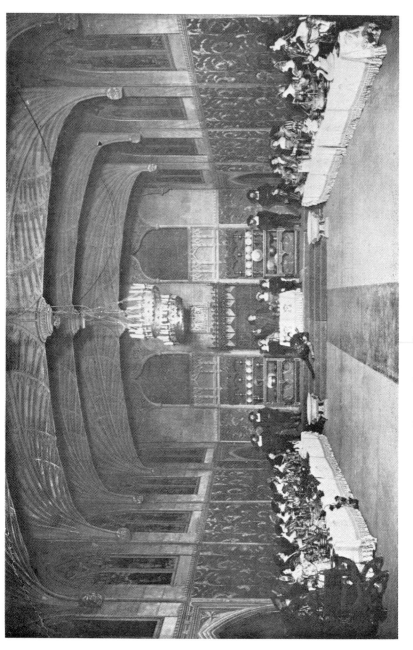

Banqueting Hall at Hampton Court
Tree's production of *Henry VIII* in New York, 1916

Colonel Newcome receives a kiss
Tree's production of *Colonel Newcome* in New York, 1917

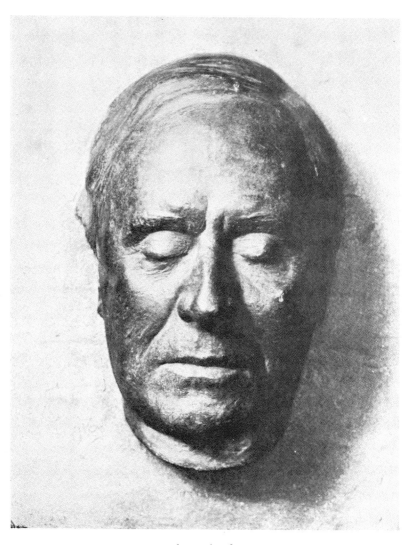

Death-Mask of Tree

directly from his, that whatever she did to vex him was done out of pique. He should have known that a woman of her character could hardly be expected, in the first uprush of wrath, to take his transgressions with indifference or toleration. She accused him of grudging her the happiness she could find in the company of others, and of criticizing her expenditure. He replied that he had denied her no extravagance and had wished her as much felicity as her nature would allow, but he did not think she had the judgment to perceive the difference between pleasure and happiness.

The most difficult period of their relationship occurred during the first two or three years of the century, when he felt that the less they saw of each other the better. Together they made each other miserable, for they were incapable of discussing their predicament with calmness. In the heat of the moment he said things which he quickly regretted, working himself up into a condition that made him harsh when he wished to be sympathetic. Her unhappiness distressed him, but the impossibility of easing the strain between them reduced him to a state of frenzy; and as they were all dependent on his ability to work, which he was incapable of doing in a constant fever of domestic broils, their temporary separation seemed advisable. Fortunately this wretched period of constraint between husband and wife did not endure.

When he could think more calmly he crystallized a life's experience of marriage, his own and other people's, in two sayings. The first: 'Which is the victim—he or she? She was, he is.' The second: 'Of all laws the marriage law is the most immoral (not excepting that relating to income tax), for it is productive of more subterfuge, lying and hypocrisy than any law that governs us.'

But he was very much of a family man with his children, to all of whom he was devoted. Viola, his first-born, was his favourite, but as Felicity and Iris grew up he became more and more fond of them. His arrival at their Chiswick home was always something of an event, and so a little awesome to the two younger ones, but he took part in their games and made them shriek with laughter over his imitations of a short-sighted man, a drunken man, a tired man, an absent-minded man. By that time Viola had grown up and was an actress in his company. His affection made him overrate her ability and placed her in the tricky position of an amateur playing leading parts in a professional company. He never criticized her, never advised her at rehearsals, but left her to the chance advent of inspiration. She wanted to be a singer, and experience as an actress gave her confidence. Her voice did not survive the ordeal of training; but while there was still hope he put on a scene for her benefit from *Hansel and Gretel* as a curtain-raiser, and when he produced Offenbach's *Orpheus in the Underworld* she had another opportunity. To oblige Florence O'Neil, who represented the Hearst papers in Paris, Tree cast O'Neil's girl-friend for a leading part in *Orpheus*. She was not good, and Viola was substituted, greatly to the annoyance of O'Neil, who watched the dress-rehearsal with Tree from the back of the circle. After Viola's first song O'Neil snapped: 'I don't think so much of your goddam daughter, Tree.' To which the latter soothingly returned: 'Mr O'Neil, neither you as a lover nor I as a father are unbiased judges.'

The period of strain between Herbert and Maud was made more bearable for her by the appearance of Viola as Ariel in *The Tempest*, by her own appearances as Agrippina in *Nero*, Mrs Mackenzie in *Colonel Newcome* and Paulina in *The Winter's Tale*, and by her husband's kindness in taking Wyndham's Theatre for a season in order that she might produce two plays there, unsuccessfully as it turned out. But the deep affection between them was manifested, suffering no further eclipse, when Maud's jaw was broken in a motor accident while out driving with Lewis Waller. She was in *The Winter's Tale* just then, and Herbert was on tour. His distress and sympathy were great, and he treated her with so much indulgence and gentleness that she began to take a philosophic view of his peccadilloes, regarding them light-heartedly as an unavoidable element of his nature. 'Poor dear Herbert!' she said to a friend: 'all his affairs start with a compliment and end with a confinement.' A man in his position received many compliments; and when, after his death, Maud described their life together, she restricted herself to such laudations. Wishing to interest Bernard Shaw in her account, she sent him a portion of it.

Between ourselves [wrote Shaw on January 9th, 1920], you are an incorrigible flatterer and a most frightful liar; but you play the widow so well that you play the lost one off the stage . . . Now if it had been me I should have blurted out everything—thus:

Nobody—no woman who reads this—can form the faintest notion of how awful a thing it is to be married to a man of genius, especially when you have twice his brains. You have to keep yourself sane, like Robinson Crusoe, by continually striking a balance between the good and evil in your lot, like this:

GOOD	EVIL
I am in the thick of everything. I know all sorts of interesting people, and am courted by them. I have the continually renewed excitement of great events like splendid productions, as if I were a queen with a coronation every three months. I am the happiest of women.	But I am married to Herbert; and Herbert is married to his theatre, to his destiny, to his work, and to everyone who plays on his feelings or on his vanity. Married to a Monster, and can't even have the Monster all to myself! I am the wretchedest of women.

How do you manage to convey all this whilst heaping flowers and wreaths on his cenotaph, and immolating yourself on his funeral pyre? ... You are a born comedian. I laugh when you cry: I laugh when you laugh: you cannot pen two lines without a delicate stroke of sincerity conveyed by an outrageous abuse of the most hyperbolical hypocrisy.

No doubt she was able to write in this fashion because the later years of their married life were much happier than the middle period. The shock of her accident, and the consequent loss of her good looks, restored their old relationship. 'Mother is so sweet and good to me', Herbert wrote to Viola from the Falmouth Hotel, Falmouth, on February 6th, 1908. 'I don't know what I should do without her, and she is a splendid nurse ... We do very little except wander along the sea front or into the town.' Henceforth she placed his interests before everything else, and no longer did she harbour resentment towards his natural sons. In 1911 she got Robert Hichens to offer his play The Garden of Allah to Herbert, at a time when Lewis Waller, acting the leading part in America, wished to produce it on his return to London; and the strength of their mutual affection was revealed in Waller's complaint to her that whenever the question of an advantage arose, either real or imaginary, she considered no one but her husband.

CHAPTER 16

Tolstoy, Dickens, Thackeray, Sheridan and Brieux

Although he kept an eye open for any modern work of fiction that could be satisfactorily adapted to the stage, Tree felt that only the great masters of the novel had provided characters and scenes almost as effective as those of Shakespeare, and some of his best work was done in dramas founded on the romances of Tolstoy, Dickens and Thackeray. He and his wife saw Henri Bataille's version of Tolstoy's *Resurrection* in Paris and at once arranged for it to be Englished, as Dr Johnson described the process, by Michael Morton. Tree used to say that 'within the rose of altruism there lurks the caterpillar of utilitarian sm', but in Tolstoy's story of atonement the caterpillar is effectually smothered by the rose and everything ends in a very moving and quite unnatural manner, the figures becoming transfigured. People love to indulge in vicarious expiation, and of course the play did well. All that need concern us here about the production in 1903 is a note in Tree's papers:

> The speech from *Resurrection*, which used to get a round of applause every night, I gave, and when the King was coming to the theatre I was warned by my energetic advisers that it would be better to omit it and be more tactful; but I thought if I did not make it I should be guilty of the very spirit that I was attacking, so I spoke it, and not without reprimand, which was conveyed to me.

From the Christlike hero of Tolstoy to the Hebraic villain of Dickens was the sort of transition that appealed to Tree. But just before putting on Comyns Carr's adaptation of *Oliver Twist*, he played a very different sort of Jew, Isidore Izard, in *Business is Business*, a play by Octave Mirbeau (*Les Affaires sont les Affaires*) first acted by Coquelin. Tree's performance was a wonderfully built-up caricature of a type of financier personified in those days by Barney Barnato, the famous dealer in South African diamonds, whose vast undertakings were eventually amalgamated with De Beers. The satire was a little too near the knuckle to fill the stalls, the patrons of which far preferred the dirty old Jew, Fagin, whom Tree next presented for their edification and who was like no one they might be asked to meet at a Buckingham Palace garden-party. To vary Pope's famous ejaculation, this was the Jew that Dickens drew, with something new: an uncannily clever portrait, softly diabolical, slyly humorous, subtly oleaginous. When he crushed an imaginary beetle, one could almost hear the crackle; when he shooed away a rat, the squeak and scamper of the vermin seemed audible. A hundred well-observed and telling touches, the wheezy laugh, the asthmatic cough, the whine, the sudden spurts of feline venom, made the disreputable creature both fascinating and horrifying. Incidentally, the line that got the biggest laugh in the play was a 'gag' which Tree introduced at one performance, getting such a roar of delight that he kept it in. Overhearing Mr Brownlow refer to Fagin as 'this old Jew', he turned to the Artful Dodger and said with indignant amazement 'D'ye 'ear that? 'E called me a *Jew!*' His was a hauntingly macabre, spicily comical performance; and though Lyn Harding as Bill Sikes and Constance Collier as Nancy were superb, it was Tree's Fagin that filled the theatre for over three months in the autumn of 1905. Or rather two theatres, for late one afternoon a dangerous fissure in the proscenium arch of His Majesty's was discovered.

I only learned this on arriving at the theatre to dress for Fagin [wrote Tree in one of his notebooks]. It was at the beginning of the run; and feeling it is always well to make capital out of one's misfortunes, I at once determined that we should open on the following night at another theatre. Such a dramatic coup, I felt, would save the situation and turn the sow's ear of misfortune into the silk purse of opportunity. I sent out to six different theatres. Among these I secured the Waldorf [now the Strand], where we opened. I announced the fact to the audience, saying, 'Just above the place where I stand there is a crack in the wall of the proscenium which is a source of danger', and I stated that we should open at the Waldorf Theatre the following night. We opened to a tremendous house and ran continually there for some weeks, until I returned to His Majesty's.

In most tragedies [continues the note] a humorous incident will intrude itself. I remember that while I was writing my speech to be delivered to the audience, under great stress, a card was brought up —the Rev. So-and-so. He was a friend of Hugh Chapman, who, in the West End of London, had a 'Home for inebriate clergy'. I said I would see him, being a friend of Chapman's. The young gentleman lurched or lilted into my room and I said, 'Can I do anything for you? Would you like a whisky and soda?' He replied, 'ThatswhatIhavecomefor.' I asked him whether he was undergoing the normal treatment. He said that was his case. I asked him, 'Is it successful?' He began 'P', when the effort of the consonant caused him to hiccup, and with great presence of mind he continued, 'arshily.' In order to proceed with my writing I introduced him to Comyns Carr, who was in my room at the time. Addressing him, he said, 'Do I understand, brother, that you too are addicted to the drink habit?' To which Carr replied, 'Alas, only intermittently.' He was a very charming young man and I believe he has done quite well since.

Tree's next Dickensian venture was a failure. Comyns Carr's version of *The Mystery of Edwin Drood* ran for a month at the beginning of 1908. 'We only do really well what we can't help doing,' said Tree, but if he could not help doing *Edwin Drood* he should have done better in the part of John Jasper. Obviously his ambition was to startle London in the way that Irving had stormed the town in *The Bells*, and he thought there was a chance in Jasper's dream. But it did not come off, because his was a delicate not a mesmeric art, and a scene that is meant to be thrilling appears absurd when it fails to thrill. What he could do really well was shown in a quiet scene with the solicitor, when he held the house by the watchful expression on his face, timing the drop of a handkerchief so perfectly that it revealed his criminality, and the silent action produced a sound of suppressed excitement from the audience.

Everyone prophesied failure for Tree's third Dickensian production, because he took the grave risk of presenting Louis N. Parker's adaptation of *David Copperfield* at the commencement of the 1914–18 war. The condition of the legitimate stage was such that he asked the leading actors to play for half-salaries, so that he could keep the theatre open. They agreed; but the moment it became clear that the show would thrive, they were all paid the remaining half of their salaries from the opening date. The play ran from December, 1914, till April, 1915, Tree doubling the parts of Micawber and Peggotty. The element of caricature in Micawber suited the tendency towards caricature in Tree, while the pathos of Peggotty brought out the emotional sensitiveness that was too often hidden under Tree's more exhibitory qualities.

But one of the oddest things about his acting was that two of his greatest triumphs were in characters of such dissimilarity that the whole of literature could not supply so antipodean a contrast. Within six months of making playgoers shiver over his grisly Fagin he was making them sob over his charming Colonel Newcome. Perhaps he never quite recaptured the pathos and beauty of his first-night performance, but this was partly due to the fact that the circumstances of his initial appearance could not be repeated. Shortly after the public announcement that he would produce Michael Morton's dramatization of Thackeray's novel *The Newcomes*, an article appeared in Lord Northcliffe's paper *The Daily Mail* with these words splashed across the page as a heading: 'Should Mr Tree be allowed to play Colonel Newcome?' Boiled down to a sentence, the writer said that an actor whose guttural accent had become intensified by playing such characters as Svengali and Fagin should not be permitted to appear as the *beau idéal* of an English gentleman and to murmur that heart-searching last word *Adsum*. Tree made a private record of the incident:

> The article was a somewhat brilliant attack. On the first night the play was a huge success, a success which was greatly enhanced by the discussion that had taken place, although it had the effect of hindering the box-office receipts before the play was produced. The enthusiasm at the end of the performance was very great on the first night, and I was called upon to make a speech. I refrained from doing so, only saying 'Ladies and Gentlemen, I think we win.' Meeting Northcliffe some time after at the Beefsteak Club, he said, 'By the bye, where is His Majesty's Theatre?' To which I replied, 'Oh, within a stone's throw of the *Daily Mail*.' However, there was no resentment in our conversation and he subsequently came round to the theatre and sat in the wings to witness my performance of Fagin in a revival of *Oliver Twist*.

Another of his notes shows him as the observant actor who profits from incidents in real life:

> At Lady Burdett-Coutts' at dinner I met old admiral Sir Harry Keppel. After dinner Lady Burdett-Coutts remained behind, and

as the others were going said to me, 'I am just going to look after the admiral, he is very tottery.' The admiral said to me, 'I will be back in a moment, I am just going to look after the baroness, she is a trifle infirm,' and they went out supporting each other. I introduced this situation in *Colonel Newcome* when I went out with the old lady.

Tree proved in this performance that, like Bottom, he could 'roar you as gently as any sucking dove . . . an 'twere any nightingale'. The tender softly-spoken old Colonel was quite as convincing as the harshly guttural Svengali or the alternately rasping and greasy Fagin. In classical work his voice was more in tune with Sheridan than with Shakespeare; he could manage the exquisite finish of Mozart, not the thunderous rhythms of Beethoven; and when in 1909 he produced *The School for Scandal*, surrounding himself with a galaxy of 'stars', he shone as brightly as any of them in the part of Sir Peter Teazle. The play can never have been so handsomely produced, nor on the whole much better acted, throughout its stage-history. Tree suffered two keen disappointments at the outset. He wanted Irene Vanbrugh for Lady Teazle and Seymour Hicks for Charles Surface, but they were engaged elsewhere. However, Marie Lohr was an attractive Lady Teazle and Robert Loraine a sprightly Charles; four actors of the old school, Henry Neville (Sir Oliver), Edward Terry (Crabtree), Hermann Vezin (Rowley) and Lionel Brough (Moses), could not have been bettered; James Hearn (Snake), H. V. Esmond (Backbite) and Basil Gill (Joseph) were worthy followers of that school; Ellis Jeffreys as Lady Sneerwell created a figure of exquisite artifice; while Godfrey Tearle gave significance to the relatively inconspicuous part of Trip. As with many of Tree's productions, the dresses, furniture and scenery were designed and executed by Percy Macquoid, who had done his work so well that Sheridan would have felt at home on the stage of His Majesty's Theatre.

After the first performance Tree gave a supper-party in the dome, and his confidential jottings afford what used to be called a sidelight on history:

One of my guests was Lloyd George, another Winston Churchill, between whom I sat. Lloyd George said, 'That is a very interesting phrase—"Many a poor wretch has sat on a hurdle who has done less mischief." ' I turned to Winston Churchill, who was at that time supposed to be somewhat vacillating in his political convictions, and asked, 'What is the difference between riding on a hurdle and sitting on a fence?' to which he promptly replied, 'The one is the road to ruin of the eighteenth century and the other is the road to fortune of the twentieth century.'

In spite of the huge expenses involved, *The School for Scandal* paid its way and would have yielded a handsome profit if Tree had not taken it off and finished the season with a Shakespeare Festival, since he wished to be acting in Shakespeare when his knighthood was publicly announced.

Relishing nothing so much as a striking disparity, his next production was *False Gods*, a translation by James B. Fagan of *La Foi* by Eugène Brieux, then the most discussed dramatist in France, whose play *Les Avariés* (*Damaged Goods* in English) provoked a hurricane of controversy because it dealt with the dangers of syphilis. Tree contented himself with the small part of the High Priest in *False Gods*, leaving the acting honours to Henry Ainley and Mrs Patrick Campbell, who in her memoirs said that she was 'curiously uncomfortable in my work in this theatre: a disturbing mixture of domesticity and art, of Society and Bohemia, of conventionality and vagary, irritated me'. Put in another way, Tree's habit of letting the acting look after itself, and leaving rehearsals at a moment's notice if anyone popped in to have a talk with him, got on the nerves of his leading lady, who would have preferred him to take some notice of her performance instead of amusing himself with quips; as when an actress in the cast spoke of the 'glorious skay' and Tree exclaimed: 'Oh my God! Remember you're in Egypt. The *skay* is only seen in Kensington.'

He was not the only person to supply entertainment at these rehearsals. The music was provided by Camille Saint-Saëns, who supervised the rendering. Tree's German conductor, Adolphe Schmidt, was not in harmony with the famous French composer, and at intervals they spluttered incoherently at each other while Tree stifled his laughter with the aid of a pocket handkerchief. The climax came one day when both Frenchman and German were more than usually inarticulate. Saint-Saëns rushed on to the stage, and, spreading out his hands in an agony of expostulation, hissed at Schmidt:

'Ze flutes! Ze flutes is too loud!'

The conductor glared back at him, and, doing his utmost to suppress the scream of rage that was almost choking him, spoke slowly through clenched teeth:

' 'Ow shall flutes play more softly as dey can?'

To which the distinguished Frenchman frenziedly proclaimed:

'But zey *do*!'

The rehearsal was suspended.

Eugène Brieux was even less pleased with the proceedings than Mrs Patrick Campbell, Camille Saint-Saëns and Adolphe Schmidt. Tree had staged an elaborate interior scene instead of the intimate one required by Brieux, who was so angry that he did not turn up at the supper-party arranged for him in the dome. Fortunately Frederick Whelen, who was Tree's reader of plays, knew where Brieux had probably gone, ran him down at Oddenino's, where he was discovered just inside the entrance-door, and enticed him back to the theatre. Tree also gave a big dinner to Brieux, so that he could meet his English fellow-authors. At this function Whelen found himself sitting next to Madame Brieux, who was stone-deaf and had a box into which Whelen had to speak loudly in French. He soon observed the entire table listening to his remarks with interest. Feeling self-conscious, he turned to his left-hand neighbour, Mrs Hecht, and spoke to her. She lifted an ear-trumpet. For the rest of the meal he was compelled to shout his remarks in English to Mrs Hecht and to bawl them in French to Madame Brieux. Noticing that Tree was enjoying his predicament, he could not doubt that it was one of that humorist's practical jokes.

At about this period the subject of a National Memorial Theatre cropped up, and Tree, who had done the work of one, spoke in favour of it, hoping to 'capture the machine', as he called it; in other words, to see that the committee appointed to manage its policy should be influenced by actors, not theorists; in different words, to make sure that he was consulted over every important question, since he had done more practical service for Shakespeare than all the scholars, all the critics, all the commentators in the kingdom put together. He did not say all this, except perhaps to himself. Suddenly it began to dawn on him that another Richard had entered the field, and furthermore one who combined practical experience of the theatre with a scholarly attitude to Shakespeare's text, and who therefore might unite the two points of view, those of the actor and the professor, and capture the machine by his dual ability. Up to this time Granville Barker had been chiefly associated with modern work, especially as an actor in Shaw's comedies, but in 1912 he obtained the financial support of Lord Howard de Walden to produce Shakespeare's plays in a modernistic style, the simple scenic effects and rapid enunciation of the actors making it possible to perform them in their entirety, Barker having learnt much about stage décor from Gordon Craig and Max Reinhardt and a lot about production from William Poel.

Here was a dangerous competitor in a region where Tree had reigned without a rival for fourteen years. He brooded on the matter intensively throughout the year 1912, and two of his comments appear in letters to Maud from Marienbad in July. The spring season at His Majesty's, just concluded, had not been prosperous, and in the autumn he intended to tour the music halls in *The Man Who Was*, after producing at his own theatre *Drake*, a patriotic play by Louis N. Parker, with Lyn Harding in the leading part. Later he hoped to visit North and South America, and possibly Australia, returning with enough money to continue his Shakespearean work in London. 'As to Barker's season at the Savoy,' he wrote, 'it is of course an attempt to seize the Shakespeare machine, and I am afraid that some of our friends on the National Theatre scheme are behind him.' He returned to the subject in another letter:

> I think that Barker is probably being backed up by some of the Shakespeare Committee, who are naturally jealous of the national work I have done.—But I will have no nonsense and shall cut myself adrift from them publicly and start the thing myself if I find any knavish tricks.—I have behaved most loyally to them throughout.

We may suppose from this that he intended to found a National Theatre at His Majesty's if the Shakespeare Committee became pro-Barker, and, as we shall hear in the next chapter, he was already gaining the collaboration of the other actor-managers.

Drake hit the patriotic mood of the hour and did enormous business, which made him drop his plan of visiting America and concentrate on future plans for His Majesty's. While acting in the provincial music halls that autumn, he gave the benefit of his meditations on sundry matters to his daughter, who was about to make her début in opera at Genoa and who had written disparagingly of his appearance on the Variety stage:

> Midland Adelphi Hotel
> Liverpool
> 4 Oct. 1912

Darling Viola

First as to your last.—You know I think as you do about most things—I mean my *instincts* jump with yours.—But there is another side to this music-hall question. Firstly, a music-hall is now a theatre, and by my present tour I shall have reached a vast number of the masses (32,000 in Glasgow alone) with whom I shall henceforth be a household-word: that is something—and it is *the people* that I want to get at—for they most want me—I mean, one does good to them —whereas one is a mere entertainment to most of our fashionables. —Then it would have been terrible to have gone bankrupt—and there is my duty to you all—so don't despise the humble means.— Some day I should like to take Shakespeare to these places—having no other entertainment on the same night—and cheap prices.— That would be a fine thing to do.—Had I known *Drake* was going to be such a success I would not have gone . . . Of course, *Drake* was a splendid thing to do—and it has stirred up the national spirit more than a thousand leading articles or speeches could.

You must tell me how money affairs are going.—I quite understand all the preliminary expenses which are necessary to the proper 'launching' of you.

As to the pretentious Barker business, I think for once humbug has o'erleapt itself and fallen on the other side.—Craig is really not much better—his talk is wonderful—a vast volume of verbal *blubber* —but believe me, little else, for I have listened to him with patient wonder and fatigue—all they can do is summed up in a single copy of 'Jugend'.—I hope to give them a taste of this quality in the Spanish play if I have the energy to do it—and we will have fun.— Bakst is very amusing—even amazing—but he is not the last word in art—only the latest!—My *Hamlet* and *Macbeth* were far simpler than any of their productions. But most of the Shakespeare plays are entirely unsuited to the impressionistic treatment—How, for instance, could they do *Julius Caesar* in this fashion?—The play would lose its reality—its direct appeal—the forum is the forum, a structure, just as Caesar is Caesar, a man.—What one wants is sincerity, directness and a reverence for Shakespeare. Craig *says* Craig is the most important thing!

No, as I remarked before, it is easy to be a genius until one does something—for to be understood is to be found out.—No, darling, throw away the worser part of post-impressionism and rest content with the eternal.—(Poor Poel—an absolute crank—and an unsuccessful crank to boot.)—I'll write you another letter about your other letter.

Your loving
Daddy

The slight misunderstanding between Tree and Barker was soon removed by the stupidity of the Shakespeare Committee, which put both their backs up and goaded them to common action. 'But what are the hopes of man?' as Dr Johnson sighed. By the end of the 1914–18 war Tree was dead, Barker had deserted the stage for a life of ease, and the Committee had dissolved into its component parts; later to be reassembled, for it is the nature of committees to go on sitting.

CHAPTER 17

The Ways of Glory

In a manner Tree's catholicity of taste and versatility of accomplishment told against him. His energies were distributed instead of being canalized, and what he gained in sympathy he lost in intensity. He was a good draughtsman, a competent speaker, a fair linguist, an agreeable writer, a humorous talker, an inspired if erratic actor and producer. His all-round ability, while lessening the force of his acting, increased its range, and no actor-manager has produced such a wide variety of plays.

His enjoyment of a good melodrama resulted in a five-months' run of David Belasco's *The Darling of the Gods* (1904), which dealt with love and honour among the Samurai in ancient Japan. It was lively twaddle, giving Tree the sinister part of Zakkuri, an atrocious villain with charming manners, played so effectively that audiences became more interested in his stratagems than in the love-story. The scenery was notably beautiful, each tableau, said William Archer, 'like a vivid Japanese print endowed with motion'. In fact, the first-night audience was so determined to applaud the settings that when Tree began a speech they showed no inclination to hear it. 'I want to apologize,' he shouted above the din. Silence restored, he discharged the following: 'I said the other day that one fool makes more noise than a thousand wise men. I apologize.' At the close of that season, and of several subsequent ones, he did something that no one but himself would have dared, devoting an evening to a single scene from each of four plays produced or revived during the previous twelve months. After such a *tour de force* no one denied his astonishing versatility, though he did not escape the charge of showmanship. 'The man is . . . hm . . . a mummer,' Irving was heard to say. Tree would not have denied it. He was.

He delighted in romantic comedy as whole-heartedly as he revelled in Machiavellian villainy, and another of his enjoyable impersonations was Paragot in W. J. Locke's *The Beloved Vaga-bond* (1908). Perhaps his Paragot was rather like a bourgeois Svengali out for a spree, but the gaiety was not forced and the Vagabond deserved his appellation. It is surprising that Tree should have refused Barrie's *Peter Pan* and Maeterlinck's *The Blue Bird*, both of which were launched with immense *éclat* by other managers. He would have been excellent as Captain Hook in the former, but after Barrie had read the first two acts of the play he decided that the author had gone mad and begged him to stop. Asked by the present writer why he had rejected it, he replied mysteriously: 'God knows, and I have promised to tell no one else.' But he was in good company. Shaw could not endure the play, and Anthony Hope neatly voiced the opinion of the in-telligent minority on this tearful children's romp: 'Oh for an hour of Herod!' Tree's contribution to the Christmas demand for youthful entertainment was Graham Robertson's *Pinkie and the Fairies* (1908–9), in which Ellen Terry played Aunt Imogen ('I do like Tree, he *does* things,' she wrote to the author), and for which Frederic Norton, whose tunes in *Chu Chin Chou* were later to be whistled on every battle-front, wrote the music.

Before we move on to what was his greatest achievement on the stage, the institution of an annual Shakespeare Festival, men-tion must be made of Tree's interest in music, an integral part of all his work. Raymond Roze and Coleridge Taylor composed a good deal of excellent music for his Shakespearean productions; Arthur Sullivan, Edward German, Paul Reubens and others con-tributed many charming things; and the interludes between the acts were so admirable that Edward Elgar declared he was never compelled to take refuge in the bar, a necessary move in other theatres. Ethel Smyth produced her opera *The Wreckers* at His Majesty's. Thomas Beecham had a season there. And in 1913 Strauss's *Ariadne in Naxos* was sandwiched into *The Perfect Gentle-man*, an English version of Molière's *Le Bourgeois Gentilhomme* by W. Somerset Maugham, who writes:

Tree had asked me to put the translation into modern English, which I did, and both he and I were rather violently attacked in conse-quence. If Tree hadn't wanted this, he could have used the very good eighteenth-century translation. Mine was never published, and has long since been lost sight of. I used to see a good deal of Tree, either at the Garrick or at my own house. He used to come to dine from time to time, and was always very good company.

Somerset Maugham was unaware that the leading part in his play *Jack Straw* had been offered to Tree, who refused it because Comyns Carr said he would lose prestige if he played at the Comedy Theatre. But Carr wanted him for Mephistopheles in the Phillips–Carr version of *Faust*.

Tree's enthusiasm for music caused him to produce *Beethoven* by Réné Fauchois, adapted by Louis N. Parker, in 1909. He knew it could not succeed because several rows of stalls had to make way for an augmented orchestra, but the play had some merit and the part gave him an opportunity to disclose a quality in his acting seldom seen at His Majesty's, that house being unsuitable for such refined and perceptive touches. One incident which those who saw the play would always remember as more vivid than reality was that in which Beethoven, while conducting his quartet, became aware of his oncoming deafness. Only an actor of Tree's faculty for spontaneous inspiration could have brought out the poignancy of such a moment. He was excellent throughout, both as the gruff and the tender Beethoven, but in this scene he was great, producing in his own evanescent medium the same emotion conveyed by the composer in the *cavatina* of his B flat major quartet. Tree had no technical knowledge of music, but a deep feeling for it. At the annual dinner of the Guildhall School of Music, when Herbert and Maud were guests of honour, Landon Ronald informed the company that he had taught Tree how to hold the baton in *Beethoven* and *Trilby*, 'the result being that in the latter the audience had the happiness of seeing Trilby singing six-eight time while Sir Herbert was beating four to a bar'. In reply Tree said that if, for purposes of his own, he did beat four to a bar, whatever that might mean, he begged them to believe that it was due to his conception of the character, not to any base ignorance, for, after all, he had played the piano as Svengali—at least, he should have admitted, his 'ghost' had.

Though he did not believe that any art could be taught, he was in favour of training, and offered the coming generation of actors a chance he had missed by founding in 1904 the Academy of Dramatic Art, wherein elocution, dancing, fencing and some knowledge of periods could be imparted. He took and furnished a couple of houses in Gower Street, started a school, appointed an administrator, lent his theatre for public performances by the students, tendered his advice whenever asked, and gave jobs to the more promising pupils. Since then many of the best actors and actresses on the stage have passed through the Academy, which has had 'Royal' tacked on to its title.

Having established his Academy, Tree demonstrated that nothing is impossible in the theatre by initiating an annual Shakespeare Festival at His Majesty's in 1905. Even now, or more especially now, it seems a miraculous achievement. He gave six plays in six days, each revived with the detail and sumptuosity of the original production. It meant of course rehearsals by day and by night for several weeks, and the strain was terrific on the actors, the scene-shifters, the lighting experts, and everyone concerned, especially the stage-manager, Cecil King, whose almost superhuman efforts were chiefly responsible for the smoothly running performances. It may safely be said that, in the matter of play-production, Cecil King was not only Tree's right hand but very often his left hand as well. Without him the Festivals would have been impossible. But Tree had the genius of extracting whole-hearted service from others and the instinct of perceiving efficiency.

These six-day Festivals, unique in theatrical annals, were repeated in 1906, 1907 and 1908, increased to a fortnight in 1909, a month in 1910, and three months in 1911, other actor-managers being brought in to exhibit their productions, F. R. Benson, Arthur Bourchier, H. B. Irving, Oscar Asche, Lewis Waller, as well as William Poel's Elizabethan Stage Society and Herbert Trench's company from the Haymarket Theatre. The Festivals were continued in 1912 and 1913, and throughout all these years occasional revivals and new productions of Shakespeare's plays were seen at His Majesty's. In short, Tree had already started a National Theatre and had obtained the support of his fellow-managers for an undertaking that was more imposing than that of any continental State Theatre in existence. F. R. Benson's excellent Shakespearean work in the provinces was not on the scale of Tree's ambitious enterprise; but its value was great, and the other managers visited Stratford-on-Avon to appear in Benson's annual season there. Tree went down to play Hamlet, and was met at the station by Mrs Benson. As they drove through the streets he seemed impressed by the gay decorations. 'Is all this kind thought for me?' he asked.

In April, 1907, at the desire of the Kaiser, Tree and his company acted for a week at the Royal Opera House, Berlin. The *pièce de résistance* was *Antony and Cleopatra*, the run of which had just finished at His Majesty's, the other plays being *Richard II, Hamlet, Twelfth Night, The Merry Wives of Windsor* and *Trilby*. The company travelled from the Hook of Holland to Berlin and back in the Kaiser's private train, and were entertained by Reinhardt and others during their stay. But the administrators of the Opera House were envious of the interest aroused by the visit and put as many obstacles in the way as possible, ably assisted by the stage-hands. Tree opened with a gala performance of *Antony and Cleopatra*. The German Emperor and his family were present and the theatre was packed with Court and military notabilities. Some difficulty was experienced in setting the first scene, but after the curtain had gone up the stage-hands walked out and no more scenery could be discovered, so the play had to start and finish on the quayside at Alexandria. The rest of the scenery was eventually found stacked behind trees in the garden. This state of affairs continued throughout the week. Properties were missing when needed; Yorick's skull was smashed; no 'supers' were available, the soldiers who had volunteered for 'crowd' work having been ordered back to Potsdam at the request of the administrators. The students in front, taught to believe that Shakespeare could only be understood in Germany, made unsympathetic noises; and the critics, convinced that Shakespeare as well as God were of German extraction but forgetting that Tree was too, did their best to crab the performances. The general public were enthusiastic, and once, after Tree had made a speech from the stage at the conclusion of the play and was in the Imperial box, the audience went on applauding for twenty minutes. 'You must address them again,' said the Crown Prince. He did so from the front of the box. The Kaiser conferred an order upon him, and the experiment was hailed in the English papers as another step in the promotion of cordial relations between the two countries.

By this time his many admirers and well-wishers were wondering why Tree had received no honour from his own monarch. After all, he had appeared as Nero in Madame Tussaud's waxworks; his three seniors, Squire Bancroft, Charles Wyndham and John Hare, had been knighted, and none of them could boast of such a record of artistic achievement as his. Maud had not been idle. In 1902 she tried to get the Lord Chamberlain, Clarendon, to obtain a knighthood for her husband, and in 1905 she asked her friend the Duchess of Rutland to use her influence in the same direction. In 1908 the famous editor W. T. Stead wrote to intimate his disappointment that the actor's name was not in the list of Birthday Honours and to ask whether there had been a hitch somewhere. Tree himself was probably ignorant of his wife's endeavours, and, not being a time-server, had never acted in accordance with his epigram: 'In order to get on one must stoop to flattery; one must learn to walk backward in order to get forward.' All the same, he did not underestimate the value of an official honour in his profession. A stage knighthood in those days was a hall-mark of distinction: it has become a trade-mark of success. Tree had attained the highest distinction as an artist, and after his friend Asquith became Prime Minister in 1908, his name appeared among the Birthday Honours in 1909. On the evening of the public announcement he acted Malvolio in *Twelfth Night*, and when he uttered the famous line 'Some achieve greatness' the performance was delayed for a considerable period while the house roared and applauded. He would not have been Tree if he had failed to get considerable comedy out of his next line, 'Some have greatness thrust upon them', and the house was equal to the occasion. In his speech at the end he expressed his pleasure that 'this honour to our art has come at a time when Shakespeare is being honoured here', but an unfriendly critic might have remarked that the Shakespeare Festival had been delayed, and the play carefully picked, to provide this happy coincidence.

The day after the publication of the Birthday Honours an old friend of Maud's told Max Beerbohm that she wanted to write her congratulations but was not sure whether, before the accolade,

the envelope ought to be addressed to Mrs Tree or Lady Tree.
'Oh, well,' said Max, 'I think there would be no harm in writing
"Lady". I'm sure that in the eyes of Heaven my brother is already
a Knight.' This is the authorized version of a much-misquoted
witticism. Arthur Pinero, who received the honour at the same
time, whispered to Tree just before the ceremony: 'Do you not
think we might have this done under gas?'

Tree was at Marienbad that summer, and heard from Viola,
who was staying with the Asquiths, that Maud had conceived the
idea of suggesting a peerage for her husband. A political crisis had
arisen as a result of the rejection of the budget by the House of
Lords, and Asquith intended to advise the King to create a lot of
new peers in order to facilitate business in the Upper House.
Eventually the power of the Lords was curtailed by a Parliament
Act which was passed by the peers under threat of these new
creations. But in 1909 there was still a hope that the difficulty
could be met by compromise; and Tree, whose common sense
indicated that he was no politician, wrote to Maud:

> Do let Viola unfold to him [Asquith] my pet plan which others
> may have thought of—of abolishing the House of Lords as it is—
> and making it a House independent of party . . . their influence
> would of course be infinitely greater, and the country, a little awry
> with party politics, would have a steady confidence in them.—I
> am so glad by the by you listened to Viola's advice—it would be
> *awful* to press me forward in that connection.

There was a deep sympathy between himself and Viola, to
whom he once wrote: 'Be sweet, dearest Viola, during all the
years, as you have been to me during all the years that have
passed. Your fond Father. And do remember to spell holiday with
one "l"!' Her wedding to Alan Parsons at St Martin's-in-the-
Fields was a popular social event. The crowds at the church were
so great that the traffic had to be diverted. But even on such a
happy-sad day in his life Tree could not keep away from the
theatre, and as they drove to the church he asked his daughter if
she would mind stopping at His Majesty's on the way. The bride
sat in her veil and train outside the stage-door while he rushed in
to make certain that the building was still intact, and having satisfied himself rushed out again. He remained silent for the rest of

their journey until, just before arriving at the church, he asked, 'Do you like Alan, dear?' As she was on the point of marrying Alan, the question seemed belated.

But before this well-publicized private event, Tree paid his grandest and most prodigal tribute to Shakespeare in a superb representation of *Henry VIII*. At the end of the acting version containing his notes for the production he pencilled the words: 'And so the injustice of the world is once more triumphantly vindicated, royal adultery is blessed by the Court of Bishops, while minor poets sing in unison their blasphemous pæans. —The fool enters weeping, in black.' He toned this passage down in the brochure he wrote, *Henry VIII and his Court*, which was his most pleasing literary exercise and remains good reading. He noticed in the Prologue to the play that the performance had originally been completed 'richly in two short hours', and he decided that 'The play must be played swiftly—and the waits quite short.' But he paid more attention to the richness than the brevity, and illustrated the history

> With pomp and feast and revelry
> With mask and antique pageantry.

He used the music written for Irving's production by Edward German, who composed additional numbers for His Majesty's, including the anthem sung at the Coronation of Anne Boleyn. No expense was spared over the scenery, crowds, dances, costumes and cast. Arthur Bourchier, a fellow actor-manager, was engaged for the King and gave the best performance of his life; Violet Vanbrugh was the Queen; Henry Ainley the Buckingham; and the rest of the acting was worthy of a better play. Tree's Wolsey was on the whole his best bit of 'straight' work in Shakespeare. It lacked the inspired moments of his Richard II, but it was all through an impressive and dignified performance, and even his voice seemed to have dropped an octave. His Cardinal was not, like Irving's, a great prince of the Church; he was the butcher's son from Ipswich, coarse, cunning, ostentatious, arrogant, avaricious, unscrupulous, an astute politician, a greedy nest-featherer. His bright scarlet robes displayed his nature, just as the subdued tones of Irving's had revealed a different disposition.

Tree suffered from his generosity in offering the part of the King to Bourchier, who was a pushing, blustering, insensitive fellow, one who never considered the feelings of others but could be courteous and ingratiating where his own interests called for such qualities, browbeating the underdog, bowing to the upperdog. He was extremely conceited, and it is just possible that a remark of Tree's had been repeated to him. At some rehearsal a gas explosion in the street shook the theatre. 'Whatever was that?' cried a startled actress. 'It's all right, my child; it's only Bourchier's head, I think,' purred Tree. At any rate, unpleasant episodes were of frequent occurrence during the run of *Henry VIII*, and Douglas Jefferies recalls that he saw Tree weeping because Bourchier had said something blackguardly. 'I've never been spoken to like that before in my life,' he complained to Bourchier's wife, Violet Vanbrugh, who was doing her best to soothe him. At a grand banquet given to the company on the stage, in celebration of the 200th performance, Tree and Bourchier made speeches at each other's expense, which did not contribute to the general joy, though an eminent dramatic critic, A. B. Walkley, was observed to smile sardonically.

The rehearsals were as colourful as the scenery. For the first four weeks they were directed by Louis N. Parker, a gentle, friendly, but deaf pageant-master whose ear-trumpet formed part of his walking-stick. Chaos entered with Tree, everything having to be done again and done differently. Calling forth one of the dancers in the Hampton Court scene, Tree commanded, 'Show me the step.' Hoping he would die of heart-failure before the attempt, the novice timidly essayed the step. 'Oh, my God! that's so tuppenny tubey', said Tree, who then explained what was wanted: 'Ladies! this dance is La Volta. Leap, for God's sake, *leap*! Don't be so suburban. Show your knees!' Another time, at the conclusion of the Coronation scene, Tree climbed on a chair and told the company that Nat Goodwin had attributed his ruin to wine, women and song: 'I don't care what you do about the first two, but for God's sake *sing*!' He was as easily overcome by emotion as he was quick to criticize. When the company presented him with a gold plate, he wept profusely and unashamedly, which touched those who were not entrenched in British phlegm.

The production was what he described as 'an obstinate success', running for over seven months in 1910–11 and playing to excellent houses when it was taken off. He soon tired of his part and relieved his tedium in the Trial scene by trying to make the guards laugh, with so much success that after one performance he addressed them: 'You gentlemen in gold—if you must laugh in this scene—er—er—*wear beards.*' He once confessed that, though not always sensible, he was always serious—'that is why I laugh—it is part of my religion to endeavour not to be earnest.' His endeavour was invariably successful with the walkers-on at His Majesty's Theatre.

CHAPTER 18

Bernard Shaw

'I am sending a letter to Tree which will pull him together if it does not kill him,' wrote Shaw to Mrs Patrick Campbell on April 11th, 1914. That same evening the curtain rose for the first time on *Pygmalion* at His Majesty's Theatre, with Tree as Professor Higgins and Stella Patrick Campbell as Eliza Doolittle; and Shaw's letter was the last shot to be fired in the fierce battle of rehearsals.

As this was one of Tree's most notable ventures, and as it was Shaw's most successful comedy, the story of its origin and their relationship is of considerable interest. They had known each other for over twenty years, Tree's admiration for Shaw's wit being as great as Shaw's amazement at Tree's oddity. For the queer thing about Tree was that, though excessively sensitive, he never resented Shaw's criticisms and recognized his genius as a dramatist when all the other managers were convinced that his plays were unactable and all the other actors thought his characters were impossible. In April, 1903, before Shaw's reputation was established at the Court Theatre, the manager of His Majesty's wished to produce a play by him and suggested that he should write one on Don Quixote. It is interesting to read, in a memorandum made by Tree at that date, that he was also considering *Œdipus Rex*, *Peer Gynt*, *Crime and Punishment*, and a drama on Joan of Arc. He discussed the subject of Don Quixote with Shaw several times in the course of the next decade. Here is Shaw's version of their talks:

'What I see,' said Tree, 'is a room full of men in evening dress smoking. Somebody mentions the Don. They begin talking about him. They wonder what he would make of our modern civilization. The back wall vanishes; and there is Piccadilly, with all the buses and cabs coming towards you in a stream of traffic; and with them, in the middle, the long tall figure in armour on the lean horse, amazing, foreign, incongruous, and yet impressive, right in the centre of the picture.'

'That is really a very good idea,' Shaw would say. 'I must certainly carry it out. But how could we manage the buses and things?'

'Yes,' Tree continued, not listening after Shaw's first words of approval, 'there you see him going down the mountain-side in Spain just after dawn, through the mist, you know, on the horse, and——'

'And Calvert as Sancho Panza on the ass,' Shaw would interrupt.

'Yes . . . Sancho, of course . . . Oh, yes,' came slowly from Tree, who was always surprised at the suggestion; and then, quickly switching over to his Falstaff vein, he began to consider whether he could not double the two parts; for, as Shaw remarked, 'your true actor is still what he was in the days of Bottom: he wants to play every part in the comedy.'

Tree's report of what passed between them differed from this:

I asked Shaw for a play once, and he wrote back giving me a full list of other living dramatists and a summary of their good points. I had an idea—I haven't altogether abandoned it—that I should like to play Don Quixote. I should like to show him as the idealist who is always right and always apparently wrong with the smaller and more practical people round him. Your idealist, you know, is really your most practical man—born before his time. I talked it over with Shaw, and he suggested that Don Quixote should begin by riding down Piccadilly, followed by Sancho Panza. I am sure Shaw could make an excellent play of Don Quixote—only I tremble lest he should hoist me with his own petard by proving in the last act that Sancho Panza was the hero after all.

Nothing came of these talks, except that Shaw eventually wrote a play for Tree that was about as unlike Don Quixote as words could make it. Shaw had always regarded Tree as a tragic and refined actor of 'straight' parts, the 'straighter' the better, and considered his appearances in comic characters merely as an imposition of personality. It was a one-sided view, but he was quite right about the one side, which found ideal expression in Colonel Newcome, Beethoven and Gringoire. In order to display this aspect to the full, framing it in a gruffness which gave individuality to the part, Shaw wrote *The Showing-up of Blanco Posnet* in 1909 for Tree to perform at a Charity matinée. 'I am rather clever at fitting actors with parts—for example, Lady Cicely–Ellen Terry, Caesar–Forbes Robertson, etcetera,' said Shaw. 'I wrote a perfect triumph of this made-to-measure art for Tree in *Blanco Posnet*, and he was simply shocked by it, absolutely horrified. Naturally I laughed and said that in that case I had no use for him as an actor.' With some difficulty this biographer extracted accounts of their interchanges from the protagonists and put together a skeleton of their duologue, which must have been a considerable amplification of what is here set down:

Shaw: I wrote Blanco for you. It will fit you like a glove. You are the only living actor who would be perfect in the part.

Tree: I'd soon be a dead actor if I attempted it.

Shaw: Why?

Tree: The audience wouldn't swallow it.

Shaw: Nonsense! They'd eat it.

Tree: And then vomit it.

Shaw: And ask for more. You exaggerate the queasiness of their stomachs.

Tree: I know the queasiness of my own.

Shaw: What makes you feel sick?

Tree: Not exactly sick, but . . . well . . . shocked.

Shaw: What shocks you?

Tree: This about God. (*Reads*) 'He always has a trick up his sleeve. . . . He's a sly one. He's a mean one. He lies low for you. He plays cat and mouse with you.' That's . . . that's awful.

Shaw: God is not such a reality to you that you can speak and think of Him like that?

Tree: I've never thought of Him as someone you could slap on the back and call by nicknames.

Shaw: Then He's not real to you: He's a mere figure of the fancy.

Tree: Anyhow, I can't see myself saying those words.

Shaw: You needn't stand in front of a mirror.

Tree: A poor joke, but your own. I tell you what! If you cut that passage and one other——

Shaw: What other?

Tree: Well, this is a bit thick. (*Reads*) 'I accuse the fair Euphemia of immoral relations with every man in this town, including yourself, Sheriff.'

Shaw: What's wrong with that?

Tree: The stalls would rise in a body and walk out of the theatre.

Shaw: So much the worse for the stalls.

Tree: And for the manager.

Shaw: On the contrary, an excellent advertisement.

Tree: Not for *my* theatre.

Shaw: Then you must build another.

Tree: For *Blanco Posnet?*

Shaw: I can't think of a better reason.

Tree: Look here, if you'll cut that bit about God and that other bit about the prostitute, I'll consider the play.

Shaw: If you cut a single syllable of a single sentence, I shan't consider letting you play it.

Tree: I think you'll find in any case that the Censor won't pass those remarks.

Shaw: Try him and see.

Tree sent the play to the Censor's office, but failed to obtain the Lord Chamberlain's licence. Following its production in Dublin, *Blanco Posnet* was again submitted to the Lord Chamberlain, who granted a licence on condition that the passages about God were omitted in presentation, upon which Shaw commented: 'All the coarseness, the profligacy, the prostitution, the violence, the drinking-bar humour into which the light shines in the play are licensed, but the light itself is extinguished. I need hardly say that I have not availed myself of this licence, and do not intend to.' In the meantime Tree had been knighted, and Shaw wrote to *The Times* (June 26, 1909), heading his letter 'The Censor's Revenge':

A few weeks ago one of the most popular of London actors and managers was found guilty by the Lord Chamberlain of attempted blasphemy, and mulcted and suppressed accordingly. Today the King makes that manager a knight. But the Lord Chamberlain . . . has not taken the rebuke lying down. An hour after I read in *The Times* of Sir Herbert Beerbohm Tree's triumph the counterblow fell on me (the accomplice in Sir Herbert's blasphemy) in the shape of the Lord Chamberlain's refusal to licence my sketch entitled *Press Cuttings*, and announced by the Women's Suffrage Society for performances at the Court Theatre on July 9 and 12. It only remains for the King to make me a duke to complete the situation.

After what had passed between Shaw and himself, Tree considered the implication that he had been an accessory in the other's blasphemy unfair, and on the spur of the moment wrote to *The Times*:

I see you have thought fit to print a letter from Mr Bernard Shaw in which he states that the knighthood was conferred on me for a base reason. I should like to state that the honour was conferred on me for a yet baser reason than that imputed by Mr Bernard Shaw. I had threatened that, unless such a distinction were conferred upon

me, I would produce *Blanco Posnet*. Need I say that the honour was
at once extended to me?

But on reflection he tore the letter up and wrote a post card to
Shaw instead, adapting the well-known lines in 'The Ancient
Mariner'—'This was the worst that ever burst from that unsilent
Shaw.' At length the Lord Chamberlain's nerves, shattered by the
perusal of *Ghosts* by Ibsen and *Damaged Goods* by Brieux, rallied
under the repeated shocks of the modern drama, and licences were
granted for the public performances of *Mrs Warren's Profession*
and *Blanco Posnet* by Shaw.

In spite of their skirmishes in 1909, Tree still hankered after a
play by G. B. S., and four years after the fuss over *Blanco Posnet*
he heard from George Alexander that an undoubted 'winner' had
been written by Shaw for Mrs Patrick Campbell, which Alexander
himself would have produced if he had not made up his mind
never again to have that lady in his theatre. This was *Pygmalion*,
the main idea of which had first entered the author's head when
he saw Forbes–Robertson and Mrs Campbell acting together
some fifteen years before. By the time the play was written Stella
Patrick Campbell had become so difficult to work with that every
manager thought twice before casting her for a part, though all
of them knew that she was the only actress on the stage who
could carry a bad play to success on her own shoulders. Tree, like
Alexander, had found her impossible in the theatre, but, unlike
Alexander, he quickly forgot unpleasantness, and when she approached him about *Pygmalion* he immediately asked Shaw to let
him hear it. A reading took place in the dome of His Majesty's,
and Tree's mind was made up before the conclusion of the third
act. 'His admiration for you and the play is ENORMOUS', Mrs
Campbell wrote to Shaw.

Neither Tree nor Alexander would have thought any less of the
play if they had known that its theme had formed an episode in
Tobias Smollett's novel *Peregrine Pickle*. It seems that Shaw himself was unaware of this because when the resemblance was
pointed out he said: 'I read Smollett's novels in my youth and
didn't care for them, but it's quite possible that the incident in
Peregrine Pickle got lodged in my memory without my being
conscious of it and stayed there until I needed it. Like Shakespeare

and Molière, I take my good things where I find them, giving them a fresh setting, a shavian philosophy and a modern meaning. I believe it has been remarked before that there's nothing new under the sun, and I dare say that Smollett pinched this idea from someone else.' The memory of his boyhood must have been as remarkable as the genius of his manhood, for the story of his Eliza Doolittle follows that of Smollett's girl almost as closely as Shakespeare's Roman plays follow Plutarch. A summary of the adventure in *Peregrine Pickle* may not be out of place:

The hero, Peregrine, meets a beggar-woman and her sixteen-years-old daughter on the road. The latter is filthily clothed and talks the language of Billingsgate, but she has agreeable features, so Peregrine buys her for a small sum of money from the beggar-woman, or as Smollett puts it, 'purchased her property in the wench', and tries an experiment which he has long contemplated. He has noticed 'that the conversation of those who are dignified with the appellation of polite company is neither more edifying nor enter-taining than that which is met with among the lower classes of man-kind; and that the only essential difference, in point of demeanour, is the form of an education, which the meanest capacity can acquire, without much study or application. Possessed of this notion, he determined to take the young mendicant under his own tutorage and instruction. In consequence of which, he hoped he should, in a few weeks, be able to produce her in company, as an accomplished young lady of uncommon wit, and an excellent understanding.'

He takes the girl home, gets his man to give her a good washing, scrubbing and rinsing, has her hair cut, and clothes her decently. He then proceeds to cure her of swearing, his most difficult job, and in a few days is able to present her at the table of country squires, where she scarcely says a word but behaves well enough to provoke no comment. He makes her repeat sentences from Shakespeare, Otway and Pope, tells her the names of celebrated players which she can introduce casually into the conversation, and teaches her to play whist. After passing the test of meeting a company of her own sex, where her apt quotations give an impression of learning and taste, she goes to London, lives in private lodgings with a female at-tendant, is instructed in dancing and French, and attends plays and concerts several times a week. At a public assembly Peregrine dances with her among the gay ladies of fashion, and her air of rusticity is regarded by them as an agreeable wildness of spirit, superior to the forms of common breeding. Then she enters the most exclusive and elegant circles, 'and continued to make good pretensions to gentility, with great circumspection. But one evening, being at cards with a certain lady whom she detected in the very act of unfair conveyance, she taxed her roundly with the fraud, and brought upon herself such a torrent of sarcastic reproof as overbore all her maxims of caution, and burst open the floodgates of her own natural repartee, twanged off with the appellation of b—— and w——, which she repeated with great vehemence, in an attitude of manual defiance, to the terror of her antagonist and the astonishment of all present: Nay, to such an unguarded pitch was she provoked, that starting up, she snapt her fingers, in testimony of disdain, and, as she quitted the room, applied her hand to that part which was the last of her that disappeared, inviting the company to kiss it, by one of its coarsest denominations.'

Peregrine is a little disconcerted by this relapse, which excludes her from the social circles in which she has been moving; and as the aristocracy feel insulted because a common trull has been palmed off on them as a young lady of birth and education, he is forbidden their houses. He feels relieved when she runs off with his valet, and provides them with money to start a tavern.

It is hardly worth mentioning that Shaw's keen interest in the science of phonetics and his witty handling of the subject lift his play far above Smollett's humorously ribald story, just as Shakespeare's *Henry IV* is incomparably superior to Holinshed's chronicle.

Since Shaw's plays demand the technique of Shakespearean actors, there was much trouble at rehearsals, neither Tree nor Mrs Campbell having learnt it. 'There is no rose without a thorn, but I have known many a thorn without a rose,' Tree once said, and for several weeks Shaw was a roseless thorn in the side of the actor-manager. Apart from the difficulty of making Tree speak the lines as the author wished them to be spoken, Shaw found it almost impossible to get on with the job of producing because Tree was completely unbusinesslike, leaving a rehearsal without a word of explanation when someone wanted to see him and on his return expecting the rehearsal to continue from where he had left off. Also, to Shaw's dismay, no one appeared to have a defined position in the theatre. Tree was surrounded by a little crowd of satellites, none of whom seemed to have any business there but all of whom interfered in the production. Shaw therefore took matters into his own hands and meddled in every department, assuming that as anyone who happened to drop in contributed suggestions the best thing he could do was to issue commands. This he did with so much authority one morning that Tree ironically remarked that plays had actually been produced at His Majesty's before *Pygmalion*. Shaw replied that he could not understand how such a miracle had been performed without his assistance. To an ordered mind like his the utter lack of method at Tree's theatre had been inconceivable until he was compelled to face the reality, and he had to adapt his nature to the preposterous conditions. The Scotsman expresses his individuality by difference of opinion, the Englishman by indifference to any opinion, and the Irishman Shaw now expressed his by both in turn. He fought, gave way, fought again, gave way again, and at length achieved some sort of production 'in the face of an unresisting, amusing, friendly, but heart-breakingly obstructive principal'.

The scenes during rehearsals were quite awful. Shaw could not treat two such histrionic monsters as Tree and Mrs Campbell in the quiet, amiable, informal manner that got the best out of the actors under Granville Barker's management. Tree, with his odd combination of sympathy and thoughtlessness, did the most unpardonable things in complete innocence. 'I never could bring myself to hit him hard enough,' said Shaw, 'whereas no poker was thick enough, no brick heavy enough, to leave a bruise on Mrs Campbell.' Yet it should be recorded that he did address the manager, 'I say, Tree, must you be so treacly?' which convulsed the staff but induced symptoms of epilepsy in the victim. Sometimes a rehearsal was stopped while Tree recovered from a shavian comment. Sometimes Mrs Campbell refused to continue until the author left the theatre. On at least two occasions G. B. S. gathered his papers together with quiet dignity and departed. Once he retired from the stage and went to collect something he had left in the dress-circle, whence he heard Mrs Campbell speaking her lines. 'Accursed woman, can't you wait till I am out of earshot?' he called out. At a dress rehearsal he begged Tree to allow others some of the limelight which he had been enjoying for thirty years. 'I've stood your insults long enough: I'll have no more of them!' exploded Tree. 'Ah, now, don't lose your temper,' said Shaw coaxingly. 'If you could forget that you are Sir Herbert Beerbohm Tree for a moment and step into the part of

Professor Higgins, we'd get along splendidly.' During one of the author's temporary absences he wrote a long letter containing much advice on how the part of Higgins should be handled. Tree entered a reflection in his notebook: 'I will not go so far as to say that all people who write letters of more than eight pages are mad, but it is a curious fact that all madmen write letters of more than eight pages.'

Stella Campbell thought it splendid of Tree to accept with gentle indifference letters that would have made a Frenchman challenge Shaw to a duel; but the truth is that most of the agitation was due to her. 'Why do you always turn your back to me at this point?' Tree asked. 'But it's a very nice back, isn't it?' blandished Mrs Pat. A chuckle from Shaw did not mend matters, and there were moments when her behaviour drove Tree screaming from the stage. For days in succession the two were not on speaking terms and Frederick Whelen was the medium through whom they exchanged messages. Whelen read plays and ran the Afternoon Theatre, which put on 'uncommercial' plays at His Majesty's, and not once in ten years did he have a cross or heated word with Tree, whose strange lack of rancour was shown in Shaw's confession that on the two occasions when he left the theatre, only to return at the urgent request of the other actors, 'Tree took leave of me as if it had been very kind of me to look in as I was passing to see his rehearsals, and received me on my return as if it were still more friendly of me to come back and see how he was getting on.' When the play was ready for production, Tree and Mrs Campbell lunched at the Royal Automobile Club with Shaw, who suddenly staggered his guests by saying: 'Have you noticed that we three people, all of us with established reputations and even eminent ones, and all of us no longer young, have nevertheless been treating one another all through this business as beginners?' They had not noticed it, but it was so palpably true that they could not gainsay it. The effect of the rehearsals on Shaw became apparent to him when the proofs of several photographs, taken just after the first night, were submitted. 'I suppressed them because they made me look like an old dog who had been in a fight and got the worst of it. But I sent one to Stella with the words "Are you not ashamed?" and another to Tree saying "This is your work".'

The great sensation of the play on the first night was the phrase 'Not bloody likely!' The audience gasped, their intake of breath making a sound that could have been mistaken for a protracted hiss. This never happened again because all future audiences knew what was coming and roared with laughter. The expression was Shaw's nearest equivalent to the exit line of Smollett's girl in *Peregrine Pickle*, but even in that euphemistic form it shook the senior generation. One of them, Sydney Grundy, erupted in *The Daily Mail*, saying that, though there was no harm in Shaw's 'incarnadine adverb' when informed by genius, 'on his pen it is poison'. In Grundy's opinion, Shaw was imperilling the liberty of the English theatre, and he declared that public indignation was gathering over a deeply-resented outrage. Perhaps Grundy's attitude was due to the hatred of jumped-up genius usually felt by talent, or to the fact that, when a dramatic critic, Shaw had described one of Grundy's plays as 'a mere contrivance for filling a theatre bill, and not, I am bound to say, a very apt contrivance even at that,' and had called a Grundeian lecture on the sex question in another play 'the greatest nonsense possible'. Whatever the cause, Grundy was incapable of seeing that it would have been easier for any other playwright to touch a star by leaping into the air than to write *Pygmalion*. But he was not the only person to express the public indignation. On May 8th the Theatrical Managers Association wrote to inform Tree, its President, that a member had complained of 'Not bloody likely!' and that 'with a view to retaining the respect of the public for the theatre' they would be much obliged if he would have the objectionable words omitted, since they lowered the standard of the profession and might result in licences being refused to managers of theatres where the play was performed. Tree got Henry Dana to reply that he declined to accede to their suggestion and that the tone of their letter was wholly unjustifiable.

Public indignation manifested itself by packing the theatre at every performance and applauding the play with gusto. Shaw called it his *As You Like It*: that is, as the public liked it; and Tree netted £13,000 out of the London run. He could have made a great deal more. 'It is quite absurd that the notice should go up at the end of a £2,000 week,' Mrs Campbell complained to Shaw.

But Tree was bored with the show, wanted a holiday at Marien-bad, and brought down the final curtain towards the close of July. He was also irritated by Shaw's lack of interest in his performance. 'Tree has only one ambition in the world, that you should be pleased with his Higgins,' Mrs Campbell told Shaw. But the author had suffered enough during rehearsals and kept away from the theatre, though in response to Tree's reiterated requests he promised to witness the hundredth performance, adding that this was tantamount to not seeing it again. But he had to redeem his promise, and sat through the hundredth (and punitive) perform-ance. He found, scarcely to his surprise, that Tree had 'contributed to my second act a stroke of comic business so outrageously irrele-vant that I solemnly cursed the whole enterprise, and bade the delinquents farewell for ever'. He also found what he expected, that Tree, who loved romantic endings, had hit on the idea of throwing flowers to Eliza in the brief interval between the end of the play and the fall of the curtain, thus letting the audience know that a marriage would shortly take place between the professor and the flower-girl, which was in flagrant opposition to the author's conception of their characters and relationship.

In several letters that passed between them Shaw tried to make Tree aware of the error, and Tree tried to make Shaw aware of the box-office. 'My ending makes money; you ought to be grate-ful,' said Tree. 'Your ending is damnable: you ought to be shot,' replied Shaw. A few days before Tree's death, he and Shaw walked home together from a Council meeting at the Academy of Dramatic Art. Tree was as youthful, high-spirited and enthusiastic as ever, making Shaw feel hopelessly old and grumpy in com-parison; and oblivious of all the emotional disturbance and nerve-testing correspondence which had taken place during the pro-duction of *Pygmalion* only three years before, Tree spoke of an early revival in terms that suggested a happy renewal of the most delightful experience of their lives.

CHAPTER 19

Strange but True

Some men inspire anecdotes, because they so frequently say or do funny things that nearly every funny thing said or done by someone else is fathered on to them. Tree's often eccentric behaviour created more anecdotes than were attributed to anyone else of his time, and since his death his personality has given rise to a sort of comical apocrypha. It is the duty of his biographer to separate the wheat of fact from the chaff of fancy, and every anecdote recounted in this book is authentic, deriving from first-hand evidence. The many other stories that are still told of him are at best suspect, and most of them are sheer inventions, though their existence is a tribute to the astonishing nature of the man.

His own notebooks inform us that a gramophone company asked him for a testimonial, and he replied that he never gave testimonials to objects of merchandise. The company begged him to favour their special case, since his own voice had been reproduced by this means. So he wrote the following: 'Sirs, I have tested your machine. It adds a new terror to life and makes death a long-felt want.' He was asked to amend this, as the public might misconstrue it; but he answered that it was not open to misconstruction. 'The immortalism must stand,' said he; but it was not used as an advertisement by the company.

Occasionally a true story about Tree seems exaggerated beyond belief, of which this is a specimen, warranted by his secretary and stage-doorkeeper. One day he left the theatre eagerly scanning the morning's correspondence. Incidentally, several people who knew him well could never recall seeing him in the street unoccupied: he was always reading a letter or a book. On this occasion he entered a hansom-cab without a word and went on reading his letters until it drew up outside his house. Tree stepped out, knocked the door, and waited, still deep in his correspondence.

The door was opened by a servant. 'Come in,' said Tree, who then returned to his cab and was driven back to the theatre, where he dictated answers to his letters; after which the driver, familiar with his habits, drove him home again and waited for his reappearance. It was a sad day for London cabbies when Tree obtained a motor-car.

Other people were sometimes less pleased by his erratic conduct. A solitary feeder at the Carlton Restaurant was surprised when a waiter conveyed to him the compliments of Sir Herbert Tree coupled with the request that 'Mr Henry Arthur Jones' would kindly spare him a minute. The lonely gentleman may have felt flattered but had to admit that his name was not Jones. When Tree heard this, he said, 'Very funny, very funny indeed; he always did like his little joke. But this is important. Please tell Mr Jones that I should feel most grateful if he would behave seriously for once. I am very anxious to speak to him.' The waiter again addressed the putative Mr Jones, who said with some heat that he was not joking and that his name was Wagstaff. On hearing this Tree dismissed the waiter with a laugh, implying that Mr Jones was incorrigible. Mr Wagstaff finished his meal first, and stopping at Tree's table on his way out spoke severely: 'I don't see why you should insist on knowing me. Surely it was enough to point out your mistake once?' Tree was astounded. 'Do you mean to tell me quite seriously that you are not my old friend Henry Arthur Jones?' The other was annoyed. 'I do, sir!' he almost shouted. 'Then you were quite right to deny it,' mildly returned Tree as he continued his lunch. He was not unaware that this scene was witnessed, a few tables away, by the real Mr Henry Arthur Jones, who retailed it when in the humour.

Another incident has been frequently misreported. During the preliminary provincial run of *The Beloved Vagabond* the company were at Cardiff, where Tree, strolling with Frederick Whelen, entered a post office. After pondering for some moments, in an attempt to discover why he was there, he approached the counter and said to the man behind it, 'I hear you sell stamps.' 'We do.' 'May I see some?' 'You may.' Tree surveyed them carefully, then pointing to a stamp in the centre of the sheet said, 'I'll take that one.' This amused Whelen more than the post office official; but another absurdity got a laugh from the station booking-office clerk at Victoria. 'Give me some tickets, please,' said Tree, producing money. 'What station do you want?' 'What stations have you got?'

Naturally, the majority of stories about Tree are linked with the theatre. He was proud of everything that concerned His Majesty's, even the 'House Full' boards when he was not personally appearing. 'Isn't it wonderful for this time of year?' he exclaimed to the stage-manager of the Haymarket Theatre, Charles Latrobe, who pointed out that 'House Full' boards were also outside the theatre opposite. 'Ah, but not so many boards,' said Tree. An actor in his company reported that he had been to a matinée of *King Lear* at the Haymarket Theatre. 'Good house?' asked Tree. 'Pretty good, but there seemed to be a lot of paper.' On which Tree, in Falstaff's voice, quoted *The Merry Wives of Windsor*: 'I see. "The leer of invitation"!'

He was not always at ease with actors, possibly because he was a little afraid they were going to ask him for a part or a rise in salary, which may have been impossible to give and was unpleasant to refuse. To one of them, whom he had met elsewhere, he explained why he had not shaken hands on his way from the stage to the dressing-room: 'Forgive me. I didn't recognize you in my disguise.' To another, who said that he had been on the stage for forty-five years: 'Really, really! Almost a lifetime, eh? Any experience?' A third, who bored his dressing-room companions with the large parts he had played with Benson and the small parts for which he was cast at His Majesty's, was advised by them to ask Tree not only to release him but to request Benson to take him back again. He did so; Tree agreed; and he then heard from his fellow-actors that they had been pulling his leg and that he had behaved very foolishly. He returned to Tree at once and begged him not to write to Benson. 'I'm afraid it's too late,' said Tree: 'I *wired*.' Sometimes the prospect of an interview made Tree more nervous than the applicant. Edward O'Neill arranged for his daughter to see the chief, and she entered his dressing-room with a beating heart. Tree was sitting slumped at his knee-hole desk so that only his head and shoulders were visible. When he saw her startled face he slid down further until nothing but his eyes and the top of his head could be seen. She gave a wild shriek and bolted down the corridor, never to go near him again.

A first meeting with the manager could be alarming and memorable. G. Dickson–Kenwin, wishing to become an actor, obtained an interview. When he was shown into the room, Tree moved quickly behind him, shut the door, and stood facing him in silence for a minute. Then said Tree: 'How do you do? Who are you? Why are you here? Sit down.' As the scared fellow obeyed, Tree revoked the order: 'Stand up! What is your name?' Dickson–Kenwin handed his card. 'My God! there's a hyphen,' said Tree. The visitor collapsed into a chair. 'That's right. Take a seat,' from Tree. Another long pause was followed by the question, 'What have you done?' As an amateur he had played Shakespearean and Dickensian parts. 'A coincidence. So have I,' murmured the manager. The other laughed feebly and hoped Tree would remember him for his next production. 'My next production. Ah, yes! Quite right. Not a bad idea. But when will that be?' Tree got up and shook hands, saying, 'It's good of you to come and see me. I have enjoyed your visit. Come again. Would you like two stalls for my play? Ask my business-manager for them. I don't say you'll get them, but you can ask. Good-night.'

An actress who eventually played leading parts at His Majesty's had an agitating first interview with her future employer. 'I had a green bird in my hat,' said Constance Collier, 'and as he talked to me my head was slightly bent and he stroked the bird continuously.' She was frightened out of her wits and did not dare raise her head until he dismissed her. At their second meeting some months afterwards she was careful to wear a different hat, and he at once asked: 'Where's that bird?'

Complacent actors were liable to have their self-possession shaken at His Majesty's. A newcomer, aware that the chief was interested in make-up, arrived on the stage at the first dress re-hearsal in an impenetrable disguise. Tree noticed him at once and drifted towards him, amazement on his face. 'How did you do it?' The actor purred pleasure. 'The result of lifelong study, eh?' The actor admitted that he had put a good deal of thought into it. 'I've never seen such shadow effects—wonderful! But you must

have been helped?' No, he had received no assistance: 'Alone I
did it!' 'A wit, too,' Tree laughed, and then in turn admired the
actor's side-view and back-view, especially the wig. 'But that's
my own hair!' Tree expressed astonishment, again seemed lost
in admiration of the front-view, and finally remarked, 'Of course
you're not *going on* like that.'

In the year 1910 a company of Sicilian actors, headed by
Giovanni Grasso, made a sensation in London; everyone went to
see them in *Othello*, and nearly everyone raved over the performance. Grasso, in the leading part, bellowed and ranted and grunted
and howled and gurgled and apparently broke every bone in
Iago's body and deluged himself with blood when slitting his
own throat, and in short turned the tragedy into a Grand Guignol
horror. Tree went to see the show, and put his finger on the main
defect: 'Very remarkable, but hardly Shakespeare's conception.
You see, Grasso's Othello would never have *wanted* a pocket
handkerchief.' He gave a supper-party to Grasso in the dome, at
the conclusion of which the Sicilian embraced his host and all the
other guests. About to enter his cab after these demonstrations,
Grasso suddenly turned and darted back into the theatre. 'He has
forgotten to kiss the fireman,' said Tree.

The man who was ready with quips for any situation was also
equal to any professional emergency. Playing at Manchester, he
once fell and dislocated his arm, which hung down helplessly
until the act was finished. A smart pull got it back into its socket,
and he finished the play with his arm in a sling, improvising a
few words to explain that the character had met with an accident
since the previous act. Alfred Noyes relates how Tree dealt with
a very tricky situation when he produced *The O'Flynn* by Justin
Huntly McCarthy in Dublin. There were a few lines in it about
the descendants of Irish kings which Tree had told the actors to
speak half-humorously. When the curtain fell on the first act an
irate man got up and denounced the play as an insult to Ireland.
A storm of hissing and booing greeted the players in the second
act. Tree at once signalled to the orchestra to play an Irish reel
which in the ordinary way would have finished the scene, and as
the music started he hissed to the cast, 'Dance! For God's sake,
dance!' They all did so; the audience ceased their hostile sounds;

and there was some applause when the dance came to an end. But Tree was not satisfied, and signed to the orchestra to play it again. More applause. A third instalment went still better, the entire house applauding. The scene was cut, the curtain came down, the actors dropped from exhaustion, and in response to a call Tree made a speech between gasps: 'Fellow-Hibernians, I am not so frightened now as I was half-an-hour ago, but I think I should explain that I lost my brogue at the Battle of the Boyne.'

Throughout the twenty years of his management of His Majesty's Theatre the posters on the hoardings advertising his plays, usually designed by Charles Buchel, were the most striking in London. 'It is difficult to live up to one's posters,' said Tree, who loved gazing at them as he went through the streets. At some provincial town Norman Forbes twitted him about the placarding of his name in colossal capitals all over the place. 'Yes, you are quite right,' Tree agreed, 'and when I pass my name in such large letters I blush, but at the same time instinctively raise my hat.'

CHAPTER 20

Actor and Producer

When Tree had been on the stage for a year the famous dramatist Dion Boucicault saw him act and expressed surprise that a beginner should know all the tricks of the trade. 'Mention one trick,' said Tree. 'You allow the gesture to precede the words,' replied Boucicault. 'Do I? Well, I'm sorry you told me, for now I shall probably do it wrong.' Which explains the success and failure of Tree as an actor. He trusted to intuition, impulse, inspiration; he put no faith in experience, judgment, teaching. 'You couldn't come to a worse person if you wanted instruction in the art of acting,' he declared. 'I simply do things as I am prompted by my instinct, as I feel they should be done.' This may be a good guide for genius, but it is worthless for talent, and as the vast majority of the human species have some sort of talent or aptitude, and scarcely six people in a generation possess genius, Tree must be dismissed as an exemplar. Indeed, there is a sense in which he must be dismissed as an actor: that is, as one who can be relied upon to attain a certain standard of performance and keep it whatever the state of his health or the waywardness of his moods. Short of inspiration, which is both rare and momentary, human beings in all professions must rely upon training and technique. A little practice is worth a lot of insight even at the elementary job of hammering in nails.

But Tree was a genius, enjoying the potency and suffering the defects of his capacity more than most of its possessors. He celebrated the obsequies of the actor-manager system with a number of unforgettable performances of 'Herbert Beerbohm Tree' in various plays of that name, though they had carelessly been given different titles by their authors. No one who saw him would have wished it otherwise, for with rare exceptions his personality was more interesting than any play he produced, his fancy more prolific than any playwright's. Even in Shakespeare no one but a pedant disliked his oddly personal interpretations, though perhaps his tremendous creation of Malvolio turned *Twelfth Night* into a sort of 'Tree Night', while the wicker-basket of mannerisms which he substituted for Falstaff convinced a lover of *Henry IV* that it should have been billed 'Herbert I'.

Roughly speaking, there were two main aspects of Tree's acting, though he could play many variations within the first. What struck all his intelligent critics except Shaw was the astonishing inventiveness he brought to the building-up of a 'character' part. What impressed Shaw, and also Max Beerbohm and Desmond MacCarthy (both of whom admired his 'character' work as well), was the imaginative delicacy and pathos which he sometimes displayed in the delineation of 'straight' romantic parts. He could not play dashing heroes or passionate lovers, but he could suggest heroism and the affection of deep sympathy.

His public reputation was founded and maintained on his mimetic genius, and the range of his ability in this respect was great. But it was not only mimicry. He was capable of creating a part on the stage just as Dickens could create a character on the page. 'The difference between Irving and Tree as actors, if I had to put it in two lines, was that Irving always made a character come to him—Tree went to the character.' Such was the opinion of Henry Arthur Jones, who had an immense admiration for Irving and had seen every famous actor of his time. In other words, Tree was metamorphic; he could feel his way into a character, make himself share the thoughts and emotions of the man he was portraying without any sense of true affinity. His daughter Iris once asked whether he thought himself like any of the characters he had played. 'Yes, I think I am like nearly all of them. I have lived them all,' he replied; and this was true from the standpoint of his advice to actors: 'Project your being into the part you are playing, so that you unconsciously become the man without study.' Two of his famous contemporaries acclaimed his versatility. 'The best character comedian of his day', wrote Mrs Patrick Campbell. 'His slightly foreign manner, distinction and elegance, and fantastic grace, gave an arresting charm to his work.' Seymour Hicks, who was familiar with the work of all the best French actors, said that 'as a character actor Tree was unrivalled.

I have never seen anyone on any stage who could run the gamut of so distinct a line of parts or who had so varied a range.'

It may be asked how this was done without study. Certainly Tree never studied in the usual meaning of that word. He absorbed his parts slowly, the actual lines coming to him with difficulty and usually suggesting something more than they said, which caused him to invent business often at variance with the author's meaning, so that in the end he created rather than interpreted his characters. His vividly bizarre Svengali could not have been mistaken for Du Maurier's commonplace figure, his Fagin was more amusing and subtle than Dickens's, his Malvolio became the focal figure in Shakespeare's comedy. Genius in an actor cannot be described: it can only be felt. But it may be roughly classified; and the difference between, say, the acting of Irving and that of Tree was the difference between bewitchment and enchantment. Irving's power compelled people to leave their world and enter his: there was wizardry in it. Tree's strength lay in his humorous charm: people sat back in comfort, delighted with the world they knew as revealed by the fanciful pleasantry of the actor.

Baliol Holloway said that 'Tree was a born miniature painter who tried to do landscapes, but his elaborate productions aroused enthusiasm for Shakespeare in people who would otherwise never have seen or read the plays.' This is true; and it has already been remarked that Tree could not speak the long speeches in Shakespeare as Forbes–Robertson and Lewis Waller could, for he lacked the gift of sustained declamation, his peculiar faculty being for flashes of intuition and observation. With Fagin's asthmatic cough he somehow evoked the existence of a fog beyond the window; with the uncouth gestures of Beethoven he made real the spiritual turmoil of the man; with the nervous glances and high quick speech of Richard II he revealed the character more clearly than actors who spoke the lines more effectively. He was able to feel thin and hungry as Gringoire, magnetic and dirty as Svengali, short and stocky as Beethoven. Playing the part of Isidore Izard he could smoke strong cigars that would have made him sick in private life; and as Sir Peter Teazle he took real snuff with relish, though off the stage a single pinch would have made him sneeze for five minutes. All this was due to his gift for living in a character he had fashioned from the hints of an author, the best moments in his acting being his own conceptions, not the playwright's.

The drawback to this inspirational form of acting is that it cannot be commanded at will. The actor who has learnt his business can go on repeating a performance without variation; even when ill his technique will help him through. But 'I have not got technique,' Tree confessed; 'it is a dull thing; it enslaves the imagination'; with the result that he never gave a repetition of a set performance, and his acting of the parts was as versatile as his choice of them. Improvising as he went along, always trusting to the right expression of the momentary emotion, his work could be as bad as it was good; he was either lost in a part or wholly outside it; and so the people who saw him act on the first night sometimes witnessed a totally different performance on the fourth. For this reason playgoers disagreed over his ability more entirely than has been the case with any other famous actor in history, and the opinions of contemporary dramatic critics are valueless. It was occasionally necessary to see him a dozen times in the same part before a true impersonation emerged. For example, his first performance of Colonel Newcome was exquisite, his second dull. His Richard II could be poignantly beautiful; it could also be affected and commonplace. There were some parts for which he was physically and vocally unfitted; and just as the poet who does not feel what he is saying writes rhetoric, so the actor who cannot feel his part overacts. Unable to impersonate Shakespeare's heroes and lovers, Tree persistently overacted them and was quite ineffective. 'It is not pace but boredom that kills,' he once remarked, and it was boredom that killed his genius even in parts for which he was suited. The long run of a play was death to his inspiration. He scarcely ever knew his lines in the early stages of a run, and this gave him the excitement which frequently issued in flashes of genius; but when he became word-perfect he lost interest and his performance went flat; he began to 'walk through' his part, to 'gag', and to 'dry up' the other actors with unseemly jokes and grimaces. He should never have played a part for more than a week, at the most a fortnight, and those who saw him in short revivals, such as the annual Shakespeare Festivals, usually saw him at his best. His personality was unique; he could be inspired; he could be brilliant; he was often surprising; he was always interesting; but being incalculable he was not in the proper sense a professional actor.

Since he was either feeling himself into a part by instinct, or wondering what else he could put into it to maintain his interest, his preoccupation with his own performance led to curious results. He looked unconscious of what the other actors in a scene were going to say, and seemed taken aback when hearing his cue to speak. In this way he avoided the commonest fault of actors: that of appearing to know the words of the previous speaker by heart. A strange episode during the rehearsals of *Pygmalion* revealed his unawareness of everything except himself. At one moment Eliza Doolittle had to throw Professor Higgins's slippers in his face. Knowing that Stella Campbell was a dead shot, Shaw planned that the slippers should be very soft. Yet when Tree received them slap in the face he had completely forgotten the incident in the play, mistook her adherence to the text for a personal assault on himself, collapsed under the blow to his feelings, and had to be nursed back to an understanding of the circumstances by his solicitous staff. 'The worst of it was,' said Shaw, 'that as it was quite evident that he would be just as surprised and wounded next time, Mrs Campbell took care that the slippers should never hit him again, and the incident was consequently one of the least convincing in the performance.'

Something of the same kind was described by Owen Nares. In *David Copperfield* Tree had to make a quick change from Peggotty to Micawber. For this purpose he descended through the stage by a lift. At the dress rehearsal the costumier Simmons and his assistants were ready beneath to help him make the change, as settled by Stanley Bell, then stage-manager. The lift descended, Tree stepped off it, and the rest of the cast suddenly heard him yelling: 'Get away! Bell! Where's Bell? Send Bell to me! What are all these men rushing at me for? Help! Where's Bell?' When Bell arrived Tree was fighting Simmons and company and frantically resisting their efforts to change his clothes. 'My God!' exclaimed Tree, 'when I got down and saw all these strange men charging at me, I thought my last hour had come. And a quick change to do on the top of it!' He was thinking himself into Micawber out of Peggotty, and had completely forgotten the arrangement to facilitate his thoughts.

A last illustration by his daughter Viola, who played the Queen in a revival of *Richard II.* It was the scene of farewell between the King and his wife, which took place in the street on his way to the Tower of London: 'Each time it seemed as if he were surprised to see me standing there, and as if we were really to say good-bye to each other for the first and last time. Then I fell on his neck, and said my speech sobbing, because at that moment I was not Richard's Queen but my father's daughter . . . He never could begin his speech at once—he was so worried by my tears . . .'

Acted as he alone could act it, this scene was the most moving in the play. It was not only that he spoke the lines with a fond tenderness; it was the way he stroked Viola's hair that made the onlooker feel the sorrow of all separations. At such moments of imaginative sympathy he transcended the art of acting and lifted the spectator out of the world of make-believe. His most perceptive critic, Desmond MacCarthy, recorded two instances of this nature. One was in *Colonel Newcome.* When the Colonel's old nurse heard of his ruin, she called to return some of the presents which he had given her in his days of affluence. It was a sentimental situation, but what made it remarkable was the way in which Tree by his gestures conveyed the comfort they felt merely in being near each other and 'the kind of unconsciousness with which he caressed her, as though the vagueness of old age had created in him the instinctiveness of childish affection'. The other was in Ibsen's *An Enemy of the People.* When Dr Stockman was inveighing against stuffy, selfish, ignoble homes, his wife, who had tried to prevent him starting his campaign, sat beside him on the platform. In the midst of his harangue about the wretched homes he put his hand for an instant on her shoulder. The gesture said plainly, 'Of course, my dear, this is not a hit at you,' and perfectly expressed their relationship. The average dramatic critic missed such subtle moments and dwelt on the clowning he had introduced to liven up the play. But then the tendency of most critics to say that if somebody had expressed something else he might have been someone else is very strong.

These spontaneous impulses in Tree's acting gave a perpetual interest to his least satisfactory performances, making them more fascinating to watch than the wholly admirable impersonations of other actors in the same characters. That he was not aware of his illuminating gleams is proved by a story told by William Mollison. At a rehearsal of *David Copperfield*, in the scene where the flight of Little Em'ly is made known to Peggotty and Ham, Tree as Peggotty suddenly put his hand on Ham's arm to comfort him, knowing that his was the more desolating loss. The action moved Mollison to tears, and when Tree failed to repeat it at the next rehearsal he summoned up the courage to speak: 'Oh, chief, would you mind my telling you something?' Tree's eyes opened with pleasure when the young actor explained. 'Was it good? You liked it?' he asked eagerly, and thereafter repeated the action.

Which shows too that he had little conceit. In spite of his huge success he remained humble about his own acting. It has already been noticed that his supporting cast often did more than support: they were allowed to shine, to win as much kudos as lay within their power. 'You couldn't play with a more unselfish actor,' testified Weedon Grossmith; 'he wished me to make as much of my part as I possibly could, and suggested that I should write it up a bit, leaving it entirely to my discretion. The parts were very equal, one was as good as the other.' This refers to a one-act play called *The Van Dyck*, in which Tree and Grossmith provided a superlatively comical entertainment. Tree shared with some men of genius a love of pure nonsense, and his way of letting-off steam might have been mistaken by silly-serious people for eccentricity bordering on insanity. In *The Van Dyck* he was able to express this element in his nature by playing a burglar who pretends to be a lunatic, and no broad farce was ever so uproariously funny as the subtle acting of Grossmith and himself. It disclosed to a later generation the peculiar quality in Tree that had gone to the creation of Spalding in *The Private Secretary*, for in filling out the part he improvised such sentences as 'A mad chaos of sea dashing drowned mermaids on a shrieking shore.' He was really an author-actor, who should have written his own plays. Had he done so he would have taken more interest in the other parts. As it was he remained almost exclusively concerned with his own, a state of mind that was amusingly exhibited on his return from a trip to Moscow and St Petersburg early in 1913. He had gone with his stage-manager Stanley Bell to see Gordon Craig's production of *Hamlet* at the Moscow Art Theatre. In the train on their way home they were discussing a play he wished to produce, and a fellow-passenger, Mrs Edward Fordham, recalled forty years afterwards one moment of their conversation. After talking for some time in level tones of the progress of the action, Tree, his eyes alight and with an ample gesture of satisfaction, proclaimed: 'And then *I* come on!'

Having created a part in a wider sense than may be claimed by other actors, he did not like to think of anyone else copying his creation, and his understudies scarcely ever had a chance to show what they could do. He never succumbed to illness, sometimes appearing on the stage when he should have been in bed. He suffered intensely from first-night nerves and usually went for an hour's fast walk before entering the theatre. The occupation of making-up helped to soothe him. He experimented in colours on his mirror before getting what he wanted, but once he had achieved the character's appearance to his satisfaction he did not take long to reproduce the effect on his face. His disguises might almost be described as important features in the theatrical world of his time. People waited for them, speculated upon them, wondered how they were done. More remarkable even than the facial alteration was the bodily transformation. As Colonel Newcome he had an erect military build totally unlike his everyday carriage and physical structure. He seemed able to transpose various parts of his body. Coming on to the stage in the costume of Sir Peter Teazle at the first dress rehearsal of *The School for Scandal*, he went up to his daughter Viola and, referring to his belly, touched it, saying, 'Shall I wear it there or' (pointing to his chest) 'here?' But the queerest of all these metamorphoses was his appearance as Beethoven. Tree was tall, lanky, blue-eyed, somewhat amorphous in face and body, graceful in gesture, vague in manner, soft in speech. There entered a short, thickset, bull-necked, agile fellow, with dark eyes, awkward movements, harsh utterance, jerky gestures and clear-cut features. The low stature was not fanciful, because men in the company, whose eyes were normally on a level with his own, looked down at him as Beethoven. Somehow his body had shrunk as he got into the skin of the part.

It will easily be guessed from the foregoing that Tree's methods as a producer, since they resembled his methods as an actor, were singularly immethodical. People like Graham Robertson who had been accustomed to the dictatorial atmosphere generated by Henry Irving or Sarah Bernhardt, those like Owen Nares who had experienced the order and calm of the St James's Theatre under George Alexander, were dismayed by the chaos and turmoil of His Majesty's, where the birth-pangs of a play were beyond belief. All sorts of people wandered about the stage or in and out of the auditorium; no one seemed to know anyone else's business; everyone seemed to interfere in other people's business. There was a lot of bawling and banging. Interruptions were so frequent that a continuance of the rehearsal resembled an interference with the natural order of disturbance. It was production by impromptu, with occasional witticisms by Tree, at which his crowd of hangers-on dutifully laughed. No member of the company knew who these people were or what they were doing. They may have been journalists or backers or composers or playwrights or painters or merely Tree's fellow-clubmen whom he had asked to drop in and say what they thought of his efforts. Advice from any of them was given, and accepted, rejected or ignored. Most of them were what a later generation called yes-men. All of them were ha-ha-men. When Tree said 'Every dogma has its day', which did service on more than one occasion, they cackled, and proceedings were discontinued by the laughter which greeted 'I shall give a banquet to my critics and on each plate I shall put copies of their articles in order that they may eat their words.' In the babel of discordant opinions that broke out at any point during a scene, Tree's voice would be heard asking plaintively, 'May I be allowed to say a word in this theatre?' or 'Could I just humbly suggest——?' and when quiet was temporarily restored some person would receive a volcanic roasting.

If he noticed that his words had really hurt anyone, he would do his best to heal the wound. 'Do you think I should apologise?' he asked Graham Robertson, who answered that it was difficult to apologize to a man who had been rude to him. 'Yes, yes, of course; I suppose so; but it seems a pity,' he sighed. He hated enmity, and expressed much of his own nature in the remark: 'Why not palliate the pangs of conversational vivisection with the chloroform of courtesy?' But not the whole of his nature, for there were occasions at rehearsal when a rather feline streak of malice appeared, probably called forth by self-complacency or stupidity or unresponsiveness in another actor. Once he walked round and round Otho Stuart at a yard's distance, examining him like a prize animal while he delivered a long speech. This, however, was not characteristic; and most of his comments were meant to be funny, not painful, as when he told an actor at each rehearsal to stand nearer the Prompt corner, until the fellow complained that he could not be seen at all, and Tree reassured him: 'That's just the effect I want.' Douglas Jefferies relates two such instances that happened to him when Israel Zangwill's *The War God* was in preparation. Having made himself up he felt rather pleased with his smart appearance as a naval lieutenant. Following a detailed scrutiny, Tree said to him: 'Very good, very good, but I think you should wear a long black moustache.' Jefferies made a rather self-conscious exit through a door, and Tree called him back: 'Mr Er—er, Mr Er—er, could you possibly open that door and go out like a—like a—well, like a man opening a door and going out.' The famous perruquier, Willy Clarkson, once criticized the natural hair of an actress, thinking it an ineffective wig. Tree explained: 'Hair is the stuff that grows on the head. How should *you* know what hair is?'

Tree may have been the first of a race of producers who have dealt in analogies to obtain the effects for which they have striven. 'I want you to play this part with a mauve voice,' he said to Constance Collier when she was cast for Calypso in *Ulysses*; and he gave the not-very-helpful hint to an actor: 'I want you to suggest—well, you know, don't you?—a cross between a whitebait and a marmoset.' Granville Barker converted this mannerism into a style, carrying it to strange lengths, since when it has passed the bounds of reason and become a form of mania. With Tree, its probable initiator, it was partly funny, partly stimulating. He was practical enough in his ordinary advice. 'Judge an actress by the way she handles an artificial rose,' he said. 'Keep your vowels and your bowels open,' he counselled young actors. When Irene Vanbrugh, rehearsing the part of Lady Teazle, bent her head as she curtsied, Tree checked her: 'Don't do that; you'll shake all the powder off your hair. In a powder period always keep your head rigid.' Playing Jasper in *Edwin Drood*, he put his hand over his mouth at a critical moment. 'The mouth gives away more than the eyes,' he remarked. In trying to reproduce the gait of a drunken man, Philip Merivale, as Cassio in *Othello*, staggered all over the place while making his exit. Tree showed him by example that a fellow in that condition walks more directly to his objective than a sober man, maintaining his balance by moving more quickly. Because of his own tendency to reveal character in sudden beams of insight, he was able in an instant to see where another actor was wrong and to set him right.

His rehearsals seemed endless to everyone but himself. Oscar Asche, who produced *Ulysses*, said that Tree was never inclined to do much till after midnight. Asche was working hard from twelve noon till six-thirty the following morning for several days before the opening date; but Tree would look in before lunch for about ten minutes; he next appeared after dinner at nine, rehearsed for two hours, left for supper, turned up again at one in the morning as fresh as a lark, and said: 'Come, let's do some *work*!' He was nearly always absent when wanted, and absent-minded when present. He demanded from his staff apparent impossibilities, which somehow became possibilities; though when he complained of the noise made by buses in the Haymarket and wrote to Sir Edward Henry suggesting that they should be diverted to Lower Regent Street, the Commissioner of Police proved intractable. He never troubled to learn the names of things, such as battens and floats. He knew what he wanted, and got it, but could not tell how it was done. Similarly he neither liked nor understood stage slang. Enlightened on one point, he imparted it to his brother Max: 'Do you know what they call the curtain? They call it "the rag".' Max being amused, Herbert started to improvise: 'My boy, the rag came down on mud,' which, being interpreted, meant that the play had failed on the first night.

Out of chaos Tree created cosmos; out of vagueness came clarity; from conditions that reminded many people of a more than usually riotous playground, there emerged a production of admirable smoothness, carefully considered detail, and unrivalled magnificence. It seemed, and was, a miracle. But perhaps miracles cannot occur without a great deal of preliminary fumbling.

CHAPTER 21

Personal

For the sake of convenience the biographer will now write in the first person.

At the age of eighteen I saw Tree in *Nero*. He opened the gate of art to me, and in doing so became my first living hero. I had never shared the usual schoolboy's enthusiasm for some team-captain who could hit or kick a ball about a field with dexterity. Clearly my real interests lay elsewhere, and Tree revealed them to me. Henceforth I spent every shilling I could lawfully or unlaw-fully obtain at His Majesty's Theatre, and when not inside it I dreamt of being there. I saw him in nearly all his famous parts, as he constantly revived his early successes, and I witnessed all his Shakespearean productions many times, with the single exception of *King John*, which for some reason he never revived. My life in a City shipping-office was made bearable by the memory or the anticipation of golden hours in the pit or upper circle of His Majesty's, and I even toyed with the notion of writing to Tree for a job. But a legacy released me from the drudgery of clerkship, and in 1909 I found myself mismanaging my brother's motor business in Brighton. That year Tree was knighted, and I was pleased to find among his papers a letter of congratulation from me pasted into a large volume containing many others of a like nature. Written from 31 King's Road, Brighton, and dated 30 June, 1909, it informed him that I had seen every play in that year's Shakespeare Festival, and requested him, as I was bringing a party from Brighton to see *Hamlet* the following evening, to do his best to finish the play by 11.30 p.m., so that we could catch the 11.50 from Victoria. I said that I had seen it the previous even-ing, when the performance did not finish till 11.45. My request must have tickled him because he wired the following morning: 'Cannot alter my conception of the part to fit midnight train but will cut a scene if you run to Victoria.' I agreed to run, and he cut a scene in which Hamlet did not take part.

Soon I made up my mind that merely to appear in a play by Shakespeare was preferable to any other form of activity, and sent him a letter to that effect. He replied: 'Come and see me, but don't be too optimistic. You should have independent means or relations with Court circles to be successful on the stage nowadays. If you have the former, why go on the stage? If the latter, the kings and queens of real life should satisfy you; though I admit we can give you the romantic article better than they, because a cardboard crown is more artistic than a top hat.'

It was a great moment in my life when I entered his dressing-room during the run of *Henry VIII* and saw Cardinal Wolsey sitting at his desk. He rose, shook hands, said, 'How do you do? Take a seat,' and resumed his. I took a seat. He leaned back and stared hard at me for about two minutes without speaking. He had sandy-grey hair and pale blue eyes, and the anxious, vaguely wondering expression on his face made me feel uncomfortable. As the silence continued I became restless. Suddenly he said: 'Don't bite your nails—it's a sign of mental stagnation.' I tried to ease the situation with a remark about the coloured sketches on his mirror. He made no reply. I felt fretful. He spoke again: 'Don't suck your thumb—it signifies lack of stamina.' This irritated me, and I asked, with some approach to irony, if he would care to write me a prescription. He instantly took his pen and wrote something on a slip of paper. Then he got up, handed me the slip, said, 'Come again after the next act,' conducted me a few steps along the corridor, and showed me through a door into the dress-circle. I read the words on the paper:

> *Disease:* Want of philosophic calm, typically modern.
> *Cure:* One performance of *Henry VIII*, to be taken weekly.
> H. B. T.

At the next interval I returned to his dressing-room. 'Who are you?' he asked. I told him. 'What do you want?' he demanded. 'Surely you can't have forgotten——' I began. 'Answer my question,' he interrupted 'I forget everything I don't wish to remember.' I now perceived that I was dealing with one who enjoyed acting a part in private life, and decided to play up to him if I could. The conversation continued. But first I ought to say that all the talks here reported were noted down immediately after they took place, and that they may be regarded as almost verbatim. In those days I had an excellent memory, and when I troubled to concentrate on a discussion, as I always did with Tree, I could reproduce it word for word with very few variations. Occasionally I showed him an account of what he had said, and though he might advise me to tear it up he never suggested emendations and always showed pleasure and interest in my Boswellian ardour. Here is our earliest conversational interchange, following his question, 'What do you want?'

'I want a job.'

'Can you speak German?'

'No, but does one have to speak German to go on the stage?'

'It would certainly be useful if you wanted to go on the German stage.'

'I don't.'

'Well, that settles it, doesn't it? Can you speak French?'

'Yes.'

'Fluently?'

'No.'

'What a pity!'

'Why?'

'Because one should always swear in a foreign language at rehearsals.'

'Is there any necessity to swear at all?'

'No necessity but a great relief.' After a pause he went on: 'Are you fond of your wife?'

'I haven't got one.'

'Yes, but are you fond of her?'

'How the dickens can I be fond of a wife I haven't got?'

'Ah, I hadn't thought of that. Have you read much?'

'It depends upon what you call reading much.'

'I mean the perusal of a vast quantity of words printed on paper and bound in books.'

'Yes, of course I knew you meant that; but to what class of reading do you refer?'

'Oh, the kind that teaches facts and figures.'

'I know nothing of facts and figures: they don't interest me.'

'That's right, quite right. Beware of the encyclopædias. A little knowledge is a dangerous thing, but a lot ruins one's digestion.'

At this moment Henry Dana, the business manager, came in, and for several minutes Tree wrestled with figures in a ledger. I watched the performance with interest. He kept turning the leaves backwards and forwards, quite unable to follow Dana's explanation, and occasionally putting his finger on some possibly conspicuous figure, saying, 'What's that?'—rather in the way a child might cry, 'Oh, look at that lovely big one there!' Forty-four years later I came across a letter he had written to Dana from America in January, 1917, and it did not surprise me to read: 'As you know, it is very difficult for me to grasp these financial matters.'

The struggle over, Dana departed, the call-boy announced the next act, and Tree told me to see him again after the performance. He then left me. But just as I was about to open the door into the dress-circle he called to me, came trotting back along the corridor, his red silken robe rustling against the walls, dragged me into his dressing-room, and asked me very confidentially: 'Have you ever been to Jerusalem?' I replied that I had not. 'How interesting!' he murmured as he drifted away down the passage.

After the final curtain I returned to his dressing-room and sat watching him remove his make-up and change his clothes. While doing so he delivered a monologue, speaking partly to me, partly to his dresser, partly to no one in particular. His remarks were disconnected, and he paid no attention to my occasional replies to questions that were not meant to be answered. Thus he soliloquized:

'How did you like the play? Wonderful production, isn't it? Have you read my brochure on *Henry VIII*? Quite a charming little essay. I wrote it during my holiday. It's always useful to have a job on hand during one's holidays; it saves one from bores who insist on interrupting one's dreams with tedious prattle about politics or mixed bathing. Did you ever see old Irving? A strange personality, but hard . . . hard . . . I couldn't get on with him at all. Quite unlike his two boys, Harry and Laurence. Such nice lads; I like 'em both . . . Don't forget to remember me to your wife . . . See that letter? It's from a girl who wants to go on the stage. She writes: "The enclosed photo will show you how attractive I am. I also send a photo of my aunt, who has the toothache." The English public doesn't really like Shakespeare; it prefers football . . . Shakespearean scholars say I am wrong in tempting people to come to the theatre and giving them a spectacle instead of Shakespeare. But I prefer a spectacle on the stage to spectacles in the audience . . . Some day you will tell me how it was you didn't go to Jerusalem. It must have been a delightful experience—not to have gone after all . . . Winkles!—yes, that's a fine occupation—picking winkles out of shells on a frosty night in Pimlico. (Are they in shells, by the way?) Take my advice: don't go on the stage—pick winkles out of shells . . . Do you believe in God? (Where's that damned stud?) Perhaps you aren't old enough. The reason old people believe in God is because they've given up believing in anything else, and one can't exist without faith in something. Besides, after sixty one hasn't the vitality to combat the instincts of the majority. God is a sort of burglar. As a young man you knock him down; as an old man you try to conciliate him because he may knock you down. Moral: don't grow old. With age comes caution, which is another name for cowardice, and both are the effect of a guilty conscience. Whatever else you do in life, don't cultivate a conscience. Without a conscience a man may never be said to grow old. This is an age of very old young men . . . Never neglect an opportunity to play leap-frog; it is the best of all games, and, unlike the terribly serious and conscientious pastimes of modern youth, will never become professionalized . . . Have you ever been in love? That is the greatest thing in life. Don't confuse love with matrimony. Love keeps you young, matrimony makes you old. Love should never be allowed to disturb the excellent economic foundation of the domestic hearth. Love is more precious than life; but a silver wedding speaks for itself . . . Why is it that we have to go to Germany for our greasepaints? . . .'

Throughout this discourse Tree kept floating to and from his inner dressing-room, apparently unconscious of his actions, his whereabouts or his company. It was entirely due to his dresser that he managed to complete his toilet. As he talked it struck me that much of his humour was due to his personality, to his way of saying a thing rather than the thing said. The eccentric mannerisms, the quick turn of the eyes and the soft purring voice made a commonplace remark sound funny. I made an excellent audience, because I laughed heartily at his impromptus, and something about me must have amused him because he entertained himself either at my expense or for my entertainment in the days to come. The moment his dresser passed him as presentable, he held out his hand, saying 'Good-bye. So nice for you to have seen me,' and I retired to the Westminster slum where I then lived to record his comicalities for posterity; because even then I felt a desire, later to become the impulsion of my biographical work, to take my hero off his pedestal and know him as a fellow-man.

Towards the end of the run of *Henry VIII* I received a wire telling me to be at the theatre on a certain date. People were being interviewed on the stage when I arrived, but my turn came at last. Three men were sitting at a table, one of whom was Tree. I was asked to give my name and a summary of my experience as an actor. While I was wondering whether to mention the work I had done as an amateur, Tree said:

'I like his legs.'

'But you can't see them through his trousers,' objected one of his companions.

'That's why I like them,' said Tree.

The other made a noise like a corncrake.

'What parts have you played?' I was asked again.

'None,' I bravely decided.

'Splendid!' exclaimed Tree, who gave no hint by his manner that he had ever seen me before; 'you will have nothing to unlearn. We must give him something really good; nothing must be allowed to stand in his way. He has a fine nose. He has a most becoming modesty. Moreover, I like his legs. We will do everything in our power to help you, Mr Er——' (he referred to a paper) 'Mr Hesketh Pearson—if you promise not to hyphen your names.' (More sounds from corncrake.) 'I will speak to Mr Dana about your contract, and you shall play the part of Bottom in *A Midsummer Night's Dream*.'

This had a volcanic effect upon his companions, who rolled

about on their chairs in a condition of glee that struck me as excessive.

'My God! I owe you an apology,' Tree went on. 'I had completely forgotten that I have already promised the well-known actor, Mr Arthur Bourchier, that he shall play Bottom. It is therefore casting no reflection on you when I say that he has the prior, not to mention the posterior, claim.' (Further convulsions from his associates.) 'But do not despair. You will get a far wider and more valuable experience by not playing it than by playing it; for you will be able to watch Mr Bourchier's performance night after night, and after a careful study of his manner and method of acting you will always know exactly what to avoid.' (Spasms from the other two.) 'In conclusion, Mr Pearson, I cannot do you a greater honour than to engage you to walk-on at my beautiful theatre for a salary of one guinea a week, extra for matinées.'

And so it came about that I appeared in *A Midsummer Night's Dream* as a courtier whose chief duty was to greet the idiotic remarks of Theseus with shouts of laughter that would scarcely have been justified had they been as witty as the best of Voltaire's. Fortunately some of Tree's quips at rehearsals were on a higher level than those of Theseus in the play. When Maud made too much fuss about the dresses of the fairies, wondering whether they should be masculine or feminine, her husband decided the point: 'Fairies are carefree, so they must be neuter.' This revival was followed by the annual Shakespeare Festival, which in 1911 opened with *Julius Caesar*, a play that contains so many characters that even I was allotted one: Publius, an ancient senator, who said exactly three words, 'Good-morrow, Caesar,' and thereafter held his peace. As it was my first part on the professional stage, I took great pains to study the carriage, gait and voice of senility. I drooped, I shuffled and I squeaked for a fortnight. Douglas Jefferies helped to make me up, and my appearance in a long white beard left nothing to be desired. Standing in the wings, just before the portentous event, I concentrated on my vocal trills, and when the cue came for my entrance I temporarily forgot the palsied walk, marching on with the vigour of youth. Perceiving my error, I was struck dumb, and A. E. George, playing Caesar, said, 'Welcome, Publius', which should have followed my 'Good-morrow, Caesar.' This tragic deprivation of my perfectly-rehearsed greeting staggered me into the physical condition necessary for my part. I shook and went limp. But it also called for a rejoinder, which I made in my ordinary voice. 'Hullo!' I said. Utterly ashamed of myself, I tottered across the stage, praying that I would fall through a convenient trapdoor. Anticipating the sack, I was not surprised when Tree came up to me at the close of the scene and fearsomely asked in his slightly nasal voice: 'What did you say to Caesar?' Too wretched to attempt an explanation, I replied simply that I had said 'Hullo!' He appeared to be re-lieved: 'Oh! I beg your pardon. My mistake. I thought you said "What ho!"' And he left me dazed. I attribute my luck in being cast for Balthazar in *The Merchant of Venice*, which followed, to the fact that as a citizen in the Forum scene of *Julius Caesar* I gave forth the line 'What does he say of Caesar?' in a manner that impressed the stage-manager, Cecil King.

Such incidents in London's leading theatre might seem in-credible to those who never knew Tree; but there were innumer-able stories of his odd conduct, from which I will select one sent me by Richard Hatteras, who interviewed him in the dome. Tree was seated at the end of a long table, dressed in riding clothes and eating a boiled egg, which he asked permission to finish, being extremely busy that day. 'What is your height?' he wished to know. 'Six feet two inches.' 'You don't look it. Stand back to back with me'—they did so in front of a mirror—'why, so you are! You're the same height as I am. It's a noble height.' Tree then said he wanted Hatteras for Valentine in *Twelfth Night*, and after explaining the part at some length slapped him on the back with the words, 'Just the man for the part!' Hatteras, delighted, assumed he was engaged. 'But the worst of it is . . . the part's gone,' con-cluded Tree. The next suggestion was that Hatteras should under-study Henry Ainley, and when that appeared to be settled he left the theatre. But before he had gone far down Charles Street the stage-doorkeeper caught him up and breathlessly said that Tree wanted him again. This time he went to the actor's dressing-room and found him making up as Fagin. Tree glared at him as if he were a complete stranger who had taken the liberty of walking into a gentleman's private sanctum unannounced. 'You sent for me, Mr Tree?' 'No . . . no!' came the answer, and then, on reconsideration, 'Yes . . . yes! I wanted to know whether you could find your way out of the theatre all right?'

King George V was crowned in 1911, and Tree gave a Coronation Gala Performance on June 27th. His contribution to the show was the Forum scene, and he asked Granville Barker to produce it. Barker prepared a pamphlet, which I still possess, containing the movements of all the citizens at each point in the scene, a job that must have taken him many hours to complete. His time was wasted. He tried, with the aid of a powerful bell, to make a mob of about three hundred actors follow his detailed stage directions; but he gave it up when Tree arrived and compelled the crowd to behave in the simpler fashion usual at His Majesty's. The arcade at the back of the theatre was closed to the public and turned into a dressing-room, drinks being served to the citizens in abundance through a window of the Carlton Hotel which opened into the arcade. The result of Tree's generosity was amusing, if unpatriotic. At the close of the entertainment everyone who had taken part came on to the stage, the Forum crowd standing on benches, each row higher than the one in front; and while Clara Butt sang the National Anthem, the sovereigns and their entourage must have thought it strange that vacancies should frequently occur in the ranks of the actors, the song being punctuated by the sound of falling bodies as one tipsy citizen followed another into the darkness behind.

Occasionally during this season Tree invited me into his dressing-room, and once I happened to remark that Sargent's sketch of him, though a brilliant likeness, made him look younger than he was. 'You don't know me as well as Sargent does,' he said, returning to the subject later with 'You ought to study the art of expression,' and again 'Go and see an oculist, my friend.' Some criticism of his acting prompted this:

'There are three kinds of dramatic critics. There are those who say the drama is going to the devil, those who say it's ascending to heaven, and those who halt between two opinions. So far as my own theatre is concerned I am inclined to agree with the second class. Of course, not one of them really knows what he is talking about. They all make statements that the intelligent public disprove. And it's the public, not the critics, who have kept Shakespeare alive. If it were possible to put on an unknown play by Shakespeare and give its author's name as John Smith, there'd not be a single critic in London with sufficient discernment to spot the poet. In Germany things are different. There the critics possess true culture and literary ability. But here I sometimes think they've sent the football reporter to our first nights instead of the dramatic critic. Perhaps it's the same person, you say? Yes, there's something in that. I must try to find out. Their extraordinary preference for what they call virile acting certainly bears out your suggestion.' (I had not contributed a word.) 'What's wrong with the English theatre is not the drama nor the actor nor the public, but the dramatic critic. Personally I have nothing but praise for the social qualities of our critics. They are delightful fellows. No words could do justice to their personal charm, their generosity, their sincerity, their patriotism, their domestic virtues—and their unfathomable ignorance!'

I spent a curious hour with Tree one spring night in 1911. Leaving the theatre after the performance, I heard his voice on the stairs behind me: 'Where are you going?' 'Home to bed,' I replied. 'Don't be rash,' said he; 'young and yet careful.' Then he gripped my arm, hailed a taxi, pushed me inside, got in himself and slammed the door. The driver left his seat, opened the door, and asked where we wanted to go. 'That is not the sort of question that ought to be put to a gentleman at this time of night,' rejoined Tree. 'Come orf it,' snapped the driver. 'He means "off"', using the term in a metaphorical sense,' Tree murmured. 'Are you going to tell me where you want to go, or shall I fetch a bobby?' demanded the man. 'Whither thou goest, we will go,' quoted Tree, 'but where thou lodgest, we certainly don't intend to lodge.' Then, seeing that the man was likely to create a disturbance, he added: 'Drive us slowly round and round the West End until we tell you to stop. If you see a man in green trousers, a top hat and spotted waistcoat, blow your horn three times and increase your speed.'

The driver, not altogether certain whether he was indulging a privileged lunatic or dealing with a Scotland Yard detective, returned to his seat and started off. Tree lay back in his corner, crossed his legs and talked. Now and then I said something, to which he paid no more attention than a grunt, and his purrings practically amounted to a soliloquy, of which I give here only those parts I remembered and noted down the same night. The dots denote pauses, some of which were long, some short. I should add that the gentleman to whom he referred so frequently had been hanged some months previously for murdering his wife, and Tree's concern over his fate must have been due to something he had recently heard in the man's favour, possibly from one of his defending counsel:

'I used to believe the world was round. Nowadays I am sure it is flat . . . Poor old Crippen! . . . Why? you naturally ask. I don't know. Possibly because I can't believe that God plays football with the planetary system. The idea is outrageous. It is horrible that a man of your intelligence should support it.' (I had not opened my mouth.) 'You have what I may call a Crystal Palace mind. I don't mean to suggest that your mind is as clear as crystal. It isn't. No Crystal Palace minds are. That is the paradox of the Victorian era . . . Poor old Crippen! . . . Don't talk so much. Talking hinders thought. I always think aloud, and I can't stand people talking when I'm thinking at the top of my voice. Do you really imagine that anything you say is of the smallest importance? Your tongue was given you to hold it . . . Poor old Crippen! . . . Once, many years ago, while I was witnessing my own imperson-ation of Hamlet—a beautiful performance—the thought struck me that I would, some time or other, produce one of Shake-speare's plays. But alas!—don't interrupt me—all our ideals escape us. Besides, it wouldn't be fair to Sidney Lee and the rest of the would-be Elizabethans, none of whom would have anything to grumble about if I stuck to the "true and perfect coppie". Their occupation would be gone, and one cannot trifle with the problem of the Unemployable . . . Does your eye ever roll in a fine frenzy? No, of course not. You would be in Hanwell if it did. As I said before, you have a Crippen Palace mind . . . Poor old Crystal! . . .'

At this point Tree lapsed into silence for about ten minutes. Then he commenced to murmur, but I only caught one phrase— 'She probably deserved it'—referable no doubt to the late Mrs

Crippen. Then silence again. I began to feel sleepy and had got into a sort of nodding condition when the taxi stopped and the driver opened the door violently.

' 'Ow long's this going on for?' he shouted.

Tree, without moving, said to me: 'Give him something on account.'

'I'm awfully sorry,' I replied, 'but I've only got half-a-crown on me.'

'My God!' he exclaimed: 'fancy inviting a man to go for a ride and then expecting him to pay for it.'

'But, Sir Herbert, it was you who invited me.'

'Yes, I know. I regard my behaviour as perfectly scandalous.'

'Oh, I beg your pardon.'

'You do not beg in vain.'

It was now the turn of the driver, who must have been a new-comer to the job, all the old ones knowing Tree well: 'I'd like you two gentlemen's names and addresses,' he said threateningly.

'I know what!' cried Tree, the light of inspiration in his eyes: 'He shall have seats. Yes, he shall have as many seats as he likes. He shall have *rows* of seats all to himself. He shall have tier upon tier of boxes and circles. We shall build a theatre to hold countless seats, and he shall have them all . . . Poor old Crippen! . . .'

I decided that it was time to talk sense:

'Will you please drive us back to His Majesty's Theatre? My name wouldn't interest you, but this is Sir Herbert Tree, a great man with curious habits.'

'Right you are, sir,' said the driver, becoming human and respectful at the same time: 'I've 'eard of 'im.'

We must have been somewhere in St James's during this incident, because I remember driving at an unholy rate through King Street, across the Square and along Charles Street. We narrowly missed another taxi in Waterloo Place, which brought Tree up with a jerk and an exclamation: 'I'm sure he didn't mean to do it,' which may have been inspired either by the driver or by Dr Crippen. At the theatre he managed to borrow some money for the taxi-driver, and then I left him. His last words were: 'Good-night, my boy . . . Why in heaven's name can't they use the Lethal Chamber?'

It was difficult for me, after that scene, to picture Tree as Macbeth, a part he essayed in the autumn of 1911. The rehearsals were more than usually nerve-fraying. Scenes were repeated again and again until the atmosphere of unexploded tempers became tense. Explosions began with the first dress-rehearsal, when Tree detonated during the Banquet scene, which was gone through twelve times, until it became clear that the only person in the play who would certainly be murdered was Macbeth. A great deal of thought had been given to an appropriate entrance for the chief character in the opening scene. It was heralded with an ear-splitting crash of thunder, and against the background of a lightning-riven sky rocks toppled and a stout oak-tree, rent to the roots, fell to earth. The shriek of the blast mingled with the sound of distant trumpets, and after the elements had run riot for a while a final flash of lightning showed the figure of Macbeth poised on a boulder. But Tree felt that the flash did not discriminate between the landscape and the figure, and asked the electrician if he had not seen lightning which illuminated *one man*. A repressed titter occurred in the stalls, which prompted him to say, 'I'm thinking of the play, not myself.' His sense of fun never deserted him for long, and when one of the Witches, buxom Frances Dillon, in flying through the air caught him full in the face and rolled him over on the ground, he joined heartily in the general laughter. Even at the height of one of his tempers, during a stage fight, he paused to have his joke, warning the Guardsmen who had been engaged as 'supers' that if one of them killed another he would be *fined*. In the middle of his speech, 'Is this a dagger that I see before me?' came the sound of thunder. He stopped to complain, but Cecil King at once informed him that it was real thunder in the heavens above the theatre. 'Ah, yes, I thought it wasn't as good as ours,' he said. My own share in these proceedings was slight but effective. At one point I carried Macbeth's shield, and while Tree was making it difficult for me to slip it on to his arm I dropped it on his toe, which received so much of his attention as he painfully hopped about that he forgot to curse me.

He took little notice of the acting of Violet Vanbrugh as Lady Macbeth, and still less of Arthur Bourchier's as Macduff; but all the Macbeth episodes were rehearsed with a thoroughness that

showed how difficult it is for an actor to attend to anything but
his own performance. For example, in the scene following the
murder of Duncan, Macbeth explains why he has killed the king's
attendants. This is how the explanation came from Tree at a dress-
rehearsal:

> Who can be wise, amazed, temperate, and furious,
> Loyal and neutral, in a moment? No man:

('Keep that light steady! What's he doing with it?')

> The expedition of my violent love
> Outran the pauser reason. Here lay Duncan,

('No, he's dead! Don't worry about him. Keep the light on me
—on my face, not my legs. Thank you. Words, please.')

> Here lay Duncan,
> His silver skin laced with his golden blood,
> And his gash'd stabs look'd like a breach in nature
> For ruin's wasteful entrance: there, the murderers,

('For God's sake don't fidget! This is a terrible scene. You
should feel rooted to the spot. Words, please.')

> there, the murderers,

('Think of that!—the *murderers*!')

> Steep'd in the colours of their trade, their daggers
> Unmannerly breech'd with gore:

('They won't be able to see me from that box. Will that gentleman oblige me by moving out of the way? Thank you. Words,
please.')

> Who could refrain—

('I wish you'd refrain from wobbling those lights!')

> That had a heart to love, and in that heart—

('I don't see terror or pity on anyone's face. I want everyone,
please, to appear *stricken*—stricken as well as rooted.')

> and in that heart
> Courage to make's love known?

('Now we'll do that again. Words, please.')

In a moment of enthusiasm Tree had asked Gordon Craig to work on designs for the scenery of *Macbeth*, and was delighted with the result. But when their collaboration began their methods did not harmonize, and Craig suggested that Tree should leave him in sole charge of the production; but in the end Tree took sole charge of the production. It cannot be said that he was good as Macbeth, but he was better than he might have been because the part did not bore him as much as most. 'It has been most interesting to me to have done *Macbeth*,' he wrote to Graham Robertson on December 1st, after he had been playing it for three months, 'it is a part in which I find fresh interest every night.'

All the same, he varied the monotony of the run by putting on Israel Zangwill's *The War God* for three performances. The rehearsals, as usual, were trying, especially to Zangwill, who was roundly informed that a good deal of his blank verse was 'mere journalism' and had to be lopped. Tree described Zangwill's physical appearance to a friend: 'his face shining like Moses, his teeth like the Ten Commandments, all broken'; and he directed a gibe at the well-known actor, J. H. Barnes, who was heard muttering to himself, 'Well, I've never been called a *baby* before!' As a rule Tree relied on Cecil King to prompt him, and could not bear to be prompted by anyone on the stage, but he never learnt his part in *The War God*, so some of his speeches were printed in large letters and stuck on the backs of seats and trees or pushed through the palm leaves that hid the orchestra. The character he portrayed was a sort of Tolstoy, whose appearance he copied, and at the end he was executed by counter-revolutionaries, a moment that must have gladdened the heart of the author after a dress-rehearsal.

Snipe-shooting in Ireland called me away from His Majesty's in the winter of 1911–12, and when I rejoined the company for *Othello* in March 1912 Tree wanted to know why I had not remained for his revivals of *The Man Who Was* and *Trilby*. I told him. 'My God!' he cried: 'what harm has the snipe done that you should wish to shoot it?' Knowing that his question was rhetorical, I left it unanswered. He was quite annoyed when I said that *Othello* did not suit him, and he implied that it was his finest

Shakespearean performance, the only substantial reason he advanced for this view being that the part made him perspire more than any of the others. A highly intelligent reading of Iago was given by Laurence Irving, and an exquisite performance of Desdemona by Phyllis Neilson-Terry. Laurence Irving was a somewhat lugubrious being, but Tree's fantastic way of saying things amused him, and he roared with laughter when Othello broke off in the middle of a speech to address the stage-manager: 'Oh, for God's sake stop people from passing in and out of that door! They look like the horrible objects that glide to and fro somewhere at the bottom of the sea.' At about this period Tree seemed more concerned with aphorisms than with acting. Several pithy comments occurred to him, and having heard their early forms it intrigued me to come across the polished versions in his notebooks over forty years after:

'Old men give advice to young men when they can no longer set them a bad example.' (There is a familiar ring about this, and I fancy Tree had heard it somewhere and appropriated it.)

'He is an old bore: even the grave yawns for him.'

'The man who said to everyone "How well you are looking!" became a millionaire.'

'There is only the difference of a letter between the beginning and the end of life—creation and cremation.'

'What a man would shrink from doing as an individual he wouldn't hesitate to do as a member of a committee.'

The annual Shakespeare Festival brought the spring season of 1912 to a close, and I left the great theatre that had meant so much to me for seven years. But though I joined Granville Barker I remained faithful to the old firm, and to the end of his life I would rather have watched Tree in a bad play than any other actor in a good one, such was the fascination of his personality. Barker's Shakespearean productions, though containing more of the poet's lines, never satisfied me as Tree's had done, largely because Tree encouraged his actors to act, while Barker made his underact. We have already seen that all the best players of the day appeared at one time or another at His Majesty's, and one of them, Lyn Harding, was the most gifted and versatile Shakespearean actor of his time. He could perform six parts in a week: Aguecheek in

Twelfth Night, the Ghost in *Hamlet*, Cassius in *Julius Caesar*, Prospero in *The Tempest*, Ford in *The Merry Wives of Windsor*, Bolingbroke in *Richard II*: and be equally good in all of them, speaking the verse superbly and playing the comedy delightfully. The only other actor I have seen in half a century who could accomplish such a feat with as much success is Michael Hordern, whose position on the stage of today is more clearly marked than Harding's was at His Majesty's, firstly because the level of Shakespearean acting in leading parts is not so high now as then (though the level of acting in the lesser parts is higher), and secondly because Hordern has a more intelligent and emotional grasp of character than Harding had.

Tree displayed generosity and sound sense in casting Lyn Harding for the name part in *Drake*, which filled His Majesty's for over six months in 1912–13. Pageantry was in the air, as it had been at the end of Shakespeare's life, and a year later came *Joseph and His Brethren*, in which Tree played the patriarch Jacob so imposingly that a company promoter was moved to say: 'Oh, if only we had you on our board of directors!' At moments the stage became an exhibition of Palestinian fauna, camels, oxen, sheep, asses and goats attracting the eyes of playgoers who would scarcely have noticed them in the street. Sarah Bernhardt, anxious to see the animals but not wishing to trespass on the manager's hospitality, sent someone secretly to engage a box. During an interval in the performance she received an envelope, on which was inscribed in a semi-illegible hand: 'I render unto Sarah the things that are Sarah's—H. B. T.' It contained the sum she had paid for the box.

My last conference with Tree took place during the run of *David Copperfield*, early in 1915. Temporarily invalided out of the army, I had returned to my job as secretary of The British Empire Shakespeare Society, for a public meeting of which I wanted the loan of His Majesty's Theatre. Entering his dressing-room, I shook hands with him and stated the reason for my visit. While I spoke he subsided wearily into a chair, still in the costume and make-up of Micawber.

'Have you seen *David Copperfield*?' he asked, taking no notice of my request.

'No.'

'Then you must see it.'

'I should like to.'

'So should I.'

'Do you think you will be able to lend us your theatre?'

'Have you seen *David Copperfield*?' he repeated, looking dreamily at me.

'I said "No".'

'Then you must see it.'

'Yes, I said I should like to see it.'

'So should I.'

'Will you please give an answer to my question?'

'Upon compulsion? Never!' he said in Falstaff's voice.

'I said "please", Sir Herbert.'

'I heard you.'

'Am I to understand——?' and I took up my hat.

'Silence!' He spoke to his dresser: 'Conduct this gentleman to the dome and give him a drink.'

I knew it was useless to protest; besides, I wanted the loan of his theatre; so I allowed myself to be put into the lift. Just as we were about to ascend, Tree poked his Micawberish head round the corner and said to the dresser:

'Explain to the gentleman, after he is pacified with a drink, that if he had seen *David Copperfield* he would not have come at the fall of the curtain to ask for a thing I am too tired to refuse . . . Take great care of him. The last man who used this lift was killed instantaneously, owing to the unaccountable habit it has acquired of dropping quite suddenly from the top floor to the bottom, just as one is about to step out of it . . . Good luck!' and he waved a farewell.

We reached our destination safely and at the dresser's bidding I made myself at home. In about twenty minutes Tree joined me, asked me to excuse him while he read some letters, and went to his desk. About five minutes passed in silence, which he broke. 'Sit down,' he said. As I was already seated, I failed to follow his trend of thought; but on looking up I saw another fellow in the room—a tall, big-boned, clean-shaven man, who nodded to me and sat down. I nodded back, handed him a paper, and went on turning over mine. At last Tree finished, said 'Ah!' several times in succession, added 'One in the eye for Whibley!' and flung himself into a roomy chair between us.

'Consider yourselves introduced,' said he, looking at the ceiling, 'because I only remember one of your names, and that wouldn't be fair on the other. This gentleman,' he continued, addressing me, 'represents an influential section of the New York press, and he wants me to tell him a lot of things about myself to prepare America for my third coming. That is chiefly why I asked you up here. You shall do the telling. I have nothing further to say.' He lay right back in his chair, closed his eyes, and gave an immediate impression of being fast asleep.

I gazed at the American and the American gazed at me. For several seconds neither of us spoke. Then he addressed the somnolent figure of the actor-manager:

'See here, Sir Beerbohm Tree, I didn't come to be introjooced to our young friend here, though I'm very glad to be acquainted with him. I want something bright and crisp about yourself to tell our folk on the other side. If you're played out, just say the word, and I'll pop in again when you're feeling spry.'

One of Tree's eyes opened slowly. 'Oh, God!' he murmured. The other eye followed suit. 'Oh, Manhattan!' he whispered.

This was enough for the American. He took out his notebook and made several entries, reading each aloud as he put it down: 'Great actor sends greetings to U.S. Pines for God's own country. Never happy since leaving Manhattan.'

Tree at once entered into the spirit of the thing. Springing from his chair, he began to walk about the room, dictating as he went, and warming to his work with many exclamations and gesticulations:

'For what are the United States? The answer is clear to anyone with an elementary knowledge of history. They are states which have been united. Why have they been united? A simple question that nevertheless demands a careful reply. They have been united because they did not wish to be separated. The point naturally arises: would they have benefited by a separation? No! A thousand times No! Why? Because they would no longer have been the United States. That, in brief, is its political history . . . I pause before I go on . . . What is its social aspect? What is its—forgive the professionalism—its apparent make-up? The reverse, I think, of its political aspect. The United States of a disunited people, a Nation of internationals, a cosmic chaos, a——'

At this point the American, who up to now had been too busy with pencil and notebook to think seriously of what he was putting down, tumbled to the fact that his leg was being pulled. He looked steadily at Tree for a moment, then closed his notebook with a loud snap, reached for his hat and stood up. I was so much interested in his movements that Tree's further discourse escaped me, though I was still conscious of the soft purring voice rising and falling. The subject of canned meat was occupying his mind when the American at length interrupted him; at least I caught a distinct reference to Chicago, pigs, porcupines, and (though the connection here was a trifle vague) trouser buttons. It was on the word 'buttons' that the Yankee cut in with the following curt and carefully-chosen words:

'Thank you, Sir Tree, thank you very much. You've got a fine place up here, but I hope you don't spend much time on the balcōny outside. It's a long drop to the street, and they haven't got padded pavements—yet. Good-night, sir. Good-night, mister.'

And with a nod to each of us he turned sharply on his heel and left the room.

'How curious!' mused Tree, as the sound of the American's footsteps died away; 'how curious! I never thought of that. . . . Padded pavements! . . . The orange-peel would lose its terror.'

He then returned to earth, and after asking me a few questions about army life he granted the loan of his theatre.

CHAPTER 22

Uniting the States

Mentally a man, temperamentally a boy, Tree had the happiest possible disposition. As we have seen, he loved to lace sense with nonsense, his light-headed nonsense being more intelligent than the thick-headed sense of others. He could not endure earnest folk, who are usually stupid; and as the majority of people associate dullness and self-importance with sincerity of purpose, he was generally regarded as flippant and superficial. He was not interested in politics, recognizing the irresponsibility with which men entrusted with the public welfare made a party game of it, as if they were playing football on an erupting volcano. He thought that speculation on religion was profitless, since man could not even understand himself, let alone the Creator, and he once nodded assent to a casual remark of mine: that many people wasted their present lives by tormenting themselves about a future life, that after death we shall know either everything or nothing, and that in either case our minds will be set at rest.

It may be that congruous work is one of the secrets of happiness, and Tree's whole being was in his theatre, though as an actor he was too imaginative for the mechanical routine of constant repetition, and as a manager too gay in spirit to treat his cares with gravity. Happiness, too, must be the outcome of a benevolent nature, and in this respect Tree's sincerity was manifested in unadvertised practical assistance whenever called upon to give it, in contributing to the welfare of those about him, in lending his theatre for all sorts of charitable and artistic objects, and in letting it to his brother-managers for as low a rent as he could take, not as high a rent as he could get. A further ingredient of happiness is detachment from the pettinesses of life, such as the desire to do the correct thing, to know the right people, to be seen in the proper places. It was necessary for Tree as head of his profession to be recognized as such by the powers that endorse distinction. His own position had been won against heavy odds, in the shadow of a man who had dominated the stage for a generation. With brains, pluck, initiative, driving power and imagination, he had taken the place of Irving; but it was not a case of Elisha inheriting the mantle of Elijah, because Tree wove one for himself and wore it with a difference but with as much distinction as his predecessor had worn his. He was therefore unconcerned with the silly subterfuges of snobbery, and was bored by the social distinctions that ministered to the vanity of so many folk, his attitude to such matters being perfectly expressed when he received the Lord Chamberlain's invitation to the funeral of Edward VII: 'I don't care a rap about the invitation, but I should have been damned angry if they hadn't sent it.' Equally he did not value the Crown orders bestowed on him by the Kaiser and the King of Italy; but they were useful as public acknowledgments of his work. He soon had cause to regret the German decoration.

Having brought the run of *Pygmalion* to a premature close in July, 1914, he set off for Marienbad, meaning to get there by car, driven by his chauffeur, Sam Wordingham, who wrote a description of what happened to them. The whole population of France was agitated by the possibility of war with Germany. At Luxembourg everyone thought the outbreak imminent, but Tree said that the present state of civilization made such a thing impossible and described the situation as 'a political game'. In Germany the game was being played more seriously, but at Frankfurt Tree remained in bed all the morning. Sam insisted that he should get up, as the English and Russians had left for their respective countries. 'He at last said he supposed he must get up, and I told him I was in favour of going home. He wondered why!' A visit to the British Consul explained why, and soon they were on their way back. 'I can't tell you,' he said to Sam, pointing to his breast; 'something seemed to break inside me when I heard it was war—wicked!—wicked!—wicked!' He refused to eat any breakfast, but had some beer, bread and cheese after an hour's run while the engine was cooling down. At a bridge over the Rhine they were stopped by soldiers. Tree got out and started to walk across the bridge. The car followed, escorted by two soldiers with fixed bayonets. After that they were held up every ten miles to show their passports. At Cologne children threw stones at their car, and some in the crowd booed them, but the place was so thickly packed with refugees that patriotic discrimination was difficult. No petrol was obtainable, the Government having prohibited its sale, and Tree caught the last train to leave the city. Their car was abandoned as well as all the luggage they could not carry. In the train he met Yvette Guilbert, who afterwards related that, having reached the Belgian frontier, they had to walk several kilometres 'in an awful heat, because the German railway cars could not leave German territory'. They bade farewell to each other at Liège: 'And, all about us, the anxieties of those thousands of people concerning their thousands of pieces of luggage, which they expected never to see again! And the thousand foolish little details of human anxiety for trunks full of clothes, while ruin and death were on the way.' Shedding their luggage as they went, Tree and Sam crossed Belgium in a train like sardines in a tin. Tree could neither eat nor drink. He said that the time would come when the man who made war would be the first in the firing-line, an ideal that may be realized by recent chemical discoveries. He also prophesied that Europe would degenerate because the best and strongest men would be slaughtered. They arrived at Ostend and had to wait many hours for a boat. Dover harbour was entered at daybreak. It was the dawn of a new age, and Tree knew it.

One of the first things he did on returning to London was to visit the Garrick Club, where he dropped into an armchair and related his experiences to Seymour Hicks. Then he jumped up and exclaimed: 'I know what I'll do—I'll send him a telegram!' 'Send who a telegram?' 'The Kaiser, my dear fellow, the Kaiser! I'll send him a telegram—that's what I'll do. I'll say, "You gave me a third-rate order for acting in Berlin—I've left you a fourth-rate motor-car for acting just as badly!"'

Most people like or dislike war because it distracts them from their private hostilities. Tree hated it because he hated all hostility, but he knew that life would not be liveable if German militarism were victorious, and he believed that its defeat would be followed by an enduring peace. Being a man incapable of feeling enmity, he could not understand that international peace will never come while there is turmoil in the heart of man, and that to expect permanent peace between nations is to believe that sparrow-hawks can lay doves' eggs. The conflict was therefore simplified in his mind as a war to stop future wars, and all his spare energies were directed to that end. He started off with a revival of *Drake*, giving all the profits to war charities. Knowing himself unsuited to the name part, he turned up at an early rehearsal saying that he was only going to read it as an understudy; but he soon deter-mined to play it, in spite of which the show ran for nearly three months. It was followed by *Henry IV*, but audiences were not in tune with Falstaff's views on honour, and Shakespeare gave place to Dickens. A successful run of *David Copperfield* was followed by two 'flops', and Tree accepted an offer to appear as Macbeth in a Hollywood silent film.

During a short holiday before his departure for America he visited Donnington Hall, where many Germans were interned. 'I rather envied them,' he said. 'I could not help feeling how delightful it would be to get behind that barbed wire and make faces at one's creditors.' Having made arrangements for the pro-duction of another pageant play, *Mavourneen* by L. N. Parker, which did fairly well, he went down to Hurstmonceux to stay with Claude Lowther. His fellow-guests were F. E. Smith (after-wards Lord Birkenhead) and Winston Churchill. The conver-sation was mainly about the war, Tree making a prophecy and a note:

> Winston talked much of his troubles over Gallipoli and seemed very manly about it. He considered that the only thing to do was for him to go into the trenches, and that he had committed the great crime of being unlucky. I told him that he should bide his time, and that he should say to the House of Commons, 'A little time you shall not hear me, and again a little time and you shall hear me.'

Having given a farewell supper to friends in the dome, Tree sailed for New York late in 1915, accompanied by his daughter Iris. He had what is now called a Victorian attitude to his own children, wishing them to maintain their innocence as long as possible. After introducing Iris to Isadora Duncan, he had said, 't see too much of her!' and now, aware that Iris would be meeting a natural son of his in America, he had asked Maud to explain the situation to her. Maud did so, telling him that Iris was not in the least perturbed. Yet he never referred to the subject on the journey, and when the boat docked at New York, and he waved to his son, he whispered to her, 'Be nice to your cousin.'

He arranged for a Shakespearean season in New York to coincide with the Tercentenary Commemoration of the poet's death, and set off for California to fulfil his contract. He wrote to Maud from The Blackstone, Chicago, on December 23rd, 1915, and spent Christmas Day at the Grand Canyon. He was received by the Mayor of Los Angeles, overhauled by the press, and on his arrival at the studio saluted by the discharge of pistols. 'Recovering from the shock, and finding myself, happily, unwounded, I raised my hat to the cheering crowd.' A five-years-old boy, popular on the films, advanced, the word 'Welcome' sewn in large letters on his long garment. 'Pleased to meet you, Sir Tree.' They shook hands. 'And how has the world been using you these last few years?' asked the newcomer. With a resigned shrug of the shoulders, the child replied: 'Well, I guess this world's good enough for me.'

Settling down in Hollywood at 1985 North Van Ness Avenue, Tree started work on the *Macbeth* film in January, 1916. With no responsibilities he was happy and carefree in spirit, and his fellow-workers voted him a 'sport'. He did not like the new medium, preferring more space and less pace, and said that 'at Los Angeles I never had any private life', but he showed intense interest in the job and enjoyed the surroundings. The picture was finished in six weeks, and every one except himself was thrilled by the preliminary 'running', at the conclusion of which he was found fast asleep in his seat.

By the middle of March he reported to Maud from New York: 'I had a rest-cure of four days in the train—wonderful after the slave-driving work through which I went at Los Angeles.' He presented *Henry VIII* in New York, the scenery having been sent over from England. It was an immense success, the press describing it as the most sumptuous Shakespearean production ever seen in the States. 'They want me to have a theatre here in the autumn and to call it "The Tree Theatre",' he wrote gleefully to Maud. Within two months all the capital invested in the production, in addition to £4,000 preliminary expenses, had been paid back, a clear profit of £2,000 had been made, and he had received a large salary. 'Not bad!' he concluded. The play could easily have run to the end of the season, but that was not his way of doing things, and he put on *The Merchant of Venice* as well as *The Merry Wives of Windsor*. On Shakespeare's birthday, Easter Sunday, both he and Sir Johnston Forbes-Robertson gave addresses from the pulpit of the Cathedral of St John the Divine. Haddon Chambers saw a lot of him and described the whole season as a managerial accomplishment of the highest order. Tree greatly valued the advice of his wife, and would frequently say to Chambers, 'I wish I could talk this over with Maud' or 'I'm certain Maud would agree with me there'; and another friend, Luther Munday, testified to the 'extravagant admiration . . . in every possible way' that Herbert had for Maud.

Meanwhile the war was never absent from his mind; and though there was a good deal of pro-German feeling in America at the time, he made speech after speech, both in and out of the theatre, for the cause of the allied powers, England and France. 'Daddy grows more and more an extempore artiste', wrote Iris, 'and makes brilliant speeches every night unprepared.' But they were not always unprepared, because Tree confessed that he used to think out his 'curtain' speeches while delivering Wolsey's farewell on the stage. Life was strenuous and he had little time for writing letters home, but he loved to hear all the family news, and when Viola gave birth to a girl he wrote, 'I hope your daughter will bring you both as much happiness as you have brought me.' He was extremely anxious to go home for a short visit at the end of the season and made arrangements to do so; but the submarine peril became acute and Maud sent cables begging him not to make the journey. He replied on June 22nd, 1916, from The Greenbrier, White Sulphur Springs, West Virginia:

> I cannot tell you how terrible was my disappointment at not going home for a little while.—I cannot now understand why the risk was considered so great—and in a way I liked the risk—for I knew people would be glad to think that I did not care much about my little self in this terrible time when they are all facing danger at home.—However, the thing is done—and in the face of that series of

cables I felt I must not cross—but it was only your final cable that determined me.—Let us hope it may have been for the best.—I could only have stayed a week or ten days.—Now we are off to California to do another three months of pictures—I don't relish the prospect. —Still it is money, money all the way! Then I am arranging to tour in October for three months—they say we shall have a tremendous tour . . .

I have been making speeches—some quite good and useful. Did you see the one about Lloyd George and Ireland? I think I shall send it to him, and ask him to let me do some work at the end of the war. Of course there are two ways—and the danger is that stupidity and passion and the flush of success in victory will make people more militant and then the result of the war will only be other wars— the whole civilized world should combine now for a perpetual peace. Even here one hears a lot of rotten 'talk talk'.—By the by I wish you would whisper in the right quarter that we ought to have social ambassadors—men of the type of Charles Beresford—the public are in the right mood for alliance—but now is the time to grapple with hoops of steel.

Iris and I are here for a few days—I was quite ill—and gout coming on apace—but I can only stay ten days as I must be off to California in that time.—I am ever so much better in these few days—so that's a good thing.—Give my love to Viola and Fit*—darling child, she is so happy about her baby coming.—Don't overwork yourself with all the charities—by the by the Bazaar in New York did splendidly—I went there and helped—it was a terrible crush, and I was 'done in' after the strenuous season—an enormous success. Have you read the Asche play? I am putting money into it.—
Good-bye—God bless everybody. Your H.

The play to which he referred was a musical show called *Chu Chin Chow*, which Oscar Asche produced at His Majesty's Theatre at the end of August, 1916, and which ran for five years. Tree had not read the manuscript, but on the recommendation of his London committee he invested £2,000 in the production, and on worldly grounds had no cause to regret the investment.

He returned to Los Angeles, but this time he did not like the job. On August 3rd he wrote to Viola from 1862 Cherokee Avenue, Hollywood:

I am doing an awful picture here—but I suppose it has to be.— I play the part of a virtuous American senator-farmer who would wear elastic side-spring boots and a toupée, has the old testament in

* Felicity.

one hand and the ace of diamonds up his sleeve. It is called 'The Old Folks at Home'—and is not entirely in my line. We have a lovely abode—garden full of oranges and lemons (their blossoms scenting the night) and an eucalyptus tree with large masses of blossom—a Jap cook—two English servants.

In a letter to Henry Dana he said 'I must swallow my antipathies and smile at the money'; but he was extremely anxious to return home and get back to worthy work, writing to Maud: 'We ought to do something to stir the people—and take them out of the hogwash they are lapping up now.—Is it not terrible? They say war is ennobling—look at the songs it brings forth!'

However, he obtained relief from the film by arranging a performance of *Oliver Twist* for the benefit of the British Red Cross Fund, and Charlie Chaplin, whom he liked very much, played the Artful Dodger. He also prepared for the press a volume of short stories called *Nothing Matters*, the profits of which were to help a fund for actors disabled in the war. It came out in January, 1917. A collection of his essays and lectures entitled *Thoughts and Afterthoughts* had been published in 1913 and reprinted several times. Another employment in these trying weeks was to go through several trunks full of the accumulated letters of thirty-five years, which he had taken with him to America. He read and destroyed them. They gave him data for the memoirs he projected but never wrote. Having lived his life unselfconsciously, his impressions, he anticipated, would be more philosophic than photographic.

Unable to face any more films, the makers of which treated him with scant courtesy, he arranged an autumn tour of *Henry VIII* and *The Merry Wives of Windsor*, starting at Boston on October 15th, and then paid a flying-visit to England, where he arrived in the first week of September. 'The call of London was absolutely irresistible,' he told a newspaper reporter. 'There is but one word for it. I was homesick.' In order to get home he was also seasick, which he considered a horrible affliction: 'I hate the landscapes on the insides of those basins.' He saw *Chu Chin Chow* at once, and summed it up in a phrase: 'More navel than millinery.' He disliked it and felt that by doing such a thing at His Majesty's his old lieutenant Oscar Asche had let the theatre down, but he tried to comfort himself with the thought that 'in these days one must not expect to get what one likes, and the public has the plays it deserves'. And there was consolation in the handsome dividends.

But he had lost some of his eager interest in the theatre. The war, his book, the films, his speeches had taken up so much of his time that he seemed less keen about plays. His brother Max noticed at their last meeting that he said not a word about acting. I was struck by the same thing. As President of the Actors' Committee for the Shakespeare Tercentenary Performance, which had taken place in his absence at Drury Lane Theatre, he went to the St James's Theatre one September morning in 1916 to present me with a silver cigarette-box, given by the Committee in remembrance of my services as Secretary. Sir George Alexander and H. B. Irving were the only other members of the Committee present. All three died while I was serving abroad.

Tree asked me how I liked the army, which I had managed to rejoin some months earlier. I replied suitably. 'Do you want to go to the front?' he asked. 'Does anyone *not* want to?' I countered, with three pairs of patriotic eyes upon me. 'I don't,' he answered emphatically, adding as an afterthought, 'at least I shan't pretend I do.' This was a most refreshing statement at a time when all the elderly men in the country went about bleating 'If only we were younger!' With a wealth of gesticulation Tree then described the inventions that were shortly to be used against the Zeppelins. He spoke of some terrifying things that our airmen were to carry, calling them 'great tentacles of fire', and as he clawed the air it seemed to me that the war would soon be over. H. B. Irving next told a yarn, straight from the War Office, about Kitchener's death. A few days before his departure for Russia he had received a wire: 'Shall Henry enter the London Academy next December?' He thought it meaningless; but after the ship carrying him had been sunk off the Shetlands, someone noticed that the first letter of each word spelt the ominous name. 'Dirty work, I should think,' said H. B. Irving. 'I must take a copy of that, Harry!' cried Tree, just like a child who had been shown a new toy. As I said 'Good-bye' I felt that he owed much of his charm to his abiding youth.

He was back in America by the end of September, the last four

days of the sea-voyage on the *Philadelphia* being of some interest
to the crew, who were conscious that a fire was raging in the
hold, but of no interest to the passengers, from whom the information was withheld. At The Plaza in New York he received
a book from Frank Harris, who also wrote him a letter which did
not arrive. Harris was then undergoing a phase of unpopularity
due to his pro-German outpourings, which, being interpreted,
were merely pro-Harris outpourings. But Tree was not the man
to ignore someone he had once known merely on account of his
opinions or because he was out of favour; and when Harris told
Constance Collier that he had received no reply to his letter, Tree
at once wrote: 'I have not had your letter—or I should not have
failed to write to you. Please ring me up here . . . Congratulations on your book.' It is pleasant to know that Tree's patriotism,
unlike that of so many eminent men, did not dehumanize him.
At the end of 1916 his daughter Iris wanted to get married at once
to Curtis Moffat, and there was much correspondence between
Herbert and Maud touching her youth and the young man's lack
of money; but they capitulated to love, and the marriage took
place in December. 'Daddy was so sweet about this,' wrote Iris.

Tree took his productions of *Henry VIII* and *The Merry Wives
of Windsor* to all the leading cities in the States, and the tour was a
triumph. Lyn Harding played the King in one and Ford in the
other. 'All the people in the company are very nice to me, especially Lyn Harding, a wonderfully clever and sympathetic man,' he
told Maud in January, 1917. He and Harding stayed up chatting
together nearly every night, exchanging old theatrical memories
until well into the early hours. Tree delivered innumerable 'curtain' speeches, always with a strong patriotic tinge. Altogether he
made more than a hundred speeches in favour of the Allies before
America joined in the war. The company finished up with a
season at the New Amsterdam Theatre, New York, where among
other novelties he presented *Colonel Newcome*, on the first night of
which he ingeniously interpolated a toast to the British Navy for
which Thackeray was not responsible. The experiment was received with roars of applause, which enabled him to add 'And let
us not forget our friends across the seas', which brought down the
house. Each performance at the New Amsterdam was the occasion

for another attempt to unite the States on the subject of the war, and several times he called on the audiences to sing the National Anthems of England, France, Russia and America. For a charity in aid of mutilated soldiers at the Metropolitan Opera House he appeared as Colonel Newcome, closing a peroration with 'Colonel Newcome begs respectfully to salute the Star Spangled Banner', which raised the roof; and whenever asked to attend any public function, he took the opportunity of putting the case for the Allies. After America had entered the war he received letters from Britain's Prime Minister, Lloyd George, and her elder statesman, Arthur Balfour, acknowledging the value of his contribution to the Cause; and at a farewell luncheon given him by the Executive Committee of the Pilgrims, the famous American orator, Chauncey M. Depew, spoke of his 'cordial service for friendly relations between our two nations'.

But all the time this 'unofficial ambassador extraordinary' to America, as he was called in *The New York Times*, yearned for home. He felt that 'It will be terrible to die without knowing the end and consequences of this terrible affair'; yet when Yvette Guilbert asked him why he was returning to England at so hazardous a moment for travellers, he replied: 'Yes, it is dangerous, but I feel I must go home. I must go.' Before leaving, he was received by President Wilson at The White House. Tree's appearance reminded Wilson of a well-known statesman, and Wilson's appearance reminded Tree of another well-known statesman, so each felt quite at ease in the company of the other. On April 28th, 1917, Herbert wrote his last letter to his wife from The Plaza, New York:

My dear Maud
   I am writing in great haste as I am due at the dentist's—I have been rather weary in health lately.—By this time I hope you will have seen by the papers that my activities are not unknown. I assure you I have done much more good here than I could have at home, though the work has not been so spectacular.—I send you copies of letters from A. Balfour and Lloyd George.—I am trying to get away about the 8th May—probably by a Spanish boat—so I should see you soon, bar accidents.—Thank Clara Butt.—I send you some newspaper cuttings.—Balfour has made a deep impression—it was tremendously important he should come.—Give my love to all the

dear ones.—I long to be home—in fact I can't bear the prison of this. Your loving Herbert Tree.

He arrived in London on May 27th, having acted as King's Messenger from Madrid, which enabled him to cross from Calais to Dover instead of by the usual Havre–Southampton route. He went down to Sutton Courtney, where Maud was staying with the Asquiths; but he preferred the London streets to the country flowers even in springtime, and in a day or two he was within easy reach of His Majesty's Theatre, his real home in spite of the Oriental pantomime then filling it nightly.

CHAPTER 23

Quick Exit

Feeling free to do what he liked for a little while, Tree plunged into social life. Somehow the shadow of war seemed less dark when he was nearer to it. Everyone was glad to see him, and he never lost the love of being liked. He was often at the Garrick Club, and attended every function to which he was invited. He saw George Alexander for the last time in a play, *The Aristocrat*, and lunched with him and the Charles Wyndhams at Alexander's house in Pont Street. He dined out frequently, and livened up every party with his gaiety. He once told the simple truth about himself when someone asked how he was. 'Oh, I'm radiant!' he replied; and now, in the spring of 1917, no one who saw him could have guessed that his radiance was about to be dimmed.

On June 16th he was staying at 7 Ethel Bay, Birchington, Kent, and going up a steep old-fashioned staircase he slipped and fell. He called for help, and the cook-housekeeper found him lying at the bottom of the stairs, holding on to the banister. 'I believe I have broken my leg,' he said. She helped him into the sitting-room, where they found that the lower part of his shoe-heel had been torn off. He rested on a sofa while she telephoned for a doctor, but when she returned he was lying on the floor, having tried to walk and again fallen. The doctor found that a tendon above the knee-cap had been ruptured. Tree was taken back to London by car next day, and entered Sir Alfred Fripp's nursing home, Netley House, 15 Henrietta Street, Covent Garden. Fripp saw him on the 18th and decided to operate on the 19th. Again the central figure in a show, Tree displayed the keenest curiosity in the preparations. He was given nothing but gas and oxygen, so that he could enjoy watching all the preliminaries in the operating theatre, generally gone through when the patient was unconscious. As the gas was administered he was heard to mutter 'Nirvana', and a moment later 'I shall see you again.' The operation was successful, and soon he was in exuberant spirits, writing a brief note to Viola: 'We'll talk things over when we meet—and may that be soon, darling! I send you £10 today to pay little debts. All goes miraculously with me—Fripp is overjoyed—and I am thankful. Loving Dad.' When the stitches were removed the wound had healed perfectly, and Tree said that he must get up at once in order to preside at a dinner of the O.P. Club. Fripp put his foot down. Tree insisted, saying that he had been accustomed to giving orders, not receiving them. Fripp laughed and said that the situation was now reversed.

The patient became impatient, refusing to lie still in bed during his convalescence and making all sorts of plans, among others for the production of a new play, *The Great Lover*, which he read so often in bed that he almost knew his part. There were many visitors, gifts and messages, and he received the attentions paid him with the surprised pleasure and excitement of a schoolboy aged 64. But the enforced rest after his accident had caused the formation of blood clots.

On Monday evening, July 2nd, 1917, he sat up in bed to eat his dinner, afterwards chatting to his nurse while she pared him a peach. He asked her to open the window. She did so, and as she turned towards him again his head fell forward. He was dead.

When his brother Max saw him early next morning his face seemed

> both familiar and strange. Death, that preserves only what is essential, had taken away whatever it is that is peculiar to the face of an actor. Extreme strength of character and purpose was all that remained and outstood now. But at the corners of the lips there was the hint of an almost whimsical, an entirely happy smile. And I felt that Herbert, though he was no longer breathing, was somehow still 'radiant'.

It was arranged that his ashes should be placed in the graveyard of Hampstead Parish Church. An air-raid began while the funeral procession was on its way to the Golders Green crematorium, and the journey was made to the accompaniment of bursting bombs and booming guns. Tree would have enjoyed the drama of his final exit, while reflecting that, with a few barrels of stones, several sheets of tin and a couple of large drums, he could have produced a more striking effect at His Majesty's Theatre.

Appendix

List of Plays produced by Sir Herbert Tree at the Theatre Royal, Haymarket, and His Majesty's Theatre: 1887-1917. (Excluding dates of their Revivals.)

PRODUCED AT HAYMARKET THEATRE

DATES	PLAYS	AUTHORS
1887	The Red Lamp (transferred from Comedy Theatre)	W. Outram Tristram
	The Ballad Monger	Adapted by Walter Pollock from Theodore de Banville's *Gringoire*
1888	Partners	Robert Buchanan
	Cupid's Messenger	Alfred C. Calmour
	Pompadour	W. G. Wills and Sydney Grundy, founded on Brachvogel's *Narcisse*
	A Compromising Case	Adapted from the French by Mrs T. E. Smale
	Captain Swift	C. Haddon Chambers
	Masks and Faces	Tom Taylor and Charles Reade
	The Duchess of Bayswater & Co.	A. M. Heathcote
1889	The Merry Wives of Windsor	Shakespeare
	Wealth	Henry Arthur Jones
	A Man's Shadow	Adapted by Robert Buchanan from the French play *Roger la Honte*
1890	A Village Priest	Sydney Grundy (suggested by *Le Secret de la Terreuse*)

DATES	PLAYS	AUTHORS
	Rachel	Miss Clo Graves
	Comedy and Tragedy	W. S. Gilbert
	Called Back	Hugh Conway and J. Comyns Carr
	The Intruder	Adapted from the French of Maurice Maeterlinck
	Beau Austin	W. E. Henley and Robert Louis Stevenson
	The Waif	Adapted by Cotsford Dick from *Le Passant*
	Peril	Saville Row and B. C. Stephenson
1891	*The Dancing Girl*	Henry Arthur Jones
1892	*Hamlet*	Shakespeare
1893	*Hypatia*	G. Stuart Ogilvie
	A Woman of No Importance	Oscar Wilde
	An Enemy of the People	Henrik Ibsen
	The Tempter	Henry Arthur Jones
	Six Persons	Israel Zangwill
1894	*The Charlatan*	Robert Buchanan
	Once Upon a Time	Adaptation by Louis N. Parker and H. B. Tree from Ludwig Fulda's play *Der Talisman*
	A Bunch of Violets	Founded on Octave Feuillet's *Mountjoys*, by Sydney Grundy
	A Modern Eve	Malcolm C. Salaman
	John-a-Dreams	C. Haddon Chambers
1895	*Fedora*	Version by Herman Merivale of play by Victorien Sardou
	Trilby	Paul M. Potter, dramatized from George Du Maurier's novel
1896	*Henry IV, Part I*	Shakespeare

PRODUCED AT HIS MAJESTY'S THEATRE

1897	*The Seats of the Mighty*	Gilbert Parker

DATES	PLAYS	AUTHORS
	Chand d'Habits	Wordless play by Catulle Mendès
	The Silver Key	Sydney Grundy
	Katherine and Petruchio	Garrick's version of Shakespeare's *The Taming of the Shrew*
1898	*Julius Caesar*	Shakespeare
	Ragged Robin	Adapted by L. N. Parker from *Le Chemineau* by Jean Richepin
	The Musketeers	Sydney Grundy, founded on the novel by Dumas
1899	*Carnac Sahib*	Henry Arthur Jones
	King John	Shakespeare
1900	*A Midsummer Night's Dream*	Shakespeare
	Rip Van Winkle	
	Herod	Stephen Phillips
1901	*Twelfth Night*	Shakespeare
	Macaire	W. E. Henley and Robert Louis Stevenson
	The Last of the Dandies	Clyde Fitch
1902	*Ulysses*	Stephen Phillips
	The Eternal City	Hall Caine
1903	*Resurrection*	Tolstoy, adapted by Henri Bataille and Michael Morton
	The Gordian Knot	Claude Lowther
	Flodden Field	Alfred Austin
	The Man Who Was	F. Kinsey Peile, dramatized from Rudyard Kipling's story
	Richard II	Shakespeare
	The Darling of the Gods	David Belasco and John Luther Long
1904	*The Tempest*	Shakespeare
1905	*Much Ado About Nothing*	Shakespeare
	[First Annual Shakespeare Festival]	

DATES	PLAYS	AUTHORS
	Business is Business	Adapted by Sydney Grundy from *Les Affaires sont les Affaires* by Octave Mirbeau
	Oliver Twist	Adapted by J. Comyns Carr from the novel by Dickens
1906	*Nero*	Stephen Phillips
	Colonel Newcome	Adapted by Michael Morton from the novel by Thackeray
	The Winter's Tale	Shakespeare
	Antony and Cleopatra	Shakespeare
1907	*The Van Dyck*	Adapted by Cosmo Gordon Lennox from the French of Eugène Fourrier Peringue
1908	*The Mystery of Edwin Drood*	Adapted by J. Comyns Carr from the novel by Dickens
	The Beloved Vagabond	William J. Locke
	Hansel and Gretel	E. Humperdinck
	The Merchant of Venice	Shakespeare
	Faust	Stephen Phillips and J. Comyns Carr
	Pinkie and the Fairies	W. Graham Robertson. Music by Frederic Norton
1909	*The School for Scandal*	R. B. Sheridan
	False Gods	Translated by James B. Fagan from *La Foi* by Brieux
	Beethoven	Adapted by L. N. Parker from play by Réné Fauchois
	A Russian Tragedy	Adapted by Henry Hamilton from the German of Adolph Glass
	The Lethal Hotel	Translated by Frederick Whelen from play by A. W. Willner
1910	*The O'Flynn*	Justin Huntly McCarthy
	[The Thomas Beecham Opera Season]	
	Henry VIII	Shakespeare
1911	*Macbeth*	Shakespeare
	The War God	Israel Zangwill

DATES	PLAYS	AUTHORS
	Orpheus in the Underground	Version of Offenbach's *Orphée aux Enfers* by Frederic Norton, Alfred Noyes and H. B. Tree
1912	*Othello*	Shakespeare
	Drake	L. N. Parker
1913	*The Happy Island*	M. Lengyel
	Ariadne in Naxos, and The Perfect Gentleman	Translation of Molière's *Le Bourgeois Gentilhomme* by W. Somerset Maugham
	Joseph and His Brethren	L. N. Parker
1914	*Pygmalion*	Bernard Shaw
	David Copperfield	Adapted by L. N. Parker from the novel by Dickens
1915	*The Right to Kill*	Adapted by Gilbert Cannan and F. Keyzer
	Marie Odile	Edward Knoblauch
	Mavourneen	L. N. Parker
1916	[Arthur Bourchier Season]	
	[Martin Harvey Season]	
	Macbeth Film	
	Chu Chin Chow	Oscar Asche and Frederic Norton
	[Oscar Asche's Season]	

Authorities

The Private Papers of Sir Herbert and Lady Tree, including letters, diary, notebooks, and other manuscripts.

Chronicle of the Beerbohm Family (compiled partly from an old German Chronicle and partly from the diary of Ernest Henry Beerbohm), by Dora Beerbohm

Personal knowledge

Private information

Herbert Beerbohm Tree: Some Memories of Him and of His Art. Collected by Max Beerbohm. n.d. (*c.* 1920)

Herbert Beerbohm Tree, by Mrs George Cran, 1907

Thoughts and Afterthoughts, by Herbert Beerbohm Tree, 1913

Nothing Matters, by Herbert Beerbohm Tree, 1917

Ellen Terry and Bernard Shaw: A Correspondence. Edited by Christopher St John, 1931

Bernard Shaw and Mrs Patrick Campbell: Their Correspondence. Edited by Alan Dent, 1952

Our Theatres in the Nineties, by Bernard Shaw, 3 volumes, 1932

Music in London, 1890–4, by Bernard Shaw, Volume 2, 1932

Days and Ways of an Old Bohemian, by Major Fitzroy Gardner, 1921

The Life and Letters of Henry Arthur Jones, by Doris Arthur Jones, 1930

Oscar Asche, by Himself. n.d. (*c.* 1929)

Both Sides of the Curtain, by Elizabeth Robins, 1940

Harlequinade, by Constance Collier, 1929

To Tell My Story, by Irene Vanbrugh, 1948

My Life and Some Letters, by Mrs Patrick Campbell, 1922

Dame Madge Kendal, by Herself, 1933

Ellen Terry's Memoirs, with additions by Edith Craig and Christopher St John, 1933

Two Worlds for Memory, by Alfred Noyes, 1953

Time Was, by W. Graham Robertson, 1931

Celebrities and Simple Souls, by Alfred Sutro, 1933

My Memoirs, by Sir Frank Benson, 1930

Mainly Players, by Lady Benson, 1926

Me and My Missus, by Seymour Hicks, 1939

Between Ourselves, by Seymour Hicks, 1930

This for Remembrance, by Julia Neilson, 1941

Studio and Stage, by Joseph Harker, 1924

Myself—and Some Others, by Owen Nares, 1925

From Studio to Stage, by Weedon Grossmith, 1913

The Truth at Last, by Charles Hawtrey, 1924
Haymarket: Theatre of Perfection, by W. Macqueen-Pope, 1948
A Quaker Singer's Recollections, by David Bispham, 1920
Alfred Fripp, by Cecil Roberts, 1932
Old Days in Bohemian London, by Mrs. Clement Scott, n.d.
The Strange Life of Willy Clarkson, by Harry J. Greenwall, 1936
My Bohemian Days, by Harry Furniss, 1919
Men and Memories, by William Rothenstein (1900–22), 1932
Kate Terry Gielgud: an Autobiography, 1953
Clyde Fitch and his Letters, by Montrose J. Moses and Virginia Gerson, 1924
Many Celebrities and a Few Others, by William H. Rideing, 1912
Final Edition, by E. F. Benson, 1940
Fifty Years of a Londoner's Life, by H. G. Hibbert, 1916
A Playgoer's Memories, by H. G. Hibbert, 1920
A Chronicle of Friendship, by Luther Munday, 1912
The Colvins and Their Friends, by E. V. Lucas, 1928
Son of Oscar Wilde, by Vyvyan Holland, 1954
Peregrine Pickle, by Tobias Smollett
Dictionary of National Biography
Periodicals

INDEX OF NAMES

Aide, Hamilton, 24, 43, 53

Ainley, Henry, 119, 137, 159, 169, 208

Alexander, George, 2, 19, 29, 31, 84, 85, 121, 134, 176, 197, 229, 233

Allan, Charles, 58, 75

Ambler, Constance, 20

Archer, William, 11, 134

Arliss, George, 75

Arthur, Sir George, 3

Asche, Oscar, 3, 105, 118, 165, 199, 227, 228

Asquith, H. H., 143, 168, 232

Asquith, Margot, 143, 168, 232

Austin, Alfred, 103

Baird, Dorothea, 91

Bakst, 160

Balfour, A., 143, 231

Bancrofts, The, 10, 16, 54, 59, 70, 84, 102, 147, 167

Baring, Maurice, 2, 145

Barker, Granville, 60, 159, 160, 161, 179, 198, 209, 216

Barnato, Barney, 153

Barnes, J. H., 215

Barrie, Sir James, 3, 163

Bataille, Henri, 152

Beerbohm, Constance, 123

Beerbohm, Ernest Henry, 6, 8

Beerbohm, J., 122, 123

Beerbohm, Julius Ewald, 6, 8, 13, 21, 22, 41, 65

Beerbohm, Sir Max, 4, 42, 62, 67, 79, 80, 81, 82, 107, 109, 147, 167, 168, 190, 199, 229, 234

Bell, Stanley, 19, 31, 196

Belloc, Hilaire, 148

Benson, F. R., 46, 47, 72, 134, 165, 166, 185

Benson, Mrs, 46, 166

Beresford, Charles, 227

Bernhardt, Sarah, 23, 63, 84, 145, 197, 217

Betterton, 116

Bischoffsheim, Mrs, 101

Bispham, David, 64

Booth, Edwin, 33, 63

Boucicault, Dion, 23, 189

Bourchier, Arthur, 119, 165, 169, 170, 206, 213

Brayton, Lily, 129

Brieux, 72, 157, 158, 176

Brieux, Madame, 158

Brookfield, Charles, 43, 61, 127

Brough, Lionel, 62, 80, 94, 113, 129, 156

Browning, Robert, 30, 31, 134

Brownlow, Mr, 153

Bruce, Edgar, 21, 22, 23, 24, 44, 51

Buchel, Charles, 188

Burbage, 116

Burdett-Coutts, Lady, 155

Burnand, F. E., 25

Butler, R., 61

Butt, Clara, 103, 209, 231

Byron, 35, 134

Caine, Hall, 2, 139, 140

Calvert, Louis, 118

Campbell, Mrs Patrick, 2, 84, 85, 86, 118, 120, 157, 158, 172, 176, 178, 179, 180–2, 190, 193

Carr, Comyns, 43, 51, 53, 127, 137, 152, 154, 164
Carr, Philip, 114
Carson, Edward, 121, 122, 143
Carte, D'Oyly, 76
Cassel, Ernest, 92, 151
Cecil, Arthur, 87
Chamberlain, Joseph, 78, 143, 144
Chambers, C. Haddon, 1, 52, 53, 79, 98, 226
Chaplin, Charlie, 228
Chapman, H., 154
Churchill, Winston, 143, 156, 157, 224
Clarendon (The Lord Chamberlain), 167, 175, 176, 222
Clarkson, Willy, 3, 198
Cleveland, President (U.S.A.), 81
Coglan, 11
Coleridge, 134
Collier, Constance, 2, 118, 133, 139, 153, 198, 230
Colvin, Sydney, 50
Connolly, 20
Constance, 148
Conway, H. B., 26, 43, 44
Coquelin, 145, 152
Corelli, Marie, 139
Craig, Edith, 11
Craig, Gordon, 11, 159, 160, 161, 196, 215
Cunard, Lady, 2
Cust, Harry, 145

Daly, Augustine, 92
Dana, Henry, 99, 102, 125, 181, 204, 206, 228
Dante, 134
Darwin, Charles, 18
De Beer, 153
Dickens, 18, 67, 152, 153, 190, 191, 224
Dickson-Kenwin, G., 186
Dillon, Francis, 213

Disraeli, 109, 113
D'Orsay, Count, 138, 139
Doyle, Conan, 140
Draper, C., 6
Draper, Eliza, 13
Draper, John, 6
Dumas, 125
Du Maurier, George, 1, 82, 83, 86, 87, 90, 191
Du Maurier, Gerald, 91, 97
Duncan, Isadora, 224

Edward VII, King, 129, 147, 168, 222
Elgar, Edward, 1, 163
Eliot, 135
Emery, Winifred, 118, 132
Esmond, H. V., 156
Evelyn, Beerbohm, 122

Fagan, James B., 157
Fauchois, Réné, 164
Fechter, 62, 63
Felicity (Tree's daughter), 74, 96, 98, 149, 227
Fitch, Clyde, 138
Fleming, George, 141
Floyd, Mrs, 33
Forbes, Norman, 129, 188
Forbes-Robertson, Johnstone, 24, 62, 72, 87, 99, 116, 141, 173, 176, 191, 226
Fordham, Mrs E., 196
Frederick, Crown Prince, 5
Frederick the Great, 5
Fripp, Sir Alfred, 1, 233, 234
Fry, 135
Fulton, Charles, 119

Gardner, Fitzroy, 91, 92, 115
Garrick, David, 104, 116

George, A. E., 207
George, Lloyd, 143, 144, 156, 227, 231
George V., King, 209
German, Edward, 56, 163, 169
Gilbert, W. S., 43, 45, 46, 57, 64, 74, 75, 76, 77, 78, 90, 91, 120, 121, 129
Gill, Basil, 119, 156
Gill, Charles F., 2
Gillette, William, 140
Gladstone, Mr and Mrs, 60
Glenesk, Lord, 113
Godwin, E. W., 11, 27, 33, 37, 38, 39, 43
Goodwin, Nat, 170
Granby, Lady, 80
Grasso, Giovanni, 187
Greets, Ben, 91
Grieg, 63
Grossmith, George, 3
Grossmith, Weedon, 119, 195
Grundy, Sydney, 58, 78, 98, 123, 125, 181
Guerbal, Count de, 25
Guilbert, Yvette, 147, 223, 231

Hampson, Sir George, 36
Harding, Lyn, 119, 133, 153, 159, 216, 217, 230
Hare, Sir John, 4, 54, 59, 64, 72, 85, 167
Harker, Joseph, 129
Harriet (Tree's sister-in-law), 4
Harris, Frank, 55, 230
Harrison, Frederick, 3
Harvey, M., 172
Hastings, 53, 127
Hatteras, 208
Hawtrey, Charles, 43, 147
Haye, Colonel John, 81, 143
Hazlitt, W., 17
Hearne, James, 156
Hecht, Mrs, 158
Helmore, Arthur, 54
Henley, W. E., 48, 49, 50, 60

Henry, Sir E., 199
Henschel, G., 63
Hering, Paul, 20
Herman, H., 55
Hickens, Robert, 15
Hicks, Seymour, 159, 190, 223
Holland, Vyvyan, 68, 69
Holloway, Baliol, 191
Holmes, 140
Holt, Emmie, 36
Home, Myra, 30
Hope, Anthony, 163
Hordern, Michael, 217
Horniman, Roy, 2
Hunt, Leigh, 17

Ibsen, H., 54, 72, 73, 84, 176
Iris (Tree's daughter), 100, 111, 147, 149, 190, 224, 226, 227, 236
Irving, H. B., 92, 165, 229
Irving, Henry, 15, 16, 23, 26, 48, 58, 59, 60, 62, 63, 66, 87, 90, 92, 99, 103, 105, 106, 108, 112, 115, 116, 117, 118, 120, 121, 130, 133, 137, 154, 162, 169, 190, 191, 197, 204, 222
Irving, Lawrence, 119, 204, 216
Izard, Isidore, 152

James, David, 26
Jefferies, Douglas, 91, 170, 198, 207
Jeffreys, Ellis, 156
Joachim, Ernest Beerbohm, 5
Johnstone, see Forbes-Robertson
Jones, Henry Arthur, 3, 55, 56, 57, 58, 65, 68, 85, 98, 114, 120, 128, 184, 190

Kaiser, The, 166, 222, 223
Kean, 71
Keats, 134
Kemble, Henry, 47, 62, 71, 127
Kemble, John P., 47, 52

Kendal, Madge, 59, 72, 118, 130
Keppel, Sir Henry, 175
King, Cecil, 165, 208, 215
Kipling, Rudyard, 81, 128, 140, 141

Labouchere, 86, 103, 143
Lamb, Charles, 17
Lang, Matheson, 119
Langtry, Mrs, 24
Latrobe, Charles, 185
Lewis, George, 96
Locke, W. J., 1, 163
Lohr, Marie, 156
Loraine, Robert, 119
Lowther, Claude, 145, 146, 224

McCarthy, Desmond, 190, 194
McCarthy, Justin Huntly, 187
McKenzie, Mrs, 150
Macklin, 53
MacLeary, F., 118
Macquoid, P., 156
Macready, 16, 62, 63, 71, 116
Maeterlinck, 72, 163
Marbury, Elizabeth, 95, 96, 98, 99, 102
Maud (Mrs Tree, née Holt), 27, 28, 30, 31, 32, 33, 34, 37, 38, 39, 40–6, 57, 74, 76, 77, 78, 79, 85, 86, 87, 90, 94, 96, 97, 98, 99, 103, 104, 109, 121, 122, 123, 125, 126, 128, 129, 130, 143, 145, 148, 150, 164, 167, 207, 225, 230, 232
Maugham, W. Somerset, 163, 164
Meredith, George, 47
Merivale, Philip, 199
Meyer, Carl, 101
Mill, John Stuart, 18
Milton, 135
Mirbeau, 152
Modjeska, Madame, 23, 24
Moffat, Curtis, 230
Molière, 177

Mollison, W., 195
Moore, A. K., 21, 28
Morley, 143
Morton, M., 152, 155
Mounet-Sully, 23, 63

Nares, Owen, 119, 193, 197
Neilson, Julia, 76, 77
Neilson-Terry, Phyllis, 118, 216
Neville, Henry, 16, 21, 156
Newton, Miss, 19
Northcliffe, 155
Norton, Frederick, 3, 163
Noyes, Alfred, 187

O'Connor, T. P., 108
Odette, 23, 24
Ogilvie, Stuart, 51, 53
O'Neill, Edward, 185
O'Neil, Florence, 150
Oxford, Lady, 35
Oxford and Asquith, Lord, 3

Page, Thomas Nelson, 81
Pape, General von, 5
Parker, Gilbert, 1, 92, 94, 95, 96, 97, 98, 100, 103
Parker, Louis N., 3, 76, 140, 154, 159, 164, 170, 224
Parry, Hubert, 75
Parsons, Alan, 168, 169
Peile, Kinsey, 141
Penley, N. S., 44
Percival, Laura, 20
Phelps, Samuel, 63, 117
Phillips, Stephen, 134–7
Phipps, C. J., 101
Pinero, Sir Arthur, 2, 19, 30, 45, 55, 84, 85, 98, 168
Playfair, Sir Nigel, 3
Poel, William, 165
Ponsonby, Claud, 43

Pope, 153
Potter, Mrs Brown, 126
Potter, Paul M., 82
Pounds, Courtice, 129
Powles, 24
Prince of Wales, The, 101, 103

Racine, 134
Radke, Henrietta Amalie, 5, 6
Rehan, Ada, 92
Reinhardt, Max, 159, 166
Rejane, Madame, 145
Reubens, Paul, 163
Ristori, 63
Robertson, G., 163, 197, 198, 215
Robertson, T., 10, 16
Robins, Elizabeth, 54
Roerdanz, 5
Ronald, L., 3, 164
Rorke, Kate, 98
Rossetti, 134
Rothschild, Lord, 101
Roze, Raymond, 61, 90, 163
Rutland, Violet, Duchess of, 143, 167

Saint-Saens, Camille, 157, 158
Samuelson, 23
Sardou, 66, 84, 85, 134
Sasvini, 15
Schmidt, 157, 158
Scott, Clement, 23, 24, 108
Scott, Sir Walter, 136
Senea, 136
Shakespeare, William, 31, 60, 61, 92,
    104, 115, 117, 130, 131, 133, 135,
    147, 153, 156, 157, 159, 176, 182,
    191, 192, 205, 210, 211
Shakespeare Company, 134, 159
Shakespeare Festival, 116, 157, 163,
    165, 193, 201, 216
Shallow, Justice, 125
Shaw, George Bernard, 1, 3, 52, 53,
    60, 61, 62, 63, 72, 73, 84, 85, 89,

92, 101, 103, 114, 118, 119, 120,
    131, 148, 150, 159, 163, 172, 175,
    178, 179, 180, 181, 182, 189,
    193
Shelley, 134
Shelton, Herbert, 119
Sheridan, 156
Siddons, Mrs Sarah, 47, 116
Simmons (a costumier), 193
Sims, G. R., 10
Smith, E. E., 143, 224
Smollet, Tobias, 176, 177, 181
Smyth, Ethel, 163
Stead, W. T., 167
Stevenson, Mrs, 49, 50
Stevenson, Robert Louis, 48, 49, 50,
    60
Stone's School, Dr., 7
Strauss, 163
Stuart, Otho, 198
Sullivan, A., 45, 61, 113
Sullivan, B., 63
Swann, Mrs, 22
Swift, Capt, 54
Swinburne, 134
Sylva, Miss, 96
Synge, Hamilton, 19, 21, 22

Tadema, Lawrence Alma, 23, 75, 116,
    145
Taylor, Coleridge, 163
Tearle, Godfrey, 119, 156
Tennant, M., 23, 80
Tennyson, Alfred, 31, 134
Terriss, William, 1
Terry, Edward, 156
Terry, Ellen, 1, 11, 18, 33, 60, 66,
    103, 118, 130, 131, 132, 163, 173
Terry, Fred, 62, 77, 118
Terry, Marion, 75
Thackeray, 152, 155, 230
Tolstoy, 152
Toole, J. L., 15, 105
Trebell, Alfred, 2

Tree, Herbert Beerbohm, (1875–)
11, (1878) 14–16, (1880) 18–25,
(1881) 27–9, (1882) 29–41, (1883)
43–, (1884) 45, (1886) 46–54,
(1891) 55, (1892) 65–71, (1893)
71–6, (1894) 77–9–83, (1895) 86–
94, (1896) 95–104–8, (1898) 108–
121, (1899) 127–9, (1901) 130,
(1902) 131, 132, (1904–6) 133–
146, (1908) 155, (1913–14) 156–
187, (1913) 217, (1914) 222,
(1915) 224, (1915–16) 225–6,
(1917) 228–34
Trench, Herbert, 165
Tristram, Outram, 53

Unruh, General von, 5

Vanbrugh, Irene, 3, 76, 85, 118, 156,
199
Vanbrugh, Sir John, 85
Vanbrugh, Violet, 118, 169, 170, 213
Vedrenne-Barker, 72
Vezin, Hermann, 31, 43, 46, 156
Victoria, Queen, 78, 81, 129
Viola (Tree's daughter), 45, 46, 78, 80,
81, 87, 90, 92, 96, 98, 136, 149,
150, 151, 159, 168, 194, 196, 226,
227, 234

Wagstaff, 184
Walden, Lord Howard de, 159
Walker, Romaine, 101
Walkley, A. B., 108, 170
Waller, L., 10, 62, 99, 118, 123,
124, 125, 126, 128, 150, 151, 165,
191
Walton, Lawson, 122
Ward, Genevieve, 21, 22, 23, 24, 27
Webb, William (solicitor), 26, 123
Wells, H. G., 145
Wernher, 96
West, Sir Algernon, 96
Whelen, F., 158
Whistler, James McNeill, 136
Wilde, Oscar, 2, 19, 25, 26, 55, 65, 68,
70, 71, 72, 85, 114, 120, 138
Wiles & Godwin, Messrs, 37
William, Emperor, 15
Wilson, President (U.S.A.), 231
Wilton, Marie (Mrs Bancroft), 11
Wordingham, Sam (chauffeur), 222
Wordsworth, 134
Wyndham, Charles, 58, 59, 72, 120,
129, 167, 233

Zangwill, Israel, 198, 215

INDEX TO PLACE NAMES

Academy of Dramatic Art, 165, 182
America, 224, 229
American Tour, 94, 95, 97, 230

Bath, 121; Pump Room Hotel, 124
Birchington, Kent, 7 Ethel Bay, 233
Bognor, West Lodge, Aldich, 124
Brighton, Metropolitan Hotel, 102; 31 Kings Road, 102

California, 227
Chicago, Blackstone Hotel, 113, 225; Opera House, 81

Donnington Hall, 224

Falmouth Hotel, Falmouth (1908), 151
Folkstone (1895), 87
Frankfurt, 222
Fripps Nursing Home, 115 Henrietta Street, Covent Garden, 233

Garrick Club, 112, 113, 114, 129, 164, 223, 233
Globe Playhouse, Park Street, Southwark, 147
Glottenham House, Robertsbridge, Sussex, 148
Guildhall, 144, 164

Highbury, 143
Hindhead, 140
Holywood, 1862 Cherokee Avenue, 227; 1985 North Van Ness Avenue, 225
Huddersfield, Theatre Royal, 20; White Hart Hotel, 20
Hurstmonceux Castle, 145, 146, 224

Isle of Man, 139

Los Angeles, 227

Manchester (1895), 90
Marienbad, 86, 122, 123, 124, 136, 146, 159, 182, 222
Moscow, 196

National Theatre, 165
New Cavendish Street (16), 74
New York, 80, 81, 98, 225; Metropolitan Opera House, 231; New Amsterdam Theatre, 230; Plaza, 230, 231; Waldorf Hotel, 96
Niagara Falls, 100
North Street, Westminster, 145, 148

Pembridge Villas, 2 Kensington, 6
Petersburg, St., 196
Philadelphia, 81; Stenton Hotel, 97
Prince's Gardens, 143

Rottingdean, Hillside, 148

249

Sloane Street (No. 77), 145, 148

Waldorf, 80, 86

Walpole House, Chiswick Mall, Chiswick, 148, 149

West Virginia, Greenbrier, White Sulphur Springs, 226

Wharf, The, Sutton Courtney, 148, 149

Wilton Street, No. 4 Grosvenor Place, 43

Also in The Lively Arts series

A Life in the Theatre

TYRONE GUTHRIE

Tyrone Guthrie was one of the first British theatre directors to be as prominent as the actors in his plays – and they included Olivier, Gielgud, Richardson, Redgrave and Edith Evans. This autobiography, irreverent and opinionated, is justifiably considered the wittiest and most candid recollection of theatrical life in this country ever published by an insider.

'Tyrone Guthrie's book is a stimulating and delightful autobiography, full of the characteristic energy and brilliance of the author.' **Sir John Gielgud**

'The most exciting and stimulating person in the theatre today, Guthrie's influence has extended from the British Isles to Australia, from Israel to Finland, from Canada to Texas. He is not only a great man of the theatre – an unpredictable and sometimes wayward genius and adventurer – but a great man in himself. His autobiography gives us a handsome slice of the man and his work. The omissions in it are typical of the man – his innumerable acts of kindness to young and old, his generosity, and the fact that so many of us owe him, largely, our careers.' **Sir Alec Guinness**

'One of the most important books on the Theatre that I have read for many a year. It is informative, witty and unpretentious, and I am sure it will be as fascinating and entertaining for the great public as it is for those of us who belong to the Theatre.' **Sir Noël Coward**

'Tyrone Guthrie is famous for his light touch when he handles a production in the theatre. Now he has produced a book of memoirs: coming from such authority they are of necessity interesting; they are also light, and easy to read.' **Sir Ralph Richardson**

'Dr Guthrie's book is hilarious, engrossing, shrewd, ironic, informative, disputatious and inspiring – a perfect mirror, in fact, of the man himself.' **New York Times**

Also in The Lively Arts series

Fun in a Chinese Laundry
JOSEF VON STERNBERG

Josef von Sternberg is best known as the director who found Marlene Dietrich for *The Blue Angel*, an association that led them to Hollywood and six more films. This autobiography is generally accepted as the most combative, irreverent, and ruthlessly honest book ever to be written about films, the stars, and the money-men.

'Half-autobiography, half vitriol, a compendium of wicked portraits from Jannings to Laughton . . . a quite unforgivable book; and I couldn't stop reading it and laughing over it.'
Dilys Powell, Sunday Times

'Von Sternberg has been a unique creator; only belatedly have we discovered just how individual was his gift for extracting thrilling, dense sensual qualities from the cold, two-dimensional image. However prejudiced by anger, by the *amour-propre* and frustrations of a too-sensitive artist fighting, on wholly unequal terms, the machine of the film industry, his opinions on the methods and aesthetics of cinema are worth hearing. . . His opinions on actors at large − his magnificent scorn of the race and his conviction that only vanity and severe psychological deprivation lead them into such a demeaning trade − are real anthology pieces, sovereign antidotes to the sort of softening adulation on which actors are generally fed.'
David Robinson, Financial Times

' . . . fascinating and educative musings on the aesthetics of the cinema.' **Gerald Kaufman, Listener**

'From its jokey title . . . to its comic index . . . Sternberg's autobiography is as idiosyncratic as its author . . . a strange mixture of innocence and sophistication, of naivety and cynicism, vulgarity and good taste, wit and humourlessness . . . extremely well written. His chapters, incidentally, on working with Emil Jannings on *The Last Command* and *The Blue Angel* are hilariously funny, and it is of considerable value to have his own account of discovering and shaping the screen persona of Marlene Dietrich.' **Philip French, Observer**

Also in *The Lively Arts* series

The Movies,
Mr Griffith and Me

LILLIAN GISH
AND ANNE PINCHOT

'Only the people who lived through an era, who are the real participants in the drama as it occurs, know the truth,' declares Lillian Gish, whose 75 years as a movie actress have included such eternal silent classics as *Way Down East*, *Broken Blossoms* and *The Wind*, and stretch to 1987, when she co-starred with Bette Davis in *The Whales of August*. Her autobiography is the most touching and revealing of all Hollywood memoirs, telling the story from birth to maturity of a great art form through her own experience and that of the first great genius of film, the director D. W. Griffith.

'No one can imagine the Hollywood of the 1920s without the image of Lillian Gish. She embodies the innocence, the emotion, the drama of that decade as no other actress does — and the story of her own life, told with exact recall and clear-eyed sentiment, is the most enthralling testimony to that glorious period that has ever come my way. It may not be so easy to see the films that made her famous, but this memoir is a satisfying substitute.'   **Kenneth Tynan**

'It was my privilege that Lillian Gish was able to portray Ophelia when my Hamlet opened in New York in 1936. She had already established her reputation on the stage, but of course I was still in awe of those luminous performances she had given us in the silent cinema. For me, this book is an outstanding account of a lady for whom truth has always been at the heart of her great artistry.'   **Sir John Gielgud**

'When Charles Laughton told me that he hoped Lillian Gish would accept a key role in the only film he directed, *The Night of the Hunter*, I knew I was in for a great learning experience. And I was right; no performer understands the film medium more thoroughly than Miss Gish. This book manages to communicate not only the pleasure we have all had from her performances, but it brings the whole history of Hollywood before us in close-up.'   **Robert Mitchum**

Also in The Lively Arts series

Groucho and Me

GROUCHO MARX

The most outrageous and voluble of the legendary Marx Brothers, Groucho's life stretched from early vaudeville to recent television. With his cigar in his mouth, he explodes with wit and iconoclasm about his life, his unconsummated loves, and the triumphs and disasters of working in Hollywood. As T.S. Eliot said of him: 'The mind boggles.'

'If anything could reconcile us to the end of the Marx Brothers, it would be Groucho's autobiography. Here life and art get together, so that the man is inseparable from our image of him.'
Benny Green

'He is the most generous of men – and that is a great tribute for me to give, as I am considered the meanest man in town. In this book, Groucho gives all – and he deserves every dime of his royalties. I'm looking for my percentage for this puff.'
Jack Benny

'Groucho brought the spirit of carnival to Hollywood. This book gives us a chance to linger over the gags that went too fast on the screen.'
Alistair Cooke

'The only thing the man can't do is sing and that gave me an opening. But he can do everything else. I envy him this book, most of his wives, and all of his talent.'
Frank Sinatra

Also in The Lively Arts series

Memoirs

ALEXANDRE BENOIS

It is impossible to visualize the great age of Diaghilev and the Russian Ballet without conjuring up the images of Alexandre Benois, who created much of its decor. Gifted with total recall, Benois provides an incomparable record of this glittering era, people with legendary personalities like Stravinsky, Prokofiev and Chagall. His own backdrop is the beautiful city of Petersburg, home to his distinguished family and which, together with his outstanding, outgoing personality, stamps every page.

'An intimate, tender, utterly truthful story of a child and his world. But what a child and what a colourful, unrepeatable world! The vivid descriptions evoke all the validity of real experience. The excellent translation by Moura Budberg, it seems to me, has all the inflections of Benois's own conversation. He writes as he speaks, in an easy flow of limpid language.' **Tamara Karsavina**

'This book, vivid and nostalgic, is as much a work of art as any of his paintings.' **Arnold Haskell**

'He writes with the warmth and limpidity that used to seem characteristic of his countrymen.' **Raymond Mortimer**

'We are simply listening to the late Monsieur Benois reminiscing in English. Personal memories are woven in with apparently artless effect. The book is limpid yet vivid and it gives the quiet, lasting pleasure of a water-colour drawing.' **Philip Hope-Wallace**

'It is so touching and gay. It brings a dear friend to life.' **Igor Stravinsky**

Also in The Lively Arts series

My Grandfather
His Wives and Loves

DIANA HOLMAN-HUNT

William Holman Hunt was a central figure in the Pre-Raphaelite Brotherhood, a painter still best known for such works as 'The Light of the World', an allegory on our failure to follow the teachings of Jesus. Hunt's private life, however, as unveiled by his grand-daughter, was a combination of passions galore, of sensuality substituting for sense, and of an eccentricity typical of the Victorian ability to combine public morality with private pleasure.

'The book is un-put-down-able.'   **Times Literary Supplement**

'Countless excellent anecdotes.'   **Auberon Waugh, Spectator**

' . . . her new extensive study of the first fifty years of Holman Hunt's own life . . . is crammed with hitherto unknown information.'   **James Pope-Hennessy, Financial Times**

' . . . anyone interested in the Pre-Raphaelites and their boy-scout-like *vie de bohème* is likely to enjoy it.'
    Claire Tomalin, New Statesman

'Her amusing new book ranges far beyond its title, throwing much tragi-comic light on the whole world of Pre-Raphaelitism.'   **John Raymond, Sunday Times**

'One has to admit that his grand-daughter is pretty quick . . . she provides a deal of fun. Even the footnotes crackle . . . Dramatically vivid.'   **Brian Aldiss, Oxford Mail**

'The author recounts in a charming prologue how her cousin Evelyn Waugh encouraged her to write this work, and Waugh himself contributed an afterpiece. But Cousin Waugh was not responsible for this work's excellence; that is all Miss Holman-Hunt's doing. Her delicate appreciation that these stormy love stories are at once ridiculous and affecting is superb, like her clean prose.'   **New Yorker**

Also in The Lively Arts series

Renoir, My Father

JEAN RENOIR

There are scarcely any parallels for this biography of one great artist by a son who achieved similar distinction in another medium, that of film. It began in 1915, when a German sniper put a bullet through young Jean's leg, and he spent his convalescence in his father's Montmartre apartment. Alone with one another, the stored-up memories and reflections of the master Impressionist's long and eventful life recounted then were to result, many years later, in this portrait, written with an unforgettable intimacy and affection. Maturity, says Jean Renoir, enabled him 'to appreciate his genius and understand his personality'.

'One can only marvel at this book, which is indispensable for anyone interested in painting and, indeed, humanity. What one would give for a similar memoir from, say, the children of Rembrandt or Rubens! For Jean has the honesty to see his father without false flattery, but with a tolerance of faults that gives dignity and stature to his irreplaceable legacy as a painter and as a man.' **Sir Kenneth Clark**

'There are two overwhelming reasons for reading this book. The first, of course, is the wealth of information and anecdote about Auguste. But the second is equally important, for it demonstrates the inspiration behind the films of Jean, who showed his heredity in masterpieces like *Partie de Campagne* and *La Règle du Jeu* and who surely would not have become one of the four greatest directors this century without that influence.'
Orson Welles

'I knew Renoir in his later years, when his triumph of will over pain and illness produced some of his finest work. Jean's biography also tells me of happier times, and it is full of warmth and wisdom about the art of painting, and the dedication needed to reach its heights.'
Pablo Picasso

Also in *The Lively Arts* series

A MINGLED CHIME

SIR THOMAS BEECHAM

This vivid, eccentric, and quirky memoir of his early life has all the characteristics of brilliance and passion that brought Sir Thomas Beecham to the forefront of British orchestral and opera conductors. His prolific output of recordings has ensured his reputation as conductor for posterity; this witty autobiography performs the same office for the man himself.

'The big tenor bell in *A Mingled Chime* is the art of music and it is rung by the artist who of all British executant musicians has established his claim internationally to the title of genius, perhaps the first Englishman to be ranked among the great conductors of the world. The smaller bells are education (public school, university, conservatoire), politics, business, literature and painting, rung by a man of the world, a connoisseur and a wit . . . A mingled chime indeed, containing a detailed and sober account of years of effort to give the British public the best opera and orchestral music . . . containing penetrating musical criticism and equally just criticism of men, shrewd and without malice. Like Papageno with his chime of magic bells he sets us dancing to his tune.' **Times Literary Supplement**

'It would be useless to attempt a summary of the good stories that Beecham relates.' **Listener**

'The author's innumerable anecdotes are told with characteristic wit. His comments on famous composers and performers are fascinating, often provocative, but always shrewd and worthy of being closely pondered. The whole book is of extraordinary interest.' **Manchester Guardian**

'What he has given us in the way of autobiography whets our appetite for more. He writes quite as well as he speaks, and we all know what that means . . . the story of his own myriad musical activities is told without the least exaggeration.' **Sunday Times**

Also in The Lively Arts series

Liszt

SIR SACHEVERELL SITWELL

Sacheverell Sitwell, who celebrated his 90th birthday in November 1987, is the modern writer most in tune with the Romantic age — as his many books on its art, its architecture and ballet have shown. His study of Liszt is the most sympathetic and engaging to have appeared this century, Sitwell making this dazzling and protean musician a living figure. Over the last three decades, the reputation and the repertoire of Liszt have been greatly enlarged through the interpretations of such pianists as Arrau, Brendel and Bolet, and conductors like Haitink. Liszt led a life that was in keeping with his fiery and tumultuous talent, and no one has been so adept as Sitwell in making coherent the conflicting strains of his temperament.

'Mr Sitwell's ability to recreate scenes from myth or history, his imaginative skill in restating the themes of music and painting in literary terms, his facility with the devices of nostalgia, are all formidable. His senses range widely, his knowledge and memory of all the arts are remarkable.'　　**The Times**

'He is not a writer of any particular age or fashion or school. He is peculiarly and refreshingly alone.'
　　　　　　　　　Pamela Hansford-Johnson

'There is no doubt that subsequent research, especially amongst Hungarian archives, will amend some of the facts of Liszt's life. But this biography will never be wholly superseded, for Sitwell brings to it so much insight, affection, and intuitive understanding of this chameleon man.'
　　　　　　　　　　　Dame Myra Hess

'Liszt and I could not be more different men. But he was my greatest Hungarian forbear, and my mentor at the piano from childhood onwards. This book summarizes for me what Liszt meant to his own generation, and why we neglect him at our peril. He made the piano that I use the expressive instrument of the soul.'
　　　　　　　　　　　　Bela Bartok

Also in The Lively Arts series

Chaliapin

MAXIM GORKY

In the world of singing, and especially in opera, few names can cast a spell equal to that of Chaliapin, the great Russian bass who died fifty years ago in April 1938. There can be few autobiographies as enthralling or as perceptive as this one, for it was originally told to Chaliapin's close friend, Maxim Gorky, one of the most compelling novelists and dramatists of this century. Gorky eventually composed this narrative from those extensive conversations, and the result is an absorbing account of victory over early deprivation to final world-wide acclaim and recognition. It is still possible to hear Chaliapin's incomparable voice on recordings. Now we can read his words.

'Chaliapin was the motive force for my own career, and I have humbly walked in his shadow. This book explains both his art and his indomitable spirit. When I first sang in *Boris Godunov*, his interpretation of excerpts was always on my gramophone. With all superb artists, a wealth of experience must be brought to bear on all their creations. Here we discover where that golden voice was mined.'
Boris Christoff

'I believe that Chaliapin's last appearance in opera was at the Theatre Royal, Drury Lane, in June 1914, the eve of the First World War. Yet even those who never heard him in the flesh can recognize his unmatched authority and power from early acoustic recordings. This book is some compensation for a new generation, who are given memorable views of a personality that was both larger than life but could yet encompass the smallest nuance of emotion and humour.'
Sir John Barbirolli

'Chaliapin was my hero when I was young, and I only regret that he did not live for me to write anything for him. This book should be in the hands of any singer who takes his vocation seriously. I know no other that so searchingly explores the making of great art, and no one who could have assembled the words as brilliantly as my friend, Maxim Gorky.'
Dimitri Shostakovich

'A story that haunts the mind as powerfully as the voice reaches our soul.'
Boris Pasternak